THE STORIES OF
WILLIAM SANSOM

THE
STORIES
OF
WILLIAM
SANSOM

With an Introduction by

Elizabeth Bowen

Short Story Index Reprint Series

BOOKS FOR LIBRARIES PRESS
FREEPORT, NEW YORK

Reprinted 1971 by arrangement with
Little, Brown and Company, Inc. in association with the
Atlantic Monthly Press

INTERNATIONAL STANDARD BOOK NUMBER:
0-8369-3786-4

LIBRARY OF CONGRESS CATALOG CARD NUMBER:
77-144171

PRINTED IN THE UNITED STATES OF AMERICA

CONTENTS

CONTENTS

INTRODUCTION

By Elizabeth Bowen

RARE is the writer with command of his powers who absolutely cannot write a short story—if he so desire, or if (as may happen) it be desired of him. Few there must be who have not, at one time or another, wanted to try the hand at this form, or found themselves seized by an idea which could be embodied in no way other than this. The writer not sooner or later tempted to try everything, if only to prove to himself that he cannot do it, must be exceptional; might one not say, defective? Incidental short stories of writers by nature given to greater space, or by need bound to the synthesis of the novel, generally warrant attention and give pleasure. Some have the *éclat* of successful command performances. Few quite misfire. Few fail to merit the author's signature or to bear the particular stamp he gives any work. Yet such stories, recognizably, are by-products. One does not feel that they were inevitable. In this, they differ essentially from stories by the short-storyist *par excellence*: the short-storyist by birth, addiction and destiny. Such is William Sansom.

William Sansom, I do not need to point out, has extended himself into other fields. One could say he has experimented *with* extension, and that there has, moreover, been no experiment he has cause to regret. His by now six novels are in a position, a foreground, of their own. And of his equal command of the 'short novel' (novelette or *novella*) has he not given us examples? His two travel books exercise a sharp, sensuous fascination: of their kind and in their own manner they are unrivalled. He has mastered the essay; he has manifested a gift for writing for children. It could be that these his other achievements eclipse, for some of his readers, his short stories —as achievements, these others have been substantial and dazzling. Yet the short story remains (it appears to me) the not only ideal but lasting magnet for all that is most unique in the Sansom art.

Here is a writer whose faculties not only suit the short story but are suited by it—suited and, one may feel, enhanced. This form needs the kind of imagination which is able to concentrate at high power and is most itself when doing so. The tension and pace required by the short story can be as stimulating to the right writer of it as they are intimidating to the wrong one: evidently they are stimulating to William Sansom. That need to gain an immediate hold on the reader (a hold which must also be a compulsive one) rules out the writer who is a slow starter: the quick starter, reacting, asks nothing better. There is also the necessity to project, to make seen, and make seen with significance—the short story is for the eye (if the mind's eye). Also the short story, though it high-lights what appears to be reality, is not—cannot wish or afford to be—realistic: it relies on devices, foreshortenings, 'effects'. In the narration there must be an element of conjury, and of that William Sansom is an evident master.

Though all the short stories written by William Sansom are not, I find, present in this collection, the thirty-three which are present have been well chosen. (That a reader should be so conscious of those missing testifies to the power those pieces had to stamp themselves on the memory and, indeed, haunt it.) Those here are, one must concede, outstanding examples of their different kinds. Kinds? One had better say, types of subject—pedantic though that sounds. The wider a storyist's range, the more unavoidable it becomes that one should classify when attempting to take stock of his whole output. From his wartime London, N.F.S. and fly-bomb period, we have, for instance, those two masterpieces, *The Wall* and *Building Alive*. Portrayal of the terrible, or of the nature of terror, reaches three of its highest levels in *The Vertical Ladder, How Claeys Died* and *Among the Dahlias*. Comedy, canine in one case, human in the other, overflows with a cheering rumbustiousness from *Three Dogs of Siena* and *A Contest of Ladies*. That extra dimension of oddness added to humans by their being in a pub or bar, or even in a hotel with the bar closed, appears in *Displaced Persons* (another masterpiece), *Eventide* and *A Game of Billiards*. Of the pursuit of man (or woman) by a fatality, not to be given the slip or shaken off, there are several examples in stories here, the most memorable, and grimmest, being

8

Various Temptations. The resignation-reconciliation theme (very pronouncedly a Sansom one when he writes of courtship, engagements to marry, or marriage) carries to their conclusions two other stories, *A Waning Moon* and *Question and Answer.*

Two of the greatest, at times awesome and certainly most curious powers of this writer appear in two kinds of story not mentioned yet. Where it comes to conveying hallucination, I know few if any who can approach him. (Kipling, possibly, though in another manner?) The fewness of 'pure' hallucination stories in this collection to me is a matter of regret—above all, I hope that this does not mean that this author is reneging on this power? We have, however, the wondrous *A Saving Grace* . . . . The other group, to be identified with the other power, are what one might nominate the great scenic stories: those in which what in the hands of another writer could be called 'background' or 'setting' steps forward, takes over, dominates like a tremendous insatiable star actor, reducing the nominal (human) protagonists to 'extras', to walkers-on. In such Sansom stories, who, what, why and how people are is endlessly less important than where they are. How this can be made to come off, and come off triumphantly, is evident in *My Little Robins, Time and Place, Gliding Gulls, Episode at Gastein, A Country Walk,* and, to a great extent, two stories already spoken of in another context (or, under another heading) *A Waning Moon* and *Question and Answer* . . . . *Pastorale* is debatable: in a sense, the couple in it defeat the landscape.

To a point, all Sansom stories are scenic stories. Corsica, maritime Provence, Scandinavia, the Highlands of Scotland, the Isles of the West and the past-haunted, mountainous Austrian spa are far from being the only robbers. In this formidable and dismaying world of the Sansom art, no 'inanimate' object is inanimate—mutely, each is either antagonist or accomplice. Influences and effluences are not only at work; they seem the determinants—to a point where mock could be made of human free will. The human is not only the creature of his environment, he becomes its plaything. For the moment, that moment, perhaps, only? But a Sansom moment, given extraordinary extension, so that during it hands may move round round the clock face, the sun set then rise, or leaves be torn from a calendar, is a Sansom story.

A*   9

THE STORIES OF WILLIAM SANSOM

This writer's timing, with its expansions and contractions (as though he were playing on an accordion, or squeeze-box) is one of the instances of the trickiness he so well uses—trickiness which (I suggested earlier) a short story not only licences and justifies but demands.

The need for the writer's obtaining compulsive hold on the reader (that is, the reader's imagination) has been referred to. Few, if any, are the occasions when the writer of the stories in this collection allows you or me to slip through his fingers. I suggest that what rivets one to a Sansom story is a form of compulsion, rather than 'interest' in the more usual, leisurely or reflective sense. The characters, the men and women protagonists, are not in themselves 'interesting'—or at least to me. In the main they are pallid; the few more coloured ones (like Miss Great-Belt, the Danish beauty-contestant in *A Contest of Ladies*) are, often, handsome wound-up automata, jerking through their small ranges of looks and gestures. The fatalism shown by most of these people is, one feels, neither desperate nor romantic; rather, it is the outcome of an incompetence which may shade off at any moment into sheer impotence. These people do not appeal to us, or attract our sympathies. But to say that they 'fail' to do so would be misleading. Why? Because it has not for a single instant been their creator's intention that they *should* (interest, attract or appeal to us, I mean). The enormous suspense element in a Sansom story is generated in no ordinary way. Since we care little for, or about, these people, do we greatly care what happens to them? Why, no! Then how are we held? We are held not by what happens but by how it happens. The substance of a Sansom story is sensation. The subject is sensation. The emotions are sensations of emotion. The crisis (to be depended upon to be 'sensational' in the accepted sense) is a matter of bringing sensation to a peak where it must either splinter or dissolve because it can no more. Or it may, sometimes, simply, ironically and altogether subside . . . . We accompany, thus, the nominal Sansom 'character' throughout the ups-and-downs of fear, or infatuation, or suspicion, or daydream-success, or amazement, or apprehension, or whatever it be. We ease off during the intermissions, let-ups and pauses allowed by the malady or the ordeal (or, it may be, the delight) only to quiver under the shock of renewed assault.

Held we are: either rooted, like the firemen looking up at the falling wall in *The Wall*, or gummed, like the youth scaling the gasometer in *The Vertical Ladder*.

A Sansom story is a *tour de force*. Readers who dislike, mistrust or resent that should turn to something other than this volume. In me these stories induce, also, suspense of another kind, call it sympathetic suspense—will they come off? It is staggering how they do. Their doing so is anything but a matter of fortuity. Nothing here is slapdash or 'got away with'. The writer has taken, and shown himself right in taking, a succession of calculated risks. He is not writing *for* effect, he is dealing *in* it, and masterfully. For his purposes, vocabulary is clearly very important—vocabulary in the literal sense, in the matter of words, yes; but also there has to be a complete command of the vocabulary of the senses. To have knowledge of, to be able to call up into what in the story is actuality, to be able not merely to convey to the reader but impose on him (almost, inflict on him) smells, tastes, sounds rendered complex or curious by acoustics or echoes, differences (as though under the touch) of surfaces, gradations of light and its watery running off into shadow —this was essential for the writer of the Sansom stories. Equally, the writing of these stories, these particular stories, as they come to us, must have been an essential for William Sansom—burdened, he would have otherwise been, with a useless faculty.

Weather is part of the vocabulary. 'The day slate-dark, the air still, the cindertrack by the cottages without life in a watered middle-day light'—is the overture to *Something Terrible, Something Lovely*. The visage of the house in *A Saving Grace* (the house from out of whose open door one by one the dead are to proceed, the dog and all, to group themselves smilingly on the lawn, as though for a photograph), is framed in 'the hour before dusk . . . when the hot afternoon is grown old and cool'. There are, again and again, in *A Country Walk*, those weather-passages betraying the terrible animosity of Nature. Such as:

The shadow of a cloud was passing over the map, it came

towards him like a fast-moving tide, heaving the hills as it came. A simple matter? Not so simple. He watched it, he began to judge whether it would envelop him or not. It came at a fast windblown pace, eating up the fields, blotting out life like the edge of a dangerous sea moving in.

The whole countryside grew more inimical. Every deep acre of this ancient sleeping earth breathed a quiet, purposeful life—and it was against him. Not now the simple material conflict with animals—the grave earth itself and the green things growing in collusion with it took on presence and, never moving, breathed a quiet hatred on to the mineral air.

Animals, birds also are part of the vocabulary—they seem, at the moments of their emergences, long to have existed *within* it, behind all words. Corsican robins, the lion at liberty in the middle of the dahlia-edged path, and those dogs of Siena—Enrico, Osvaldo, Fa. And, in the Hampstead garden, 'isolated at the very top of a tall sapling, crouched on the tapering end of this thin shoot so that it bent over under the weight like a burdened spring . . . a huge dazed cat'.

The Stories of William Sansom speak for themselves. A peril of introduction is that it can go on for too long. So this breaks off, though there could be more to say.

The Wall

IT was our third job that night.

Until this thing happened, work had been without incident. There had been shrapnel, a few enquiring bombs, and some huge fires; but these were unremarkable and have since merged without identity into the neutral maze of fire and noise and water and night, without date and without hour, with neither time nor form, that lowers mistily at the back of my mind as a picture of the air-raid season.

I suppose we were worn down and shivering. Three a.m. is a meanspirited hour. I suppose we were drenched, with the cold hose water trickling in at our collars and settling down at the tails of our shirts. Without doubt the heavy brass couplings felt moulded from metal-ice. Probably the open roar of the pumps drowned the petulant buzz of the raiders above, and certainly the ubiquitous fire-glow made an orange stage-set of the streets. Black water would have puddled the City alleys and I suppose our hands and our faces were black as the water. Black with hacking about among the burnt up rafters. These things were an every-night nonentity. They happened and they were not forgotten because they were never even remembered.

But I do remember it was our third job. And there we were—Len, Lofty, Verno and myself, playing a fifty-foot jet up the face of a tall city warehouse and thinking of nothing at all. You don't think of anything after the first few hours. You just watch the white pole of water lose itself in the fire and you think of nothing. Sometimes you move the jet over to another window. Sometimes the orange dims to black—but you only ease your grip on the ice-cold nozzle and continue pouring careless gallons through the window. You know the fire will fester for hours yet. However, that night the blank, indefinite hours of waiting were sharply interrupted—by an unusual sound. Very suddenly a long rattling crack of bursting brick and mortar perforated the moment. And then the upper half of that five-storey building heaved over towards us. It hung there, poised for a timeless second before rumbling down at us. I was thinking of nothing at all and then I was thinking of everything in the world.

In that simple second my brain digested every detail of the scene. New eyes opened at the sides of my head so that, from within, I photographed a hemispherical panorama bounded by the huge length of the building in front of me and the narrow lane on either side.

Blocking us on the left was the squat trailer pump, roaring and quivering with effort. Water throbbed from its overflow valves and from leakages in the hose and couplings. A ceaseless stream spewed down its grey sides into the gutter. But nevertheless a fat iron exhaust pipe glowed red-hot in the middle of the wet engine. I had to look past Lofty's face. Lofty was staring at the controls, hands tucked into his armpits for warmth. Lofty was thinking of nothing. He had a black diamond of soot over one eye, like the White-eyed Kaffir in negative.

To the other side of me was a free run up the alley. Overhead swung a sign—'Catto and Henley'. I wondered what in hell they sold. Old stamps? The alley was quite free. A couple of lengths of dead, deflated hose wound over the darkly glistening pavement. Charred flotsam dammed up one of the gutters. A needle of water fountained from a hole in a live hose-length. Beneath a blue shelter light lay a shattered coping stone. The next shop along was a tobacconist's, windowless, with fake display cartons torn open for anybody to see. The alley was quite free.

Behind me, Len and Verno shared the weight of the hose. They heaved up against the strong backward drag of waterpressure. All I had to do was yell 'Drop it'—and then run. We could risk the live hose snaking up at us. We could run to the right down the free alley —Len, Verno and me. But I never moved. I never said 'Drop it' or anything else. That long second held me hypnotized, rubber boots cemented to the pavement. Ton upon ton of red-hot brick hovering in the air above us numbed all initiative. I could only think. I couldn't move.

Six yards in front stood the blazing building. A minute before I would never have distinguished it from any other drab Victorian atrocity happily on fire. Now I was immediately certain of every minute detail. The building was five storeys high. The top four storeys were fiercely alight. The rooms inside were alive with red fire. The black outside walls remained untouched. And thus, like the lighted carriages of a night express, there appeared alternating rectangles of black and red that emphasized vividly the extreme symmetry of the window spacing: each oblong window shape posed as a vermilion panel set in perfect order upon the dark face of the wall. There were ten windows to each floor, making forty windows in all. In rigid rows of ten, one row placed precisely above the other, with strong contrasts of black and red, the blazing windows stood to attention in strict formation. The oblong building, the oblong windows, the oblong spacing. Orange-red colour seemed to *bulge* from the black frame-work, assumed tactile values, like boiling jelly that expanded inside a thick black squared grill.

Three of the storeys, thirty blazing windows and their huge frame of black brick, a hundred solid tons of hard, deep Victorian wall, pivoted over towards us and hung flatly over the alley. Whether the descending wall actually paused in its fall I can never know. Probably it never did. Probably it only seemed to hang there. Probably my eyes only digested its action at an early period of momentum, so that I saw it 'off true' but before it had gathered speed.

The night grew darker as the great mass hung over us. Through smoke-fogged fireglow the moonlight had hitherto penetrated to the pit of our alley through declivities in the skyline. Now some of the moonlight was being shut out as the wall hung ever further over us. The wall shaded the moonlight like an inverted awning. Now the pathway of light above had been squeezed to a thin line. That was the only silver lining I ever believed in. It shone out—a ray of hope. But it was a declining hope, for although at this time the entire hemispherical scene appeared static, an imminence of movement could be sensed throughout—presumably because the scene was actually moving. Even the speed of the shutter which closed the photograph on my mind was powerless to exclude this motion from a deeper consciousness. The picture appeared static to the limited surface sense, the eyes and the material brain, but beyond that there was hidden movement.

The second was timeless. I had leisure to remark many things. For instance, that an iron derrick, slightly to the left, would not hit me. This derrick stuck out from the building and I could feel its sharpness and hardness as clearly as if I had run my body intimately over its contour. I had time to notice that it carried a foot-long hook, a chain with three-inch rings, two girder supports and a wheel more than twice as large as my head.

A wall will fall in many ways. It may sway over to the one side or the other. It may crumble at the very beginning of its fall. It may remain intact and fall flat. This wall fell as flat as a pancake. It clung to its shape through ninety degrees to the horizontal. Then it detached itself from the pivot and slammed down on top of us.

The last resistance of bricks and mortar at the pivot point cracked off like automatic gun fire. The violent sound both deafened us and brought us to our senses. We dropped the hose and crouched. Afterwards Verno said that I knelt slowly on one knee with bowed head, like a man about to be knighted. Well, I got my knighting. There was an incredible noise—a thunderclap condensed into the space of an eardrum—and then the bricks and the mortar came tearing and burning into the flesh of my face.

Lofty, away by the pump, was killed. Len, Verno and myself they dug out. There was very little brick on top of us. We had been lucky. We had been framed by one of those symmetrical, oblong window spaces.

Difficulty with a Bouquet

SEAL, walking through his garden, said suddenly to himself: 'I would like to pick some flowers and take them to Miss D.'

The afternoon was light and warm. Tall chestnuts fanned themselves in a pleasant breeze. Among the hollyhocks there was a good humming as the bees tumbled from flower to flower. Seal wore an open shirt. He felt fresh and fine, with the air swimming coolly under his shirt and around his ribs. The summer's afternoon was free. Nothing pressed him. It was a time when some simple, disinterested impulse might well be hoped to flourish.

Seal felt a great joy in the flowers around him and from this a brilliant longing to give. He wished to give quite inside himself, uncritically, without thinking for a moment: 'Here am I, Seal, wishing something.' Seal merely wanted to give some of his flowers to a fellow being. It had happened that Miss D was the first person to come to mind. He was in no way attached to Miss D. He knew her slightly, as a plain, elderly girl of about twenty who had come to live in the flats opposite his garden. If Seal had ever thought about Miss D at all, it was because he disliked the way she walked. She walked stiffly, sailing with her long body while her little legs raced to catch up with it. But he was not thinking of this now. Just by chance he had glimpsed the block of flats as he had stooped to pick a flower. The flats had presented the image of Miss D to his mind.

Seal chose common, ordinary flowers. As the stems broke he whistled between his teeth. He had chosen these ordinary flowers because they were the nearest to hand: in the second place, because they were fresh and full of life. They were neither rare nor costly. They were pleasant, fresh, unassuming flowers.

With the flowers in his hand, Seal walked contentedly from his garden and set foot on the asphalt pavement that led to the block of flats across the way. But as his foot touched the asphalt, as the sly glare of an old man fixed his eye for the moment of its passing, as the traffic asserted itself, certain misgivings began to freeze his impromptu joy. 'Good heavens,' he suddenly thought, 'what am I doing?' He stepped outside himself and saw Seal carrying a bunch of cheap flowers to Miss D in the flats across the way.

'These are cheap flowers,' he thought. 'This is a sudden gift, I shall smile as I hand them to her. We shall both know that there is no ulterior reason for the gift and thus the whole action will smack of goodness—of goodness and simple brotherhood. And somehow . . . for that reason this gesture of mine will appear to be the most calculated pose of all. Such a simple gesture is improbable. The improbable is to be suspected. My gift will certainly be regarded as an affectation.

'Oh, if only I had some reason—aggrandizement, financial gain, seduction—any of the accepted motives that would return my flowers to social favour. But no—I have none of these in me. I only wish to give and to receive nothing in return.'

As he walked on, Seal could see himself bowing and smiling. He saw himself smile too broadly as he apologized by exaggeration for his good action. His neck flinched with disgust as he saw himself assume the old bravados. He could see the mocking smile of recognition on the face of Miss D.

Seal dropped the flowers into the gutter and walked slowly back to his garden.

From her window high up in the concrete flats, Miss D watched Seal drop the flowers. How fresh they looked! How they would have livened her barren room! 'Wouldn't it have been nice,' thought Miss D, 'if that Mr Seal had been bringing *me* that pretty bouquet of flowers! Wouldn't it have been nice if he had picked them in his own garden and—well, just brought them along, quite casually, and made me a present of the delightful afternoon.' Miss D dreamed on for a few minutes.

Then she frowned, rose, straightened her suspender belt, hurried into the kitchen. 'Thank God he didn't,' she sighed to herself. 'I should have been most embarrassed. It's not as if he wanted me. It would have been just too maudlin for words.'

Something Terrible, Something Lovely

THE day slate-dark, the air still, the cindertrack by the cottages empty and without life in a watered middle-day light—and young Nita came running, running home from school. Her satchel swung behind her, the blue exercise book fluttered its white leaves in her windmill hand, thin long legs and young-boned knees pranced before her like the separate legs of a pony careering the rest of her along. High on the brow of the slope that led down to the cottages she was already singing it out: 'Dody! Dody!' so that her young voice shrill with life and so excited echoed round the black cindered emptiness of that path, sang in and out of the bricked cottage yards, rained against blind windows, rose and died with the tops of the green elms above the grey roofs, above the smoke that seemed to smell of cooked meat and coal.

Dody, her younger cousin, was squatting in the yard winding a little gramophine. The gramophone disc rotated at a wild speed, hurrying round ever faster to tin out a shrill voice that pranced up and down, as though its very bladder were bursting among the blazers and the pier-stage somewhere down the dark tin horn, screaming among the old jazz instruments to get off the stage and out of the box: 'Swanee, Swanee, How I love you, *How* I love you . . .' When Nita banged through the wooden yard gate and clustered herself feverishly down, all in one piece, satchel, hat, skirts, curls, like a bird alighting with wings askew by Dody's ear, the gramophone went on singing. She put her arm round Dody's neck and breathlessly whispered into her ear. Dody's eyes went round and fascinated, her mouth pressed itself small as though she would cry: the voice kept whispering, Nita's eyes opened and shut and rolled with every terrible word, her head waved from side to side, retreated, then back came those lips, wet and hot with breath close to the ear. 'I saw it . . . there, right in front it was, plain as day . . . I don't know how

19

long, I'm sure . . . anyone could see . . .' In short, dreadful gasps the whispers came out, the chattering secret. A silence, long and wise, as the two girls squatted and gazed at each other. Then from Dody a deep, heart-blown sigh. From Nita a nod, then emphatic quickening nods, one after the other, racing up to get breath to tell it all again, the lovely terrible thing.

For nothing like this had ever happened before—that was plain from the start. There had been terrible things before, as when the sweetshop woman fell on the line two summers ago, on a hot afternoon, and the train had run right over her. That was terrible, especially as it had been a picnic afternoon, hot and all the flowers out—but it was funny, too, when they made jokes afterwards about strawberry jam. And there was the time when the Leadbetters had suddenly gone: one day there were all the Leadbetters, seven of them from Granny Leadbetter to little Angela, living in the cottage one door from the end—and then the next day they'd gone, there were no Leadbetters! A van had called, people said, in the night. Not a stick of a table or a chair was left in the cottage. The cottage was there still, Number Six still, but no Leadbetters! And nobody would say why or how. People knew, but there was something awful that they would never tell. They frowned, they pressed their lips into ruler-lines. 'Don't ask no questions,' they said, 'and you know what you won't be told none of.' Nita and Dody had asked for weeks, they had stood outside Number Six and peered into the windows. They had rattled the back door and kicked the empty bottles. The newspaper man had even left the Sunday paper sticking in the letterbox, the dead letterbox. Since then, no Leadbetter had ever been seen. They had gone in a hush. There was something nasty about the Leadbetters.

Those events were memorable but they were memories only, misted and vague as the uncley sort of God one heard stories about in Sunday School. But here—here was something new, alive, overwhelming, something that was happening now, at the very minute, as the clock ticked, as the church bell tolled! The church bell just then tolled suddenly, like some great celestial dustbin-lid beaten against the grey sky, and then started its measured echoing march through the September Wednesday noon. The children whispered frantically. The gramophone whirred round grating and clicking; the singing had stopped. All about that little yard, with its washing hanging abandoned, its pramwheels and cans and its derelict wooden hutch—all this stayed empty and desolate as the cinderpath. But the children felt none of it. They saw none of the lowering green leaves against that slatey sky with its white-bottomed clouds, nor the vegetable green of the little leaves climbing the elm-trunks, nor the old tin shelters with the weeds in them and the jars of dried paintbrushes, nor the allotment beyond, nor the blanched grey of the walls of the seven cottages—a scene of only grey and heavy green and cinder-black.

'What shall we do? What shall we do . . .?' chattered Dody to Nita and Nita to Dody, making backwards and forwards glances wise and sophisticated, lunatic and tender. At eight and nine years of age their faces were old in gesture, their expression poised into magical replicas of feelings that they seemed to expect rather than experience. And suddenly Nita was saying over for the twentieth time, '*Who* could have done it? Who *could* have done it?' Dody jumped up and clapped her hands and began dancing. 'Dody knows, Dody knows what we'll do . . .' she sang, chanted, repeated hopping round the yard with her eyes brilliant and mad. She suddenly ran back to Nita and said what was very simple, but to these two an idea of impossible daring, a breath-taking stroke. 'It was a boy done it,' Dody said. 'So we'll do it back on the boys!'

They both gasped. Nita's hand was up at her mouth. She was going to cry or to laugh, something was bursting in her. But all she did was to say in a little voice, not exactly her own: 'What'll we do then?'

Dody laughed and screamed delightedly: 'We'll do it back on the boys . . .'

'What? What though?' whispered Nita, who knew.

'The same, the same!' screamed Dody, then clapped her hand over her mouth.

Nita nestled close up to her, took her arm, ran over to the corner of the yard, then whispered more slowly but with her eyes bright with appetite for the words she knew would come but only wanted to hear

over and over again: 'Tell, tell! Tell me what we'll do, Dody . . .'
Dody bent her head and whispered it again.

Their hot dinner never seemed to be going to end, though that in itself was delicious. Nita's Mum, in her apron still, gave them their mutton boiled juicy grey and the white wet potatoes. And all through Nita and Dody kept tittering, staring at each other across the cruet with fearful eyes, then looking down at their plates and spooning round the barley in that gluey pale gravy. Nita's Mum kept asking them what was the matter. Then they hung their heads, continuing on a lower plane and with slanted eyes the same exchange of secret glances and held giggles. Once Nita sang out, 'Oh dear, what can the matter be?'—but Dody, crammed with barley, nearly choked herself, and at this Nita's Mum lost patience and told them to go straight up to their bedroom without any pudding. And that was just what they wanted, to slide out on the linoleum, with the blessed door closed behind them, to leap up the stairs away from the white table-cloth and its bread-crumbs, up to the bedspread where they just burst themselves laughing and where Nita suddenly stopped and said confidentially: 'Tell, tell.'

Half an hour later Dody said, 'Where's your box? We'll need the you-know-what . . .'

Nita's face fell, suddenly blank, as though now there was something to hide. She fidgeted. Then she looked up tearfully. 'I forgot, I haven't got any.'

Dody jumped up appalled. 'Where is it? Where is it?' And when Nita pointed miserably to the washstand where, between the soap-dish and the white water-jug a pencil-box jutted out woodenly—she ran across the room and fingered it open in a second. Inside there were ink-stains, a green Koh-i-noor, a stub of pink rubber stabbed with black pencil-marks, two paper-clip-hair-pins. Dody turned round wailing, 'There isn't any. There isn't any . . .'

At which Nita sat bolt upright and said, thoughtfully, tragically, slowly: 'At any rate, I've still got my penny.'

'Your penny!'

'My penny.'

SOMETHING TERRIBLE, SOMETHING LOVELY

'PENNY!'

In a moment they were chattering again, the penny was out, they were fingering it with love, and Dody said again and again: 'We can get lots of it now.'

'Lots of what?'

'Lots of you-know-what!'

'When?'

'Oh, now, now, now now now . . .'

Nita rose then to her feet, a dreadful pallor straining her face with age and sickness. 'Oh,' she said, 'it's Wednesday!'

'*Wednesday!*' Dody mouthed after her, as though she were munching something she would never swallow. 'Shop's shut!'

That night they knew they would do it tomorrow. That night was as long as one of the nights sometime before Christmas, when Christmas is near yet still will never hurry nearer, as long too as the nights of early bed in the summer when the windows were open and the music of the fair came so clearly across the common. That night the windows were open too, but outside it was dark, dark and warm, telling about the winter in the wrong way, without any cold, and thus in a queer way threatening; like some Monday nights in the kitchen with the washing about, when nobody could be bothered with you, when the minutes stopped altogether and no treats lay ahead. Tonight though, there was something ahead, but still there was the waiting, and so the room lay deadly and the electric light beaming out at the back dull and unmoving.

They were told off for bed early, as soon as that September dark came down, and when they had washed nestled near on the big pillow, sucking the stringy ends of the white coverlet, making caves in the pillow and telling, over and over again, telling. Word for word Dody knew and Nita knew exactly what was to happen, but the words themselves had to be repeated, and each time marvellously they brought the picture succulently clear.

'When'll we go to the shop?' Nita whispered.

'In breaktime.'

'What'll we ask for?'

'Chalk.'

'A ha'penny-worth?'

'Pennyworth! A whole pennyworth?'

Then there was a giggling, and suddenly Nita stopped. Her voice sounded terrified, and as though it wanted to be terrified. 'And what if someone sees? What if one of the boys comes round the corner, just then, and *sees?*'

Dody mouthed fiercely, idiotically with her tongue stuck out in the dark: 'We'll run and run and run and *run!*'

But the telling could only last minutes at a time. In between they lay in silence, thinking hard, the thoughts racing, but far too fast for the minutes, or for the long-drawn-out darkness marked only by faint noises from downstairs, from Nita's mum's cough, from Dad's rustling paper. The light from the stairs came though the door and made a patch like a clown's hat on the ceiling. There was a soapy smell.

Once, much later, as they were at last nearly asleep, Dody pushed her head nearer and whispered, much nearer than before, and as though she had been thinking of this all the time: 'I say, Nita . . .'

Nita whispered: 'Yes?'

'I say you don't . . . do you?'

A pause, fearful and long. 'Don't what, Dody?'

Dody breathed quickly. 'Love Stan?'

The pillow heaved up, it was Nita turning and pressing her face hard into the pillow, gritting her teeth, stopping herself from saying anything, from crying, from laughing, from screaming, from showing any of herself even in the dark. The dark whirled round her like a blush. But then her head was up again and she laughed: 'Who, me? What do you take *me* for?'

The next day was dull and low-clouded as before, the pale smoke from the cottage chimneys pencilled up paler than the sky, almost white against the dying green of the beeches above: pencilled, then blew suddenly down untidily on to the roofs, as though some huge invisible bird had swooped past. There were the beginnings of small winds, but the day was too heavy for them; the grey roofs seemed to shine against such a weight of dullness.

SOMETHING TERRIBLE, SOMETHING LOVELY

Though Dody and Nita had awoken early, breakfast was a scramble—and they went off to school much earlier than usual. But outside the school gates and in the playground there lay a vast emptiness, as though nothing were ever to happen again—nobody there, the doors open, and the clock outside resting its gold hands at half-past eight. That clock seemed to have stopped. And when at last the other children came first drifting then running hot-faced in, and school was assembled, the other clock in the inky oak classroom seemed also to keep stopping. So the morning dawdled, stopping and dragging, towards eleven.

At half-past ten their excitement returned, they began to feel the eyes of the others, their secret grew huge and vulnerable again. Earlier, Nita had stared blushing at the book, sure that the others knew and were looking and laughing at her: but soon, when she had looked round, it had been disappointing to see that no one at all was taking any notice of her. Now, at twenty-five to eleven, the feeling came back: soon they were to do this thing and so it seemed that everyone knew about it. By five to eleven they were looking at each other and at the clock, it seemed an endless time—when a miracle happened! The Mistress suddenly shut the book from which she had been reading and herself looked up at the clock. Just then the clock jumped a minute forward, and this must have decided her, for she smiled and said: 'All right. Off you go—*quietly*, children.'

They walked to the door and then bolted down the steps and out on to the asphalt, out through the gate and never stopped until they were at the shop. Nita handed over her penny clasped hot and stayed outside while Dody went in. The shop-door bell rang loud and crisp like a tram-bell, much too loud, startling, so that Nita looked fearfully up and down the street. If the boys heard, they would know—for sure, for sure! But there was only a soldier in washed blue sitting on a bench, two old ladies with shopping baskets looking at a cat. The cat rubbed itself up against their black skirts and the ladies laughed, one stroked it with her stick. The street had an empty look, no cars, no bicycles, and thus it seemed all the more empty for the ringing and echoing chattering cries of all the children hidden away in the playground round the corner. The bell clanged again and Dody crashed out holding something small and hard

25

against her breast, and nodding with her chin right in, and holding out urgently one hand to drag Nita in the direction her legs seemed already to be running. They ran together, away from the school, and Dody whispered: 'Yellow and white pieces she gave me—lots—come on . . .'

Up the road, up the steep road, higher and higher up to the asylum! The asylum tower, purple and green, stood out above them, very near, but the asylum wall was really much further away when you were down in the streets. And the streets suddenly ended, the common began. They raced along, hurrying against the minutes, the fifteen minutes of Break, and came to where the may-bushes started and the ground rose to meet the beginning of the tall asylum wall.

Here a chalky, scrap-grass path led in between the may-bushes. Along this they ran, along by the rainy smell from under the bushes. The wall came suddenly, and then the path continued straighter between the wall, high and purple and iron-spiked on the top, and the dark underneath of the straggling may-bush wood. The may stopped, and the other bushes withering dark-green with their dusty crimson berries—and Nita stopped too. Dody stopped. They could peer out now at the huge asylum wall curling out into the open, standing high and commanding over the open common. Deep purple and darker glazed bricks, severe and authoritative, glowered at the open grass that fanned away on all sides, down from it. This wall was the summit point of the common, the place to which everyone eventually walked—and now Nita pointed in its direction and whispered: 'Look! Look! *There!*'

They looked round then fearfully. No one in sight. Only the bare common, gorse, chalk-patches, dying grass. They left the may-bushes and raced off up towards the wall, two small figures growing smaller up the slope, growing murky like half-seen flies in all that dull, dead common-land.

Later, when they had gone, the wall still stood glowering out over the empty common. Once a watery sunlight opened up and for a moment chalk boulders and something metal like a can winked weakly, the pale copper-green asylum cupola glittered into transient life. Then it was as dark, darker than before. A single cyclist was drawn slowly as on a string across some distant intersecting path.

SOMETHING TERRIBLE, SOMETHING LOVELY

The leaves of the few straggling trees hung still, dark green and hardened, shrunk to the last point before they would turn colour. And on the wall, intimately lonely among the greater loneliness of the weather and that wide vacant space, there could be read two messages written in chalk, white on the purple brick, spidery and scrawled straight capital letters, words that looked bare and cold out there in the open:

NITΛ HOBBS LOVES STΛN CHUTER.

Λ long chalk line had been drawn through this, and underneath was written emphatically, with yellow first letters to each word:

THE PERSON WHO WROTE THIS IS DAFT.

Displaced Persons

HAVE you watched Time eating at a place? The bearded jaws tearing unseen at the air of a still room, the stiller for so many silent people, the stiller for a drying-off of thought and of those motions of building that alone can compensate for the wolfish mouthfuls of living every minute hugely lost? The voracious bearded jaws, biting off the air, always up somewhere near the ceiling, between the frieze and the quiet electric cord?

The Indian House stood furnaced in melancholy red by a September sunset; such a light was brassy, spacious, and seemed to glow up from below, underlining thus the shadows and the tall empty windows of that immense Indian-built warehouse in such a way that a sense of desolation and black-veiled sorrowers, of a Second Coming made a funeral of the Indian part, of the brownish plastered facade of an already mournful London evening. But there were no black-bowed figures, no figures at all, the pillared and domed warehouse stood irrevocably empty, consumed within by its own void and on the outside, reflecting on mogulish plaster screens and friezes, by the faraway funeral red. Such a dead design was of course accentuated by the business in its forecourt, where there were piled and strewn huge chunks of grey granite and rough white marble, material for the grinding of tombstones. Strange wooden hoisting devices stood about, lashed and poised, like derelict siege catapults. But the tombstone industry was silent, it was past six o'clock, the only movement was to be sensed across the road, across the tramlines and under the overhead wires, where the doors of the Admiral's Discretion stood open.

Inside, in the wan electric light, between walls of faded orange, they were drinking. Little noise: they talked, worriedly, in whispers, leaning slightly towards each other. When the bell of the cash-till rang, one of them started, looked up for a moment bewildered; he shook his head and then, as though there was nothing else to be done, slowly as though the whole world and the rest of time were empty and could provide no further move, slowly the hand reached to his waistcoat pocket and from there he drew out a small silvery machine. With this, without looking, sinking back, he rolled a cigarette. He had the face of a pale pike, grey all over and greyer where the stubble grew; on his head was pulled down hard a fawn-coloured homburg with a greased silk brim.

This man was sitting in that untidy corner improvised by the door bolted open. Along from him, on the same polished pine bench perforated by so many holes, a small straight-necked woman in navy-blue serge sat alone; her hair jet-black, her cheeks flushed with rouge, the very white skin at the back of her neck grained with black ticks where she had been shaved for her shingle, her eyes hardly visible under the felt of a pale blue hat. She was looking at a picture hanging on the wall above, a military scene framed in fumed oak. When this woman with the straight neck and the blinding hat looked up, her whole body had to swing back so that she could see at all. Now, at such a tortured angle, she watched a grey Cardigan charging his Light Brigade into the fly-blown Russian cannon at Balaclava. After a while, a long while, as the electric clock pounced on, as the September sunset through the frosted glass burned darker, as the beer slowly sank in the glasses all around, as this beer then tasted round the teeth and the palates of those mouths and sank again to wash pooling behind waistcoats and the grimed elastic of corsets— after a while, the woman pursed her lips, swung herself vertical, took a peck at the stout-glass, and then with a slight brown froth on her upper lip re-elevated herself towards Cardigan. She remained in this position, strained; but more as if she were waiting for something to happen there in the bar than for Cardigan to make a move.

Indeed this same sensation of waiting hung over all those others who stood singly or in groups round the semicircular bar. They all faced inwards, as though the expected and long-awaited happening might only occur at the pivot of their yellow pine semicircle, the central point where the cast-metal cash-till stood beneath its awning of draped Union Jacks and cards into which were stitched little bottles of aspirin tablets. To either side of the till stood and leant the two bar-tenders, sallow women of uncertain age, one spectacled and frizz-haired, the other taller and sleeker and provided with a jaw so enormous that it was weak—but both pale and slightly moist of skin. They also were waiting. Leaning with their backs to the bottles they stared vacantly just above the heads of the people who circled them. When one or other of the drinkers motioned for his glass to be refilled, one of these attendants would walk over the intervening space—and what a fine, round space, with the drinkers hemmed so close against their pale wood railing!—and enquire the nature of the request still with her eyes raised just so slightly above the drinker's head. And these drinkers would receive their new glasses mournfully and remain staring inwards towards the till.

But some talked. There was a naval captain accompanied by two ladies and an elderly man wearing a cap, a stiff white collar and a tweed coat. This elderly man carried the rough walking-stick of the retired. And the ladies! One had dyed her hair blonde, so that from behind she looked quite like a young girl; but that the bobbed hair hung straggled over a neck that shrunk away from it—and, of course, when she turned her head, one saw the face of disaster, painted in bright American colours, lifted, stitched up, the new-born virgin of fifty with thin fallen-in lips and every line pouched to a fever-pitch of anxiety: anxiety, but for the eyes, pale, filmed, popping out but not caring. Her sister wore the unmistakable marks of the tropics, the ancient tan, the melancholy wasted skin and the iron-grey hair, the seedy sportswoman and bridge-queen into whose attire there always crept the touch of silk that once had brought an *hauteur* to the far-flung club of stranded values where, for so many long and now finished years, her honeymoon had slowly set. The naval captain had eyes with a furtive, trustless twinkle. He stood drowned in a dark naval raincoat. The four of them drank long watery whiskies—and often nodded. Yet, however much they nodded, however many times they reasserted the rightness of the world, they too seemed to be waiting: the woman with the blonde hair often looked up at that pouncing clock, the elderly gentleman coughed and turned away and turned back again, the naval captain and his sportswoman stood opposite each other and jigged from toe to heel, like automatic toys, without ever stopping.

30

Two white-faced boys then lurched in, giggling. But when they faced up to the bar, the realization of some manly inheritance turned their cheeks suddenly red, as though a neon gas was momentarily infused into them, and then as quickly the new colour faded, so that their faces were white again, faintly greyed with oil—and they ordered ginger beer and bowed their heads over a black bicycle bell. Youth was to have its watery fling! Two others, older, idler, with strapping padded shoulders and about them a sprinkling of brassy gold, on their fingers, their ties, in their teeth—these two with their flat pints leant eagerly over the little balls in the pin-table machine. Eager, and thin-lipped. But between such feverish pulls and pokes at the machine, these two also lounged back and looked up at the clock, at the door, at the fading light; they were waiting, like the others, for the something that would never happen.

But, surprisingly, it did. Suddenly into this hushed air, with its whispers, its shufflings of feet, its dead chinking, and above all and over everything its pervading, soundless whirring of the small yellow electric light bulb, that constant thing, unshaded, throwing its wan unmoving light straight at the top corners where the ceiling met those strange orange walls—now into this hush there broke a sudden huge sound. It exploded in from the street, with no warning—the deafening metal burst of a barrel organ.

What happened then was ubiquitous, the same small movement jerked all that drinking room, all the faces of the drinkers—each face moved slowly round towards the door and there hung, for a second as if out of joint, pressed forward slightly off the equilibrium of the neck; mouths opened for breath, more breath; eyes blank but in their fixedness intent upon peering through the fog of shock. Everybody looked at the door. Nobody saw anything.

The barrel organ must have been placed just beyond the upright jambs, probably on the pavement neatly squared with the wall so that the room formed an extra sounding box; indeed, something new and dark was flushed against the frosted glass. The pike-faced man was staring straight into the bolted door, some six inches from his stony bewildered snout. The naval officer and those others had stopped talking, the bar-girls had each lowered their eyes so that now they peered through the drinkers instead of above them. The bicycle bell lay abandoned in the oily boy's hand, slackly extended forward, as if it were offered to the door as a warm wet present. The pin-table youths had struck subtly the attitude of boxers, toes preened, shoulders high and heads forward—while behind them their last little silver balls went hurrying round the garish presentation of a painted, modern city, flashing on lights in the urgent accumulation of silver, red, green, yellow and pale-blue skyscrapers, among meteor planes and overhead railways, among the short skirts of citizens dressed in rubbery romanish-mediaeval toguettes of the twenty-first century. These lights, in fact, provided now the only movement, they snowballed on and off, faster and faster like a gale warning. And the gale, the metal-belling wind churning through the door rushed straight about that room, entering it and filling it immediately like a flood-wind, grasping round the crevices among the bottles, under the bar, up to the corners at the very ceiling, down underneath the serge-skirted woman's ankles, round and about Lord Cardigan and everyone who was there, filling, fillling the void absolutely. And when this in that thunderous second was done and the place was a block of sound—so other small movements hesitated and began. Smiles! Nods! Shufflings of feet! For at last the explosion was recognized to be music, and well-loved music, a tune of warmth and reminisence, a war-time tune:

> 'Bless 'em all, bless 'em all,
> The long and the short and the tall——'

This music rang round the bar, again and again, a circling tune that came back every few seconds to where it had started and then went off again, round and round, waltzing and merry despite its metal fibre.

But merry to no applause. For one by one, like the lights on the pin-table, the smiles cut out. The faces dropped. The heads turned back towards the bar. The shufflings of feet, the beginning of a dance, stopped. The morose emptiness returned; and with it, unceasing, whirling round the room, the giddy music continued. There was no echo. The sound was hard, bright, filling the empty room with metal rods that clashed for breath; only that sound, exact, reporting without echo.

The drinkers drank without flinching. It was suddenly plain—
they were beyond flinching, just as they had been beyond keeping
up the first smile that had for a moment seemed to warm them. It
was just not worth it.

I was reminded then of two things, both strangely to do with big
dogs—perhaps dogs with faces so heavy and eyes as mournful as
those that now gazed in again at the cash-till. One of these dogs was
the bloodhound once seen at the bottom of an escalator in a Tube
station. This dog sat like a rock on the platform at the very edge of
the immense progression of upward moving empty stairs. His master
tried to urge him on, patting, whispering, purring, whistling, and
once even kicking. But move the dog would not. He sat absolutely.
He sat and stared sadly at the ceaseless stairs emerging from the
ground and travelling emptily upwards to Heaven. He seemed to be
nodding and saying to himself: 'There, that's another thing they've
done . . .'

The other dog is to be found in a quotation from Henri de Mon-
therlant. He writes: ' . . . And for a long time the baron, sitting in his
chair, kept that beautiful gravity of face that men get—it almost
gives them the illusion of thoughtfulness—when they lose money.
Then he sighed. Newfoundland dogs often have a little humidity
at the commissure of the eyes, falling like tears. Why do Newfound-
lands dogs cry? Because they have been tricked.'

The Vertical Ladder

AS he felt the first watery eggs of sweat moistening the palms of his hands, as with every rung higher his body seemed to weigh more heavily, this young man Flegg regretted in sudden desperation but still in vain, the irresponsible events that had thrust him up into his present precarious climb. Here he was, isolated on a vertical iron ladder flat to the side of a gasometer and bound to climb higher and higher until he should reach the vertiginous skyward summit.

How could he ever have wished this on himself? How easy it had been to laugh away his cautionary fears on the firm ground . . . now he would give the very hands that clung to the ladder for a safe conduct to solid earth.

It had been a strong spring day, abruptly as warm as midsummer. The sun flooded the parks and streets with sudden heat—Flegg and his friends had felt stifled in their thick winter clothes. The green glare of the new leaves everywhere struck the eye too fiercely, the air seemed almost sticky from the exhalations of buds and swelling resins. Cold winter senses were overcome—the girls had complained of headaches—and their thoughts had grown confused and uncomfortable as the wool underneath against their skins. They had wandered out from the park by a back gate, into an area of back streets.

The houses there were small and old, some of them already falling into disrepair; short streets, cobbles, narrow pavements, and the only shops a tobacconist or a desolate corner oil-shop to colour the grey—it was the outcrop of some industrial undertaking beyond. At first these quiet, almost deserted streets had seemed more restful than the park; but soon a dusty air of peeling plaster and powdering brick, the dark windows and the dry stone steps, the very dryness altogether had proved more wearying than before, so that when suddenly the houses ended and the ground open to reveal the yards

34

of a disused gasworks, Flegg and his friends had welcomed the green of nettles and milkwort that grew among the scrap-iron and broken brick.

They walked out into the wasteland, the two girls and Flegg and the other two boys, and stood presently before the old gasometer itself. Among the ruined sheds this was the only erection still whole, it still predominated over the yards, towering high above other buildings for hundreds of feet around. So they threw bricks against its rusted sides.

The rust flew off in flakes and the iron rang dully. Flegg, who wished to excel in the eyes of the dark-haired girl, began throwing his bricks higher than the others, at the same time lobbing them, to suggest that he knew something of grenade-throwing, claiming for himself vicariously the glamour of a uniform. He felt the girl's eyes follow his shoulders, his shoulders broadened. She had black eyes, unshadowed beneath short wide-awake lids, as bright as a boy's eyes; her lips pouted with difficulty over a scramble of irregular teeth, so that it often looked as if she were laughing; she always frowned—and Flegg liked her earnest, purposeful expression. Altogether she seemed a wide-awake girl who would be the first to appreciate an active sort of a man. Now she frowned and shouted: 'Bet you can't climb as high as you can throw!'

Then there began one of those uneasy jokes, innocent at first, that taken seriously can accumulate an hysterical accumulation of spite. Everyone recognizes this underlying unpleasantness, it is plainly felt; but just because of this the joke must at all costs be pressed forward, one becomes frightened, one laughs all the louder, pressing to drown the embarrassments of danger and guilt. The third boy had instantly shouted: 'Course he can't, he can't climb no higher than himself.'

Flegg turned round scoffing, so that the girl had quickly shouted again, laughing shrilly and pointing upwards. Already all five of them felt uneasy. Then in quick succession, all in a few seconds, the third boy had repeated: "Course he bloody can't.' Flegg had said: 'Climb to the top of anything.' The other boy had said: 'Climb to the top of my aunt Fanny.' The girl had said: 'Climb to the top of the gasworks then.'

Flegg had said: 'That's nothing.' And the girl, pressing on then as she had to, suddenly introduced the inevitable detail that made these suppositions into fact: 'Go on then, climb it. Here—tie my hanky on the top. Tie my flag to the top.'

Even then Flegg had a second's chance. It occurred to him instantly that he could laugh it off; but an hysterial emphasis now possessed the girl's face—she was dancing up and down and clapping her hands insistently—and this confused Flegg. He began stuttering after the right words. But the words refused to come. At all costs he had to cover his stuttering. So: 'Off we go then!' he had said. And he had turned to the gasometer.

It was not, after all, so very high. It was hardly a full-size gasometer, its trellised iron top-rail would have stood level with the roof-coping of a five- or six-storey tenement. Until then Flegg had only seen the gasometer as a rough mass of iron, but now every detail sprang into abrupt definition. He studied it intently, alertly considering its size and every feature of stability, the brown rusted iron sheeting smeared here and there with red lead, a curious buckling that sometimes deflated its curved bulk as though a vacuum were collapsing it from within, and the ladders scaling the sides flush with the sheeting. The grid of girders, a complexity of struts, the bolting.

There were two ladders, one a Jacob's ladder, clamped fast to the side, another that was more of a staircase, zigzagging up the belly of the gasometer in easy gradients and provided with a safety rail. This must have been erected later as a substitute for the Jacob's ladder, which demanded an unnecessarily stringent climb and was now in fact in disuse, for some twenty feet of its lower rungs had been worn away; however, there was apparently some painting in progress, for a wooden painter's ladder had been propped beneath with its head reaching to the undamaged bottom of the vertical ladder— the ascent was thus serviceable again. Flegg looked quickly at the foot of the wooden ladder—was it well grounded?—and then at the head farther up—was this secure?—and then up to the top, screwing his eyes to note any fault in the iron rungs reaching innumerably and indistinctly, like the dizzying strata of a zip, to the summit platform.

Flegg, rapidly assessing these structures, never stopped sauntering forward. He was committed, and so while deliberately sauntering to appear thus the more at ease, he knew that he must never hesitate. The two boys and his own girl kept up a chorus of encouraging abuse. 'How I climbed Mount Everest,' they shouted. 'He'll come down quicker'n he went up.' 'Mind you don't bang your head on a harp, Sir Galahad.' But the second girl had remained quiet throughout; she was already frightened, sensing instantly that the guilt for some tragedy was hers alone—although she had never in fact opened her mouth. Now she chewed passionately on gum that kept her jaws firm and circling.

Suddenly the chorus rose shriller. Flegg had veered slightly towards the safer staircase. His eyes had naturally questioned this along with the rest of the gasometer, and almost unconsciously his footsteps had veered in the direction of his eyes; then this instinct had emerged into full consciousness—perhaps he could use the staircase, no one had actually instanced the Jacob's ladder, there might yet be a chance? But the quick eyes behind him had seen, and immediately the chorus rose: 'No you don't!' 'Not up those sissy stairs!' Flegg switched his course by only the fraction that turned him again to the perpendicular ladder. 'Who's talking about stairs?' he shouted back.

Behind him they still kept up a din, still kept him up to pitch, worrying at him viciously. 'Look at him, he doesn't know which way to go—he's like a ruddy duck's uncle without an aunt.'

So that Flegg realized finally that there was no alternative. He had to climb the gasometer by the vertical ladder. And as soon as this was finally settled, the doubt cleared from his mind. He braced his shoulders and suddenly found himself really making light of the job. After all, he thought, it isn't so high? Why should I worry? Hundreds of men climb such ladders each day, no one falls, the ladders are clamped as safe as houses? He began to smile within himself at his earlier perturbations. Added to this, the girl now ran up to him and handed him her handkerchief. As her black eyes frowned a smile at him, he saw that her expression no longer held its vicious laughing scorn, but now instead had grown softer, with a look of real encouragement and even admiration. 'Here's your flag,' she said. And then she even added: 'Tell you what—you don't really have to go! I'll believe you!' But this came too late. Flegg had accepted the climb, it was fact, and already he felt something of an exhilarating glow of glory. He took the handkerchief, blew the girl a dramatic kiss, and started up the lowest rungs of the ladder at a run.

This painter's ladder was placed at a comfortable slant. But nevertheless Flegg had only climbed some ten feet—what might have corresponded to the top of a first-floor window—when he began to slow up, he stopped running and gripped harder at the rungs above and placed his feet more firmly on the unseen bars below. Although he had not yet measured his distance from the ground, somehow he sensed distinctly that he was already unnaturally high, with nothing but air and a precarious skeleton of wooden bars between him and the receding ground. He felt independent of solid support; yet, according to his eyes, which stared straight forward at the iron sheeting beyond, he might have been still standing on the lowest rungs by the ground. The sensation of height infected him strongly, it had become an urgent necessity to maintain a balance, each muscle of his body became unnaturally alert. This was not an unpleasant feeling, he almost enjoyed a new athletic command of every precarious movement. He climbed then methodically until he reached the ladderhead and the first of the perpendicular iron rungs.

Here for a moment Flegg had paused. He had rested his knees up against the last three steps of the safely slanting wooden ladder, he had grasped the two side supports of the rusted iron that led so straightly upwards. His knees then clung to the motherly wood, his hands felt the iron cold and gritty. The rust powdered off and smeared him with its red dust; one large scrap flaked off and fell on to his face as he looked upwards. He wanted to brush this away from his eye, but the impulse was, to his surprise, much less powerful than the vice-like will that clutched his hands to the iron support. His hand remained firmly gripping the iron, he had to shake off the rust-flake with a jerk of his head. Even then this sharp movement nearly unbalanced him, and his stomach gulped coldly with sudden shock. He settled his knees more firmly against the wood, and though he forced himself to laugh at this sudden fear, so that in some measure his poise did really return, nevertheless he did not alter the awkward knock-kneed position of his legs patently clinging for safety. With all this he had scarcely paused. Now he pulled at the staunchions of the iron ladder, they were as firm as if they had been driven into rock.

He looked up, following the dizzying rise of the rungs to the skyline. From this angle flat against the iron sheeting, the gasometer appeared higher than before. The blue sky seemed to descend and almost touch it. The redness of the rust dissolved into a deepening grey shadow, the distant curved summit loomed over black and high. Although it was immensely stable, as seen in rounded perspective from a few yards away, there against the side it appeared top heavy, so that this huge segment of sheet iron seemed to have lost the support of its invisible complement behind, the support that was now unseen and therefore unfelt, and Flegg imagined despite himself that the entire erection had become unsteady, that quite possibly the gasometer might suddenly blow over like a gigantic top-heavy sail. He lowered his eyes quickly and concentrated on the hands before him. He began to climb.

From beneath there still rose a few cries from the boys. But the girl had stopped shouting—probably she was following Flegg's every step with admiring eyes. He imagined again her frown and her peculiarly pouting mouth, and from this image drew new strength with which he clutched the rungs more eagerly. But now he noticed that the cries had begun to ring with an unpleasant new echo, as though they were already far off. And Flegg could not so easily distinguish their words. Even at this height he seemed to have penetrated into a distinct stratum of separate air, for it was certainly cooler, and for the first time that day he felt the light fanning of a wind. He looked down. His friends appeared shockingly small. Their bodies had disappeared and he saw only their upturned faces. He wanted to wave, to demonstrate in some way a carefree attitude; but then instantly he felt frustrated as his hands refused to unlock their grip. He turned to the rungs again with the smile dying on his lips.

He swallowed uneasily and continued to tread slowly upwards, hand after hand, foot after foot. He had climbed ten rungs of the iron ladder when his hands first began to feel moist, when suddenly, as though a catastophe had overtaken him not gradually but in one overpowering second, he realized that he was afraid; incontrovertibly. He could cover it no longer, he admitted it all over his body. His hands gripped with pitiable eagerness, they were now alert to a point of shivering, as though the nerves inside them had been forced taut for so long that now they had burst beyond their strained tegument; his feet no longer trod firmly on the rungs beneath, but first stepped for their place timorously, then glued themselves to the iron. In this way his body lost much of its poise; these nerves and muscles in his two legs and two arms seemed to work independently, no longer integrated with the rhythm of his body, but moving with the dangerous unwilled jerk of crippled limbs.

His body hung slack away from the ladder, with nothing beneath it but a thirty foot drop to the ground; only his hands and feet were fed with the security of an attachment, most of him lay off the ladder, hanging in space; his arms revolted at the strain of their familiar angle, as though they were flies' feet denying all natural laws. For the first time, as the fear took hold of him, he felt that what he had attempted was impossible. He could never achieve the top. If at this height of only thirty feet, as it were three storeys of a building, he felt afraid—what would he feel at sixty feet? Yet . . . he trod heavily up. He was afraid, but not desperate. He dreaded each step, yet forced himself to believe that at some time it would be over, it could not take long.

A memory crossed his mind. It occurred to him vividly, then flashed away, for his eyes and mind were continually concentrated on the rusted iron bars and the white knuckles of his hands. But for an instant he remembered waking up long ago in the nursery and seeing that the windows were light, as if they reflected a coldness of moonlight. Only they were not so much lit by light as by a sensation of space. The windows seemed to echo with space. He had crawled out of bed and climbed on to a chair that stood beneath the window. It was as he had thought. Outside there was space, nothing else, a limitless area of space; yet this was not unnatural, for soon his logical eyes had supplied for what had at first appeared an impossible infinity the later image of a perfectly reasonable flood. A vast plain

of still water continued as far as his eyes could see. The tennis courts
and the houses beyond had disappeared; they were quite submerged,
flat motionless water spread out immeasurably to the distant arced
horizon all around. It lapped silently at the sides of the house, and
in the light of an unseen moon winked and washed darkly, concealing great beasts of mystery beneath its black calm surface. This
water attracted him, he wished to jump into it from the window
and immerse himself in it and allow his head to sink slowly under.
However he was perched up too high. He felt, alone at the window,
infinitely high, so that the flood seemed to lie in miniature at a great
distance below, as later in life when he was ill he had seen the objects
of his bedroom grow small and infinitely remote in the fevered reflection behind his eyes. Isolated at the little window he had been
frightened by the emptiness surrounding him, only the sky and the
water and the marooned stone wall of the house; he had been
terrified yet drawn down by dread and desire.

Then a battleship had sailed by. He had woken up, saved by the
appearance of the battleship. And now on the ladder he had a
sudden hope that something as large and stable would intervene
again to help him.

But ten rungs farther up he began to sweat more violently than
ever. His hands streamed with wet rust, the flesh inside his thighs
blenched. Another flake of rust fell on his forehead; this time it stuck
in the wetness. He felt physically exhausted. Fear was draining his
strength and the precarious position of his body demanded an
awkward physical effort. From his outstretched arms suspended
most of the weight of his body. Each stressed muscle ached. His body
weighed more heavily at each step upwards, it sagged beneath his
arms like a leaden sack. His legs no longer provided their adequate
support; it seemed as though they needed every pull of their muscle
to force themselves, as independent limbs, close to the ladder. The
wind blew faster. It dragged now at his coat, it blew its space about
him, it echoed silently a lonely spaciousness. 'Don't look down,' the
blood whispered in his temples, 'Don't look down, for God's sake,
DON'T LOOK DOWN.'

Three-quarters up the gasometer, and fifty feet from the ground,
Flegg grew desperate. Every other consideration suddenly left him.

B*   41

He wanted only to reach the ground as quickly as possible, only that. Nothing else mattered. He stopped climbing and clung to the ladder panting. Very slowly, lowering his eyes carefully so that he could raise them instantly if he saw too much, he looked down a rung, and another past his armpit, past his waist—and focused them on the ground beneath. He looked quickly up again.

He pressed himself to the ladder. Tears started in his eyes. For a moment they reeled red with giddiness. He closed them, shutting out everything. Then instantly opened them, afraid that something might happen. He must watch his hands, watch the bars, watch the rusted iron sheeting itself; no movement should escape him; the struts might come creaking loose, the whole edifice might sway over; although a fading reason told him that the gasometer had remained firm for years and was still as steady as a cliff, his horrified senses suspected that this was the one moment in the building's life when a wind would blow that was too strong for it, some defective strut would snap, the whole edifice would heel over and go crashing to the ground. This image became so clear that he could see the sheets of iron buckling and folding like cloth as the huge weight sank to the earth.

The ground had receded horribly, the drop now appeared terrifying, out of all proportion to this height he had reached. From the ground such a height would have appeared unnoteworthy. But now looking down the distance seemed to have doubled. Each object familiar to his everyday eyes—his friends, the lamp-posts, a brick wall, the kerb, a drain—all these had grown infinitely small. His senses demanded that these objects should be of a certain accustomed size. Alternatively, the world of chimneys and attic windows and roof-coping would grow unpleasantly giant as his pavement-bred eyes approached. Even now the iron sheeting that stretched to either side and above and below seemed to have grown, he was lost among such huge smooth dimensions, grown smaller himself and clinging now like a child lost on some monstrous desert of red rust.

These unfamiliarities shocked his nerves more than the danger of falling. The sense of isolation was overpowering. All things were suddenly alien. Yet exposed on the iron spaces, with the unending winds blowing aerially round him, among such free things—he felt shut in! Trembling and panting so that he stifled himself with the shortness of his own breath, he took the first step downwards. . . .

A commotion began below. A confusion of cries came drifting up to him. Above all he could hear the single voice of the girl who had so far kept quiet. She was screaming high, a shrill scream that rose in the air incisively like a gull's shriek. 'Put it back, put it back, put it back!' the scream seemed to say. So that Flegg, thinking that these cries were to warn him of some new danger apparent only from the ground Flegg gripped himself into the ladder and looked down again. He glanced down for a fractional second—but in that time saw enough. He saw that the quiet girl was screaming and pointing to the base of the iron ladder. He saw the others crowding round her, gesticulating. He saw that she really had been crying, 'Put it back!' And he realized now what the words meant—someone had removed the painter's ladder.

It lay clearly on the ground, outlined white like a child's drawing of a ladder. The boys must have seen his first step downwards, and then, from fun or from spite they had removed his only means of retreat. He remembered that from the base of the iron ladder to the ground the drop fell twenty feet. He considered quickly descending and appealing from the bottom of the ladder; but foresaw that for precious minutes they would jeer and argue, refusing to replace the ladder, and he felt than that he could never risk these minutes, unnerved, with his strength failing. Besides, he had already noticed that the whole group of them were wandering off. The boys were driving the quiet girl away, now more concerned with her than with Flegg. The quiet girl's sense of guilt had been brought to a head by the removal of the ladder. Now she was hysterically terrified. She was yelling to them to put the ladder back. She—only she, the passive one—sensed the terror that awaited them all. But her screams defeated their own purpose. They had altogether distracted the attention of the others; now it was fun to provoke more screams, to encourage this new distraction—and they forgot about Flegg far up and beyond them. They were wandering away. They were abandoning him, casually unconcerned that he was alone and helpless up in his wide prison of rust. His heart cried out for them to stay. He forgot their scorn in new and terrible torments of self-pity. An uneasy feeling lumped his throat, his eyes smarted with dry tears.

But they were wandering away. There was no retreat. They did not even know he was in difficulties. So Flegg had no option but to climb higher. Desperately he tried to shake off his fear, he actually shook his head. Then he stared hard at the rungs immediately facing his eyes, and tried to imagine that he was not high up at all. He lifted himself tentatively by one rung, then by another, and in this way dragged himself higher and higher . . . until he must have been some ten rungs from the top, over the fifth storey of a house, with now perhaps only one more storey to climb. He imagined that he might then be approaching the summit platform, and to measure this last distance he looked up.

He looked up and heaved. He felt for the first time panicked beyond desperation, wildly violently loose. He almost let go. His senses screamed to let go, yet his hands refused to open. He was stretched on a rack made by these hands that would not unlock their grip and by the panic desire to drop. The nerves left his hands so that they might have been dried bones of fingers gripped round the rungs, hooks of bone fixed perhaps strongly enough to cling on, or perhaps at some moment of pressure to uncurl their vertebrae and straighten to a drop. His insteps pricked with cold cramp. The sweat sickened him. His loins seemed to empty themselves. His trousers ran wet. He shivered, grew giddy, and flung himself frog-like on to the ladder.

The sight of the top of the gasometer had proved endemically more frightful than the appearance of the drop beneath. There lay about it a sense of material danger, not of the risk of falling, but of something removed and unhuman—a sense of appalling isolation. It echoed its elemental iron aloofness, a wind blew round it that had never known the warmth of flesh nor the softness of green fibres. Its blind eyes were raised above the world. It was like the eyeless iron vizor of an ancient god, it touched against the sky having risen in awful perpendicular to this isolation, solitary as the grey gannet cliffs that mark the end of the northern world. It was immeasurably old, outside the connotation of time; it was nothing human, only washed by the high weather, echoing with wind, visited never and silently alone.

And in this summit Flegg measured clearly the full distance of his climb. This close skyline emphasized the whirling space beneath him. He clearly saw a man fall through this space, spread-eagling to smash with the sickening force of a locomotive on the stone beneath. The man turned slowly in the air, yet his thoughts raced faster than he fell.

Flegg, clutching his body close to the rust, made small weeping sounds through his mouth. Shivering, shuddering, he began to tread up again, working his knees and elbows outward like a frog, so that his stomach could feel the firm rungs. Were they firm? His ears filled with a hot roaring, he hurried himself, he began to scramble up, wrenching at his last strength, whispering urgent meaningless words to himself like the swift whispers that close in on a nightmare. A huge weight pulled at him, dragging him to drop. He climbed higher. He reached the rop rung—and found his face staring still at a wall of red rust. He looked, wild with terror. It was the top rung! the ladder had ended! Yet—no platform . . . the real top rungs were missing . . . the platorm jutted five impassable feet above . . . Flegg stared dumbly, circling his head like a lost animal . . . then he jammed his legs in the lower rungs and his arms past the elbows to the armpits in through the top rungs and there he hung shivering and past knowing what more he could ever do. . . .

How Claeys Died

IN Germany, two months after the capitulation, tall green grass and corn had grown up round every remnant of battle, so that the war seemed to have happened many years ago. A tank, nosing up from the corn like a pale grey toad, would already be rusted, ancient: the underside of an overturned carrier exposed intricacies red-brown and clogged like an agricultural machine abandoned for years. Such objects were no longer the contemporary traffic, they were exceptional carcasses; one expected their armour to melt like the armour of crushed beetles, to enter the earth and help fertilize further the green growth in which they were already drowned.

Claeys and his party—two officers and a driver—drove past many of these histories, through miles of such fertile green growth stretching flatly to either side of the straight and endless grey avenues. Presently they entered the outskirts of a town. This was a cathedral town, not large, not known much—until by virtue of a battle its name now resounded in black letters the size of the capital letters on the maps of whole countries. This name would now ring huge for generations, it would take its part in the hymn of a national glory, such a name had already become sacred, stony, a symbol of valour. Claeys looked about him with interest—he had never seen the town before, only heard of the battle and suffered with the soldiers who had taken it and held it for four hopeful days with the hope dying each hour until nearly all were dead, hope and soldiers. Now as they entered the main street, where already the white tram-trains were hooting, where the pale walls were chipped and bullet-chopped, where nevertheless there had never been the broad damage of heavy bombs and where therefore the pavements and shop-fronts were already washed and civil—as they entered these streets decked with summer dresses and flecked with leaf patterns, Claeys looked in vain for the town of big letters, and smelled only perfume; a wall of perfume; they seemed to have entered a scent-burg, a sissy-burg, a town of female essences, Grasse—but it was only that this town happened to be planted with lime-trees, lime-trees everywhere, and these limes were all in flower, their shaded greenery alive with the golden powdery flower whose essence drifted down to the streets and filled them. The blood was gone, the effort of blood had evaporated. Only scent, flowers, sunlight, trams, white dresses.

'A nice memorial,' Claeys thought. 'Keep it in the geography book.' Then the car stopped outside a barracks. The officers got out. Claeys said he would wait in the car. He was not in uniform, he was on a civil mission, attached temporarily to the army. It does not matter what mission. It was never fulfilled. All that need be said is that Claeys was a teacher, engaged then on relief measures, a volunteer for this work of rehabilitation of the enemy, perhaps a sort of half-brother-of-mercy as during the occupation he had been a sort of half-killer. Now he wanted to construct quickly the world of which he had dreamed during the shadow years; now he was often as impatient of inaction as he had learned to be patient before. Patience bends before promise: perhaps this curiosity for spheres of action quickened his interest as now a lorry-load of soldiers drew up and jumped down at the barrack-gate. One of the soldiers said: 'They're using mortars.' Another was saying: 'And do you blame 'em?'

There had been trouble, they told Claeys, up at the camp for expatriates—the camp where forced labourers imported from all over Europe waited for shipment home. A group of these had heard that a released German prisoner-of-war was returning to work his farm in the vicinity of the camp. They had decided to raid the farm at nightfall, grab as much food as possible, teach the German a trick or two. But the German had somehow got hold of a grenade—from the fields, or perhaps hidden in the farmhouse. At any rate, he had thrown it and killed two of the expatriates. The others had retreated, the story had spat round, before long the expatriates were coming back on the farm in full strength. They had rifles and even mortars. The news got back to the occupational military and a picket had been sent over. The mortars were opening fire as it arrived: but they were stopped, the expatriates respected the British. Yet to maintain this respect they had to keep a picket out there for the night. Not all the polskis or czechskis or whoever they were had gone home. A few had hung about, grumbling. The air was by no means clear.

When the officers returned, Claeys told them that he had altered his plans, he wanted to go up and take a look at this expatriates' camp. He gave no reason, and it is doubtful whether he had then a special reason; he felt only that he ought to see these expatriates and talk to them. He had no idea of what to say, but something of the circumstances might suggest a line later.

So they drove out into the country again, into the green. Rich lucent corn stretched endlessly to either side of the straight and endless road. Regularly, in perfect order, precisely intervalled beeches flashed by: a rich, easy, discreet roof of leaves shaded their passage as the foliage met high above. Occasionally a notice at the roadside reminded them of mines uncleared beyond the verges, occasionally a tree bore an orderly white notice addressed to civil traffic. And occasionally a unit of civil traffic passed—a family wheeling a handcart, a cyclist and his passenger, and once a slow-trudging German soldier making his grey way back along the long road to his farm. But there was nothing about this figure in grey-green to suggest more than a farmer dressed as a soldier; he walked slowly, he seemed to be thinking slowly, secure in his destination and free of time as any countryman walking slowly home on an empty road.

All was order. Birds, of course, sang. A green land, unbelievably quiet and rich, sunned its moisture. Each square yard lay un-concerned with the next, just as each measure of the road lay back as they passed, unconcerned with their passing, contented, remaining where it had always been under its own beech, a piece of land. And when at last the beech-rows stopped, the whole of that flat country seemed to spread itself suddenly open. The sky appeared, blue and sailing small white clouds to give it air. Those who deny the flatlands forget the sky—over flat country the sky approaches closer than anywhere else, it takes shape, it becomes the blue-domed lid on a flat plate of earth. Here is a greater intimacy between the elements; and for once, for a little, the world appears finite.

The carload of four travelled like a speck over this flat space. And

Claeys was thinking: 'Such a summer, such still air—something like a mother presiding heavily and quietly, while down in her young the little vigours boil and breed . . . air almost solid, a sort of unseen fruit fibre . . . a husk guarding the orderly chaos of the breeding ground. . . .'

Such a strict order seemed indeed to preside within the intricate anarchy—success and failure, vigorous saplings from the seeds of good fortune, a pennyworth of gas from the seeds that fall on stony ground: yet a sum total of what might appear to be complete achievement, and what on the human level appears to be peace. And on that level, the only real level, there appeared—over by the poplar plumes? Or by the windmill? Or at some flat point among the converged hedges?—there appeared one scar, a scar of purely human disorder: over somewhere lay this camp of ten thousand displaced souls, newly freed but imprisoned still by their strange environment and by their great expectations born and then as instantly barred. On the face of it, these seemed to represent disorder, or at most a residue of disorder. But was this really so? Would such disorder not have appeared elsewhere, in similar quantity and under conditions of apparent order? Were they, perhaps, not anything more than stony-grounders—the disfavoured residue of an anarchic nature never governed directly, only impalpably guided by more general and less concerned governments? Was it right to rationalize, to impose order upon such seed, was it right—or at least, was it sensible? It was right, obviously—for a brain to reason is itself a part of nature and it would be wrong to divert it from its necessitous reasoning. But right though reason may be, there was no more reason to put one's faith in the impeccable work of the reasoning brain than to imagine that any other impressive yet deluded machine—like, for instance, the parachute seed—should by its apparent ingenuity succeed. Look at the parachute seed—this amazing seed actually flies off the insensate plant-mother! It sails on to the wind! The seed itself hangs beneath such an intricate parasol, it is carried from the roots of its mother to land on fertile ground far away and set up there an emissary generation! And more—when it lands, this engine is so constructed that draughts inch-close to the soil drag, drag at the little parachute, so that the seed beneath actually erodes the

49

earth, digs for itself a little trench of shelter, buries itself! Amazing! And what if the clever little seed is borne on the wrong wind to a basin of basalt?

Claeys was thinking: 'The rule of natural anarchy—a few succeed, many waste and die. No material waste: only a huge waste of effort. The only sure survival is the survival of the greater framework that includes the seed and all other things on the earth—the furious landcrab, the bright young Eskimo, the Antiguan cornbroker— every thing and body . . . and these thrive and decay and compensate . . . just as we, on the threshold of some golden age of reason, just as we are the ones to harness some little nuclear genius, pack it into neat canisters, store it ready to blow up all those sunny new clinics when the time comes, the time for compensation. . . .'

Just then the car drove into a small town on the bank of a broad river. Instantly, in a matter of yards, the green withered and the party found themselves abruptly in what seemed to be some sort of a quarry, dry, dug-about, dust-pale, slagged up on either side with excavated stones.

It was indeed an excavation; it was of course the street of a town. This town was dead. It had been bombed by a thousand aircraft, shelled by an entire corps of artillery and then fought through by land soldiers. No houses were left, no streets, The whole had been churned up, smashed and jig-sawed down again, with some of the jig-saw peices left up-ended—those gaunt walls remaining—and the rest of the pieces desiccated into mounds and hollows and flats. No grass grew. The air hung sharp with vaporized dust. A few new alleys had been bulldozed through; these seemed pointless, for now there was no traffic, the armies had passed through, the town was deserted. Somewhere in the centre Claeys stopped the car. He held up his hand for silence. The four men listened. Throughout that wasted city there was no sound. No distant muttering, no murmur. No lost hammering, no drowned cry. No word, no footstep. No wheels. No wind shifting a branch—for there were no trees. No flap-ping of torn cloth, this avalanche had covered all the cloth. No birds—but one, a small bird that flew straight over, without singing; above such a desert it moved like a small vulture, a shadow, a bird without destination. Brick, concrete, gravel-dust—with only two shaped objects as far all round as they could see: one, an intestinal engine of fat iron pipes, black and big as an up-ended lorry, something thrown out of a factory; and leaning on its side a pale copper-green byzantine cupola like a gigantic sweet-kiosk blown over by the wind, the tower fallen from what had been the town church. This—in a town that had been the size of Reading.

Almost reverently, as on sacred ground, they started the car and drove off again. Through the pinkish-white mounds the sound of the motor seemed now to intrude garishly. Claeys wanted only to be out of the place. Again, this destruction seemed to have occurred years before; but now because of the very absence of green, of any life at all, of any reason to believe that people had ever lived there. Not even a torn curtain. They wormed through and soon, as abruptly as before, the country began and as from a seasonless pause the summer embraced them once more.

Claeys stood up off his seat to look over the passing hedges. The camp was somewhere near now. The driver said, two kilometres. Surely, Claeys thought, surely with that dead town so near the men in this camp could realize the extent of the upheaval, the need for a pause before their journey could be organized? Surely they must see the disruption, this town, the one-way bridges over every stream far around, the roads pitted and impassable? Yet . . . what real meaning had these evidences? Really, they were too negative to be understood, too much again of something long finished. It was not as if something positive, like an army passing, held up one's own purpose; not even a stream of aircraft, showing that at least somewhere there was an effort and direction. No, over these fields there was nothing, not even the sense of a pause, when something might be restarted; instead a vacuity stretched abroad, a vacuum of human endeavour, with the appalling contrast of this vegetable growth continuing evenly and unconcerned. That was really the comprehensible evidence, this sense of the land and of the essence of life continuing, so that one must wish to be up and walking away, to be off to take part not in a regrowth but in a simple continuation of what had always been. For every immediate moment there was food to be sought, the pleasures of taste to be enjoyed: what was more simple than to walk out and put one's hands on a cap-full of eggs, a pig, a few fat hens? And if a grey uniform intervened, then it was above all a grey uniform, something instinctively obstructive, in no real sense connected with the dead town. The only real sympathy that ever came sometimes to soften the greyness of this grey was a discovery, felt occasionally with senses of wonder and unease, that this uniform went walking and working through its own mined cornfields and sometimes blew itself up—that therefore there must be a man inside it, a farmer more than a soldier. But the grey was mostly an obstruction to the ordinary daily desire for food, for fun, for something to be tasted. The day for these men was definitely a day. It was no twenty-four hours building up to a day in the future when something would happen. No future day had been promised. There was, therefore, no succession of days, no days for ticking off, for passing through and storing in preparation. There were in fact the days themselves, each one a matter for living, each a separate dawning and tasting and setting.

Suddenly Claeys heard singing, a chorus of men's voices. A second later the driver down behind the windshield heard it. He nodded, as though they had arrived. The singing grew louder, intimate— as though it came from round a corner that twisted the road immediately ahead. But it came from a lane just before, it flourished suddenly into a full-throated slavic anthem—and there was the lane crowded with men, some sitting, others marching four abreast out into the road. The car whirred down to a dead halt. The singing wavered and stopped. Claeys saw that the driver had only his left hand on the wheel—his other hand was down gripping the black butt of a revolver at his knee. (He had never done this driving through German crowds earlier.)

'It's not the camp,' the driver said. 'These are some of them, though. The camp's a kilometre up the road.' He kept his eyes scanning slowly up and down the line of men crowding in the lane's entry, he never looked up at Claeys. Then the men came a few paces forward, though they looked scarcely interested. Probably they were pushed forward by the crowd behind, many of whom could not have seen the car, many of whom were still singing.

Claeys stood upright and said: 'I'd like to talk to these . . . you drive on, get round the corner and wait. I don't want that military feeling.'

The men looked on with mild interest, as though they might have had many better things to do. They looked scarcely 'displaced'; they had a self-contained air, an independence. There was no censure in their stare; equally no greeting; nor any love. Their clothes were simple, shirts and greyish trousers and boots: though these were weather-stained, they were not ragged.

Claeys jumped down. An interest seemed to quicken in some of the watching men as they saw how Claeys was dressed — béret, plus-fours, leather jacket. It was because of these clothes that the military in the car gave Claeys no salute as they drove off; also because they disapproved of this kind of nonsense, and this may have been why they neither smiled nor waved, but rather nodded impersonally and whirred off round the corner. They might, for instance, have been dropping Claeys after giving him some sort of a lift.

So that Claeys was left quite alone on the road, standing and smiling at the crowd of expatriates grouped at the entrance to the lane. The car had disappeared. It had driven off the road and round the corner. There, as often happens when a vehicle disappears from view, its noise had seemed to vanish too. Presumably it had stopped. But equally it might have been presumed far away on its journey to the next town.

The men took a pace or two forward, now beginning to form a crescent-shape round Claeys, while Claeys began to speak in English: 'Good afternoon, mates. Excuse me, I'm Pieter Claeys—native of Belgique.' None of the men smiled. They only stared hard. They were too absorbed now even to mutter a word between themselves. They were searching for an explanation, a sign that would clarify this stranger. They were unsure, and certainly it seemed unimpressed. 'Good afternoon, comrades,' Claeys shouted. 'Gentlemen, hello!'

Without waiting, for the silence was beginning to weigh, he turned into French. 'Suis Claeys de Belgique. Je veux vous aider. Vous permettez—on peut causer un peu?'

He repeated: 'Peut-être?' And in the pause while no one answered he looked up and above the heads of these men, feeling that his smile might be losing its first flavour, that somehow an embarrassment might be dissolved if he looked away.

The country again stretched wide and green. Claeys was startled then to see sudden huge shapes of paint-box colour erecting themselves in the distance. But then immediately he saw what they were —the wings and fuselages of broken gliders. They rose like the fins of huge fish, tilted at queer angles, grounded and breathlessly still. Difficult at first to understand, for their shapes were strange and sudden, and of an artifice dangerously like something natural: brightly coloured, they might have been shapes torn from an abstract canvas and stuck wilfully on this green background: or the bright broken toys left by some giant child.

Claeys tried again: 'Gijmijneheeren zijt blijkbaar in moeilijkheden. Ik zou die gaarne vernemen. . . .'

The Dutch words came ruggedly out with a revival of his first vigour, for Claeys was more used to Dutch and its familiarity brought some ease again to his smile. It brought also a first muttering from the men.

They began to mutter to each other in a Slav-sounding dialect— Polish, Ukrainian, Czech, Russian?—and as this muttering grew it seemed to become an argument. Claeys wanted instantly to make himself clearer, he seemed to have made some headway at last and so now again he repeated the Dutch. This time he nodded, raised his arm in a gesture, even took a pace forward in his enthusiasm. But now one of the men behind began to shout angrily, and would have pushed himself forward shaking his fist—had the others not held him.

It was not clear to Claeys—he felt that the Dutch had been understood, and yet what he had said was friendly . . . he began to repeat the words again. Then, half-way through, he thought of a clearer way. He broke into German. There was every chance that someone might understand German; they might have been working here for three years or more; or anyway it was the obvious second language. '. . . So bin ich hier um Ihnen zu hilfen gekommen. Bitte Kameraden, hören Sie mal. . . .'

The muttering rose, they were plainly talking—and now not to each other but to him. The crescent had converged into a half-circle, these many men with livening faces were half round him. Claeys stood still. Overhead the summer sky made its huge dome, under which this small group seemed to make the pin-point centre. The green quiet stretched endlessly away to either side, the painted gliders stuck up brightly. No traffic.

'. . . Bitte ein Moment . . . ich bin Freund, Freund, FREUND. . . .' And as he repeated this word 'friend' he realized what his tongue had been quicker to understand—that none of his listeners knew the meaning of these German words. They knew only that he was speaking German, they knew the intonation well.

He stopped. For a moment, as the men nudged each other nearer, as the Slav words grew into accusation and imprecation, Claeys' mind fogged up appalled by this muddle, helplessly overwhelmed by such absurdity, such disorder and misunderstanding.

Then, making an effort to clear himself, he shook his head and looked closely from one man to the other. But the composure had gone: they were all mouth, eyes, anger and desire—they were no longer independent. And this was accumulating, breeding itself beyond the men as men. They had become a crowd.

Knowing that words were of no further use, Claeys did the natural thing—wearily, slowly he raised his arm in a last despairing bid for silence.

An unfortunate gesture. The shouting compounded into one confused roar. One of the men on the edge of the crowd jumped out and swung something in the air—a scythe. It cut Claeys down, and then all the pack of them were on him, kicking, striking, grunting and shouting less.

Claeys must have screamed as the scythe hit him—two shots thundered like two full stops into that muddle, there was an abrupt silence and two men fell forward; and then another shot and the men scattered crying into the lane.

Those three soldiers came running up to Claeys's body. They shot again into the men crowding the lane; but then the men, bottled up in the narrow lane, suddenly turned and raised their arms above their heads. The soldiers held their fire, their particular discipline actuated more strongly than their emotions. Two of them kept their guns alert, gestured the men forward. They came, hands raised, shambling awkwardly. The other officer bent down to Claeys.

He was almost finished, messed with blood and blue-white where the flesh showed. He was breathing, trying to speak; and the officer knelt down on both his knees and raised Claeys's head up. But Claeys never opened his eyes—they were bruised shut, anyway. And no words came from his lips, though the officer lowered his head and listened very carefully.

Through the pain, through his battered head, one thought muddled out enormously. 'Mistake . . . mistake. . . .' And this split into two other confused, unanswered questions, weakening dulling questions. Broadly, if they could have been straightened out, these questions would have been: 'Order or Disorder? Those fellows were the victims of an attempt to rule men into an impeccable order, my killing was the result of the worst, that is, the most stupid disorder. . . .'

But he couldn't get the words out, or any like them. Only—weakly, slowly he raised his right hand. He groped for the officer's hand, and the officer knew what he wanted and met the hand with his own in a handshake. Claeys just managed to point at the place where the men had been, where they still were. Then his head sank deep on to his neck. Again the officer knew what he wanted. He rose, his hand still outstretched from Claeys' grasp, like a hand held out by a splint. Then he started over towards the men.

Instinctively, for this hand of his was wet with blood, he wiped it on his tunic as he walked forward. Without knowing this, he raised his hand again into its gesture of greeting. There was a distasteful expression on his face, for he hardly liked such a duty.

So that when he shook hands with the first of the men, proffering to them, in fact, Claeys's handshake, none of these expatriates knew whether the officer was giving them Claeys's hand or whether he had wiped Claeys's gesture away in distaste and was now offering them his congratulation for killing such a common enemy as Claeys.

A Saving Grace

THE hour before dusk, when birds begin to rustle about their perches in the bushes, when the hot afternoon is grown old and cool. The house stood empty across the garden. Some windows were shut, others open; but since the sun was falling somewhere to the left and behind, this garden side stood veiled now in light shadow. Each of the windows, whether open or shut, presented a black rectangle without reflection. Their white sills and frames emphasized such a black rigidity, and within no curtains could now be seen— for the curtains were dark as the new shadows prowling now inside each hidden room. In that warm late-afternoon light the grass of the lawn—high and uncut—glowed liquid. Light shone through the transparent tegument of each green blade, though the tallest tips like feathered spears were tarnished with the sun's ageing gold. The grass led straight to the veranda, with its thin white pillars, its white trellised ironwork hung over with green creeper. From this veranda four black windows peered, and in the centre two glass doors stood open revealing a great mouth of darkness among the other blind dark eyes. In such a still air, the house isolated and empty seemed in some way to be moving within itself. One remembered that here was no deserted place—that it was furnished with well-known things, that only for the evening was it empty of people. The vibrations of living had never deserted it. It seemed merely to wait, busying itself quietly about many unseen duties—accumulating perhaps a little dust, sinking by a millionth of a fraction into the earth, expanding here with the heat and there contracting again into itself. It seemed concerned with holding itself together, holding itself in readiness for the return of its children, holding and waiting.

Meanwhile the sun stretched itself over a sky that widened with the cooling of the day. Such evenings, tranquil and clear, cloudless and of a still pristine loveliness—may seem not so much true in

57

themselves as of the memory of other such times, immobilized in the past, irretrievable. They are thus themselves imperfect—for the other lost evening assumes the real raiment of perfection. The entity of such times is made up of a sadness, of the word 'nevermore'. They breed a lost melancholy that is not unpleasurable: rather, it is to be tasted, drunk like some opiate potion of non-desire, for reminiscence of this kind is no more than the ghost of hope, the remainder of hoped-for evenings evoked by the first summer weather now re-collected, hopes that were perhaps never realized but which in themselves became the blood of life and now even as memories still invigorate with a shade at least of their ancient ambition.

Thinking thus . . . pondering that after all such melancholic mysteries are never so curious but have their explanations—so often in the simple terms of this or that biological decline—thinking and looking idly across the lawn at the house, the creeper-hung veranda, I was surprised suddenly to see not as before the empty dark square of the open french windows but instead the figure of a woman standing framed by the same inner darkness. She seemed to be wearing white, a broad white hat and a flowered white dress reaching to the ground. It looked from my distance like a dress cut in the fashion of some years past, and I thought—some visitor for a charity, some elderly parishioner wearing the dress of summers ago who had now wandered in through the open front door? So I was rising to show myself—when the figure moved, advanced and I saw who it was. Moreover, a large dog, a Great Dane, came pounding out behind her. I knew both. I sat down. They were my Aunt Hester and the dog Daniel. They had both been dead for what—thirty years?

Both Danny and Auntie Hester I knew well. Danny was my father's dog, a close companion; Auntie Hester was not a real aunt, but a neighbour, intimate with the family, who had looked after me during my mother's absences (how well I remember her veil, her wide feather-brimmed hats, the air of perfume about her and the strangely exciting atmosphere of the furniture of her house so different to ours. I suppose Aunt Hester might have represented the first breath of a woman other than mother, a stranger, intoxicating even to a child and fabulous). So, knowing them indeed so closely, feeling at the sight of them never criticism but always a close and safe affection—for the first second I felt nothing odd about their appearance, they were in my mind too familiar. Death cannot age, no change can waste the shape of memory—so this picture, momentarily realized after a pause of several decades, hardly at all seemed strange. Until reason came to say they were dead.

I heard all the old stories croak: 'Pinch yourself.' I did. It made no difference. Aunt Hester walked onto the lawn, and with Danny panting his tongue out beside her she stopped and remained standing somewhere between the white tubs of wallflowers. She stared towards me, though not quite directly—more at the trees beyond my shoulders. The feeling was that she was looking through me—rather than I, as tradition would suggest, might have been looking through her. She was certainly not transparent, certainly as solid as she had ever been: the sun managed to catch and glow palely in the top of her white hat, she threw a dark shadow along the ground to her right.

Then—through the same window—stepped Mr Chisholm! Sun-yellowed flannels piped his long bowed legs, stretched tightly at his paunch, and above the striped shirt and rowing tie sat a straightly perched straw boater. His down-stretching brown moustaches draped with gravity the roundness of his redly genial face, his eyes glared a ceaseless weak exasperation. He too was dead.

But I had scarcely realized his whole presence before my real aunt, Aunt Connie, same out. She advanced, stopped, and stood with the other two. (None of them seemed aware of the other's presence, no word was spoken, no greeting made.) Connie was the Aunt with the bone. In her cupboard, deep behind the cheeses, she had said she kept a long and thin white bone. With this from time to time she had terrified me. Her dark hair piled into an overhanging loaf on her frowning forehead, her pale eyes with their dark circles, her long teeth—these had lowered over me when sometimes I was alone in her charge and she had discovered a misbehaviour. 'Well,' she would say, pressing her lips against her teeth, 'well, do you want a taste of my bone? Do you want a feel of Aunt Connie's nice white bone?'—then a pause, and slower—'Shall—I—get—my—BONE?' Yet, Aunt Connie was as dead as the others, long ago asleep under the granite angel.

Then the shapes of Ella and Bridie came out, edging and quicker than the others, as though their black uniform and white cap-strings might soil the air, the pathway of masters and mistresses. They stood close together, away from the others and a little behind. And, instantly, as though chasing these their maids came my father and my mother, leading by the hand a young sister May. May had died in a fire one night in a boarding-house by the seaside—she had been only sixteen: my father and mother had come back from a concert to find the fire already dying down. Father now took up the centre of the group, with mother at his side, smaller than him, sallow and wistfully shrunken against his huge black-coated frame. He stood erect, his hair and beard as black as ever, his six-foot of height and great corpulence giving somehow the impression of an immense black-coated butcher, a man of thick white muscle and strong blood, certain of the stance of his boots and the blunt thud of his chopper.

In a line they stood—Aunt Hester, Danny, Mr Chisholm, Sister May, Mother, Father, Aunt Connie and Ella and Bridie. They stood without moving, though they were real enough; you could sense a bloom of living about each figure, as though beyond the immediate eye a small rising and falling of breath could be sensed, an emanation of breath that can be felt from the most immobile sleeper but never from the dead. And from each one, darker than the more luminous shade of the veranda, extended fur-black lengths of shadow propping them up against the pinked gilt of that falling sun behind. A solar exercise: of the nature of a photograph.

It is difficult to express the acceptance of these my dead that I felt at that moment—can one recollect, for instance, some almost parallel episode of unusuality and the way in which one's sense of personal ignorance placed this firmly, in the first startling second, within the reasonable plan of expected existence? Say—you are sitting in a boat moored to the side of a creek. It is your boat. The oars drift at the rowlocks; the painter rope at the bows is knotted loosely round an old pole protruding from the mud. You are idling, enjoying the sun, waiting for the time when the lobsters will be on sale in the cottage up the track behind you. So far, so good . . . then abruptly a figure looms between you and the sun. Breathing heavily, this figure is—you find—stepping into your boat, rocking your boat, picking up your oars. With eyes now fully opened you see that this is an old man in a fisherman's blue jersey, that already he has cast off the painter, and that the boat and the two of you are drifting out quietly over the leaf-green waters of the creek. The man picks up the oars. He rows! He says nothing. Once he looks at you, and without smiling, but gravely affable, nods. What, *what* do you do? . . . It's simple. Nod back. There is no other answer. You might think you would be saying: 'And who in heaven's name do you think you are?' or: 'Don't you know—you're in the wrong boat?' Or something similar. But these would be absurd, you could say nothing of the kind—for this mans' absolute sureness of purpose, his passive calm, his lack of all effusive gesture, his nodding acceptance of yourself makes question impossible. He must, you admit, in that first upsetting second be right. It is you who probably have made some mistake. And so, though no reason as yet asserts itself, you decide to wait. Then—exactly then—is the moment of acceptance. No conscious reason has asserted itself. But since you admit his action to be right, you admit that somewhere, beyond your instant understanding, there is a reason quite logical for his visitation to your boat. You must assume your own ignorance, you give him a lien on a place, certain but as yet uncertified, in the scheme of things. In fact, although perhaps questioning the exact reason—you have nevertheless accepted it. So you are rowed across the creek.

It turns out of course that some minutes previously, when you waved away a fly, this man who was the casual ferryman of the creek thought you were beckoning to him. He expected no further word, the district was taciturn, visitors known to be superior and silent to the natives. Moreover, he had a tumour of the palate. And think of it as you will, that tumour was the only coincidental ex-traneity. It could all have happened, and doubtless every day does, without such tumours.

In such a way, then, it was necessary to accept for those first perplexing moments the phenomenon of this group of dead people. It may seem in retrospect to have been a far more difficult case of 'acceptance'. But that is not so. The shock of sudden appearance was the same; the absence of all relation to usuality; the passive surety of their stance; the first moment of questioning one's own senses—in fact, of admitting them to be right. So that in extension, alone in the garden and in such a queer evening sunlight, the immediate muddled assumption was that I was perhaps a fiction of my own imagining, my adolescence was a dream, these my known adult superiors were alive as they always had been. And even then, quickly confirming my own adulthood from the material shirt and trousers beneath my eyes—nevertheless I could only be sure that even if these people were in fact dead, that then it was my own conception, that death entailed disappearance, which was at fault. What, at that lonely moment in real fact, had I to prove that death meant that they should not be there? An idea in my mind—that only. Instinct? There was nothing to confirm instinct. No written letters, no orders, nobody at my side to agree me right or wrong. I was alone—that is important—alone in a deserted garden, and with a mind shocked and therefore in the first place, self-admittedly, not to be trusted.

So—they were there, nine old friends, in a row. But not for long did they remain passive. For a time—how long I cannot think, such periods expand and contract outside the ordinary measurements of reason—they stood motionless, caught in the solar moment, immobilized in the photograph. And as in a photograph, their insistence on *being* grew as one searched further into the picture. Now as the sun sank lower, the shadow of the house welled forward and overcast their few colours in a monochrome suspense. They became more of a photograph, more faded, pitched in the lesser light of a lilac evening shade. There seemed, to loom above as in many dulled paintings and photographs, an appalling cloud like the emanation of God—a weight not so much of darkness as of an exclusion of light. It was as though some giant jelly-fish of doom hung over us the little fishes: or as though a fine black wind were passing. But now it failed to pass, it remained, hung on the air, grew steadily more ominous. With it, my awareness of the character of my old friends asserted itself. I felt the awe of the dark days clouding again my adult temples.

If they remained so still—then there was a reason for this? Waiting? For what? It was beyond knowing—yet now the supposition of such a pause, the pause that cannot be without an active ending, insisted upon some future threat. They were waiting, in fact, for something to happen. Something growing within themselves? A quiet malevolence simmering, soon to leap into the thunderflash of attack? Aunt Connie's thin bone? Father's dreadful butchery of the brows? The melancholy never-ness of my dear, unattainable Hester? The twilight was thickening, intensifying like the quiet mauve shadows in the dead hearts of these silent nine. . . .

Midges danced like white powder-flecks in the low-angled glint of the sun. The dew seemed already to be falling. The leaves, the deepening shadows grew moist. An emptiness, premonitory of the long dead night, seemed to be echoing across the world. Still I waited—then abruptly the sun disappeared. The photograph turned to deeply-dusked violet. The white clothes began to glow, the dark gathered into garments of fustier gloom. My senses ached for movement, the long tension seemed to be redoubling itself, gathering, running like a dark wave mounting up into itself, rearing ever higher to its all-flooding, mountainous descent. . . .

Now, at this last toppling, edge-heavy moment . . . out of the window came dancing, tumbling another figure. Absurdly short, round, bright-coloured ginger and purple and brown and pink! Simultaneously the sun blazed out again—it had been hiding behind a chimney! With a high whinny of laughter the little figure tumbled out, hands on hips—and proceeded then without pause to dance an in-and-out jig along and around the line of motionless figures! I could scarcely fix him, he moved so fast—but gradually he came together, a man, short, stout, chestnut-haired; with cheeks mauvely red with laughter; with hair thick-growing and waved on his head and round his devil-arched eyebrows; with gold teeth flashed in a white melon-laugh; with deep red side-whiskers cut square like long hatchets; with a blue shaved strength on his chin; with violet shirt, a pink tie, a gold-brown jacket and a summer promenader's white trousers striped brown; with a huge red dahlia roaring from his buttonhole, diamonds glittering his fingers, a pearl studding his tie! Never stopping he grimaced and giggled, postured and roared, bent himself double, kicked his legs in the air—never for a second did he stop moving. He jigged, he danced, he tumbled. He flashed his smile up at Father, down at May. He threw kisses, slapped backs. The sweat you could see gleaming all over his round carmine cheeks, his stout belly held firm with effort. And all the time he kept singing: 'Kunckle, Kunckle—Kunckle's come!'—Then belabouring his balloon-pot with both short arms: 'Play some music on the big, bass drum!' One moment he was a ball, the next a cupid spreadeagled in the air. He did tricks, trick after trick—he primp-walked suddenly away with his head turned backwards, you didn't know whether he was coming or going! He balanced himself on his hands, scissoring his tubby legs in the air! He put his hands on his knees and waggled them to and fro so you didn't know which hand was on what knee! He wiggled his feet only and travelled like a fat pillar of coloured salt sideways! He conjured a stream of flags from Aunt Connie's open mouth, he took bright paper flowers from the seat of Mr Chisholm's pants! Rabbits jumped from Father's pockets, Aunt Hester's bloomers fell elasticless to her feet! The two maids' apron-bows were tied together behind, they went circling round like a blind sack-race! On thoughtful May's head sat Kunckle's gay trilby, while Kunckle himself now trailed the streaming bows of a bonnet! Kunckle! He blazed like a full brass band! He sang like a singing saw! Clown! Hofnacque! Hocricane!

And gradually, like wax melting, the stiffness left that line of figures, one after another they moved their heads, shifted their feet, turned their eyes from their queer lost horizons to Kunckle dancing around them; the stiffness left their shoulders, their erect necks— it was as if a thousand fibres and small muscles had eased each a thousandth of an inch. As rigidity declined, so did the premonitory dangers. Like the raising of a shadow, like that candle-red sun laughing out from behind the black chimney, disaster lifted and a warmth was kindled between them. No more could that stiff relationship—with its set afflictions and its hard rule, its aggressive tensions for fear the rule may be broken—no more could the dread casting of private position gather its cruel eminence: Kunckle had thrown it with his somersaults. So that now Father burst suddenly into a gigantic laugh, so that Mother's strained face softened to a smile and she took three steps forward and round and back, then curtsied down to May. And Chisholm and Hester were linking arms in a skirl of lancers. Ella and Bridie were bent double back-to-back with red laughter, May was dancing like some long-legged fairy, and at the centre of this strange and tolerant momentum, this circling and posturing of amused figures on the lawn in the last summer sunglow, this graceful motion of people leaning together with the sway of their drapery surfing about the faster dance within—at the centre stood Aunt Connie conducting musically the movement with a white and slender wand, her bone!

Last, I caught sight of Kunckle—irrational lovable, tasteless Kunckle, like a tubby puffy steam-engine he was prancing off into the veranda, I saw his coat-tail flying and the white striped paunch of his bottom pistoning off into the dark doorway. He paused once —to look round, flourish his hat, blow a fine perspiring kiss back to the garden—and then he was gone! But his company remained long after. Long after, until, somehow, the figures of my old acquaintanceship melted—and I was again alone with this empty, human house.

Various Temptations

HIS name unknown he had been strangling girls in the Victoria district. After talking no one knew what to them by the gleam of brass bedsteads; after lonely hours standing on pavements with people passing; after perhaps in those hot July streets, with blue sky blinding high above and hazed with burnt petrol, a dazzled head-aching hatred of some broad scarlet cinema poster and the black leather taxis; after sudden hopeless ecstasies at some rounded girl's figure passing in rubber and silk, after the hours of slow crumbs in the empty milk-bar and the balneal reek of grim-tiled lavatories? After all the day-town's faceless hours, the evening town might have whirled quicker on him with the death of the day, the yellow-painted lights of the night have caused the minutes to accelerate and his fears to recede and a cold courage then to arm itself—until the wink, the terrible assent of some soft girl smiling towards the night . . . the beer, the port, the meat-pies, the bedsteads?

Each of the four found had been throttled with coarse thread. This, dry and the colour of hemp, had in each case been drawn from the frayed ends of the small carpet squares in those linoleum bedrooms. 'A man,' said the papers, 'has been asked by the police to come forward in connection with the murders,' etc., etc. . . . Ronald Raikes—five-foot-nine, grey eyes, thin brown hair, brown tweed coat, grey flannel trousers. Black soft-brim hat.'

A girl called Clara, a plain girl and by profession an invisible mender, lay in her large white comfortable bed with its polished wood headpiece and its rose quilt. Faded blue curtains draped down their long soft cylinders, their dark recesses—and sometimes these columns moved, for the balcony windows were open for the hot July night. The night was still, airless; yet sometimes these queer cause-

66

less breezes, like the turning breath of a sleeper, came to rustle the curtains—and then as suddenly left them graven again in the stifling air like curtains that had never moved. And this girl Clara lay reading lazily the evening paper.

She wore an old wool bed-jacket, faded yet rich against her pale and bloodless skin; she was alone, expecting no one. It was a night of restitution, of early supper and washing underclothes and stockings, an early night for a read and a long sleep. Two or three magazines nestled in the eiderdowned bend of her knees. But saving for last the glossy, luxurious magazines, she lay now glancing through the paper—half reading, half tasting the quiet, sensing how secluded she was though the street was only one floor below, in her own bedroom yet with the heads of unsuspecting people passing only a few feet beneath. Unknown footsteps approached and retreated on the pavement beneath—footsteps that even on this still summer night sounded muffled, like footsteps heard on the pavement of a fog.

She lay listening for a while, then turned again to the paper, read again a bullying black headline relating the deaths of some hundreds of demonstrators somewhere in another hemisphere, and again let her eyes trail away from the weary greyish block of words beneath. The corner of the papers and its newsprint struck a harsh note of offices and tube-trains against the soft texture of the rose quilt—she frowned and was thus just about to reach for one of the more lustrous magazines when her eyes noted across the page a short, squat headline above a blackly-typed column about the Victoria murders. She shuffled more comfortably into the bed and concentrated hard to scramble up the delicious paragraphs.

But they had found nothing. No new murder, nowhere nearer to making an arrest. Yet after an official preamble, there occurred one of those theoretic dissertations, such as is often inserted to colour the progress of apprehension when no facts provide themselves. It appeared, it was *thought*, that the Victoria strangler suffered from a mania similar to that which had possessed the infamous Ripper; that is, the victims were mostly of a 'certain profession'; it might be thus concluded that the Victoria murderer bore the same maniacal grudge against such women.

At this Clara put the paper down—thinking, well for one thing she never did herself up like those sort, in fact she never did herself up at all, and what would be the use? Instinctively then she turned to look across to the mirror on the dressing-table, saw there her worn pale face and sack-coloured hair, and felt instantly neglected; down in her plain-feeling body there stirred again that familiar envy, the impotent grudge that still came to her at least once every day of her life—that nobody had ever bothered to think deeply for her, neither loving, nor hating, nor in any way caring. For a moment then the thought came that whatever had happened in those bedrooms, however horrible, that murderer had at least felt deeply for his subject, the subject girl was charged with positive attractions that had forced him to act. There could hardly be such a thing, in those circumstances at least, as a disinterested murder. Hate and love were often held to be variations of the same obsessed emotion—when it came to murder, to the high impassioned pitch of murder, to such an intense concentration of one person on another, then it seemed that a divine paralysis, something very much like love, possessed the murderer.

Clara put the paper aside with finality, for whenever the question of her looks occurred then she forced herself to think immediately of something else, to ignore what had for some years groaned into an obsession leading only to hours wasted with self-pity and idle depression. So that now she picked up the first magazine, and scrutinized with a false intensity the large and laughing figure in several colours and few clothes of a motion-picture queen. However, rather than pointing her momentary depression, the picture comforted her. Had it been a real girl in the room, she might have been further saddened; but these pictures of fabulous people separated by the convention of the page and the distance of their world of celluloid fantasy instead represented the image of earlier personal dreams, comforting dreams of what then she hoped one day she might become, when that hope which is youth's unique asset outweighed the material attribute of what she in fact was.

In the quiet air fogging the room with such palpable stillness the turning of the brittle magazine page made its own decisive crackle. Somewhere outside in the summer night a car slurred past, changed its gear, rounded the corner and sped off on a petulant note of acceleration to nowhere. The girl changed her position in the bed, easing herself deeper into the security of the bedclothes. Gradually she became absorbed, so that soon her mind was again ready to wander, but this time within her own imagining, outside the plane of that bedroom. She was idly thus transported into a wished-for situation between herself and the owner of the shop where she worked: in fact, she spoke aloud her decision to take the following Saturday off. This her employer instantly refused. Then still speaking aloud she presented her reasons, insisted—and at last, the blood beginning to throb in her forehead, handed in her notice! . . . This must have suddenly frightened her, bringing her back abruptly to the room—and she stopped talking. She laid the magazine down, looked round the room. Still that feeling of invisible fog—perhaps there was indeed mist; the furniture looked more than usually stationary. She tapped with her finger on the magazine. It sounded loud, too loud. Her mind returned to the murderer, she ceased tapping and looked quickly at the shut door. The memory of those murders must have lain at the back of her mind throughout the past minutes, gently elevating her with the compounding unconscious excitement that news sometimes brings, the sensation that somewhere something has happened, revitalizing life. But now she suddenly shivered. Those murders had happened in Victoria, the neighbouring district, only in fact—she counted—five, six streets away.

The curtains began to move. Her eyes were round and at them in the first flickering moment. This time they not only shuddered, but seemed to eddy, and then to belly out. A coldness grasped and held the ventricles of her heart. And the curtains, the whole length of the rounded blue curtains moved towards her across the carpet. Something was pushing them. They travelled out towards her, then the ends rose sailing, sailed wide, opened to reveal nothing but the night, the empty balcony—then as suddenly collapsed and receded back to where they had hung motionless before. She let out the deep breath that whitening she had held all that time. Only, then, a breath of wind again; a curious swell on the compressed summer air. And now again the curtains hung still. She gulped sickly, crumpled and decided to shut the window—better not to risk that sort of fright again, one never knew what one's heart might do. But, just then, she hardly liked to approach those curtains. As the atmosphere of a nightmare cannot be shaken off for some minutes after waking, so those curtains held for a while their ambience of dread. Clara lay still. In a few minutes those fears quietened, but now forgetting the sense of fright she made no attempt to leave the bed, it was too comfortable, she would read again for a little. She turned over and picked up her magazine. Then a short while later, stretching, she half-turned to the curtains again. They were wide open. A man was standing exactly in the centre, outlined against the night outside, holding the curtains apart with his two hands.

Ron Raikes, five-foot-nine, grey eyes, thin brown hair, brown sports jacket, black hat, stood on the balcony holding the curtains aside looking in at this girl twisted round in her white-sheeted bed. He held the curtains slightly behind him, he knew the street to be dark, he felt safe. He wanted to breathe deeply after the short climb of the painter's ladder—but instead held it, above all kept quite still. The girl was staring straight at him, terrified, stuck in the pose of an actress suddenly revealed on her bedroom stage in its flood of light; in a moment she would scream. But something here was unusual, some quality lacking from the scene he had expected—and he concentrated, even in that moment when he knew himself to be in danger, letting some self-assured side of his mind wander and wonder what could be wrong.

He thought hard, screwing up his eyes to concentrate against the other unsteady excitements aching in his head—he knew how he had got here, he remembered the dull disconsolate hours waiting round the station, following two girls without result, then walking away from the lighted crowds into these darker streets and suddenly seeing a glimpse of this girl through the lighted window. Then that curious, unreasoned idea had crept over him. He had seen the ladder, measured the distance, then scoffed at himself for risking such an escapade. Anyone might have seen him . . . and then what, arrest for house-breaking, burglary? He had turned, walked away.

Then walked back. That extraordinary excitement rose and held him. He had gritted his teeth, told himself not to be such a fool, to go home. Tomorrow would be fresh, a fine day to spend. But then the next hours of the restless night exhibited themselves, sounding their emptiness—so that it had seemed too early to give in and admit the day worthless. A sensation then of ability, of dexterous clever power had taken him—he had loitered nearer the ladder, looking up and down the street. The lamps were dull, the street empty. Once a car came slurring past, changed gear, accelerated off petulantly into the night, away to nowhere. The sound emphasized the quiet, the protection of that deserted hour. He had put a hand on the ladder. It was then the same as any simple choice—taking a drink or not taking a drink. The one action might lead to some detrimental end—to more drinks, a night out, a headache in the morning—and would thus be best avoided; but the other, that action of taking, was pleasant and easy and the moral forehead argued that after all it could do no harm? So, quickly, telling himself he would climb down again in a second, this man Raikes had prised himself above the lashed night-plank and had run up the ladder. On the balcony he had paused by the curtains, breathless, now exhilarated in his ability, agile and alert as an animal—and had heard the sound of the girl turning in bed and the flick of her magazine page. A moment later the curtains had moved, nimbly he had stepped aside. A wind. He had looked down at the street—the wind populated the kerbs with dangerous movement. He parted the curtains, saw the girl lying there alone, and silently stepped on to the threshold.

Now when at last she screamed—a hoarse diminutive sob—he knew he must move, and so soundlessly on the carpet went towards her. As he moved he spoke: 'I don't want to hurt you'—and then knowing that he must say something more than that, which she could hardly have believed, and knowing also that above all he must keep talking all the time with no pause to let her attention scream—'Really I don't want to hurt you, you mustn't scream, let me explain—but don't you see if you scream I shall have to stop you. . . .' Even with a smile, as soft a gesture as his soft quick-speaking voice, he pushed forward his coat pocket, his hand inside,

71

so that this girl might recognize what she must have seen in detective stories, and even believe it to be his hand and perhaps a pipe, yet not be sure: '. . . but I won't shoot and you'll promise won't you to be good and not scream—while I tell you why I'm here. You think I'm a burglar, that's not true. It's right I need a little money, only a little cash, ten bob even, because I'm in trouble, not dangerous trouble, but let me tell you, please, *please* listen to me, Miss.' His voice continued softly talking, talking all the time quietly and never stuttering nor hesitating nor leaving a pause. Gradually, though her body remained alert and rigid, the girl's face relaxed.

He stood at the foot of the bed, in the full light of the bedside lamp, leaning awkwardly on one leg, the cheap material of his coat ruffled and papery. Still talking, always talking, he took off his hat, lowered himself gently to sit on the end of the bed—rather to put her at her ease than to encroach further for himself. As he sat, he apologized. Then never pausing he told her a story, which was nearly true, about his escape from a detention camp, the cruelty of his long sentence for a trivial theft, the days thereafter of evasion, the furtive search for casual employment, and then worst of all the long hours of time on his hands, the vacuum of time wandering, time wasting on the café clocks, lamp-posts of time waiting on blind corners, time walking away from uniforms, time of the headaching clocks loitering at the slow pace of death towards his sole refuge— sleep. And this was nearly true—only that he omitted that his original crime had been one of sexual assault; he omitted those other dark occasions during the past three weeks; but he omitted these events because in fact he had forgotten them, they could only be recollected with difficulty, as episodes of vague elation, dark and blurred as an undeveloped photograph of which the image should be known yet puzzles with its indeterminate shape, its hints of light in the darkness and always the feeling that it should be known, that it once surely existed. This was also like anyone trying to remember exactly what had been done between any two specific hours on some date of a previous month, two hours framed by known engagements yet themselves blurred into an exasperating and hungry screen of dots, dark, almost appearing, convolving, receding.

So gradually as he offered himself to the girl's pity, that bed-clothed hump of figure relaxed. Once her lips flexed their corners in the beginning of a smile. Into her eyes once crept that strange coquettish look, pained and immeasurably tender, with which a woman takes into her arms a strange child. The moment of danger was past, there would be no scream. And since now on her part she seemed to feel no danger from him, then it became very possible that the predicament might even appeal to her, to any girl nourished by the kind of drama that filled the magazines littering her bed. As well, he might look strained and ill—so he let his shoulders droop for the soft extraction of her last sympathy.

Yet as he talked on, as twice he instilled into the endless story a compliment to her and as twice her face seemed to shine for a moment with sudden life—nevertheless he sensed that all was not right with this apparently well-contrived affair. For this, he knew, should be near the time when he would be edging nearer to her, dropping his hat, picking it up and shifting thus unostensibly his position. It was near the time when he would be near enough to attempt, in one movement, the risk that could never fail, either way, accepted or rejected. But . . . he was neither moving forward nor wishing to move. Still he talked, but now more slowly, with less purpose; he found that he was looking at her detachedly, no longer mixing her image with his words—and thus losing the words their energy; looking now not at the conceived image of something painted by the desiring brain—but as at something unexpected, not entirely known; as if instead of peering forward his head was leant back, surveying, listening, as a dog perhaps leans its head to one side listening for the whistled sign to regulate the bewildering moment. But—no such sign came. And through his words, straining at the diamond cunning that maintained him, he tried to reason out this perplexity, he annotated carefully what he saw. A white face, ill white, reddened faintly round the nostrils, pink and dry at the mouth; and a small fat mouth, puckered and fixed under its long upper lip: and eyes also small, yet full-irised and thus like brown pellets under eyebrows low and thick: and hair that colour of lustreless hemp, now tied with a bow so that it fell down either side of her cheeks as lank as string: and round her thin neck, a thin gold chain just glittering above the dull blue wool of that bed-jacket, blue brittle wool against the ill white skin: and behind, a white pillow and the dark wooden head of the bed curved like an inverted shield. Unattractive . . . not attractive as expected, not exciting . . . yet where? Where before had he remembered something like this, something impelling, strangely sympathetic and—there was no doubt—earnestly wanted?

Later, in contrast, there flashed across his memory the colour of other faces—a momentary reflection from the scarlet-lipped face on one of the magazine covers—and he remembered that these indeed troubled him, but in a different and accustomed way; these pricked at him in their busy way, lanced him hot, ached into his head so that it grew light, as in strong sunlight. And then, much later, long after this girl too had nervously begun to talk, after they had talked together, they made a cup of tea in her kitchen. And then, since the July dawn showed through the curtains, she made a bed for him on the sofa in the sitting-room, a bed of blankets and a silk cushion for his head.

Two weeks later the girl Clara came home at five o'clock in the afternoon carrying three parcels. They contained two coloured ties, six yards of white material for her wedding dress, and a box of thin red candles.

As she walked towards her front door she looked up at the windows and saw that they were shut. As it should have been—Ron was out as he had promised. It was his birthday. Thirty-two. For a few hours Clara was to concentrate on giving him a birthday tea, forgetting for one evening the fabulous question of that wedding dress. Now she ran up the stairs, opened the second door and saw there in an instant that the flat had been left especially clean, tidied into a straight, unfamiliar rigour. She smiled (how thoughtful he was, despite his 'strangeness') and threw her parcels down on the sofa, disarranging the cushions, in her tolerant happiness delighting in this. Then she was up again and arranging things. First the lights —silk handkerchiefs wound over the tops of the shades, for they shone too brightly. Next the tablecloth, white and fresh, soon decorated with small tinsels left over from Christmas, red crackers with feathered paper ends, globes gleaming like crimson quicksilver, silver and copper snowflakes.

(He'll like this, a dash of colour. It's his birthday, perhaps we could have gone out, but in a way it's nicer in. Anyway, it must be in with him on the run. I wonder where he is now. I hope he went straight to the pictures. In the dark it's safe. We did have fun doing him up different—a nice blue suit, distinguished—and the moustache is nice. Funny how you get used to that, he looks just the same as that first night. Quite, a quiet one. Says he likes to be quiet too, a plain life and a peaceful one. But a spot of colour—oh, it'll do him good.)

Moving efficiently she hurried to the kitchen and fetched the hidden cake, placed it exactly in the centre of the table, wound a length of gold veiling round the bottom, undid the candle-parcel, and expertly set the candles—one to thirty-one—round the white-iced circle. She wanted to light them, but instead put down the matches and picked off the cake one silver pellet and placed this on the tip of her tongue: then impatiently went for the knives and forks. All these actions were performed with that economy and swiftness of movement peculiar to women who arrange their own houses, a movement so sure that it seems to suggest dislike, so that it brings with each adjustment a grimace of disapproval, though nothing by anyone could be more approved.

(Thirty-one candles—I won't put the other one, it's nicer for him to think he's still thirty-one. Or I suppose men don't mind—still, do it. You never know what he really likes. A quiet one—but ever so thoughtful. And tender. And that's a funny thing, you'd think he might have tried something, the way he is, on the loose. A regular Mr Proper. Doesn't like this, doesn't like that, doesn't like dancing, doesn't like the way the girls go about, doesn't like lipstick, nor the way some of them dress . . . of course he's right, they make themselves up plain silly, but you'd think a man . . .?)

Now over to the sideboard, and from that polished oak cupboard take very carefully one, two, three, four fat quart bottles of black stout—and a half-bottle of port. Group them close together on the table, put the shining glasses just by, make it look like a real party. And the cigarettes, a coloured box of fifty. Crinkly paper serviettes. And last of all a long roll of paper, vivid green, on which she had traced, with a ruler and a pot of red paint: HAPPY BIRTHDAY RON!

This was now hung between two wall-lights, old gas-jets corded with electricity and shaded—and then she went to the door and switched on all the lights. The room warmed instantly, each light threw off a dark glow, as though it were part of its own shadow. Clara went to the curtains and half-drew them, cutting off some of the daylight. Then drew them altogether—and the table gleamed into sudden night-light, golden-white and warmly red, with the silver cake sparkling in the centre. She went into the other room to dress.

Sitting by the table with the mirror she took off her hat and shook her head; in the mirror the hair seemed to tumble about, not pinned severely as usual, but free and flopping—she had had it waved. The face, freckled with pin-points of the mirror's tarnish, looked pale and far away. She remembered she had much to do, and turned busily to a new silk blouse, hoping that Ron would still be in the pictures, beginning again to think of him.

She was not certain still that he might not be the man whom the police wanted in connection with those murders. She had thought it, of course, when he first appeared. Later his tender manner had dissipated such a first impression. He had come to supper the following night, and again had stayed; thus also for the next nights. It was understood that she was giving him sanctuary—and for his part, he insisted on paying her when he could again risk enquiring for work. It was an exciting predicament, of the utmost daring for anyone of Clara's way of life. Incredible—but the one important and over-riding fact had been that suddenly, even in this shocking way, there had appeared a strangely attractive man who had expressed immediately an interest in her. She knew that he was also interested in his safety. But there was much more to his manner than simply this—his tenderness and his extraordinary preoccupation with *her*, staring, listening, striving to please and addressing to her all the attentions of which through her declining youth she had been starved. She knew, moreover, that these attentions were real and not affected. Had they been false, nevertheless she would have been flattered. But as it was, the new horizons became dreamlike, drunken impossible. To a normally frustrated, normally satisfied, normally hopeful woman—the immoral possibility that he might be that murderer would have frozen the relationship in its seed. But such was the waste and the want in lonely Clara that, despite every ingrained convention, the great boredom of her dull years had seemed to gather and move inside her, had heaved itself up like a monstrous sleeper turning, rearing and then subsiding on its other side with a flop of finality, a sigh of pleasure, welcoming now any-thing, anything but a return to the old dull days of nothing. There came the whisper: 'Now or never!' But there was no sense, as with other middle-aged escapists, of desperation; this chance had landed squarely on her doorstep, there was no striving, no doubt—it had simply happened. Then the instinctive knowledge of love—and finally to seal the atrophy of all hesitation, his proposal of marriage. So that now when she sometimes wondered whether he was the man the police wanted, her loyalty to him was so deeply assumed that it seemed she was really thinking of somebody else—or of him as another figure at a remove of time. The murders had certainly stopped—yet only two weeks ago? And anyway the man in the tweed coat was only wanted *in connection with* the murders . . . that in itself became indefinite . . . besides, there must be thousands of tweed coats and black hats . . . and besides there were thousands of coincidences of all kinds every day. . . .

So, shrugging her shoulders and smiling at herself for puzzling her mind so—when she knew there could be no answer—she re-turned to her dressing-table. Here her face grew serious, as again the lips pouted the down-drawn disapproval that meant she con-templated an act of which she approved. Her hand hesitated, then opened one of the dressing-table drawers. It disappeared inside, feeling to the very end of the drawer, searching there in the dark. Her lips parted, her eyes lost focus—as though she were scratching deliciously her back. At length the hand drew forth a small parcel.

Once more she hesitated, while the fingers itched at the knotted string. Suddenly they took hold of the knot and scrambled to untie it. The brown paper parted. Inside lay a lipstick and a box of powder.

(Just a little, a very little. I must look pretty, I *must* tonight.)

She pouted her lips and drew across them a thick scarlet smear, then frowned, exasperated by such extravagance. She started to wipe it off. But it left boldly impregnated already its mark. She

77

shrugged her shoulders, looked fixedly into the mirror. What she saw pleased her, and she smiled.

As late as seven, when it was still light but the strength had left the day, when on trees and on the gardens of squares there extended a moist and cool shadow and even over the tram-torn streets a cooling sense of business past descended—Ronald Raikes left the cinema and hurried to get through the traffic and away into those quieter streets that led towards Clara's flat. After a day of gritted heat, the sky was clouding; a few shops and orange-painted snack-bars had turned on their electric lights. By these lights and the homing hurry of the traffic, Raikes felt the presence of the evening, and clenched his jaw against it. That restlessness, vague as the hot breath before a headache, lightly metallic as the taste of fever, must be avoided. He skirted the traffic dangerously, hurrying for the quieter streets away from that garish junction. Between the green and purple tiles of a public house and the red-framed window of a passport photographer's he entered at last into the duller, quieter perspective of a street of brown brick houses. Here was instant relief, as though a draught of wind had cooled physically his head. He thought of the girl, the calm flat, the safety, the rightness and the sanctuary there. Extraordinary, this sense of rightness and order that he felt with her; ease, relief, and constant need. Not at all like 'being in love'. Like being very young again, with a protective nurse. Looking down at the pavement cracks he felt pleasure in them, pleasure reflected from a sense of gratitude—and he started planning, to get a job next week, to end this hiding about, to do something for her in return. And then he remembered that even at that moment she was doing something more for him, arranging some sort of treat, a birthday supper. And thus tenderly grateful he slipped open the front-door and climbed the stairs.

There were two rooms—the sitting-room and the bedroom. He tried the sitting-room door, which was regarded as his, but found it locked. But in the instant of rattling the knob Clara's voice came: 'Ron? . . . Ron, go in the bedroom, put your hat there—don't come in till you're quite ready. Surprise!'

VARIOUS TEMPTATIONS

Out in the dark passage, looking down at the brownish bare linoleum he smiled again, nodded, called a greeting and went into the bedroom. He washed, combed his hair, glancing now and then towards the closed connecting door. A last look in the mirror, a nervous washing gesture of his hands, and he was over at the door and opening it.

Coming from the daylit bedroom, this other room appeared like a picture of night, like some dimly-lit tableau recessed in a waxwork-show. He was momentarily dazzled not by light but by a yellowed darkness, a promise of other unfocused light, the murky bewilderment of a room entered from strong sunlight. But a voice sang out to help him: 'Ron—HAPPY BIRTHDAY!' and, reassured, his eyes began to assemble the room—the table, crackers, shining cake, glasses and bottles, the green paper greeting, the glittering tinsel and those downcast shaded lights. Round the cake burned the little upright knives of those thirty-one candles, each yellow blade winking. The ceiling disappeared in darkness, all the light was lowered down upon the table and the carpet. He stood for a moment still shocked, robbed still of the room he had expected, its cold and clockless daylight, its motionless smell of dust.

An uncertain figure that was Clara came forward from behind the table, her waist and legs in light, then upwards in shadow. Her hands stretched towards him, her voice laughed from the darkness. And thus with the affirmation of her presence, the feeling of shock mysteriously cleared, the room fell into a different perspective—and instantly he saw with gratitude how carefully she had arranged that festive table, indeed how prettily reminiscent it was of festivity, old Christmases and parties held long ago in some separate life. Happier, he was able to watch the glasses fill with rich black stout, saw the red wink of the port dropped in to sweeten it, raised his glass in a toast. Then they stood in the half-light of that upper shadow, drank, joked, talked themselves into the climate of celebration. They moved round that table with its bright low centre-light like figures about a shaded gambling board—so vivid the clarity of their lowered hands, the sheen of his suit and the gleam of her stockings, yet with their faces veiled and diffused. Then, when two of the bottles were already empty, they sat down.

Raikes blinked in the new light. Everything sparkled suddenly, all things round him seemed to wink. He laughed, abruptly too excited. Clara was bending away from him, stretching to cut the cake. As he raised his glass, he saw her back from the corner of his eye, over the crystal rim of his glass—and held it then undrunk. He stared at the shining white blouse, the concisely corrugated folds of the knife-edge wave of her hair. Clara? The strangeness of the room dropped its curtain round him again, heavily. Clara, a slow voice mentioned in his mind, has merely bought herself a new blouse and waved her hair. He nodded, accepting this automatically. But the stout to which he was not used weighed inside his head, as though some heavy circular hat was being pressed down, wreathing leadenly where its brim circled, forcing a lightness within that seemed to balloon airily upwards. Unconsciously his hand went to his forehead —and at that moment Clara turned her face towards him, setting it on one side in the full light, blowing out some of those little red candles, laughing as she blew. The candle flames flickered and winked like jewels close to her cheek. She blew her cheeks out, so that they became full and rounded, then laughed so that her white teeth gleamed between oil-rich red lips.

Thin candle-threads of black smoke needled curling by her hair. She saw something strange in his eyes. Her voice said: 'Why Ron— you haven't a headache? Not yet anyway . . . eh, dear?'

Now he no longer laughed naturally, but felt the stretch of his lips as he tried to smile a denial of the headache. The worry was at his head, he felt no longer at ease in that familiar chair, but rather balanced on it alertly, so that under the table his calves were braced, so that he moved his hands carefully for fear of encroaching on what was not his, hands of a guest, hands uneasy at a strange table.

Clara sat round now facing him—their chairs were to the same side of that round table, and close. She kept smiling; those new things she wore were plainly stimulating her, she must have felt transformed and beautiful. Such a certainty together with the un-accustomed alcohol brought a vivacity to her eye, a definition to the movements of her mouth. Traces of faltering, of apology, of all the wounded humilities of a face that apologizes for itself—all these were gone, wiped away beneath the white powder; now her face seemed to be charged with light, expressive, and in its new self-assurance predatory. It was a face bent on effect, on making its mischief. Instinctively it performed new tricks, attitudes learnt and stored but never before used, the intuitive mimicry of the female seducer. She smiled now largely, as though her lips enjoyed the touch of her teeth; lowered her eyelids, then sprang them suddenly open; ended a laugh by tossing her head—only to shake the new curls in the light; raised her hand to her throat, to show the throat stretched back and soft, took a piece of butter-coloured marzipan and its marble-white icing between the tips of two fingers and laughing opened her mouth very wide, so that the tongue-tip came out to meet the icing, so that teeth and lips and mouth were wide and then suddenly shut in a coy gobble. And all this time, while they ate and drank and talked and joked, Raikes sat watching her, smiling his lips, but eyes heavily bright and fixed like pewter as the trouble roasted his brain.

He knew now fully what he wanted to do. His hand, as if it were some other hand not connected to his body, reached away to where the parcel of ties lay open; and its fingers were playing with the string. They played with it over-willingly, like the fingers guiding a paintbrush to over-decorate a picture, like fingers that pour more salt into a well-seasoned cook-pot. Against the knowledge of what he wanted the mind still balanced its danger, calculated the result and its difficult aftermath. Once again this was gluttonous, like deciding to take more drink. Sense of the moment, imagination of the result; the moment's desire, the mind's warning. Twice he leant towards her, measuring the distance then drawing back. His mind told him that he was playing, he was allowed such play, nothing would come of it.

Then abruptly it happened. That playing, like a swing pushing higher and then somersaulting the circle, mounted on its own momentum, grew huge and boundless, swelled like fired gas. Those fingers tautened, snapped the string. He was up off the chair and over Clara. The string, sharp and hempen, bit into her neck. Her lips opened in a wide laugh, for she thought he was clowning up suddenly to kiss her, and then stretched themselves wider, then closed into a bluish cough and the last little sounds.

Building Alive

AS on a fleet and smooth naval pinnace, intricate with grey cocks and rope and white-painted enumeration—we six on the Heavy Fire Unit drove swiftly through the quiet Sunday streets. Sometimes at odd corners or through a breach in the skyline of tall buildings the huge buff plume showed itself, calm and clean as sand against a pale bluish sky. We as well felt clean, in our blue flaired tunics and silver buttons, too clean for what was coming, conscious of this and awkward at a time when smudged khaki and camouflage net were the equipment of action. The streets were too clean; there were no people, the people were all hidden away cooking their Sunday dinners; one church bell pealed ceaselessly to an empty town caught in the Sunday pause.

Then, gradually, the immaculate polish showed a ruffling, stray scraps of paper suggested the passing of a crowd, a weed of splintered glass sprung up here on the pavements, another and invisible weed seemed to be thrusting the window frames from their sockets and ahead, as this tangle grew denser, the street hung fogged with yellow dust.

Our destination lay within the dust. Once inside it was easy to see, only the outer air had painted it opaque. But it was like driving from the streets of a town into sudden country; nothing metropolitan remained to these torn pavements, to the earthen mortar dust and the shattered brick returning to the clay. The fly-bomb had blasted a pause within the pause of Sunday morning.

Ambulances already. Two or three people stood about, hand-kerchiefs to their red-splashed faces. In the silence a loud-speaker called for silence. The rich living voices appealed to the dead rubble, coaxing it to make tapping noises. And men with long detecting poles weaved to and fro through the mist like slow shrimpers. We were ordered round the debris to search the broken buildings on either side.

82

At the top of the first flight of stairs, dark and rickety, a light shone through a crack in the unhinged door. The door came off easily. A single shadeless electric bulb hung over a tailor's table, shone weakly and yellow against the large daylit window beyond. On the table lay a pair of trousers, an iron, slivers of glass and splashes of red blood, comet-shaped, like flickings from a pen. Every lightly fixed furnishing of the room had shifted—bales of cloth, doors, chairs, plaster mouldings, a tall cupboard—all these had moved closer and now leant huddled at strange, intimate angles. Plaster dust covered everything. There was no space left in the room, there was nobody in the room. The blood led in wide round drops to the door, the tailor must have been 'walking wounded'. Had he been one of those outside, fingering blindly for the ambulance doors? The yellow bulb on its single string burned on, the only life in this lonely Sunday workroom, the only relic of the tailor's shattered patience.

Then, under the steady burning of this bulb, against its silent continuing effort, other sounds began to whisper. My number two, Barnes, looked at me quickly—the building was alive. Our boots had thudded on the stairs. Now for a moment, no more, they were quiet. They were silent, the light was silent, but falsely—for beneath these obvious silences other sounds, faint, intractable, began to be heard. Creakings, a groan of wood, a light spatter of moving plaster, from somewhere the trickle of water from a broken pipe. The whole house rustled. A legion of invisible plastermice seemed to be pattering up and down the walls. Little, light sounds, but massing a portentous strength. The house, suddenly stretched by blast, was settling itself. It might settle down on to new and firm purchases, it might be racking itself further, slowly, slowly grinding apart before a sudden collapse. I saw Barnes glance at the ceiling; he was thinking of the four floors still hanging above us; he was thinking perhaps, as I was, that the raid was still on and that any other explosion within miles might rock through the earth and shake the whole lot down. Walking in such houses, the walls and floors are forgotten; the mind pictures only the vivid inner framework of beams and supports, where they might run and how, under stress, they might behave; the house is perceived as a skeleton.

Then through the stripped window came further sounds—a distant explosion from the south, and above this the purposeful drone of a second bomb flying louder every moment. The gallows that would mark its course! To each dreadful roof gallows along the bomb's course a black sock would rise to swing like a sentence rather than a warning of death. The sound approached like a straight line. It approached thus for many people . . . everyone on the half-circle of its sound fanning forwards would attach the bomb to themselves. It could drop anywhere. It was absolutely reasonless. It was the first purely fatal agent that had come to man for centuries, bringing people to cross their fingers again, bringing a rebirth of superstition.

Down in the courtyard they were carrying a man out from the opposite block. We caught a glance of him through the twisted framework of an iron footbridge. They had laid him on a blanketed stretcher on the grey rubble. He lay still, bloodless, only his face showing, and that plastered with the same sick grey dust. It lay evenly on him, like a poisonous mask—he looked gassed with dust. Once he struggled, his head turned from side to side. He seemed to be trying to speak. It was as if his real face, clean and agonized, tried to be free and show its pain.

Now, in the long moment it takes these bombs to fly their swift distance—now the drone was already changing its note. The first remote aerial wavering, like a plane engine far up and away, had strengthened and bolted its direction upon our area. It was coming all right. We waited, though there was no time to wait, no real time but only the expansion of a moment so alert, and listened then for the drone to sharpen itself into the spluttering drum-beat of a jet-engine. But beneath this sound, separated from us by widths of sky, the little murmurs of secret life, fearful in their intimacy, could still be heard. And still fixed in a second's glance at the wounded man below, our eyes absorbed the whole courtyard, the waste of rubble between tall, torn office buildings. The iron bridge hung darkly between. Across it a new nest of broken pipes splayed up, a hydra head of snaky lead, but halted, paused like the rest of it. Only the oncoming sound moved deliberately, but this too was fixed, mounted on a straight, straight line that in its regular, unvarying crescendo provided only an emphasis to the stillness of the courtyard. A whole architecture, all that had ever been built, all the laborious metropolitan history had been returned to its waste beginning. The virgin scrap, the grey mortar earth, the courtyard wall torn and stripped into the texture of ancient moon-burnt rock—all these passed, taking breath. Only the little sounds sucking themselves in hinted at a new life, the life of leaden snakes, hesitating and choosing in whispers the way to blossom.

The drone was diving into a roar. We crouched down beneath the window. My eyes now near the floor found themselves facing a gap some three inches wide where the outer wall had loosened itself from the floorboards. The wall was leaning outwards. I saw my hand steady itself on a book of cloth patterns; the fingers were bleeding, the hand removed itself instinctively from the cleanish cloth, cut itself again on more glass on the floor. The bomb was above. We held our breaths, not in all that sound daring to breathe for fear we might miss the cut-out. It seemed much darker near the floor . . . the floor grew as dark as childhood. Only the amazing crack in the wall remained clear, gaping its draughty mouth. The noise grew deafening, a noise now as heavy as the shadow of a wing. Then, in a burst of anger, it seemed to double up on itself, its splutter roared double, it was diving, at four hundred miles an hour, without ever cutting out, heading like all mad anger unrestrained on to the fragile roofs. . . .

The wall, like a rubber wall in a Disney cartoon, sprang out at my eyes, bulging round, then snapped back into its flat self. That happened, distinctly. Whether despite the crack it had actually expanded into so round and resilient a curve, or whether the noise and the windclap of the explosion jarred this round illusion within my own round eyes—I do not know. But that happened . . . just as the silence fell again, just as the glass rain spat again, just as an iron tank went tumbling down outside, and—it seemed a long time after the explosion, we were already up at the window—the wall of the building opposite across the courtyard wobbled and then heaved its concrete down on the wounded man and his rescuers below, burying them finally. It seemed, even at that time, extra hard for the man on the stretcher.

Swiftly the life of the house blossomed. The trickling from the pipes gushed free, cascading noisily into the courtyard. Tiles, plaster, gutter fragments and more glass lurched off the roof. A new growth was sprouting everywhere, sprouting like the naked plumbing, as if these leaden entrails were the worm at the core of a birth, struggling to emerge, thrusting everything else aside. But the house held. It must have blossomed, opened, subsided upon itself. We raced down the stairs to the concrete mass below.

As we picked, hopelessly, at the great fragments, it was impossible to forget how hard it was on the man on the strecher. It seemed, stupidly, that he alone had had no chance.

Three Dogs of Siena

THE Italians love their dogs. And their dogs love the Italians— it is probably to show something of this love that these dogs take such care to reproduce themselves, not in the dull matrix of formal breed, but in most brilliant assortment, in a profusion of wild and unpredictable shape ever a surprise and a joy to their delighted masters. What we would call the 'mongrels' of Italy are more than an essay in democratic procreation: they are an unceasing pleasure to the eye of those who love the individual, the purely creative rather than the creatively pure, the fresh. Not only joy but genius distinguishes this variety. Nowhere but on the ancient peninsula famed for its fecundity in noble and inventive works could such hounds occur.

One day three such dogs arrived in the Tuscan town of Siena. 'Taken for a visit?' they would have said, 'And who is taking whom?' For so full of joy and industry were these fortunate dogs that in everything they preceded their masters, running always forward, smelling out the fresh ground first. Their names—it turned out later —were Enrico, Osvaldo and Fa. They came from Naples, Genoa and Venice. They were owned by three brothers resident in those cities, who now for a period had come to be reunited in Siena, the town of their birth, for the wedding of their younger sister. However, names are poor descriptions for such dogs. They must be studied in all particular, observed in the detail of their spectacular creation. First, Enrico.

Enrico was a dark-brown dog, almost Umbrian—though he came in fact from the yellow Neapolitan quays. Stoutly built and heavy, he was not tall enough for his broad body—though muscular legs supported firmly this solid barrel. The brown hair grew short in tough whorls on his back, but down from his chest and stomach it hung sternly shaggy. His face was his great glory—it was nearly the face of a mandrill. Thick-snouted, bristling with what at first seemed disapproval, it proclaimed the thinker, yet a tough thinker, ruminant but muscular for the fight. His eyes were pale liver-coloured, with bluish rims that circled them completely; but very often one could see nothing of his eyes, nor could he himself see quite where he was going, for a heavy shag sprouted from between two ears the shape of small oast-houses and sprang forward in a wave like one great bristling didactic eyebrow. In a curious way this eyebrow seemed to part as it fell on to his snout proper, and to either side it combed away, becoming a beard to drink up Enrico's strong slavering. At the other end—it was a good way—there occurred the stump of a thick rat-like tail bent backwards and curled up sharply to its bitten spatulate; this revealed perhaps too boldly a bare posterior, hairless again as a mandrill, and not well-looking—but possibly this was not Enrico's fault; possibly he never knew quite how it looked, it was so far away.

Fa came from Venice, his fur was white as his native Istrian marble. He was a fluffy dog, always laughing. At first sight one took him for a Pomeranian—he had all the powder-puff fur and bright black eyes, ever-pricked ears and slender trotting legs. This at first —but then as in a dream, or in some distorting mirror, one saw that all these pretty characters were strangely exaggerated; the white fur sprouted like a clown's frill; the little legs spun so thin and delicate that in motion little Fa seemed to travel on wheels; the inquisitive ears rose inches high, like paper squills. But his tail was Fa's greatest pride—instead of a fur ball this joyful member flowered into a high spreading fan, beautiful but overweighted as the sail of a felucca, and as such particularly helpful with a following wind. However, Fa's was perhaps mostly an eccentricity of character. His laugh, his perpetual busy trot, his ever-bright eye and his spirited soprano bark singled him out always as the life and soul of any street, a true lover of life. He liked often to walk on three feet. He was so called after the fourth phonetic of the singing scale, having arrived at a similar stage in a litter of eight.

Osvaldo—Osvaldo could claim in his way to be the finest of the three, if one spoke of earthly finery, of the feathers that make the bird. A big dog, by and large Osvaldo had grown to be the shape of a hyena—his front shoulders rose several inches higher than his tapering thin haunches. But such haunches never slinked, Osvaldo was no cur, that slendering was meant for speed. In other ways too he seemed contrived for speed—his long wolf-like nose thrust streamlined forward; his ears grew huge and round, the trumpet ears of a flying-fox; his grey body was covered with tan-coloured spots, so that such a fur had some of the look of feathers, like the feathery pelt of some griffin-beast from a wilder world; and his tail fled away in a long streak—though normally he carried it curled. But his eyes! His eyes were bright yellow, as yellow as a leopard's! These it must have been that gave him, for all his speed, such a strange impassive expression. Never the glimmer of a laugh, never a message of anger could be sensed from that motionless face. One never knew what he thought. He seemed away with his yellow eyes on the far horizon. Genoa had been his birthplace.

The three had first met in Florence. They had become instant friends. Florence had been selected as a convenient junction for Siena, and a most pleasurable few hours must there have been spent between the platforms and a nearby restaurant. They had then taken an afternoon train for Siena, a train of good wooden carriages, and had arrived after dark. So that on their first night in the hilltown the three dogs had not had the chance to see anything of their new home—though the journey in the fading summer light had offered many pleasing prospects. The dark lines of cypress outside Florence had proved interesting, a pleasant strolling place where many enquiries might be satisfied; all over the low, unexhausting hills these trees had occurred, in competitive groups or singly, like darts thrown at random into the brown earth by a fond divinity. Then, as the earth turned redder and Siena approached, there came the strange perspective of the vines, each planted singly, twisted helter-skelter figures, intertwined and loving, but statuesque, arrested in movement and in no way disquieting to the interested dog. But to Siena itself they arrived enclosed in the dark carriage— it proved quite a drive from the station to the higher town walled on its crest of hill. They had spent the night comfortably enough enclosed in a small yard. The gate had been locked, and nothing of the precincts could be seen.

The next day dawned warm and sunny; the air was filled with fresh smells from the good Tuscan earth. This not only proclaimed the joys of country life, but indicated also that there had been a day or two's rain recently—so now the weather would be fine. Good weather, then—and a new town to explore. At breakfast there had been one small drawback—the remains of a pasta flavoured with dull tomato sauce instead of the good meat gravy of Bologna. But who knew what the bins and gutters of this place might provide, a town known to be centred in rich, fertile country? At last the gates were opened, and the three friends stood sniffing on the threshold of their new adventure.

But not much time was spent standing still! A second only for three noses to appraise the air, a glance to left and right—and they were racing off. However, as is often the case, that first dash was little more than its explosive gesture—in fact they all ran in different directions, noses to the ground, and instantly circled back to the gateway. It was a ritual—and now fleet Osvaldo, betraying in his yellow eyes nothing of his intentions, took charge and wheeled the party off along the road to the left—uphill. Mandrill-faced Enrico plodded his muscles behind. Little Fa became a brisk third, though sometimes he ran forward and completed a circle round Enrico. They travelled at a lively trot, searching the sidewalls as they went.

The road led steeply upwards between tall houses of red brick. It was narrow, a kerbless street of a kind they must all have known —the cobbles met with clean precision the dark-red perpendicular of the walls. But for a time—such indeed was the precision of the Sienese mason—one might have thought this the precinct of some well-ordered private mansion. No debris littered the stones, no stones nor brick nor plaster had fallen from those well-kept walls. Nor were there any projections of any kind—no door-steps, door-posts, lamp-posts, trees—nothing that might invite the pause for consideration. Iron torch-brackets occurred frequently, but these had been placed too high for practical purposes; and the graceful architects had moulded those surrounds to their doorways so neatly that nothing obtruded, no pilaster jutted from the fine-fitted frames.

Then shops occurred—and shops could never occur in private passages. But such ordered self-contained shops! What sort of town was this? They grew uneasy. As the industrious file plodded on, they passed not a single bin, no brushed pile of warm refuse. The sober red-bricked mediaeval streets wound narrowly up and down, arched and turreted, with never a buttressed invitation—not grim, but richly grave, precise and cleaned as no town they had ever known. Frowning behind his forward hair, Enrico must have remembered the alleys of Naples, redolent of life and all odour. Osvaldo's fox-like ears would have trembled to the unheard echo of the bustling Genoese arcades. Small Fa's great tail fanned blindly for the warm resistance of all those exudations that thickened the air above the green canal by which once he had lived.

But what was it they sought, truly, bowling along at such urgent speed, sometimes on three legs, sometimes cavorting dangerously sideways, frisking and plunging—yet always continuing forward, in what was plainly an agreed single file, with searching nose and rolling wary eye? Certainly it was not, in the main, food. Nor was it another matter that, with such stores as they had retained carefully for this expedition, must have weighed heavily. It was something deeper. It was without doubt the need to find evidence of their own existence.

This they could do only through the help of others. The search for food is automatic. But the urgent cry for testimony is a different affair. A dog alone in a stone street might well wonder whether he existed, the suspicion that he was no dog could breed dangerously among the dry mirrorless stones. What proof was there? To glance down at a paw, to whip round one's head at a remote, diffident tail? What did that prove? After a moment of illusion, of pleasant relief . . . nothing. Naturally one's dog brain attributed to itself paws and tail, fur and flank; but—how be sure that this was no deception? Impossible. Proof must be sought elsewhere: it could be found only in the movements and essences of others, the clash with unfamiliar bodies and with feelings foreign to one's own intimate brain. These others were at best other dogs, but other creatures would do—cats, men, and in a more distant fashion the rats and small bodies of one's prey.

Suddenly Osvaldo stopped dead, feathery front legs splayed stiff, his fishlong snout sniffing upwards, yellow eyes peering at the wall above, fox-ears primed for intelligence. Enrico and Fa bowled to a halt and stood quivering. But they never looked up. Instead they gazed from side to side, sometimes glanced anxiously at Osvaldo, but above all pretended not to notice anything extraordinary. Here was etiquette—a pronouncement would come in good time. They stood like dogs that pause suddenly in the middle of a game, panting, abruptly indifferent to each other . . . yet patently pretending this.

High up on the wall was set a stone tablet. Sculptured in relief, Osvaldo saw the effigy of a large woman-dog with sow-like udders nourishing two naked human children who squatted beneath. He stood peering curiously. What could this mean—were the dogs here magically transformed into humans, was it another feature of this strange town? A glint of unease showed in his yellow eye as, turning his nose rather away in embarrassment, his fixed pupil revealed a thin crescent of the bluish-white. Romulus and Remus, ancient colophon of Siena, sat drinking above, impassive, cherubic, unconcerned with the passing of new wolves.

One has seen dogs pause in question before mirrors; or grow startled at the sight of an unaccustomed object—a parasol, a tall hat. Some bridle at the phantom of blue spectacles, others growl at the movement of a rag flying in the breeze. What in fact do they see —what do they *know*? Their eyes are never more alert, the finest intelligences are cocked in their ears—a certain uneasiness underlies. Perhaps an instinct, long lost to our human systems, perceives emanations of evil (we know that such instincts exist, as with the polarization in a dog travelling over unknown distances back to a former home). Or perhaps once it has been frightened by something looking the same—though in this case such a selection is queer, it balks at a parasol and disregards a walking-stick, and this only on certain days. Or does a keen appreciation of the angles of light—which again we have lost—describe around the object an abstract image of some unfavourable beast? Certainly the dog that sees himself in mirrors—and only in certain mirrors—behaves as if this might be so. He does not imagine as we do that he sees himself. What more likely he suspects is the presence, the significance, and so the threat of an alien that bears upon his own life. From his mood, his cautious sniffing and startled eye, he shows not outright alarm but suspicion and unease. His attitude is like that of the man, say, who sees written before him the words 'good and evil'. Suddenly he notices how this is almost exactly 'God and Devil'. The blood rushes to his head. Letters the same! Meaning the same! He stumbles for the dictionary of etymologies. And then the appalling truth is learned—all four words spring from different roots, it is nothing but coincidence! But this, staring at the words, he cannot really believe. Science has explained it. But for him, staring still uneasily from the sides of his eyes at these words, there is still suspicion; around his thought flutter birds of great significance, for a long time he will remain uneasy. In such a way Osvaldo looked up at Romulus and Remus. He must have known the wolf was not real—but he had his suspicions, he felt not sure.

And if this indeed was the case—what bewilderment Siena held in store for him! What a distracting plethora of porcupines and elephants, giraffes and unicorns and all those others that form the signs of the seventeen Sienese districts, and which everywhere are emblazoned in chivalric colour on the red walls. But, of course, this was not to be—though much worse threatened these unfortunate dogs. For the moment Osvaldo gave one deep growl and then—as they will—suddenly lost all interest. He appeared suddenly to forget what he was doing—and glanced curiously at the street itself, waking from a daydream. Then wheeled and was off at a trot. The others tossed their heads, seemed to jump as excitedly as if this were the first intimation of a walk that they had ever received, and followed. They disappeared round a corner.

In a town as small as Siena, we who moved constantly about the marvellous streets of course kept meeting other such industrious walkers. Those three dogs seemed to occur everywhere. More than the little girl with the birdcage who gave out printed fortune slips, more even than the mournful young man with a black eye and his arm in a sling who must have been much knocked about in the recent Palio. The Palio, furious horse-race galloped in mediaeval costume round the Campo of Siena, had been over a week. The crowds had departed, the tempers of the various districts or contrade that competed had cooled—for this animal race was as fiercely contested as it was picturesque; it was no show for tourists, but a traditional trial of strength between the contrade, as alive now as when first, centuries ago, it had grown into being; the jockeys with their round helmets thrashed each other as freely as they thrashed their ponies, bribery and tricks and competitive tempers rose high.

But now the parades, processions and pageantry of the great day were a week over—though there still remained certain ceremony to be completed. Now and again one saw bands of Sienese dressed in mediaeval clothes come drumming up the streets. Contrary to what might have been expected, this distinctive people dressed up so carried no feeling of the operette: they looked real, conclusively. In their stripes and scalloping they marched against walls of dusky red, dark old true walls—each man's face was a face seen in a mediaeval painting. The brownish, ochreous faces were unchanged—and in themselves they were as distinctive from other Italian types as, for instance, are the people of Arles from others in South France. A feeling of pride and fine breeding is sensed. And here they lived in a town that was as preserved as their traditions and their own bodies. A town austere but mellow—kinder than Florence, yet as with many such mediaeval cities resonant of the sense of death. Well-preserved in its graven self—and also well-kept from day to day . . . its clean stone streets contrasted strongly with the streets of other cities. One wondered, again idly, what the three dogs thought about it. And soon, as if we had called them, though the town was really too small to count it a coincidence, they appeared. Suddenly racing down under an arch into the main square, the shell-shaped Campo.

Industrious as ever, they travelled fast. Noses to the ground, heads tossing, tails and behinds wagging separately like the afterbodies of ants or rumba dancers. That was their way of coursing the streets—but here, here suddenly striking into the magnificent open ground of the Campo, they skidded to a halt, stupefied. Enrico and Osvaldo stood sniffing the space like incurrent lions, while small Fa bounced to and fro between them on his stick legs, a small messenger between those larger craft. What—whatever could be going on in such ever-searching minds? Had they seen and stopped stupefied at the sight of the seventy or eighty marble posts that ringed the course

94

of the Campo? Had such sudden generosity in this reserved city overwhelmed them? Had Enrico glanced up for a moment at the blue
sky and seen rising, rocketing up against it, the tremendously high
campanile? This delicate square tower of dark-red brick, so slender
in proportion to its needling height and the vertiginous pale castella-
tions bulging heavily at its far summit—this most beautiful erection
of man that seemed ever to be moving upwards, which seemed in
fact to be flying, rocketing, spearing itself in vertical flight into the
wheeling heavens, this so vertical tower that gave us a glimpse that
the world is round—what did it signify to Enrico's liver-coloured
eye, suspicious through the hair-mop? Could his wondering, almost-
intelligent mind have registered its proportion, so that it appeared
to him as a giant pillar, an exquisition too great for him, but of the
right shape and thus innately satisfying? Worldly as he must be,
Enrico turned his head down again to the cobbles, the nearer posts
of rough stone that ringed the Campo—but there might, there might
have been a glimpse of understanding in that second's attention, a
possibility that was borne out by what later we were to see, in the
episode that finally unseated these furry ones.

Now, they hastily addressed themselves to the first of the posts—
and then continued round the fan of the race-track, rehearsing their
own intimate Palio. Unspoken words seemed to circulate between
them. No barking, but rolls of the eye—the whites of their eyes
rolled like those of negroes against the coloured fur, while Fa's black
jets gleamed with a dark, clownish radiance—rolls of the eye that
seemed instantly to be understood, indicating a different direction
or a different post, and above all a call to industrious joyful companionship. Episodes and encounters marked their progress. Here
at the hub of the town more was likely to happen—although the
Campo itself, because of its curious tilted shape and its quiet historical recession, seemed always more deserted than other Italian
squares. Nevertheless at one point Enrico, running along, was seen
suddenly to wheel; he returned nosing to what he had nearly
passed—a scrap of ham-rind left like miraculous manna by the
sweepers. His pace had nearly taken him beyond it, but that square-
nostriled mandrill nose had saved him. Now he settled his mouth
down to the scrap, and with mournful eyes began to eat. As he

munched the pupils were raised thoughtfully, showing a lugubrious droop of white beneath, and those whole eyes, stricken with the conscience of sin, moved slowly from side to side. He was like a man weighed with sorrow—or a child doing what he knew was wrong. In some curious way he seemed to be listening to his stomach. It was notable that this was the one occasion when the news of a discovery was not circulated to the others.

But the others! The others had found at last a brother animal—not one but two, a brother each. Osvaldo had found a cat, and Fa had looked up suddenly to find a dog sitting almost invisible in a dark doorway. Fa abruptly stiffened—shocked, outraged. He raised his small self to what he must have imagined was a monstrous size. On the points of his paws, on inexorably stiffened legs, with neck erect and eyes implacably averted, he walked up and down quivering in front of this sitting Sienese dog. It was an exhibition of outrage, cold outrage. The Sienese, fat and well-groomed and almost well-bred, took no notice whatever.

With Osvaldo it was different; perhaps because his meeting was with a cat. And such a cat—fat, sleek, striped, heraldic! The dogs of Italy do not chase cats like their brash northern brothers. There was no reason for the cat to do other than continue to sit and gaze across the Campo—with imperturbable placidity that must have seemed remarkable to the excitable Genoese. That huge dark-striped cat, in the erect posture of some heraldic beast, simply sat and considered the Campo. Osvaldo stood opposite, his head hung, his paw half-raised, blinking his yellow eyes uncertainly. In Genoa the cats were lean and thin-jawed; their kittens were as meagre as large mice; they moved all the time, creeping and slinking. Nothing was more different than this well-fed, gloss-coated monster.

But in neither case could anything be done, the Sienese animals made no move whatsoever. Finally, Osvaldo turned away, shaken, from his cat; and Fa made longer and longer circles away from his dog, so that soon he could appear to walk away naturally, unconcerned. Enrico alone had profited—and that not overmuch, the rind had been tough and salt.

Such, then, were the minor encounters of these three eager lovers of life. Before the following day, we saw them again twice: once down by one of the town's gates, down past a long pink wall surmounted with leaves green against the blue, where one saw the town end unencumbered by suburbs, and the gentle dark-ribbed patchwork of the Tuscan fields map out to the horizon beyond; where those dogs had found two other dogs making love, and as dogs will, were circling the indifferent couple with excited sallies and a jabber of barks—animated as the chatter at a tea-party on the mention of human love. And again we saw them, of all things, trooping out from the cathedral door, industriously pacing the marble mosaics, disappointed and possibly ejected from that extraordinary hall, having no interest in the lofty rows of popes' heads, the graven fruit decorations and the striped totem pillars that give that place a cold exotism, as of a tufted African village frozen into stone. No, they were not to be touched by such ceremonies of stone —they went in search of life.

The next day they found it. Some time in the late afternoon we were at the hotel window, looking out on to an odd interjunction of roads running at different levels that complicated pleasantly the view. Of these, the main road was embanked, and thus passed slightly above eye-level from our window, while a short gully of steps descended from it to the lower street beneath. Presently as if it were a matter of course, the three dogs came pounding in their ceaseless single file up the lower road. And at the same moment, from along the upper road, came the sound of a kettle-drum and marching feet.

The dogs heard it, erected their ears, faltered and stopped. From where they stood they could see nothing of the upper road, they could only hear the marching feet, which now came to a halt, and the kettle-drum which ceased to tap and began a long, mounting, death-like roll. They stood there listening—it was plain they did not like what they heard. Enrico and Osvaldo stood with tongues lolling, panting quietly, heads lowered listening; Enrico's shaggy forehead appeared furrowed with thought, listening for some unpalatable truth; Osvaldo searched blindly with his visionary eyes, but his lowered head seemed to be waiting for the whip to fall. Fa stood erect, tremendously rigid, his small pink tongue pouting straight out forward—at first sight one thought he might be wild with laughter. Meanwhile, we could see what in fact continued on the upper road. A group of the Porcupine Ward, the Istrice, had come marching with flags towards their votive church and had stationed themselves there on the way to perform a sbandierata, a flourish of flags.

The drummer had planted himself, feet astride and firm, in the centre of the road. With implacable elbows he drew from the drum its ceaseless coil of sound, ever more rigid, ever growling out a greater power. Four or five of the others had stationed themselves at intervals along the road. These men carried standards, flowing white flags of great width, upon which were emblazoned patterns and the dark effigy of a crouching porcupine: these flags they twisted in the air with graceful mastery. Each man wore a parti-coloured black-and-white mediaeval jacket and hose; each wore a mediaeval cap, and showed thus underneath a grave clear-shaped mediaeval face; the quarterings and stripes of black and white, splendid colours of the dark-red city, showed bravely against walls of that ubiquitous dark burning.

In all principal elements there was nothing in that scene to suggest that the centuries had passed—suddenly in front of one on the everyday street, in the sunlight, was flashed the flesh-and-blood mediaeval happening. The clothes did not behave as stage properties, muscles rippled within them and the bodies were filled with the true blood. With strong grace they wielded the heavy flags, twisting and furling and swinging them above their heads, slewing them down to the ground like cabers, hanging back against their weight and deftly manipulating their hands in a music of equipoise and inspired motion. The huge banners swam through the air like coloured winds, like bubbling swathing smoke, viscous heavy elements beautiful on the moving air. Fiercely toothed patterns sprang into being, vanished in a sweeping furl. A porcupine appeared high above, sat for a moment in chivalric splendour, vanished. All the whole flags and their staffs were tossed suddenly high up, as if they themselves leapt, hesitated in the upper air, sank down more slowly into the hands of the standard-bearer. Then again great circles—and still from the drum a constant drumming, the drumming never ceased. It seemed as though the flags themselves were alive and trying to wrestle away like wild birds from their athletic captors. It was a battle between flags and men.

Windows had opened, heads had appeared. Several passers-by had paused to watch. But these did not disturb the truth of that scene, they themselves were the anachronisms, a drab intrusion upon the splendid brick and the bright designs of livery. The pageant succeeded: a small gilt procession will triumph over mundane crowds—but here, by how much more was their success achieved! Then, of course, we saw that other intruders were at work. The dogs. Osvaldo was climbing the steps.

He took one look, drew back crouching—gave a whelp of fright, and loped shivering down the steps, tail between trailing legs. The others looked at him sharply, sadly.

A pause—it seemed for reflection, for necessary indecision. Then carefully, slowly, with a hesitation that never quite asserted itself, the three of them, no longer in single file, but abreast climbed the steps. They stopped before the top. Below the very last step they stopped, and stood there furtively pointing their nose over the top, as if it were a parapet: small Fa had to raise himself on two legs. Six uneasy eyes flickered with distrust as they watched the flags; one recognized the germ of hysteria. What they saw could not have been flags—but great wrestling coloured shapes pouncing on the wind, zooming low over the men that fought them. Nothing quite similar had been seen before: except, though much smaller, in the shape of birds.

Were these then giant birds of fierce colour that had descended in droves upon the town, sharp of beak and horrid-eyed? Remorseless, lidless, steel-eyed birds? Eagle-giants to tear out the vitals, thrusters and squawkers, great feathered bolts of muscle and iron claw, divers and risers, vile destroyers of gravity? Bones and feathers and cruelty—but as for feathers, one could not quite see, they flickered and furled so swiftly: were they snakes, was it fire, or worse —animated sharp-teethed cloths, living cloths headless and limbless, savage with consuming life, unclean and unknown? . . . Whatever this was, it had never before been seen, it was dangerous. And there was no smell.

On rolled the nerve-searing drums, the dogs stood still—poised to move in two directions at once. They were stretched—by their legs and tails lowered and moving backwards, by their noses extended forward to draw in the air with anxious sniffs. Their eyes showed the white; and because they were interested and thus grew lively, appeared again most considering, wise, intelligent. Patricians' careful eyes they cast on those unearthly flags—and then, as nothing happened, as the flags made no attack, they took courage. Enrico—as if he were taking the pipe from his gruff and bearded muzzle—gave a low growl. One could not hear this for the drums, but the sound could be seen vibrating his body, one lip was raised. And Fa, propping himself alongside, heard it, heard it as a sign, realized the mounting of confidence, and quickly, in his excitable way, raised his muzzle in a peppering of short white barks. Osvaldo continued to stare with nerveless yellow eyes—and then presently he too raised his long nose into a position almost vertical, like the elevation of a sky-gun, and set up a long, unbroken howl.

The flags swooped and tossed, bellied and swirled in the rising sbandierata; the drummer's elbows held their noise in an iron grip; the dogs mounted their howls and barking in chorus. But a deadlock is never satisfactory for the lively ones. One cannot stay still—any action is preferable, backwards or forwards. And these three dogs from the sea could no longer contain themselves. Buttressed with barking, their confidence rose—and suddenly as one they raced forward at the nearest flag. It was circling low on the ground, they tore at its swiftly-moving swathe—and got their faces soundly lashed; for a moment they were lost, enveloped, blinded in a fog of silk; then up fled the great banner and circled thrashing at the higher air, the dogs crouched dazed—and then they were leaping at it, throwing themselves high like bags of limp dog, snapping, snarling, barking their last breath.

They looked then like three sacks erratically bouncing—Fa's white ball moving faster but lower than the larger brown two others. Ears well back, eyes quick with long white fury, teeth open, they gathered themselves and leapt at the enormous bird threatening from above. This was no plaything—they fought hysterically. One knew it instantly when for a moment the flag circled lower and menaced, with no illusions of dogged valour, for a second they cowed back guarding themselves . . . and meanwhile the standard-bearers plied their flags, they had no time in their exertion to watch the dogs. Nevertheless, the ritual of the sbandierata dictated that soon the banners should descend. The dogs leapt higher.

The Italians love their dogs as they love life—but they also love ceremony, and in all ceremony there is the touch of death. The will to live may also be the will to die. Whether it is a rite of harvest or marriage or church, death resides somewhere in the pomp, the order, the finality—and what is always a sense of immolation. All life for the time is suspended, a pause in living comes to revere the solemn act. There prevails an echo of all past sacrifice, solemnly one remembers the many years this rite has been preserved over the graves of others. There is an awe in the very finality resident in ceremony—all completion is a symbol and desire of death. A city such as Siena, grave and crenellated, stony and austere beyond its sun-warmed colour, is hung around with the cold breath of dead, glorious history. Other cities, as Naples, can bear their past differently, can vibrate with life so much that their time-scarred ground, repository of the ancients, seems the more fertile for its buried old ghosts, and death is so fortuitous and facile a part of the daily struggle that it is neither welcomed nor revered. But not so Siena, the quieter, cleaner, graver city of mediaeval calm.

The drummer suddenly shook his head to one of the people watching. This man took the message and dashed forward, doubled up, to kick Osvaldo sharply on his bony flank. Osvaldo gave a yelp, looked round astonished at this man, hesitated—wondered why he had been attacked; was he not in battle for a brother man against the dangerous bird? And then receiving another kick, slunk sorrowfully away to the side of the street. Enrico was dealt with similarly —small Fa saw what was coming and followed.

They sat in a doorway, framed by the severe stone lintel. Their eyes glanced with apprehension at the drummer, at those watching; the kicks had not hurt, but the meaning was absolute. Sometimes their heads turned to the flags and revolved with them. In a nearby doorway sat a Sienese cat, well-fed, tranquil, heraldic. It seemed at last that Osvaldo, Enrico and Fa had assumed some of the same sedentary pose. They seemed to be considering the fatal words, that breath of the worm that says: 'Perhaps it is time to settle down. . . .' Contentedly to die.

When a minute later the sbandierata was over and the drumming group marched away and was lost along that narrow street, they were still sitting there. Life, it seemed, was over; trotting was done. No more now but to sit in doorways, to sit and wait. Calmly to await the cold breath. They had been touched by the city, they had been permitted to see beyond the veil. No more to do but wait, satisfied, content, half-dead already.

Pastorale

ONE first heard a sound like low-toned cowbells, like many cowbells crushed and chorded together—and then round the narrow corner of old grey walls nosed the chromium grill, the long bonnet, and then all the pale gleaming length of a torpedo-shaped roadster. It wheeled noiselessly, thick-tyred, up the soft earth street, and stopped at the centre of the village. That was not far, the whole squat clump of the inner village hardly extended more than four of its lengths round the long automobile. But how it took charge of the graven, shabby place! Each house was built thickly of dark rock, windows were so small that one noticed no curtains—and the irregular street, rather a space between houses than a street, was all brown beaten earth, with a few cobbles, a slash of crumbling tar. Grey and dust-brown—the colour of the mules that sometimes trudged through like white-lipped fools.

Against such earthen textures the pearl-pale car shone with a princely lustre; the chromium flashed precious silver, the clean canvas of its hood sat reefed like Parisian cloth, the luggage of yellow pigskin and gold clasps told the tale of Pullman seats and luxury. At the wheel sat a young lean dark man; the sun flashed on his oiled hair, on the platinum watch glittering from his soft glove, on the white card he now studied. The woman at his side, her face like a soft white nut in its rich brown hat, peered over—and then, with eyes screwed, looked up at the house above in disbelief.

I thought that they must have been given an introduction to the pension, perhaps from the Syndicat d'Initiative back at Ajaccio. This mountain village, Piana, lay half-way up the jagged coast; one needed a recommendation. I was about to call down to Madame Paolo that there were customers—when through the lace curtains I saw that old black cormorant already bustling about the car, bowing and smiling, tugging at the luggage; she must have been at her own window below minutes before me, shadowy eyes rapacious behind the curtain. The man and woman hoisted themselves out of the car; the seats were set low; it was an effort to haul oneself out from such a comfortable car, the woman showed much awkwardly opened leg. But this in no way discomfited the peasant boys, who stood absorbed with respect at such new-arrived wonders. The couple never paused to wish these onlookers a good day, they seemed not to see them. But when Madame Paolo tried to lift a big suitcase, the man smiled pleasantly and took it from her.

A little later, it must have been four o'clock, I went downstairs to the parlour that served as both dining-room and entrance hall. The man and woman were sitting at one of the tables, drinking coffee and goat's milk. Neither looked up as I came down the bare wooden stairs. It was a small room, holding three large tables, and draped about with a curious assortment of art-nouveau and early-jazz ornaments left long ago by forgotten commercial travellers from France. It had a very closed-in atmosphere. It would have been difficult to imagine any estrangement between strangers in such a room—but neither of these two looked up as I came down. Nor when I asked through the kitchen door for my own coffee and chestnut cake. When Madame Paolo brought this she walked round to the other table and asked whether they required anything more; the man answered politely, but impersonally, and had turned back to his coffee while Madame Paolo was still smiling. In such rooms, in a strange village, and with all the mountains and rolling maquis wild outside, it is exceedingly difficult to remain impersonal. One is in a shelter more than a lodging-house.

Since they were so firmly absorbed in one another, I could watch them quite closely. This was not comfortable, the atmosphere was so aloof; but certainly one could feel no fear of indiscretion. At length it occurred to me what probably they were—and what they did prove to be: they were a couple sufficiently young in marriage still to be interested in themselves beyond any other person. Not so young as to feel themselves performers; not old enough to wish for others to perform.

One has seen them everywhere in hotel lounges, or in one's home-town masquerading as one's friends. In the hotel lounge they sit together in their armchairs, he turning over the pages of a book, she with a writing-pad on her knees. They never speak, but one senses from them a stronger air of intimacy than from all others in the lounge. They never look up at other people. They are absolutely incurious about the world without them. Older couples will show the searching eyes of escape. Unmarried people will be searching for immurement. But these two will sit solid, an affectionate brother and sister arranging some funeral visit; but how warm, how enviable a funeral—how armoured, wonderful! And as for those who pretend still to be one's friends—see them, for instance, as hosts at dinner. Watch them exchange private messages of the eyes, grow silent as they dismiss the conversation to speak anxiously of some intimate affair of their building which has been growing at the backs of their minds throughout dinner, watch them spring to their feet as you, the old friend, apologize for the need to leave early. And how enviable their glance as the door closes, how real the small things they will say—deeper than all the first passionate words. And how empty one's back feels—walking away from the eyeless smiles, wishing even for the lance of malice, but receiving from them nothing, absolutely nothing. . . .

In this case, their evident prosperity increased such an armour. In mainland towns it would not have so obtruded; but here on the poorer island such prosperity fired into magnificence, their rich leather and tweed looked soft and fabulously of the town. One inferred immediately that the man must have something sinister in his dealings—but really, he could have been a well-off young merchant or professional man who had looked after his money. He was a lean man, dark-eyed, polished in his tweeds as a Parisian; manicured, muscular, silk-tied. The woman sat smooth and plastered in on to herself, in the sheath of her dress, in her close-set hair; nowhere a strand astray, but fired here and there with a jewel, and with over this smoothness a loose coat draped and askew to proclaim ease, to accentuate what sat tight and unruffled within. They sat silently drinking their coffee, looking for the most part down at the table, at their hands, or to the furniture a foot on either side. They spoke little—at first glance one would have considered them unbearably tired of each other. But when they did speak—they looked straight into each other's eyes, without flinching, pulling no false expression! They smiled without laughing, without twitching! They neither raised their voices nor kept them low! When the woman asked for a cigarette, she took it without thanking him: yet he was thanked.

Outside the weather was bright and fine, a hot November sun mixed with the clear high air and the breeze of autumn. No mountain chill, only a deep invigoration—like a cool old wine, a yellow wine. I walked out by the church, a rounded plaster basilica washed pale and sudden pink against the grim grey of the other village buildings; old men, moustached and corduroyed, sat smoking on benches against the wide circular end of the church—through the day they moved round slowly, as on a wheel, with the sun. I climbed up the road, then took a hill-path. It was steep, one mounted quickly. It was a path and a brook combined, so that upwards one trudged from stone to stone with the mountain water coursing down in between. Very soon the village lay far below. One saw the roofs huddling in round the church—in that broad, sharp mountainscape like a huddle of sheep round their pink shepherd, pathetic, blind, but nuzzling safe.

A climb of ten minutes on those slopes brings out the heat and sweat, and already the country is as wild as anywhere farther. I saw a mound of moss and brush and climbed off the path on to it; once there had been a stone goat-pen there, and the old circle of stones remained, a curious fairy-ring, and good to sit on. The ground was thick with dark olive moss, above the great chestnut woods blazed yellow up the mountain, below the green maquis of cystus and sweet-smelling scrub stretched down and down, past Piana, to the eucalyptus groves by the warm sea—to Porto, little port for the loading of chestnuts, cork and granite. All was vegetated, mountains thickly carpeted with a smell of herbs and the rich brown taste of chestnuts. Occasionally a small wood of arbutus pricked the green with scarlet berries; far above rose the mauve mountain-tops, beneath stretched the wide and lovely blue of Porto's gulf, ridged with red stone. All the time I could still see that polished car and its tailored companions.

They must, I thought, be from the mainland, motoring from

Ajaccio right up the coast to Calvi. At Calvi, sleek with yachts from Cannes, they would come to rest in their grand hotel of balconies and bathrooms. What, I wondered, would they think when they found there was not even a bucket in the pension, nothing at all to be done but wander into the chestnut woods with one's copy of the *Sampiero*? Then I remembered their armour—of course this would protect them. Nothing could disturb such equanimity. They would smile, remember that the journey was being broken only for one night, and indeed wander out into the chestnut woods—with perhaps a copy of *Le Temps*. That was in itself a small matter—but it suggested again the exasperating notion of that armour, their carapace of incuriosity against which no one in the world could prevail. *No one*—the absolute quality of such armour frightened. Here was something at last impeccable, a dreadful example of the perfection that man is supposed never to achieve. Indeed, it might not be constant, there was the certainty that time would corrupt it . . . but nevertheless for a time, and perhaps for as concrete a time as a year or two years, their state would remain an immaculate truth. Evanescence may be a condition of life, but against this generality there is the real measure of time—minutes, hours, years. Pleasure for a year is more desirable than for a minute; so, more valuable. What the two had, for all present purposes, was a solid armour. Nothing would undo them. Accident, malice, affection, the chestnut wood— they were proof against each eventuality. Lawyers might write their letters of doom—they would look at each other, inter-telegraph their two-ness, and then deal with matters, unsuccessfully or not, it made no difference. Friends might deliver their invitations, they would nod their dual head—and know that the friends would get no little piece of them, not one fragment, they would go only to come back.

And of course they would be favoured by systems—I was walking back downhill to Piana again, having the idea to walk through the village and beyond to the Calanches, to watch again that sonorous eruption of red rock, a landscape unique in Europe—by simple systems and habits. By their clothes one could judge that they were part of a set section of society. There would be behaviour permitted and things not done, standards that would aid considerably the impulse of agreement; many questions would never be posed, originalities of wish would not have to be agreed—nodding was made easy. They would not, of course, be proof against small disagreements, rows of the ruffled nerve—but these would soon be straightened out: the disagreement would never include anyone or anything else. They would suffer neither jealousy nor envy, nor any desire for escape; such rows would be physical, nervous reflexes, headaches essentially within the armour.

I passed the car, now in shade, but still gleaming. What would they be doing upstairs in the bare white-washed bedroom? It was difficult to imagine them making love, they looked too intimate. But in fact they would have been satisfied often and well with each other—or the armour would have creaked. So upstairs above their car, while the leather travelling clock and the ivory hairbrushes sat quite still on the dressing-table, they might have been doing whatever they wished? Writing letters—each was as evidently sensible as the other in the case of these two, how could one interfere, even to guess?

The road out of the village became a first-class cliff motor-road, snaking about round a deep gorge, but neatly walled, and smoothly surfaced. It was quite a walk to the Calanches, and as one travelled this road—intensely alone in such a wild geography, as alone as the ringing of one's boots—the sea opened far out down to the left. It was not, of course, miles or even far—it was the illusion of distance seen from a height. Now the broad sea with its corrugation of hair-size wrinkles looked like blue beaten steel, like the steel of a lacquered fire-iron: away out a large white cloud drifted, hanging down two vicious white tails that tried to be waterspouts. Ahead lay the Calanches. A quarter of an hour later I was among them.

Here the vegetation to either side ceased—one walked along a road suspended between precipitous cliffs of fierce red granite, a steep convulsion of weird rock that seemed to glow still with the fire of its first spawning. This was a dead land, a canyon, but on one side open frequently to the far-down echoing sea. Promontories of dreamlike twisted red rock towered away down to that sea, gulches and gullies dreaded down to the great blue gulf—and each one of ten thousand pinnacles of rock was smoothly sculpted into a strange hooded shape. Holes and sockets stared as though blown by the wind, whistling silently with siren invocation. Nothing moved. All those fantastic sculptures stood still—coy tourists simpered that one looked like an elephant, that another was for all the world a bear—but they were in fact simply figures, figures standing inevitably as themselves and nothing more, figures deep in thought about themselves, their stone thoughts cowled and draped with red stone, ponderously waiting for motion. An aeolian music sang round them, but it was too ancient a sound for human ears.

For human ears! But there, along the road leaning on the wall and watching this vast colloquy of still stone souls, stood two soft humans, tweeded and diamonded, but nevertheless soft skinfuls of flesh, those two of the contented car! They stood watching the sun sink on the Calanches, close in their companionship, proofed in their tegument of quiet passion. Theirs were no linked hands, no leaning and pressing together of bodies that searched for the other's comfort—they could stand side by side, with the cool air between them, sure of each other's presence and affection and without need for the flesh of reassurance. And then the sun with remarkable swiftness changed its golden blue for red, for gilt red reflective of hot coral and the branding iron. The sea turned purple, great stretches of olive milk appeared—and above the sky darkened, and began to shine with the phosphorescences of night; but overpowering everything, the Calanches started to glow, to burn, to blaze with hot red light. Now all those standing figures, those pinnacles of graven thought took on deep shadows—burning red themselves with projected movement, invested with misery, black shadows under their eyeless cowls and tapering behind them. One felt the sea itself would steam for the immersion of these sad hot creatures; ice-green lichens that here and there occurred were burnt up and vanished in the broad consuming glow.

Alone thus with the rock and the sea stood the two whom nothing could assail. As the sun sank farther, the contortion upwards of all that rock showed itself more plainly—here suddenly was a vista such as Blake drew, a thousand souls in anguish moving upwards, the silence now a mute chorus of despair, each cowl griefed and crying.

But I had been wrong. Their armour was not immaculate, those two were town-dwellers. The woman straightened herself, and gave a little shiver. They turned to each other, their eyes must have met, they seemed to hunch their shoulders and then hurried quickly away, back walking fast to the car, to the safety of their room.

My Little Robins

THAT notable engineer first made his appearance one night on the Ligurian Sea, on the Ajaccio passage.

At nine or ten o'clock I was sitting huddled in a corner of the second-class saloon. One heavily shaded light burned above a flap-table that served, with its four or five bottles, as a bar. The rest of the saloon faded off on all sides into darkness, the darkness of bulwark-shaped walls and a portholed fore-partition: in the darkness lay passengers in all the humped and sprawled positions of shipboard sleep. They lay among the litter of their suppers—bread-rind, cheese-crumbs, wine bottles—and the crumpled shreds of newspaper in which all that food had been wrapped; among the first pale reachings of vomit; against shoulders and on laps, on Corsicans sailing back to their native island, on Corsican nieces visiting their old aunts in mountain villages, on Corsican entrepreneurs of Ajaccio, on the sons of Corsicans returning from their universities in France, on Corsican travellers in chestnuts and granite and wood, on long-moustached migrants homing again, on matriarchs intent upon the hearths of their first brooding—on all these who were bound together by the second-class look, dark and roughish, bound with the wicker-basket and the peasant spattering that distinguish both ships bound for islands and ships of the inland seas, rough ships that ply the Black Sea, the Caspian, the local Baltic and this the Ligurian Sea bound for Ajaccio in French Corsica.

And now into this sleep-smelling saloon, shuddering from the engines aft, dusky with the cramp of travellers, there stepped the bright-blue dungarees of an engineer. He entered firmly, straight from his engines, with a seaman's tread; stood for a moment wiping some of the oil from his hands; stepped over to the circle of light over the makeshift bar. Disregarding the passengers, he fingered a packet of cigarettes from his dungaree pockets, held it high to drop a cigarette unsoiled into his mouth, then ordered a pastis. He held the milky glass outstretched, curling out one long finger in a gesture of stiff delicacy—and drank. This man's presence was forceful—instantly one was affected. There was nothing odd in what he did—though later it was to prove otherwise. The appearance in the second-class saloon of a ship's worker, an ordinary engineer, was not unusual to any but a few northern passengers accustomed to firmer disciplinary divisions on larger and colder ships. It was more his personal figure; and, of course, some essential power beneath this.

He did not look like what an engineer might be supposed to look. He was a tall, thin, gangling man, with a beaked nose and dark bright eyes that peered forward with the look of an angry scholar. His thin stomach arched in, his knees knobbled and bent forward, his arms held bonily akimbo, he moved—and he moved all the time, he never stopped—like an agitated don doing his best with a fox-trot. Often the scholarly, the nominally unworldly, lurch and stumble not so much because their bodies have been misshapen by the length of their books, as by a deficiency in ordinary vanity—they have never worshipped bodily grace in a manner personal enough to imitate it; they are neither nervous nor preoccupied, simply they have never learned. But this is often compensated by a delicacy of smaller movements—gestures of the hands, inclinations of the head, reclinations of the whole body. Thus also the engineer: his hands, long-fingered, black-oiled, fluttered beautifully; the movements of his head followed fluently the thoughts of his mind, and even standing his whole body was sitting—he drooped relaxed. He wore dark sunglasses, and perched on his head a blue cap crumpled like a képi from the Crimean war.

He never stopped moving. As he took his glass and first surveyed it, he arched further backwards, and then as he drank revolved slowly with his lips to the glass, scrutinizing the deep half-circle of sleepers; simultaneously he managed to speak to the barman and wave with his free hand to one of the passengers who was still sitting upright and awake. Now taking his drink he gangled over to this man, and started an intense gesticulated conversation. His body swayed, his hands fluttered, his nose pecked, his eyes rolled. He spoke in French in either a Provençal or Italian dialect. It was difficult to understand all he said—but it had to do with prices, the loan of a gun, and the sale of something he had brought from the mainland. It was plain now that some of his volatility was moved by the common Mediterranean need for commerce, for using each moment as a street-corner; yet this too he managed with a curious distinction. The other man said little, sometimes shrugged his shoulders—his was the situation of the approached. But finally, as if forces had been slowly gathering inside him, he too began to talk, without pause, giving with definition his own idea of the matter; he pointed suddenly to his stomach, and began to talk faster and louder. The engineer opened his arms wide, and managed at the same time to move his shoulders up and down in a series of hopeless shrugs. Impossible, the shoulders said, hopeless. The other man drew from his pocket a note—twenty francs. The shrugging ceased, the engineer took the note—though indeed still as if there could be no hope, with down-pressed lips that expressed also something of the worthlessness of all money—and went shuffling and lurching from the saloon. In a few moments he returned, carrying bread and a huge dish of soup. The man nodded and began to eat. Just then, I suppose, my eyes closed and I was off to sleep.

I was to see much of this engineer, but I did not catch sight of him again until quite late the next morning.

We put into Ajaccio early—at dawn. The great U-shaped gulf, long enough to contain two thousand ships, received us with grey swelling waters, while on either side the black mountainous coast-line raced out to sea; the first pink light burnt its foundry-glare into a chilled grey sky, a red glow had already painted the curious Iles Sanguinaires with the wet of new blood. Those three sinister islands stood off the cape in a line that seemed to move. Well inside lay Ajaccio and its few sprouting palms.

Even at that distance the town, huddled down low against the dark mountains, looked poor and squalid. And then, as we neared its long façade, and as the ship seemed to fly through the water with each flat square-windowed building marking its speed, that grey light showed clearly the scabrous texture of each wall, the cracked and peeling and stained surface of decay. Later, when the sun had risen and I was warming over a glass of coffee on the Cours Napoléon, the sun threw into sharper definition the ulcerous scars, the gutter-soaked patches that smeared the walls of all those tall barrack-like buildings. The kerbs had fallen away, sand from the pavements had run in rivulets out on to the pocked carriageway of this the main street of the capital; no soft grasses and lichens pursued such decay, but instead only sand and powdered asphalt giving with their dull ochreous aridity the tone of the town, a town of huge barrack-buildings, dry palms and now leafless plane-trees, of Senegalese troops and occasional statues of Napoléon, of garbage in the streets and a wide main square of sand, of sand and the tricolour. Two main avenues converged on that immense sandy Place Diamant; along one, the Cours Napoléon, men in many clothes were already sipping their pastis and talking.

I was to know later that in these lines of cafés and bars there was no dancing, only pastis and cards—this was much a garrison town, a port for sailors and land-locked soldiers, upon which one could feel written in the sand and round the monuments and over the acres of blighted plaster the hideous word 'caserne'.

Suddenly I saw again my engineer. He was dressed as before—pale-blue overalls, képi, black glasses; he was thus sharply visible among the khakis and corduroys and greys of the growing crowd. He came gesturing and gangling from the dark door of a bar, as fast as if he had been ejected, holding under one arm a package and in the other the arm of a much shorter and fatter man whom he now dragged at speed along the street. Both men talked fast and without pause, even in their linked position managing to turn their faces close and vehement. They disappeared down one of the steep side streets to the Rue Cardinal Fesch.

Having nothing particular to do but look at the town, I rose and followed. They had chosen this little street for a transaction, and now stood, still gesturing and exploding, between a foot-high mass of cabbage and dung and one of the leaning housewalls with its fat china drainpipe. Then, at some climax, the engineer flourished his parcel, tore off the brown paper, and stood for a moment without talking, his wide black glasses staring wonderstruck at the beauty of what was revealed—an American army jacket and breeches. The smaller man showed instant disgust, looked up and down the street for something, anything amusing. But at the same time his left hand fingered the material of the jacket. The engineer was talking again. The small man kept shrugging his shoulders. At last, with the down-drawn lips and heavenward eyes of a dying martyr, he shuffled in his pocket and brought out some notes. He took the clothes, handed the engineer the notes. A pause. Then the blue form of the engineer exploded. He rose on his toes, bending over the other man like a furious bird, hands wide outstretched like eagle's wings, his nose-beaked head pecking forward with every emphatic word. The smaller man parried this by staring up at him with his head on one side, a small smile of unbelief cocking the corner of his mouth—a sceptic child surveyed his hysterical uncle. But the volcano proved too much, its force grew until the smile disappeared. A last shrug of his shoulders. Then reaching into a pocket that small man drew forth a handful of red cylinders. Cartridges. And these instantly the engineer took, hiding them, subsiding and simultaneously throwing a hand of affection on his adversary's shoulder. They then parted on the best, on the face of it, of terms.

The engineer walked quickly up into the main street again and disappeared into a bar. I stood waiting for him to come out—fascinated by such volatility, by such an exquisite performance of the Mediterranean pantomime of buy-sell, where the marks of pity and contempt, ennui and obsession, despair and joy, are seen publicly at their finest extremes. That concession to the blind eye of the police when one moves off the main street yet deals in the open! That etiquette of silence while the other talks! That entrance at a predetermined point of the score into inspired duet . . . but now the engineer came bursting out from the bar with a shotgun under his arm. This altered his manner absolutely, the shotgun slaughtered innocence. With his dark glasses gazing obsessedly ahead, he strode off to the Place Diamant, whose circuit he made, keeping to the wall.

Along past the dark yellow military hospital, down the sea-wall with its row of stunted palms like elephant legs tufted wearily with green feathers. Along the road that skirts the side of the gulf, a road marked by a gradual scarcity of building, a greater decrepitude in the roadway, by refuse dumps and isolated half-finished concrete tenements, by bones and offal and driftwood lying puddled in the red rockpools: and always by the attempt of public work to be worthy of a capital, but an attempt forlorn, abandoned at its start, as though some tremendous force of nature had weighed too heavily down on the hopeless community of human hearts. A weight of nature was implemented—for now to either side the majesty of this island of mountains began to impress itself. Those mountains on the far side of the gulf raced their black humps far into the sea, snow on their peaks glittered like sugar in the sun, pockets of poisonous wool drifted longingly across the valley cuts; while to the right of our road rose the near slopes of the maquis, small ascending mountains thickly covered with aromatic scrub, so that they looked smooth and furry, like convulsed green baize.

The engineer walked fast, bouncing on his toes, throwing his elbows back and jolting like a professional walker. His head under that képi now searched the terrain to the right: he might have been looking for one of the few scattered villas that straggled about the slope. On he went. We passed a sudden, then endless cemetery of bright stone house-tombs, each built much more stably than the houses back in the capital—sealed evidences of Corsican pride and familiarity with death. Abruptly the cemetery ceased and the road grew houseless and wild, with no embankment against the gulf, and growing on either side wet green cactus studded with yellow flowers. The Iles Sanguinaires moved like a line of ships in the distance. The maquis rose unwalled on our right.

The engineer stopped, glanced keenly up the hill-side. Very quickly he took cartridges from his pocket—I saw them flash red as they were snapped away into the gun. Then he was off climbing up the steep, rough incline. He climbed like a frog, spreading his hands and long thin legs to grasp branches and to grip the greyish boulders, thrusting forward his body against the gradient. It was hardly prudent to follow him immediately—on a road my presence might have been coincidental, but on the pathless maquis not. I waited.

In fact, was it prudent to follow him at all? There he went, purposely armed, intent on some firm direction—probably some goat-herd's shack, some outlying cottage. The morning paper had already told me that the day before, yesterday, there had been a

shooting in the main café in Ajaccio—a husband seated with his
wife and another man had suddenly risen to his feet and shot this
other man bluntly in the stomach. And some time in the recent past
a night-club manager had shot a sailor in the neck for disturbing his
orchestra with an impromptu on the accordion. There had been
bullet holes in the mirror of another café. And the Corsican is re-
nowned for his history of proud summary justice. Whatever then
the engineer would do might involve me, if I remained so close—
either as an accomplice, or as a witness. Or the engineer himself
would shoot me as a spy? However . . . the affair was too mature to
abandon. Besides, we were in the country, with no easy diversions.
So I decided to climb up into the maquis at a parallel distance from
the engineer, to climb faster and thus higher than him, so that I
could look down on his direction. With the cover afforded by scrub
it would be fairly simple to remain unobserved—and my suit was
grey, where his was bright-washed blue.

A sweaty climb under the rising sun. The maquis is a strange
mixture of hard and soft things, of sudden aromatic carpets of herb,
of eruptions of hard grey boulders, of soft arbutus and cystus, and
then of spiny cactus. But mostly it feels soft, looking so moss-green,
the hill-top a high ridge of green fur against the blue sky; the air
smells sweet as so many odorous plants are crushed by the heel.
Though it was steep and tiring, the climb was a joy: a sense of great
freedom among such windwashed luxuriance in the warm winter
sun made me forget the engineer. Or postpone him. But arrived at
last at my eminence I took cover, and looked round. He was nowhere
to be seen. I felt in my haversack for the glasses, and then began to
scrutinize carefully the intricate shrub.

No sound. No movement over all the expanse of rolling lichenous
sward—only sometimes the silent glint of a bird skimming the low
branches, or curving up suddenly like a feather kicked on hot air.
The arm of scented green stretched out to sea—for this was the thick
upper arm of a cape—and on either side extended, far and near, the
sea. No forest murmur here, no trees to move in those slight breezes
that fanned the two shores: it was deadly set, like a painted plaster
model. In ancient times pilots knew this island from a distance
because of the perfume that drifted far out over the sea, a perfume

of flowering scrub that caused those ancient oarsmen to call it the Scented Isle. But now it was winter, warm but flowerless—and still.

The black sockets of my binoculars traversed slowly. Up the slight hills, down suddenly into the overgrown ravines, past a ruined goatherd's hut, over a circle of stones that had once based a sheep-pen or a Genoese watch-tower. Suddenly I saw the peaked blue képi, a pale-blue tropical bird above a bush of myrtle. The man was crouched, moving sideways with the gun stealthily creeping to his shoulder. The dark glasses were fixed emotionless and ruthless on something at the centre of a circle he was making; my glasses were focused clear on those dark others. A slow movement, trying to make no sound—and in the binoculars there was an augmented silence. Over all, the immense quiet of the day.

It was difficult to move the binoculars off him. At such a moment he might have made some decisive move, disappearing into the bush. But at length, as his movements seemed to remain so steady, I shifted those black circles carefully across. There was nothing.

I searched in vain—for a hut, for some other man's movement, for the movement of a branch that might show up some other man. But there was nothing—and I knew by the direction of his glasses that he was anticipating no long shot. Whoever he was after lay close. No movement, no life in that scrub—only suddenly a pinpoint of colour that intensified the strange stillness. A robin sat on one of the branches. Its orange breast caught the sunlight, it was opening and shutting its beak as if trying to sing—for of course no sound came.

It did not seem possible. At first I discarded the idea. But as the minutes passed the truth emerged; irrefutable and, through the glasses, of strange isolated power. The engineer was stalking that robin. I switched the glasses to and fro, certainly the gun's barrel was trained on the little bird's level. But—why not shoot? Then, as the engineer quietly lowered his head to the gunsight, it was plain to see why he held his fire. He had been moving round *behind the robin*. Some deep amazing instinct had instructed him to shoot this little bird in the back.

For a long time the scene stayed fixed. That man's head was now lowered to the sights, so that the peak of his pale képi ran parallel with the gun. It looked more than ever like a bird, or like some false effigy of a bird, a pointed blue-beaked thing like a carnival mask, like the cruel disguise of some grotesque bird-watcher's hood. And a few yards across the scented foliage, whose every fragile leaf was set so still, there sat the other bird, the real little bird. With its back turned. So that the two made a silent unmoving procession of birds. Not a leaf shivered; they were like leaves seen on a cinema film, bright and unreal. The figure in the képi seemed cast in wax. Only the little bird's mouth could be seen faintly moving—perhaps eating. That small movement only accentuated the silence, as though the bird were singing without sound.

Suddenly it rose in the air, blasted by a sudden wind, and then with scattering wings dropped. At the same time the foliage behind shivered. Then a drift of smoke came, and a prancing blue figure—just as the echoing shot-sound cracked as if behind my ear. I kept the binoculars fixed, my two holes of vision showed the blue figure thrashing excitedly in the tangled shrub, eagerly pouncing then lifting aloft, with a backward-leaning motion of triumph, a small furry ball of grey and orange.

Some hours later, having lunched in Ajaccio, I saw him again. He was talking to two elderly Corsicans. He held in his hand a small bunch of little birds—three at least were robins. These he brandished in the faces of the two old men, who seemed annoyed and looked pointedly away. This time I determined to hear what was said. They were standing at a point that I could approach without seeming inquisitive.

They were standing near to the old fountain in the barrack wall. Here, in a stone recess behind an iron railing, was a place where old men habitually forgathered. Such old men stood there for hours, leaning on the iron railing, gossiping, gazing at the passers-by of the Place Diamant and past them across the sandy waste to the leprous line of houses stretching to the gulf-wall, at the gulf and its sombre mountains beyond. The engineer and his two acquaintances were standing outside the railing. It seemed that only the poorer went inside, men who had had their day; and somehow they must have formed a focal point for street standing, because it was around here that a ragged crowd always loitered and talked. This I now joined.

After a few hours on the island my understanding of the patois was growing clearer. They spoke Corsican—not the romance language of the midi, but a mixture of French and Genoese. The two old men were pure islanders. They wore the wide curl-brimmed black hats, the long jackets of chestnut brown corduroy, the bright-scarlet cummerbunds that still form a much-worn national dress among the older country-people. And Ajaccio, besides being a caserne, still retained some of the feeling of a large market town, it attracted people from the hills, the farmers, the millers, the sons of labourers and gentlemen and bandits. These old two, with their lean high cheekbones and their draped moustaches, were Corsicans of old stock, men of the bandit days. Their bearing was proud.

Such pride, such granite unconcern must have proved a formidable barrier to the engineer's commerce. But a barrier that perhaps he welcomed, as many small illnesses are welcomed, for the passionate pain they provoke. There was no doubt that he was now in pain. He had pushed his dark glasses on to his forehead, agonized eyebrows reached up to them like the stretched legs of frogs, his dark searching eyes glittered, his lips seemed to move in a motion faster than the flow of words—and all the time that small wedge of little birds fluttered between his mouth and the stern eyes of the two disapproving old men. The old men—perhaps owners of a restaurant, perhaps of good wives—were potential buyers of the robins. One of them said:

'I have offered you six francs the bird.'

He said this without vehemence, as having stated not a price but some patriarchal law. He said nothing further, only pulled slowly at a tooth under his moustache. The engineer burst into an appeal of despair—for ten francs the bird. Ten francs! Ten small francs for the most savoury, the delicious little bird! Shot even that morning, fresh from eating the odorous maquis—the exquisite bird of the red throat!

But obduracy had hardened in the veins of those old men. Many Mediterranean peoples buy, sell, bargain, run after coins bright and round as their sun, run after them without shame and with laughter, even without avarice and only as a reasonable means to an end. These Corsicans are different. Centuries of fighting against imperialists from the mainlands, against Spain and France and always Genoa, have welded them into firm communities, groups of the family and of the village and of the island. Their need was always to be self-provident, independent in their mountains and thence independent in their hearts. That which they own they give freely—but they will fight bitterly if it is snatched by force. Such a pride does not allow them to bargain. They state their view, their fair price. It is the last word.

Infuriating for the sinuous engineer. This one was now driven by his sunsoaked frenzy into a beatification that soon rose far beyond his wares, rose from praising the dead bird to a lyric of the bird alive, the bird he had shot, but of whose life and beauty he was deeply aware. Of course, he exaggerated:

'Fine, the little rouge-gorge! High in the maquis she sits, her breast shines like the red arbutus. Small, yes, but up there in the green it is the only little person that is alive—like a mouse she darts among the low branches.'

As he spoke his eyes rolled, his fingers played with air as lightly as birds' wings—this shooter of birds in the back. But transported now, it was plain that while killing birds he loved them, or knew their live mystery, their freedom. I who while eating flesh condemn any joy in its killing was astounded—it had never occurred to me that you could love these things exactly at the same time as killing, that in fact the processes of loving life and killing it for one's own survival could occur in the same brain at the same time, fully, without the trammelings of pity. To all this the old men just nodded. They too knew.

'There was the sky, blue and wide, the great sky, and up flew the little bird, its red breast shining in the sun, I saw the red, I aimed. . . .'

Of course he never saw the red. Nor did he see what I saw—thrushes I had eaten at lunch, little naked birds served whole and still on thick toast. Birds featherless as fledglings, with their beaks and big-lidded eyes shut and saurian, baby pterodactyls. A delicacy, for their flesh was nurtured on the aromatic scrub. Others in the restaurant lifted the birds with their fingers and picked with their teeth at the heads.

'I sprang forward! I picked her up, and she was still warm. See, only this morning, warm and fresh from the herbs of the maquis. . . .'

And there he was tacked back again on to his selling course. The flight of fancy was over. But it had been real. He was no poet, he was an engineer and apart from his looks a not uncommon one. Yet, here he was one of a curious breed—the breed of the loving hunter. No regrets, he faced up to the cruelty of life and lived his part of it; and he loved life. An aesthete of the open field, he saw his prey as a thing of beauty. But he saw it according to the scale of his own animality, not with sentiment as a fellow creature. It could only have been love that gave him such joy in killing. He cared much more than on the score of prowess. He cared much more than an ordinary lover of beauty—the debased aesthete who is held to be all heart and sympathy, but who so often becomes the most intolerant of men, a creature refined beyond generous living. But here was the predatory aesthete, a fine mind if a dark one.

However—his words were now of no use—the thoughtful patriarchs rebutted him with their pride. They made no further offer, but simply let him speak himself back into silence. As for him— perhaps he had the whole afternoon to spare and a whole town of buyers to try, or he was defiant on his own terms. In any case, he suddenly turned away, and with a brief word of parting went striding fast round the corner into the afternoon crowd of the Cours Napoléon. I followed. Once round the corner he stopped, undecided. He was still quivering with his extraordinary vehemence, more alive and alight than ever. He paused, one could hear him raging inside: 'Where now, where now with my little robins?' Suddenly he decided; in his awkward but swiftly efficient way he darted away into the crowd, into the mixed moving mass of corduroy and dark blue and Latin black and Senegalese red and all the patched-up khaki that made the fashionable throng of this capital street. He disappeared. But I was to see him frequently throughout the afternoon—before the tumultuous evening ever began.

In such a small town it is difficult to avoid meeting again such an acquaintance—particularly as my own afternoon was spent wandering and looking. Thus I saw him in the market town by the quay, out by the railway station with its earnest small trains winding off up the mountains to the old capital of Corte, in a cool stone restaurant spacious with pots of plants and lean tailless dogs, in a bar whose fixtures were of the Empire's gold and mahogany, in one of the cavernous dark shops sacked with grain and pasta. Each time he was bargaining, brandishing the robins. Not only with the imperturbable Corsican, but with other more vociferous Latins. As the hours passed, so the feathers of the little birds grew fluffed and scragged. But it seemed no one would pay his price; perhaps he deceived himself by applying the higher prices of the mainland to the simpler island economy. It seemed, at all costs, such a small transaction; but the engineer had plainly become obsessed. The transaction had become more important than the profit. Besides, many other small deals could be seen loitering round those streets—there was one tall Senegalese walking slowly from restaurant to restaurant like a priest in his red fez, a single blue-black crayfish weaving its worried feelers from his purple-black hand.

Towards four o'clock the sun grew milky and disappeared, massive clouds came lowering in from the sea. The ochreous town grew pale beneath a giant darkness. An hour later, the storm had still not broken. Still it massed strength, piling up weight upon weight of cloud, darkness upon darkness. It was about then, at five o'clock, that I noticed a crowd taking a direction: everyone seemed to be moving down from the Cours and the big Place towards the harbour, in fact towards another square enclosing yet another statue of Napoléon and at the same time the Hotel de Ville.

It was outside this pillared and balconied seat of government that a large crowd now collected. A newly elected deputy was formally taking over his office. Ajaccio had assembled to acclaim him. Now they waited, strolled, chattered, milled; a feeling of storm, of tense expectation, of suppressed revelry tautened the air— and suddenly all the electric lights were switched on. Wired among the branches of the plane and palm trees covering this little square, the yellow bulbs blazed gaudily, lit up the autumn leaves, cut themselves bright against the slate-dark sky above. Through the tall window of the balcony a glittering glass chandelier shone, telling of rich official pomp, of soft ambassadorial feet within.

All Ajaccio! That hot, seedy crowd gathered to the centre of their sun-soaked town with not much more purpose than just to gather, to stir into life. Throughout those latitudes townspeople gathered for the evening parade, for the strolling and passing and turning about in their thousand twilit squares; but this was more—some came with political feeling, others stirred patriotically, for all there was the expectation of an 'occasion'! So they stood about on the sandy ground under the plane-trees and palms, all eyes on the central yellow building with its chandelier, with its draped swathe of tricolour, with its ionic portico and its old red carpet frayed and holed. Blue-uniformed cadets lined the entrance. A loud-speaker attached to the balcony roared out music from a gramophone—Viennese waltzes, giddying javas, jazz. That loudspeaker seemed to be made all of wire, it grated so. And so also the bell that suddenly chimed five from the clock-tower—a thin wiry bell shrill above the metal music; and the wired feeling of the electric lights among the branches—through the warm air all these makeshift wires galvanized the night. The yellow tower steadily grew paler against the monstrous cloud looming indigo above; soon its stucco seemed to shine against so much darkness; then, from far across the mountains, there flickered sudden violet flashes, like shadows of light growing huge and as swiftly gone—the pagan lightning crossed the mountains with angry leaps, bewildered the electric night.

Such giant violet flickerings made the little square smaller, exaggerated the dreadful clarity of those high wide mountain spaces above. The town huddled closer; nursing its shoddiness; boasting its claim with bright-yellow bulbs and loud music. And several little boys were already letting off ground fireworks, so that crimson and green flares began to colour the crowd, casting fantastic shadows, while small drifts of smoke drifted a light fog here and there.

Napoléon stood moveless in white marble, encircled in his grove of withered palms. Four lions slobbered at his feet, their mouths green with moss over which slow water trickled; it seemed that these lions, snub-faced as pekingese, dropped their saliva as the townsfolk themselves spat, with no ejaculatory effort—it was too hot—only leaning their heads aside and letting the saliva fall. By the railings of this statue a small dark man in khaki plus-fours was tearing up long strips of white paper for makeshift confetti; past him walked two fine dark beauties, black-eyed nubiles of the south, their hair a chemical gold; a group of middle-aged men passed—grey sweaters, brown boots, black hats, silver bristles, striped dusty trousers—and their women with them, shapeless in black; a muscle-chested brown young man in a striped singlet, with a white cap set squarely over his head—the cap had a great white button round as his roving eye; two naval airmen, quiet in their disciplined nonentity, their fear; a large girl with high flat cheek-bones like her thick-boned ankles, as if an olive-skinned Swede; youths slouching quickly, swinging their arms, kicking at odd stones, vigorous and laughing braggishly at each other; a man in khaki breeches and woollen stockings, a motor-racer's leather cap flapping over his ears; Senegalese; Tunisians; Italians; French—and suddenly, thin and knobbly in pale blue came jerking along that engineer! Now his glasses were off. He still held in his hand the bunch of robins.

As he came round the railings and took a course diagonally across the square, his sharp inquisitive face pecked in every direction, his eyes darted everywhere—no one in that whole crowd could have escaped him. Then, as usual, he disappeared into a bar.

This bar lay down towards the sea end of the square, whose lower end was open to the quay. It was a cavern bar, with a wide opening like half a huge egg. When I came in, the engineer had already engaged himself heavily with another man, a short man (they all looked short against his long figure). This man wore a leather motor-coat with a fur collar, American army boots and breeches, a beret. As always the blue képi was lowered down at his face, before which swung the robins. However, this time there was a difference. The engineer now held a glass of pastis in his free hand. Moreover, the shorter man had also taken a glass of pastis, and perhaps more than one. He hardly played his part in the discussion of the robins correctly, he was unserious, he smiled, he laughed, he interrupted the engineer to lay an arm on his shoulder, protesting his delight in seeing his old friend the engineer, declaiming and pouting his manly love with a puffing of cheeks and a bracing of biceps. Worse, he praised the robins.

'Oui, mon Dominique, fine birds! Beauties!'

'Eh?'

'Beauties! And good shooting, Dominique, mon cher.'

'Ah. Mm. But you are right. You see them, you know. There's no more to be said. I'll——'

'Yes, old fellow, good shooting. Dominique knows a rifle. Remember, Dominique, the night at Porto when——'

'For you especially, for you my old friend, I offer them for only twelve francs the bird. Twelve! No more.'

'—the night you enaged the good macaronis——'

'Listen, Emilio, the birds——'

'Ten macaronis and a beautiful machine gun, phat-ta-ta-tat. And my Dominique with his old rifle, jumping about in the dark, firing from here, there and everywhere like twenty men. By God, you could not blame them.'

'Emilio, I shot them this morning, five of them.'

'Macaronis?'

'Macaronis hell—*red-breasts!*'

'Ah, the beauties.'

'Emilio—ten francs the bird.'

But already Emilio was signing for two more pastis making large round generous signs with his muscular hands, so that two double glasses of the milk-white absinth faced them on the zinc. With an abrupt gesture of impatience the engineer tossed back his first glass, then took up the new one. For a moment he said nothing, but looked down darkly at the robins. Emilio went on to talk of old times in the maquis. Behind them a weak electric light cast the shadows of its bracket across a wall alive with menacing shapes, giant brown sunlowers on an oil-green paper. The paper had been laid over previous embossed decorations, and now bulged and receded, rose and fell without moving. Two bicycles stood against a wicker table. Outside, through the dark arch of the entrance, the Place des Palmiers showed brightness and movement, the crowd was still growing, the flare and smoke of more fireworks veiled it with a sense of furnaces, of carnival. Music echoed across the warm air like the throbbing steam-music of a fair. Emilio had begun a marching-song.

The engineer suddenly emptied his glass and called for two more. He frowned, and as if making a decision emptied also his new glass of pastis. Then, at the top of his voice, he began trying again to sell the birds to Emilio. He shook the birds savagely. One or two small feathers floated down to the wine-stained floor. But Emilio went on singing, now with closed eyes, feet marching up and down, his forearm bunched to slope an imaginary rifle. So that the engineer Dominique's voice rose also louder, he began to rave. I moved away to the arched door. Emilio, who was neither acting nor insensitive that he was being spoken to, occasionally broke off in the middle of his song to pat the birds and enquire after Dominique's family.

'And your *mother*? How is your *mother*? Lola, how is *Lola*? A big girl? Beautiful?'

'All their lives they have been feeding on the maquis, the herbs. Emilio, eight francs, you rob me.'

Emilio had turned away and was paying much more—sixty francs —for two large pastis. As indeed previously the engineer had done— he who had spent a day trying to sell five birds for about fifty francs. But it was the transaction, not the profit. But now suddenly the arm holding the little birds drooped low, another blue arm reached out to Emilio's neck—and softly, with an oddly open mouth, the engineer began to croon. He sang in a sweet tenor the same song as Emilio, holding tremulously on to the sustained notes. His whole rapacious face took on the look of a thin old woman transported by sentimental thoughts; now wide open, his lips disappeared thinly stretched to show—a shock—that he had no teeth. The black hole of a mouth looked like one black sunglass.

I could hear gusts of their talk—for every so often they stopped singing and, embracing, exchanged greetings and reminiscence. The glasses of pastis, strong drink of wormwood that first tastes weak, came and went. They grew more and more friendly. Sometimes one said:

'Eh, Dominique!'

While the other, leaning back the better to survey his old friend, would intone his reply with a frown of loving bravado:

'Emilio!'

Outside, the tension had reached some sort of a climax—the

appearance of the deputy seemed to be due. The crowd had grown thick round the portico of the hotel, I could see the brass instruments of a band flashing dully about the bottom steps. From this centre the square beneath those trees was forested with groups of people, black against the lights, against the whitish firework smoke. Not a crowd dense as in a great city, but a large crowd dispersed, populating the whole square. The plane branches and their dried November leaves made a ceiling of the electric light, such foliage looked papery, like illuminated theatrical trees. Such a ceiling a few feet above the people's heads existed throughout all the twenty-four hours of all southern towns—in daytime the leaves enclosed with shade the pavement, while all light and energy lay high in the sunlit air above; at night at the same level the shade became reversed, the dark inactive night stretched its black vacuum above, while beneath the same low ceiling all was light and movement.

'Chestnut cakes at Piana—remember? Fresh from the wood!'

'The Rizzanese—a real river that, fine cold water!'

'Ah! le petit vin blanc—
Qu'on boit sous les tonnelles.'

Now they were singing together the generous little waltz-tune. Their movement as they swayed, as the engineer beat time with his bunch of birds, seemed, with the sound of their singing, to fill the dark little bar. Outside night had not yet fallen. There was still in the air, besides the occasion and the music and the fireworks, that excitement, that air of prelude that charges the twilight air with promises of night. Against now a sky the colour of dark iron, the façades of the buildings shone incandescently white, pearl-coloured, pale as bone. Only the decorated Hôtel de Ville broke the regularity of these square façades with their black regular windows; the Hôtel de Ville with its clock-tower, its coat-of-arms, its ionic pillars, its balcony, its brave draping of the blue, white and red flag of France.

'Emilio, old friend, listen! A mark of esteem in honour of our meeting, in celebration of the Deputy. His Honour. Emilio—a gift —I *give* you the birds!'

'Uh?'

'The birds, my little robins! I give them to you.'

'What?'

'For nothing!'

'Eh?'

'There, take them.'

'But . . . well, many thanks. Many, many thanks.'

'Ah!'

'But——'

'Yes?'

'But Dominique, my Dominique——'

'Ah! le petit vin blanc.'

'But Dominique, I cannot take them. I must pay. Here, fifty francs.'

'No!'

'Forty francs.'

'You insult me!'

'Take twenty.'

'If you insist.'

'There!'

'Now. Permit me to offer you a pastis.'

A murmur came from the crowd, and this rose to a shout. Behind me the singing stopped. Those two had heard the shout. Now with cries of 'the Deputy!' they were running past me and out through the door. Through the crowd they dodged, the long engineer first, Emilio on shorter legs zigzagging behind. They ran like children, like enthused students—not worrying whom they bumped, laughing and letting arms and jacket flap wildly. The engineer's arms were free, he no longer held his robins.

Over by the steps now everyone and everything had collected. A passage had been cleared by cadets and police. Down this the old red carpet, dusty and holed, stretched its royal channel. As it finished, so there began the band, an elderly and jovial group of players in assorted clothes—from plus-fours to breeches of corduroy —but each wearing a dark jacket and an old peaked cap. They looked like railwaymen; but each held proudly his brass or silver instrument, and one man was already bent backwards against the weight of his big bass drum. Several small boys ran about in the aisle carrying white boards on sticks. On the boards were written 'Vive la Republique!' and 'Criez le 20 Octobre!' And on all sides the crowd, old and young, men and women, pressed forward, singing, jostling, shouting, and all waving long strips of white paper.

A brief hush. Movements occurred at the back of the hall inside. The loudspeaker music abruptly stopped. The band raised their instruments to their lips. And on the steps there emerged the deputy and a little procession of officials.

At the same moment the loudspeaker above the balcony burst into music louder, faster, wilder than any before. But it was not the Marseillaise, nor a Corsican anthem, nor any martial song at all. There came the hot thunderous cacophony of negroes—'Washboard Blues!' Simultaneously the band began to play—but only the loud thumping of the big drum could be heard above the loudspeaker. The procession began to move down the steps and away. Instantly—for the crowd stood only three feet off on either side—they were mobbed. The air flew with white paper strips. A hundred arms reached forward to touch the deputy. Shouts, cheers, wild whistling. From all sides a battery of fireworks burst—green, yellow, Mephistophelian red. Through all this, the procession struggled away as it could, fighting through the smoke and colour and laughter, then turned sharply right into the Rue Fesch. The famous old street, narrow and winding, was filled to the walls of its tall houses with a jostling mass. All along its serpentine way the people crammed. Away in front, growing dimmer, the beat of the big drum echoed. After it, flexing like a dragon, wound the procession of all Ajaccio. Banners swayed, arms tossed hats high, the dragon swarmed waddling on a thousand unseen legs.

Then I saw for the last time that tall blue képi—higher than the rest of the crowd but caught in it, laughing and fighting and struggling as he was borne along, as now he receded from me, dragged away, drowned it seemed in the moving swelling devouring sea, the sea of hats, caps, fezzes, hands, arms, faces. . . .

I walked back to the bar. There on the floor half beneath the wicker table lay the little robins, ruffled, deflated, their skinny eyelids closed tight, their short beaks shut, and all around like bright puffs of dust the small feathers.

Gliding Gulls and Going People

TWO girls in high shorts, thin plump thighs redly raw in the blue cold; a blood-filled man in black broadcloth, his big stomach carrying him like a sail along; a queer-eyed girl in a transparent white mackintosh; an old gentleman and an old lady eyeing each other, strangers yet; a young man, curly-haired and hard-fleshed, whose frank grey eyes bristled with sneaking contempt; two wives in soldier-peaked hats, navy and nigger, cheery and cake-loving; a small lean man in blue serge and a woolly chequered cap whose friends and family, at his expense, flowed round him only to exclaim and demand.

Such were some of the six hundred lined up raggedly along the quayside waiting for several strolling ample officers to give them permission to embark. Already the gulls, thick and dark as snow-flakes above, gliding and hovering and always crying, had showered them over with confetti and streamers of white—so that in all their darkish throng they looked like wedding guests come to a white funeral.

The driven smell of kippering smoke blew in gusts from sheds about. Red lead of funnels shone orange against the metal-grey water, corrugated tin sheds stepped like large mauve flamingoes on their thin pile-legs, tarred black sheds nudged blue-washed weather-boards of a chandler's, barrels and buckets and drum and feeding-carts spent oil and oil, everywhere oil—these salt things with a huddled rigging of masts made up the quay of Mallaig, mainland port on the Sound of Sleat opposite Skye. A place of high rubber boots, of seaman's wool, of oilskins against the fresh wind and the white bright light. And all those people walked straight off the train and from the hotels along the quay to board this excursion steamer to the sea-loch Scavaig and the dark monstrous Cuillins.

Although their greatest wish was for a refreshing cup of tea, the navy and the nigger hats remained for some minutes in dumb confabulation on the departing glories of those weird mountains above the Kyle of Lochalsh. Leaning over the rail, while the ship throbbed below and the gulls questioned the air about, their ample bodies almost touched. In speechless approbation they regarded those mountains, some black, some lizard-green as shafts of sun spotlighted them from the indigo anger of clouds above. A wild improbable mass, sun-green and rock-black abstraction, nothing here of the human world, across the metal water huge and towering as a threat from old Norse gods—for even here in Scotland there was the feeling of being on top of the world, on a barren place uncongenial to man.

Little of Scotland, much of cold Viking ferocity. Yet—those two in their dear pleasure saw Scottish hills, they saw what on a hundred calendars had been dreamed and painted for them. Though none were to be seen—stags stood about in cosy might, and there was heather for these two, everywhere surely a purple mass of heather, 'a veritable blaze of colour', warm paintbox purple. And where now the sun shone sickly green, was there not a golden glow? Gold touching russet? Winking on crofter's cottage, neat-thatched, washed clean white? Of course one had to admit it was very wild, had one not? But then one expected wildness from these dear Scottish hills, homely hills so glenny and good.

So despite the fresh wind the two ladies stood and surveyed their calendar imposition. A smile for each other, a knowing nod, and once more they turned to the scene and their eyes became distant—pleased, pleased that they had come and that what they expected was there, most content and kindly in the dream picture made by their eyes upon the real scene. Then, as if enough was as good as a feast, they turned to each other and sighed—and one, simply and from the generosity of her heart, said the first thing that came to her: 'How I wish Ellen were here, she *would* have enjoyed it so.'

The other sighed, 'Yes'; and then together they turned to the companion-way and a cup of good warming tea, eager now to discuss the interesting topic of Ellen.

GLIDING GULLS AND GOING PEOPLE

But they were not the only two on deck—as they staggered along, as laughing they clutched each other and in their thick coats clutched the companion-way, they passed in between that hard-eyed young man and on the other side of the doorway the girl in the pale mackintosh: and further on stood those two girls in such high cold shorts.

The young man saw nothing of the great receding mountains, nor did he see Mallaig grown small like a doll's town under its confetti of gulls—he saw nothing but the girls. And those eyes under their short lids, bitter and ambitious, lustful, swivelled warily between the two grouped and the one sitting. Where was the better chance? Those two with their legs bare nearly to their bottoms—they looked something, Two out together on the spree, hikers probably, they had wool caps and oilskin jackets and bloody great boots with spikes. Their legs looked funny all bare from boot to bum—still they were legs, young legs and soft if indeed cold. Fine place to choose for a spree though, and there was your youth movements for you, giving girls outlandish ideas like coming to this iceberg, and outlandish was the word. Still, two together was always something, two chances in one, and each would vie with the other for his attentions, they would smile the larger and give great willing looks. Till he chose one, and then the other would mope, and that was always the worst of two—it became three's no company. Still. And yet—that other in the natty mack sitting alone, she might want company on any account, and he'd be well in nice and easy. A bit snooty? But the snooty ones turned out often enough the best, they knew what they wanted. And there she was settled, not reading, nothing but looking out at that bloody cold sea. She looked lonely enough. Still. He knew better than to go straight up. Might get a back-hander, the old one-two. Perhaps a gentle enquiry: 'Excuse me, miss—I see you have a map there, would I be right in thinking those the Cuillins? They aren't? Why, it must be a pleasure to know as much as you, it's difficult being a stranger in these parts.' And all that. Or drop his gloves at her feet? Or simply lurch across her, as if the ship had done it—that often brought a laugh.

He put a match between his teeth, and ground those small in-growers viciously into the wood. Pretending to look at none of them he walked stiff-legged over to the rail and placed himself exactly between them. He wrinkled up his short forehead into deep horizontal furrows—those that looked casual, as though he were emptying a full mind the better to perceive new things—and gazed blindly out to sea. So he stood for minutes, and the gulls glided and swooped around. Sometimes these hung on the air at the speed of the ship, and turned their faces inward, curious, looking him in the eye. The bare girls in oilskins were throwing them bread-chunks from a screw of coloured comic. They laughed and their screams came down on the wind, and though they were so near those screams sounded like an echo. The gulls adroitly caught the pieces in mid-air—at which always the girls burst into fresh screams. So it was very easy for the young man first to smile amiably and then fully to burst laughing with them as one particular gull missed its piece.

But the girls acted strangely. Together, with no sign between them, motivated like twin puppets, they stared straight at him: their eyes blanked up: they were looking through him: then as if they had never seen him they both turned to gaze slowly out to sea. Their two faces plainly said: 'There is no one on the ship but us, but her and me.' And oh bored, bored the young man too looked out to sea—the match snapped in his teeth, snapped at this trick he knew so well, snapped that two such oilskinned bums should prink themselves into such importance. He said softly to himself, spitting out the match: 'Sod that then.'

A minute later he turned casually the other way, taking a quick squint at the girl sitting there still alone in her white gummy mackintosh. Taking a breath he moved away from the rail, walked across to the companion-way door just by her side, seemed there to trip, to stagger, to drop his gloves and all he had and lurch all over her.

Meanwhile that fat man in black was nowhere to be seen. But on the way from their warming cup of tea the two matrons passed very near where he was, they glimpsed through a glass porthole into a small wooden room and saw there a mass of black already it seemed asleep.

GLIDING GULLS AND GOING PEOPLE

They saw his bulged black waistcoat jutted into the little wood flap-table, they saw the empty beer-bottles and the little wicked whisky glasses like chessmen on that board, they saw his hands pouched with blood resting sideways and almost on their backs palms upward in sleep. 'Is he ill, then?' they thought. Then worried by this they agreed he must be all right—though what he came on such a trip for just to sit inside and drink it was difficult for their lives to think. There he sat, his red chin lurched deeply down on his black waistcoat top, his large black hat overshadowing like poet or priest. And there, after they had passed on their way to the ladies' lounge, he continued to sit; a figure framed by the inquisitive port-hole, more of a round picture hung on the wall than a person inside who at some time, impossibly, might move.

The lean-faced little father from Liverpool remained on deck. He and all his family sat huddled in chairs behind the funnel, all nestled and rugged like wealthy emigrants. Father tough and lean-faced beneath his checked cap nodded a superior approbation of the air—he had blown some money on this trip, he was going to enjoy it, he was in command—and he smoked his cigarette from an arm held bent with muscle, holding it between finger and thumb and with little finger curled out in showful ease. He turned to Mother and pointed sternly with this superior hand:

—See, Ma? Muck there, the Isle o' Muck.

Mother turned to the horizon, where she saw far away a shapeless piece of rock. She nodded, pleased and satisfied:

—Muck it is? Well.

Father peered at her from beneath his great peak, together their eyes gravely conspired. They both nodded, satisfied. They had experienced the Isle of Muck, Muck could be crossed off, it was there still, nobody had been tricked. And instantly was forgotten—Father was back at the sports page and Mother began at her brood:

—Alfie, stop touching, it's the Captain's. Clarie, make Alfie leave the bleedin' funnel be.

The ship churned on into the sullen sea, great bullying iron pushing into cold waters of mineral green. To starboard now was

135

a corner of Skye, to port there came slowly harsh Eigg and thunderous Rum. But that cold-eyed young man saw nothing of those
coming islands he might have come to see, he sat to starboard with
his plastic girl. He had succeeded. Whether or not she knew it was
a dodge scarcely mattered. If she had known, then at least it acted
like an excuse. She was simply willing to speak and sit with him·
And from then on there began the fearful old tragedy—innocence
enchanted by vice.

His tight face unscrewed into a hung-open sham of courtesy, his
forehead creased up in horizontal humble enquiry, he asked:

— Excuse me, Miss—I see you have a map there, would I be right
in thinking those the Cuillins?

Her face brightened, she became alive not in pleasure at expressing what she knew but simply in talking to that man:

— No, not here, they're further up. See right up there where we're
going. But you can't see the tops, the tops are in cloud.

— Indeed? Why, it must be a real pleasure to know as much as
you, it's difficult being a stranger in these parts.

— Oh, I'm not a stranger. I've lived here all my life. Over in
Mallaig.

— Now, that's interesting that's interesting. Lived in these parts
all your life, have you? *Have* you, now.

— Well I *think* all my life. You see—

— What's that, *think? Think?*

— You see—

— Come off it, you're pulling my leg, you can't tell *me* you don't
know where you've been all your life, a smart girl like you. Telling
me you don't know who you are next.

— That's it, I don't really.

— Uh?

— Of course I know I'm me. But who me is I couldn't ever be
sure.

— Ho?

— I'm a changeling.

— Wassat? *Wassat?*

— They say I'm a changeling.

She stared at him waiting, her deep dark eyes moist between the collars of her plastic mack, against her halo hood of water-white. In those eyes there lay a slight cast. But that young man saw no eyes, he was looking at her lips, hoping like hell nothing more like what he had heard would come. Somehow the boot had got on the wrong foot, he should have been doing the talking and now she had gummed up the works with this fancy stuff. What the hell was a changeling, anyway? He furrowed up his brow in perplexed sympathy, coughed, then remembered—it was the old doorstep dodge. He cooed:

— Orphan, eh? Poor kid, no mum nor dad. Doesn't seem to've done you a packet of harm though. Not by the look of you. Foundling, eh?

— No. Changeling.

— Ah, you mean foundling. Foundling's what you mean.

— No, *changeling*. They say when you're a baby someone comes and changes you with another baby. I've been sort of queer all my life. That's why mum and my sisters say I was changed. The fairies come and changed me, I'm like a fairy, see?

— Fairies? Come off it.

— I am, I really am.

— Oho.

She's nuts, he thought. A nice balls-up—fairies. He edged a bit away from her. Then a slow, rich, gluey smile stretched his mouth. His eyes stared still hard scheming. This wasn't so bad after all? If she was nuts, she might be that much easier? You sometimes got round a soft-head easier.

He got towards her:

— I get you. That's interesting what you say, real interesting. Tell you what, you and me's going to have one. Drop of nice port wine, eh?

— Well . . .

— Come on, do you handsome a parky day like this.

— Well, I'd not say no to a cup of tea now . . .

— Cupper tea? That what fairies drink?

— Now you mustn't laugh . . .

— Whatever you say, princess. Lead the way.

Now chuckling together, he falsely and she in real delight, they rose and staggered off against the wind to the companion-way. For one moment, before going down, they paused—she pointed to where a gull stood high and solitary on the summit of the after flag-pole. It stood with the careful genius birds have for showing up statues. Other gulls wheeled and swooped round, but that one stood stiffly still and careful. The girl tittered:

— I wonder what he's thinking up there.

He looked quickly up, then shrugged—eyes already on the companion-way and action:

— Ask me. Just ask *me*.

That man in black in the wooden bar with a grunt woke up. He looked startled, turned to the empty bench beside him and said:

— What's time? We there?

Receiving no answer he looked with suspicion round the rest of that bare wooden cabin, saw his empty whisky glasses in front and again grunted. It was a final grunt. Stretching his huge stomach more, he put both hands in pockets at the same time, drew out with one hand a red silk handkerchief and with the other a small black book, blew his nose and commenced to read at the same time. Once a dark shape flashed winging by the porthole. He brushed it away from his page like a fly, but never looked up. The engine throbbed with his silence.

The engine throbbed, the boat shuddered, and now that Liverpool father was up and standing by the rail with a pink-faced scrubbed old gentleman. Perhaps his silk white hair made this old man look so clean—or perhaps it was the little old lady who fitted so neatly near his arm. She wore a straggled tippet round her throat, from this her live little face came like a small round vegetable. From time to time, as the three talked, these two looked at each other with twinkling affection. The Liverpool man was saying:

— Turbines, steam turbines, that's what they are. And I'm *telling*

138

you. I'm telling *you*—it won't be long before *you'll* be seeing Diesels
along this line. Diesels, you'll see.

He was looking with small fury at the old man. His checked peak
thrust forward, the lines deep in his cheeks dragging his mouth down
in scorn. But it was the scorn of approval; scorning all other times,
astonished by this world of plenty that rained Diesels. The old man
nodded:

— Times are changing. It's a turn of speed they're after.

The old lady smiled up at him:

— That's it.

The checked cap nodded emphasis. Then the old gentleman
went on:

— But us'll have in mind the old paddlers, won't us, madam?
Foof foof foofle foof—that's the stuff to give 'em!

He churned wide with his hands, turning them round like
paddle-wheels. The old lady pressed her small face backwards with
laughter. The man with the cap relaxed, and again in approval
nodded:

— Ay, they did their turn rightly and no one's goin' to say a word
agin' 'em.

Creeping up nearer on the starboard came Eigg and Rum, queer
masses of rock and mountain riding the sea aloof and insolent as
battleships. Unique shapes—Eigg low like half a huge whale of grey
stone cut open and exposing its great scar of ribbed blubber: Rum
lowering behind, mountainous and jagged, black against the silver
sunlight like a giant tooth extracted and roots upmost planted in the
sea. People looked, and looked away consumed with their own
affairs. The gulls flew round and round, pacing the ship, swooping
up and down, planing no one knew how or where or why, on a
voyage instinctive but unaware. Their piping over the cold green
sea came and then was lost on the wind.

Those militant fanciers of cake, the navy and the nigger, had
already confessed to an empty feeling in their tum-tums, and now
stood at the head of a small queue forming far down in the ship
outside the glass-doored dining-saloon. Inside the doors stewards

stood, themselves a scattered queue, also waiting. No one moved. The clock only slowly wound the minutes forward across its marine and brass-bound face.

Since no teas were then served, the young man had thankfully been able to guide his changeling to a port and lemon. They sat in the small bar, as far away as possible from the man in black. That was not far.

The fat man, deep in Johnson's tour of the Hebrides, with these in fact passing unseen through the dark bulwarks, had no wish to speak to them. But being there he spoiled the young man's hopes of privacy, and so this one kept the steward behind the bar in conversation. Talk to impress his changeling, talk of two men together. On he talked. The steward only nodded.

— Wouldn't suit me, this job. I like to get going. How much do you pull in a week? Chicken-feed. Me, I'm the best man on the road. Give me a good line and I'll sell it to anybody. Mind you it's got to be a good line, you can't sell a dud. Not even me, I can't.

He paused and looked round with wonder at himself to the steward. The steward gave him back a grim look. He went on quickly, now thumping the bar:

— Know what I do? I take night trains. So I get there early. None of your nine o'clocks. Seven, that's me. Like this I can go to my hotel and then I have a bath and then I change and then I'm there for my first call at *ten minutes past nine*. On the dot. *And* fresh. What's that?

Somewhere distantly in the ship a gong droned, approached and retreated and was lost. The steward sighed taciturn, seamanly relief. Looking hard at the young man he said:

— *That's* your dinner.

As the young man and the pleased girl rose, as the fat man reminded drew from his pocket still reading a bag of sandwiches, as those two motherly ones at the head of their queue victorious and satisfied swept through the glass door into the dining-saloon, as all over the ship others—the check-cap, and his brood, the old gentleman and his new old lady, the healthy cold girls purpling in their short pants and everyone else aboard who had paid eighteen shillings for this most enjoyable round trip—as everybody turned from their places to the companion-way and the blind bowels of the dining-saloon, so Eigg and Rum came magnificently at last into full view.

And the ship, naked of sightseers, ploughed past them.

Empty decks as empty as the great rock-mass of near Eigg, empty as the mineral cold sea, empty as the wide northern sky whistling forlorn over this part whose life showed no warm profusion and few things chose to live. On the long scarred face of grey Eigg a little grass grew. The wind-dried salt emptiness of those seas was not changed since the dragon-headed longboats ran through, since that desolate day when the raiding Macleods of Skye came in their fierce craft to board the island and light at the cave-mouth a suffocating fire that smothered to death all the women, children and men of Eigg driven there to shelter. Similar winds must have driven across in those days, similarly the mountains to either side must have loomed. And the faraway white sun must have shone its pale light on similar clouds scudding like wet canvas. All around, mountains and misted horizon and metal-green sea would have lain as empty in those days as now, as when that lonely steamship, the only moving thing in view, dogged its midget course past drama into greater drama. Gigantic mountainous Rum came to port—and at last the Cuillins topped in vertiginous cloud towered terribly to starboard.

Yet no one saw. Even the gulls, questing open-eyed round, had swooped to the sea and were pecking the first plate-emptyings thrown out in the ship's wake.

The ship turned in past shark-curing Soay and entered more sheltered water, the sea-loch Scavaig. Dinner was finished and most of the passengers had come on deck again. A sharp new wind had risen that brought sudden whirls of spray spiralling like furious little waterspouts: these, coming from nowhere, bidden it seemed by an unseen presence, heightened the uneasy feeling of that strange precipitous place. They had entered into the first reaches of the dark Cuillins.

So that now—whether from a certain uneasiness that hung in that place, or from a sense of satiety and arrival, or from a bewildering wonder as to what should happen next—now all those different ones stood about the decks and stared at the grey rock that surrounded them. The ship's engines stopped. Then they started again: but churning backwards. One did not know quite what was happening. Yet all the time the ship slewed nearer the rock. And they had reached the end of the loch, they drifted dangerously in the small cove-like end which was no bigger in radius than some five lengths of the ship. Could one then control a ship so unwieldy in such short space? But the captain must know. And one saw that though not exactly a harbour, there was some sort of a stone jetty built out from low-lying rock. Could one then land here?

Really, in all that sharp rock? But it was on the schedule to land.

Already a motor launch had put off from the jetty and was spitting over the hundred yards or so to the ship. Yet how was one to get into that boat? So low down? There must be some difficult seaman-ship here—would not each passenger be involved? That father in the checked cap thought for a terrible moment: 'Breeches-buoy?' And thought: 'Women and children.' And thought of his wife swinging helpless and fat out in the cradle over horrible water.

The iron sides of the ship invited sharp rock. One felt that a sound would echo for years round and round that hard place. If one shouted. Nobody shouted.

And above, as though the cold and friendless near cliffs were not menacing enough a great dark jagged Cuillin blasphemed black against the highest sky. So they stood not knowing. And then per-ceptibly, having come up, there began a movement down. Soon all the passengers had sheeped onto the inside stairs and were standing queued and pressed on those steep steps inside. Brass-bound and embellished with the framed monochromes of life-belts and statistics of draught, those stairs led to where a door had been opened miraculously in the ship's very side just above the waterline. Pressed together, not knowing what was coming but herded and willing, they waited.

Somewhere up above, from the upper deck perhaps to that extra-ordinary door below, sailors were shouting to one another. There came a shuffling at the front of the queue—an oilskinned man from the launch had stepped up into the ship, he was making his way along to where a short fat bluff double-breasted officer stood. Together these two, talking closely, disappeared through a door into some most watertight-looking part. The people waited. They grew silent. There was no more to be said.

Waited and waited. The ship rolled slightly. Nobody knew quite how near those rocks they were now.

Then up above, quite suddenly, and for some reason that will never be known, one of the circling seagulls swooped into a wild ellipse and headed off. Low on the water it flew straight as a line back across the lonely miles to Mallaig.

After waiting minutes, those who formed the last half of the queue gradually dispersed. Having no valuable precedence, being far up the staircase by the deck, they thinned and straggled up for air and to see.

It had been promised in the itinerary that a landing would be made here at the end of the loch. For with a short walk inland one could really see the Cuillins, feel the Cuillins—and lying just out of sight was the inland Loch Coruisk, a still water closed in forever by frowning cliffs. This was reputed to be the most desolate and terrifying place in the British Isles. Something one should see. And now— to their surprise—those who climbed again on deck saw that in fact the launch was putting off again, empty but for one passenger, a rough-looking man in broadcloth. The ship still lay safely in the centre of that cold claustrophobic cup of water. But now there was more commotion on the stairs, the people parted and climbing up came that great figure in black. Impassively he passed, gripping his book, and his stomach carried him off the staircase and straight back to the bar. The cold-eyed young man, letting him pass, thought: 'Well, that's that'. For the whole twenty minutes he had been trying to persuade his changeling to stay behind in the empty ship. He had described in detail the trivial nature of a Loch Coruisk he had never seen. But the changeling allowed nothing to alter her mind. She liked nature. Especially in her new white mack.

Yet a further commotion followed the fat man up the stairs. The whole queue had turned and now were slowly remounting the stairs, grumbling with surprise, laughing with surprise, unsurprised and silent. There was to be no landing—the water was too low from the level of the jetty. Last of all came those who had made certain to be first, the nigger and the navy caps—now for the moment undone.

— And all this way too!

— They ought to know. Telling us and then not.

— I was never so surprised.

— What I mean is they ought to know. The captain ought, really. What I mean is it's his job. It's his job, isn't it, Cora?

— I was never so surprised.

But not for long. A few stairs higher, and it was all over. The future had to be looked to. Already the boat was moving homeward.

— There, we're moving! It won't be long now.

Already visions of home presented themselves. After the first dismay, all minds had turned to thoughts of home. Watches were consulted. Ideas of the length of the homeward trip were exchanged. The father with the checked cap, eagerly always pacing the deck and admiring the mechanical prowess of the ship, had found again that old lady and gentleman:

— We'll be ashore by four o'clock! She's making a pretty turn. Twelve knots, I'm reckoning. We've the wind behind us and all.

The old gentleman made no reply. This was unfair, such a statement called for argument. So the checked cap repeated, intruding his chin:

— Twelve knots, I said.

The old gentleman nodded:

— I expect you're right. Yes. Twelve knots.

So the other said:

— Well. Well then could you tell me the time, the time it is now, the right time?

— I'm afraid I haven't a watch.

— What about the missus?

The old man turned and smiled. His eyes twinkled. The old lady pressed her chin into her fur, blushing, though her pale cheeks showed no colour.

— She's not my missus.

He looked down twinkling at her small beaming face:

— In fact—my dear—I don't even know your name, do I?

He turned back to the checked-cap man and said slowly, emphatically and softly, as though telling a story from a long time ago:

— You see, this has been my lucky day.

So the ship went churning back past Soay and Rum and Eigg and distant Muck. The sun paled low, silvering the western waters, giving to all those islands lying Atlanticwards a romance of lost lands. Islands reaching out towards some place irrevocable, a place that only might have been, and now in a visionary moment at end of day shown somehow as a real possibility. Perhaps for the first time many of those people began to look at what was passing with moved hearts, with curious regret.

They stood about the decks in groups, or sat sheltered on the long wooden seats to leeward by the funnel. They had fallen silent and their eyes were on the sea. The homeward journey rests the soul, nothing to be done but to arrive. A shorter journey—no danger of surprise, no new climates to assail.

And in this very relaxation the senses may at last blossom. For the first time the journey is seen as it is, for the first time it is felt to be sliding away forever from grasp. Never again, nevermore. Evanescent as the water at the ship's keel, the white ephemeral wake, water that marks the passage, white and wide, that melts and vanishes in personless flat green. A journey made, no more. Soon forgotten. Thus the deep iron sides of the ship sailed on relentless homewards—leaving behind the magic of the westering sun, flying on what felt a following wind, sailing ever faster home.

Even that cold-eyed young man seemed to feel some of this melancholy beauty of a journey ending. He stood by the ship's rail half hidden by the curved white prow of a life-boat, his changeling tucked in his arm. He never tried to kiss her. His eyes rested, a shade softer, on the horizon and the last of those great receding island shapes. He had planned, complacently, to make no kiss until they were ashore. He had told himself that by holding off he would impress her with trust of himself—and provoke her at the same time with a wish to entice him. This decided, he could relax the better, he could give himself to the scene.

But the man in black still sat in the bar. He read on with comfort and seclusion of the Doctor's journey two centuries before: within the square of his book it was warmer, more defined too, than the great and gusty outside.

Gulls circled and swooped high round the wind-proud mast, swooped low to kiss the water—but among these too there were thoughts of home, some suddenly took off ahead of the ship and flew swiftly arcing to where now Mallaig began to show its colour and indeed its own white smoke of gulls.

They drew in, the *Pride of the Isles* and her wool-wrapped passengers. Steam of gulls and smoke from the curing-sheds greeted them. The black iron touched the hard stone quay, great ropes flung out to the bollards and winches, small dock machines began to grind, the first burnt smell of kippering blew over all. So stationary things looked! Here the hotels and the houses and the long-legged sheds had stood all that while waiting, not moving up and down but settled and dry and, most of all, stationary. Suddenly it came over many how dull all these things were. Homely and welcoming—but dull, dull, dull.

Yet as soon as they had set foot on the quay this feeling vanished. The solidity of the land claimed them, here it was safe and sound, one could relax here as—with on the calmest seas always some gentle motion—one can never relax on a boat.

First ashore were those two matrons. Only pausing to rebutton once more their coats, to set homewards their scarves and the peaks of those two hat-caps, they set off at once along the quay. Their direction had been planned long before.

— It was a lovely, lovely day.

— It was worth every shilling we paid. But I shall be glad to be home.

— A nice sit-down, Cora. A nice cup of tea.

Soon after the mother and her brood came stumbling down the gangway, clotted together like one large animal disturbed in the unloading process. Behind, with the nonchalance of a drover, came the father. He kept a wary eye on the mechanisms of landing—on hawsers, bollards, gangway and all practical arrangements. That eye never questioned 'why' a thing was—but always 'how' is it done?

Then he took a last look up at the ship and was gone.

The man in black, staggering a little from weight or alcohol, hurried at speed down the gangway, carried as always by his own great momentum. He took no last backward glance. He carried it in his hand, in the little black book.

The old gentleman and the lady were among the last to leave, they had lingered as long as possible. Now they too came slowly, unsurely down that difficult slope. At the bottom the old gentleman turned, and with courtesy handed his new lady off. His eyes were watering in the cold, his shoulders bent, he breathed harder from even this slight effort: together they turned and passed along the quay.

Suddenly the changeling, who still stood at the deck-rail, started to wave. The young man by her side started. He had been waiting casually, feeling he had so much time, pleasurably possessive. But now that plastic white arm was pumping up and down, that face was smiling excited! She was looking somewhere down along the quay. He said quickly, eyes hard, lips thin:

— Hello what's this? What's up?

— It's him! I thought he'd never come!

— Him? Oo?

— My boy.

— Wassat you said?

— My boy that I'm engaged with.

— Christ.

— I *beg* your pardon.

— Nothing, oh nothing. Oh nuts. So long.

— But I wanted you to meet . . .?

He was already at the gangway, dancing down with long stiff strides, his mackintosh belted tight and hard round him.

Those two girls with the high shorts had their oil-cloth capes on, and these capes reaching just to the bottom of the shorts at the top of their blue legs gave them a look of naked pixies. Together they stooped by the door of a kippering hut. Inside, the little dark kippers hung above a fire of cinders spread over the floor. Each kipper looked like a small ebony god in a temple full of incense braziers. The girls giggled: then turned away. The young man eyed them, considering. But they simply turned, hands in pockets. And with heads bent trudged off down the quay. Heads bent, two together walking intent only on themselves, talking, walled-in and unassailable as young and pretty girls can surely be.

Soon, when the sun set, the gulls themselves stopped circling. The white-streaked quays grew quiet. The gliding gulls had gone to roost, the people going . . . gone.

Time and Place

ROSE paused by a girl whom he found not at all attractive—and who was as plainly not interested in him—and said casually:

— Seems to have cleared up. I'm going out for a walk.

Indifferently, looking first at him and then across the hotel lounge to where a pale sun was now watering raindrops on the window, she nodded. It should keep fine for his walk.

They were about the only ones left in the hotel. Several elderly people still sat quietly in corners—in the empty hotel it was a shock to come across them, suddenly in mirrors or nearly indistinguishable among large furniture and ornament—but these two were the only rather young people left. The others had decided on various excursions—a steamer to the mainland, a coach trip to the crofts on Bunessan and the blue clarity of Iona. On the previous night Rose and the girl had been introduced. After a few disinterested words they had each turned back to their friends. They had not, until now, exchanged another word. And now he suddenly said:

— Care to come along?

The emptiness weighed. After the morning hours, after the dripping of the rain, the sun invited purpose. There was shopping to be done along the quay—but that too would be lonely. So that simply for the sake of a companion, the girl found herself agreeing. At least some sort of conversation would pass the time. She had come to that place for a holiday, with hope. But quickly, after a day's examination of her fellow-guests, and those others in the small town, she had given this up. Now her day depended on the arrival of the steamer from the mainland. The morning steamer had come and gone. No one had landed.

At once, as she agreed, Rose regretted his invitation. Quickly he said:

— I'm going a fair few miles, you know. Up above the woods, up to the high ground. It's very boggy.

In spite of her disinterest, such a small assault on her pride had instantly to be countered. She yawned and sighed:

— I can always turn back if I feel like it. If I want. I'll just go up and get some shoes.

Thus Rose was left alone. It occurred to him even then that he might slip out alone, leave a message with the porter. Then he shrugged. It was appalling to be landed with this Anne-Marie— that title in itself was irritating, Anne-Marie, why two names? And what was the surname . . . MacDougal, MacDowell? Yet as soon as it occurred that he might still go out alone, the emptiness weighed down again and the idea of a companion became preferable. The vacant morning reimposed itself. From nine until eleven standing by the bedroom window, eyes near the window frame where the raindrops hung in a wet line, where the blind cord flapped its monotony, where dark mornings in the empty house of childhood shadowed his memory. The tide had been full—flat deep grey water rose to a few inches from the promenade level. Rain and this brimming full water made a fresh-water lake of the sea; the railings and a line of lime trees planted along the little tarmac promenade made it more of a rainwashed lakeside. No salt invigoration. It was full flat water, grey, wet, drenched.

So that with relief, almost pleasure, he saw Miss Anne-Marie Mac-something descending again the stairs.

Out on the quayside, in the clearing air and the warm sun, his last regrets evaporated. A small place; a shallow crescent of houses lining the small inner curve of the anchorage; stone houses of classic proportion, and several of them painted bright black with corner-stones scalloping white up the sides. Now patches of blue intruded high in the clearing sky—and the deep water of the anchorage, belted with trees down to its edge, began to show a rich opaque Prussian green. Anne-Marie had kept him waiting up in the hotel. And now among the water-front shops she remembered a little shopping. At first he was resentful. But the delay scarcely mattered. he leant on the quay-rail and felt the late blossoming of fair weather. A deep-sea liner, buff against the green water, sent a launch spider-ing shorewards with passengers. Several stick-masted yachts swung slowly at anchor. Otherwise the water was empty across to the

mainland mountains. Gulls filled the air—swooping, feathering the
water, yelping like lonely puppies; one in the distance dropped its
white like a torn letter against the deep green of the trees. Rose
liked those trees, there quickened in him always an unexplained
excitement when the land-locked trees grew their green leaves down
against the salt water's edge.

Finally the girl was ready and they started. They walked off the
promenade, up among the trees towards the higher moorland that
lay beyond. They talked little: and then at arm's length. There was
the intent of their feet to keep them occupied, to fill the silence with
purpose. All they said was ready-made, expected question and
expected answer. Perhaps Rose said, knowing it well:

— That liner, that's from Liverpool, isn't it? Cruising out to the
Outer Hebrides?

— Mm. She comes every ten days.

Sometimes they smiled. But never as close friends might—in
delight at the strange and beautiful things they passed; instead
they exchanged the manufactured, the familiar. Anne-Marie said:

— Rain before eleven, fine before seven.

— It's an old Scottish custom.

— Spanish, not Scottish.

A pause, for Rose to digest that. Then:

— Anyway, the rule doesn't hold here. It'll rain any time.

Thus together, eyes more on the road than the passing scene, he the
set brown-haired Londoner, she the loose-boned chestnut Scot, both
tweeded and mackintoshed, they passed to the end of the quay where
rose the mottled stones of a distillery and where the warm vegetation
began. Passed the skeleton of an old boat cradled like a midsummer
dreamer among tall yellow irises formed exactly round its sunken
shape; passed from the harbour and entered the northern tropic of trees
and moss and shrub, lushly wet. There in a sheltered part of the Mull
island warm air from tropic America fanned into being a secondary
hothouse—rhododendron, wild iris, giant foxglove, the chinese drip of
fuchsia flowered among ash and beech and fir and the great mosses that
suckled high up their branches. A thick motionless colloquy, sparing
no morsel of soil, green with aquarium magic scentless and odoured
only with the decay of rain-logged wood shredding softly into earth.

Yet out of this soon they walked, to higher land where a belt of corn grew and a light wind played, where the fields were marked with grey stone walls and meadows of sorrel and marguerite smeared the green with soft pink. Why hadn't Miss MacDougal gone with the others to Iona? MacDowell, please, was her name. He was so sorry, he was at times a trifle deaf in one ear: the war. Oh, had he been in the war then? Indeed he had—in France and Holland and Germany. . . . So to the steady swing of their bodies, in the cleared air up towards the moorland, they talked of the war. Miss Mac-Dowell, who was thirty-five, listened to his story with uneasy awe: she saw it as a sheel-torn field of Flanders mud, mud of the first war muddled with air-raids and the names of new German generals. They passed up to the higher, wilder ground: passed two solitary hikers with long bare legs and huge boots and pale plastic cloaks, passed the last stone wall and met their first black-faced sheep; passed the last flowers, tall bells of vampire foxglove praying among the grey bones of a dead bramble.

It was after they had walked a mile out on to the moor, up the rising hills and down into shallow valleys, across wet bogland and skirting small precipices of rock, that quite suddenly the clear sky filmed over, lowered itself, and threw down a splashing of rain. The rain came at them on the wind as if a shower of water was thrown, obliquely, the thin spray from a bucket tossed.

— That's torn it—

— Better get to shelter, said Miss MacDowell.

But looking round they saw there was neither tree nor wall nor hut—only the gentle raise and fall of the moor. Then the rain burst down, thrashing and drenching: yet in the next minute it was blown on, there remained no more than a light, misty drizzle. They stood bowed in their mackintoshes, hoping for it to stop, standing close together. It did not stop. But down came the sky—and gently, gently they were drowned in mist. The prospect round them faded slowly—so slowly one was not sure whether it was the mist or a raindrop in the eye that blurred the view. Soon they could see only for a dim hundred yards around them. The wind had dropped, it was very quiet. The deep echoing boom of a siren came ploughing up from the Sound. It ceased, the echo died. Again the silence.

— Well, said Rose.

They both laughed. It was shocking and peculiar—one moment sunshine, then rain, then such a sudden mist. At that time, too, there was wonder in the abrupt desolation—wonder at the disappearance of the world and a sense of awe that they and they alone stood on what was left. Rose looked round and struck again the bright note. His voice, even to him, sounded lonely and amplified, it seemed refracted from the muffling lonely wall wreathing round them:

— Nice day for a walk! You know—you should have turned back before.

— What's done's done. Anyway, you can say you've seen a real Scotch mist.

— I think it's more than that, it's cloud.

And she to whom also these island mists were strange, also peered round. She frowned and pulled her mackintosh closer.

— You never know when it'll lift. We'd better start off back.

— Anything you say, you're the native.

— Not of here I'm not.

They started walking: but after two or three paces stopped and looked at each other. Each intently had taken a different bearing: they were faced roughly in the same direction, but now a yard apart. The girl pointed, she was sure it was their way. Rose looked for a moment down with doubt at a group of white moss-mounds that seemed to have been his mark. Doubtfully still, but thinking that she was more used to the country than he was, he followed where she began again to tread. The ground was soft with bog, sponged with water: once off the drier hummocks and one was in—ankle-deep, knee-deep, perhaps more. They went picking their way down one long slope and then up another. They stood at the top and looked round. It seemed exactly the same. And then from somewhere down and far off—it seemed this time from a greater distance—the steamer siren sounded again. Rose peered towards the echo:

— Hello, that's moved.

— She must have reached the pier—that was the putting-off siren.

— May not. May have been a freighter from Oban. Is there a late-morning passenger-boat?

— I don't know.

— I thought you did.

— I've only been here two days. You're not being sarcastic, are you?

— Wouldn't think of it.

He paused. Then:

— Anyway, we don't know where it came from. It's no guide. And this place looks like the last. Are you sure we're right?

She waited before answering—and then a sense of growing loneliness overcame what might have been obstinacy.

— Tell the truth, I'm not. Only I think—

— Not much use thinking in this lot. Look, let's try over here, there might be something we remembered.

They trudged then off at an angle, again down into some declivity and up a further hill. Once more they stood peering, but once more there was no landmark, nothing they remembered. It seemed, too, that the mist was closing in.

There was nothing to do but try again, and then again. They stopped talking—from the effort of walking that difficult ground, from a need to listen, from a feeling for the oppressive silence itself. The silence became a presence. Once Rose raised his voice suddenly and called: the call vanished into the mist, drowned and muffled, so that he felt it went no further than the misted wall beyond which stood no one, nothing. It was absurd, demeaning—he never tried again: the sound of his voice enclosed them further. At length, tired from the struggling blind walk, they stopped.

— We'll have to wait here till it lifts.

She nodded, saying nothing. And for a while they stood listening. Both listened for the note of a steamer, for anything to confirm the existence of a world that must have lain close at hand but seemed now to have vanished forever, nor indeed ever to have been. But now no steamer called: the Sound might have been miles away or near—beneath a precipice falling off just at the edge of what ground they could see. Weary, silent, smelling only the mist-smell, seeing only the sour-green bog—for the first time they realized how the white curtain made a circle round them. Until then they had possessed a direction. Now there was none, they had turned all ways, there remained not even an imagined idea. And all around, bellying a little but most regular, there hung the circular blindness. It edged the ground. It hung domed low overhead. They stood under a domed lid, and wherever they looked it was circular and perpetual, round and round, and round overhead. It seemed too—but gently, slowly—to be thickening still and closing in. But perhaps that was the illusion of their eyes straining for some point of definition—any mark for their human eyes. They moved a little, a few paces: but wherever they moved they remained still in the exact centre of the circle, it was impossible to get away from the centre.

From the grass grew only pale hummocks of sphagnum and the white bog-cotton. The cotton on its thin stem came to look like wisps of wool mist, the huge sponged moss-lumps like fog-clouds heavy on the ground. Rose began to count the hummocks—hoping for some relation between them that he might remember. As he counted, he noticed that the girl beside him was shivering. It was not cold.

He hesitated, then raised his arm to comfort her. An arm on her shoulder might help, she would be afraid. And just then as he touched her he felt the breath of a need to protect her, the lonely woman, the weak small-boned one. But just then too he saw on the edge of the mist a sudden shape, a defined shape of rock grey against the white mist. His arm feeling towards her changed to a shaking, pointing arm:

— Look!

They stood held for a second in hope. Then abruptly the ground beneath them began to recede, they were rushing headlong back, slipping with the earth itself at the speed of avalanche. Rose's arm swung back and clutched the girl, her hands gripped into his raincoat. Then as suddenly they stopped, the ground held firm—and from the direction of the stone, the stone now disappeared and distant, they heard a plaintive gargling baa-sound. A sheep had been moving forward.

But this time there was no laughter. Their hearts pumped relief, they simply stood and after some seconds came to realize they were still embraced. But still neither moved. Only Rose after a while took gently the edge of his open raincoat and pulled it over her shoulder, so that she was closer to him and protected within his cloak. He muttered again, less to speak than to soothe, that the only thing was to wait and that it would be all right in the end.

They were both of the same height, perhaps of the two she was the taller. But now close to him instinctively she had slacked her figure, so that in fact her head was inclined on his chest and beneath his throat, she was resting snaked against him and his head felt towered and capable above. Damply her hair-smell rose—it was fresh, feminine, lightly stirring. His protective hand held her thin brittle shoulder: poor bones, with a pathos of slight flesh trying to cover them—but warm. Careful not to seem abrupt he drew her closer; his hand shaking with tension felt how simply its muscle could break such bones; his mind above the hand felt a wave of chivalric honour that it could control such an impulse, that it could be trusted not to hurt but to protect. And with this sense of chivalry, remembrance of romances read inspired him to feel his circumstance —he felt how she must be smelling the manly tweeded smell of his coat, and how he stood like some literary knight with his embracing raincoat proof against not merely the frightening mist but all high peril.

In fact, there was no danger that could not simply be avoided. They had simply to stay there until the mist lifted. Only a restless wandering, an unlucky precipice or a lapse in the peat could hurt them. Rose knew this quite well; he chose to stay. But safety of the body is no haven for the mind: that sheep had baa-ed close, it had sounded the nearness of other living things. It made no further sound. The silence thus dropped down more than ever intensely, it became possible—a dangerous suspicion quickly dismissed, quickly recurrent—that the sheep had never been.

It all closed in absolutely. Pocketed, will-lessly drifting, a thickness came upon them and even their domed periphery was gone. Now, nothing but the white. It was easy to breathe, but it looked difficult. The stuff wreathed about them slowly, at times opening a little to frame a hopeful vista of a few yards, then closing. All the world gone, the map Rose knew contorted restlessly near—Loch na Keal, Salen, Tobermory drew nearer in his mind; but at the same time it grew possible to fear they had never existed. The whiteness enveloping bore down its pillow on their eyes—their nerves in such a steady loneliness stretched for some sign, some relief, anything at all by which things might be known. But nothing. And to Rose peering the nothingness began slowly to wheel, there came the heave of the beginning of an infinitesimal rotation—and quickly he looked down at the head beneath him. Her eyes were pressed close in under his raincoat. He saw the hair, the extraordinary intricate hair, and a gratitude for its presence filled him—he bent down his lips. Even then it occurred to him that he should move away, make some gesture of separation. But his lips touched her hair and the girl made one small clutching movement at the jacket she was gripping —she who probably with open eyes in the darkness of his jacket reversed exactly his comforting romance, smelled the myth of his tweed and knew how she offered the scent of her hair. Rose pressed his lips deeper.

He began to take off his raincoat—somehow one arm after the other, so that they were never parted—and let it drop down on the moss. Close together, she with her head curiously bowed, they knelt down, fumbled the mackintosh straight on the soft yielding hummocks, together sat and then stretched themselves down. The silence that had drummed them gradually receded—with faces pressed together a closer world was made intimate with the other drumming of blood-pulse and heavier-growing breath, of the rustle of clothes and all other small sounds.

Once—perhaps minutes, perhaps much later—the mist tried to reassert itself. A roaring sound whispered up from nowhere, a thunderous sound that grew huge and filled all the air round—but sounded to Rose's intimate ear as distant as a sound in a dream. For a moment its intensity woke him, alerted some faint pull of reason: Thunder? Lorry? Whirlpool—the flat waste of milling water, the dark hole hubbing round its roared descent? . . . he opened for a moment his eyes and saw vaguely that the sound had stopped and that above, incredibly high in the mist, peering through with kindly outraged interest, hung the great curved neck and head of a horse. Apocalyptic, pagan, a classic lordly beast—it disappeared. Not ever fully awake to it, he closed his eyes and sank back into what was of stronger presence.

157

Later that evening, long after the mist had lifted and silently they had returned, long after the detailed and not unembarrassed accounting of their adventure to fellow-guests in tea-lounge and cocktail bar, and shortly after a dinner eaten separately at two ends of the cold dining-hall—Rose walked down from his bedroom again to the public rooms. Through intersecting doors he caught sight of her. Her back was half-turned; he paused for a moment watching her profile bent over an illustrated paper. She was alone. He hesitated, almost started in her direction, then still on the wide stairs turned down towards the front door. She was dressed as on the previous night, her hair was arranged as previously he had known it, she had assumed again all the garment of his previous disinterest, of the wan atmosphere of the lounges of hotels.

She for her part had not been reading. She had sat particularly in that chair to be seen and to see the stairs from an inclined and obvious mirror. As he had appeared, she too had noticed with a sense of disappointment how he no longer looked like the man on the moor—only a mild and not attractive man moving self-consciously down in evening clothes. But as from her hidden eye she saw him change his direction, there came a harsh moment of anger and loss—for she of her nature as a woman considered herself to have given rather than taken. Then that, at least for the time being, was overcome; with a heart full of resentment she rose, replaced carefully the magazine, and rejoined her friends.

A World of Glass

CELLS become writers. Writers are solitaries and cells are solitary: here I can sit in imposed solitude, free from my pity of solitude self-imposed, absolved from all decision and responsibility and all question of selecting diversions of the outside world. Physically I can choose practically nothing: mentally I am freer than before. I must simply sit here and serve my sentence. It was, of course, for assault.

Assault, and I think justified. That is why I refused any concession that might have been offered, and decided to let them all do with me just what they wished. I did not think it would turn out as well as this. And so, in moderate and pleasantly austere comfort, with none—or at least very little—material seduction, I can sit within these six walls—for here the ceiling and the floor are as much walls as the walls themselves—and let my mind and my pen run free. Not surprisingly, they run upon the course of events that led to my arrest: not upon the arrest itself, which was a small matter, but upon the emotions—and they were as strong as I will try to tell—that preceded the affair.

I shall never forget the terrible beauty of the journey to Trondhjem: and the beauty of Trondhjem itself. To travel to a place in circumstances of mounting beauty, mounting with no moment of regression, and then to find that after those long elating hours the destination is no dross of achievement but is even more beautiful than all the rest, that it expands about one like a great flower whose petals unfold the final, endless, sleepening glory—that is an experience seldom to be enjoyed. We began at Oslo. Early morning. A great black monster of a steam train. An empty carriage with cushions of carmine velvet. And throughout the day mounted through long

Norway, from slush to snow, from snow to deeper snow, proceeding both up the map and on to higher ground. Which together makes for a most pleasing sensation.

From the warm, almost the hot carriage—it was invigorating and fresh to watch the snow. No fierce peaks and sharp summits to disturb a gentle skyline, but instead a good rolling of high distant hills that swam around the wide perspective with a rise and fall of waves: often these were fir-capped, when the snow-back stood fringed against the sky with short rich bristles. For this was no barren country. And all the way up the line one passed small stations, dark brown wooden stations eaved with dragons' heads in the Viking manner. The station officials wore high black fur caps, and in their black uniforms they looked like a fierce contingent of Turkestan police. The ticket collector on the train also—but his red round face and bucolic Norwegian address belied the Turk: he was always up and down the carpeted corridor outside announcing the imminence of unpronounceable stations, and when on this journey I say 'we', it is of him and the engine and myself that I speak, for I was alone at the time.

By midday we had passed through the ski-ing country, where, apart from the beauty of the snow, there was at certain stations a spirit of festivity as red-capped skiers left the train and sought sleighs to take them out to their snowy places of holiday. But some time after that the real country began, the skies changed, a frozen magnificence charged the air with a peculiar magic. Great lakes appeared, ice-bound, their miles to the horizon furred with wide-fanning flat snow. Near the shore frozen waves lay ridged like skin under a microscope: logged on the banks piles of fresh stripped wood shone like pigskin. Icicles as thick as tree-trunks hung their green glow from rock ledges, and where waterfalls had been struck solid they hung in rows like monstrous teeth: but cruelly as these were shaped, their glass made music of them: over everything the far-gleaming sun and its greening sky played strange tricks of transparency. Such a sun! It hung and travelled all day on the horizon so low that losing heat it grew in complement larger—it gleamed more than shone. It gleamed like a force of great candlepower over the wide land, turning the snow to lavender and pink, greening the icicles and greening the sky; and the sky itself receded infinitely, it became more transparent than itself, it provoked in its pale green a visible sense of infinity. Yet this was no true Arctic sun—although we were travelling near to the polar circle: it shone not on a barren land, but on a snow-laden gentle place rich with cream-coloured birch and black fir. On such country its low long beam cast everything into a strange clearness—in the same way, though a thousand times clarified, that a lowering sun on a summer's day clears and stills the air just before evening. Everything seemed set in glass, transplendent, motionlessly clear.

So the day passed as we steamed on through the snows, higher ever north. The sun set early. The last thing I can remember was the passing of a river, swift-flowing water of bottle-green that pooled and snaked down between the rocks and ice and moussed snow, disappearing one knew not whither, and in the cold air smoking. Then the light was gone, the snows grey—and soon after we ran into a blizzard.

Three-quarters way up, three-quarters way penetrated north, and with the ominous fall of night—some ancient listening God pressed the loud-pedal and sent the great pianoforte of his mountain scorn into action. Now from the warm and easy carriage nothing was to be seen: only the drive of snow hailing by, and the white steam and smoke of the forward engine driven down past the windows by the weight of the wind. Up and up, winding along the white track into a blank curtain of white: only at stations could anything be seen, and these—with their snow-swirling lamps, their dark-stamping figures, with the high-funnelled great engine steaming its monstrous black iron against the snow—these could only remind me of scenes dreamed over from novels of the Russian nineteenth century. From the warm red-covered lighted carriage one saw passing along the curtained corridor travellers in fur caps and astrakhan, ladies with white fur collars and once a curious ermine bonnet. The feeling was of Russia—for all our first impressions are allied quickly with previous knowledge, with things nearly similar—but it was not exact: for there were the names of stations passed—Hjerkinn, Kongsvoll, Driva; and there were the Viking dragons uptilting like pagoda eaves from the roof-beams of each wooden station; and there was the recent memory of standing in wonder at the fine dark beauty of the retrieved Viking ships themselves, abstractions of dark curved planking as beautifully draped as a classic robe, objects indeed that must take their place with the other few abstract, complete, Parthenon beauties of the world. This was Norway of Haakon and no tsarist Russia.

We steamed out of the blizzard into clear cloud-high height. A hidden moon shone a starshine light over the snow, giving to things mysterious visibility but no exact shape. Then the train passed through the last station, and curled round towards Trondhjem. There was a stirring in the corridors. People who had sat still for twelve hours rose to get their luggage out first—to save a minute. This movement I find irritating, and always swear to remain seated until the train is cleared. But as usual I became infected, started pulling at my bags, and as usual missed the sight of the entrance into my town of destination. A grinding of iron brakes, a jolt of luggage, and the train came expiring its last steam to a halt. Outside, a babel of fresh faces to receive us the stiff and weary.

There was not much to do that night but get to the hotel and go to bed. I had a mixed impression of crossing a river from the station, entering streets wide and squarely laid, and many of the muddled sensations with which a new town receives one. I remember a busy sense though the streets were empty, a solid feeling after the fluid day on wheels, and a sense of unconfessed astonishment that lives were really lived here all the time without one's presence and not even in the knowledge of one's existence. Yet perhaps because of this and because of the alerted nerves of journey a new city is always a place of great promise and possibility: a feeling so often punctured absolutely after a day's acquaintance.

Next morning I parted the old lace curtains—it was a barish room, Ibsen in remnant, with a horse-hair sofa and a brass lamp that might have once burned oil—parted those curtains and looked out on to the wide snow-covered street. Instantly the amazing impact came—no dragons, no dark wood! Instead—a white-painted classic town! Suddenly this—at three degrees below the polar circle!

It was of course a reversal of everything expected. But it was only a beginning to the confusion that followed. I went downstairs to take a walk quickly, taking no overcoat—and naturally after a few steps along the pavement felt it too cold and returned. Perhaps, after all, breakfast first. I asked for the restaurant. I was shown it. And again the confusion arose—for that unbelievable restaurant was a palm garden and no potted place from warmer latitudes but a real palm garden growing in real earth real big palms. I remember flipping the snow from my glove on one large tropical frond that stretched with the stealth of a bird-eating spider near my table. So. One could only sit coffee-less and muddled in such a place. Moreover, lighted Christmas trees had been placed at regular intervals among those palms and exotic plantains and the whole was turfed in an earthy basin circled with granite pillars of an oldish Nordic style. A fountain made water music in the centre.

As I sat there muddled the porter came through. A gentleman to see me. A gentleman? A gentleman from the newspapers.

I was travelling unannounced. My real name was not the one by which I was generally known. All the way up through Copenhagen and Gothenburg and Oslo I had been received and interviewed. It was a necessary, and not at all times unpleasant, duty. There is a flattery about it that never entirely fails, however often the process has occurred: nevertheless it is also a duty, and as a duty it must sometimes call for the pleasure of being avoided. It was such a pleasure that I had promised myself on this last lap of the journey before taking ship for the British Isles. But I had forgotten that the Oslo papers are read in Trondhjem: and, anyhow, that there is a telegraph between journalists. Perhaps it was this very stupidity that made me suddenly say 'No!': and knowing this refusal to be of little use, made me get up from the table breakfastless (it was, to give the reporter his due, eleven o'clock) and demand the backstairs exit to reach my room. There, rummaging quickly for sunglasses, a drab old scarf, and putting on my overcoat and soft hat twisted ridiculously down over my eyes, I felt myself disguised (to no one, of course, but myself) and left the room angrily just as the telephone was beginning to ring.

So here I was, some time after eleven, slipping into the side-streets, all guilt on my tail, simply for the sake of avoiding a ten-minute conversation. It was absurd: yet how often one clings to such first decisions with bone-brained vigour—and it may be that obstinacy in such small matters trains one for resolution on more important principles: but I hardly think so, it is more a strength to be able to change one's mind.

For some time walking the streets I felt myself followed, I thought everyone looked too curiously into my face, I imagined the whole town conspiring against me. Once I tried to telephone the hotel to *forbid* them to admit any more reporters, but the instrument, the little øre pieces, and the thought of the Norwegian voice answering defeated me. And soon after a small boy in the street asked me the time. I knew it was that because he pointed to a clock. I could not answer in Norwegian. The boy looked astounded, then hurt. It was a foolish moment, standing there falsely dressed and apparently unable to read a clock. Perhaps the boy lost forever what faith he had left in adults.

However—with all these confusions the particular quality of that town surprised and exalted me. It is a small town, but the streets are wide. The streets seem wider than the houses which range them, houses of not more than two storeys. These are of planked wood. Planked wood painted white, but a white greyed or creamed so by the purer white of snow, white coloured as softly as some gentle shade of hand-made paper. And at the doors there are pillars of carved wood, with carved wood capitals and pediments, and the windows are set with classic regularity. There are some small palaces and there is also a royal residence, the largest wooden building in Europe, a fine white-painted low-lying mansion windowed with lavender blinds, pedimented with a red regalia like a scarlet royal seal, gilded occasionally and touched with wrought iron. Then there are the great apothecaries' houses, designated by emblems such as The Swan, throughout Scandinavia the largest of the old shops, and in themselves like small hospitals. Trondhjem has much the look of an American colonial town, with its wide perspective and wooden classic builidngs—yet it is finer, and there is the snow to throw everything into greater relief; and here and there a yellow toy-like tram gives an air of business. Wherever you walk, too, you come to water, for the town is nearly encircled by its lazy oil-green river Nid, bestower of the town's old Viking name Nidaros. That name in itself added a confusing charm—a false Greek word among derived Greek architectures in the snowbound north. And one must never forget the sun, lying so low, beaming everywhere its curious inexact light.

It was after I had been walking for almost an hour that I met the girl. I remember leaving the streets—which I had already traversed more than once, for the town is pleasantly limited—and deciding to have a good look at the rivermouth harbour. So once more down broad Mungkegaten to the waterside wharves. And I remember then being glad of those ridiculous sunglasses, because at every gap between houses, when one was walking laterally to the sun, the great candlemass hidden below roof-level shone out with tremendous power, at eye-level it struck just as though one had chosen to look the sun in the eye, it nearly knocked one down.

Resting on something—a barrel, a smoked-fish-crate, a wood railing?—I looked out over the packed fleet. I remember coughing —and then feeling both self-conscious of the noise and of the mist of my breath on the air, for exactly then I noticed her standing quite near. I felt she might have mistaken this for the beginning of an intrusion. But it was she who intruded. She moved along nearer me —for she also had been simply standing and looking, and said pleasantly something in Norwegian.

I stuttered back:

— Kan ikke Norsk—I cannot speak Norwegian, I am English.

— Oh, you speak English? I too. We all speak English. You are English?

— Yes. I am on my way to England.

— From Trondhjem? There is another English man here in Trondhjem now, he came yesterday, a famous actor. You know him?

It is easy to adopt the disguised lie, difficult to speak the lie direct. But after a suspended moment, I did. I said I had not seen myself. And what a beautiful morning it was.

She answered immediately, with a strange enthusiasm:

—It is, it is. That's what I said first. The sun isn't warm but the light is lovely. The ships so still. . . .

For a while she went on like this. She seemed too enthusiastic about the weather, strangely so for a modern-looking girl—but then I remembered how all Scandinavians were devout lovers of nature, they love with an elemental love not far removed from their ancient sun and forest worship.

— I do like how open it is, and how gentle the hills round—no steep mountains. . . .

— Then you are on a visit too?

— Oh, no, I live here. I've always lived here.

She too was wearing sunglasses: but I could see from the high lift of her cheek-bones that her eyes would have that curious Mongolian tilt so fascinating among the Norwegians with their china-blue eyes.

— And you have seen our statue to King Olav?

— One could hardly miss it. Yes, it's most striking.

— And our cathedral?

— I am against the cathedral. Too much fuss is made of it—few people speak of what is much more beautiful, the town itself and its elegant houses.

— . . . . that's the first time I've heard—but I think you are right. And the warehouses, did you see? . . .

Her hair was blonde. She wore one of the youth-caps, a red woollen thing with a becoming tassel. Round her neck was a soft wool scarf of Norwegian pattern, a black spiky design on plaster-grey. Her skin against the wool looked fresh and soft. I went on talking:

— The warehouses, yes. Perhaps that view from the little bridge down the Nid to the sea is one of the most beautiful things I've ever seen, ever.

— . . . the warehouses lining up on either side on their stilts, we used to call them giants. . . .

— But such extraordinary colours—olive, maroon, dark ochre, they're the colours of oil-paint, of a painting of Breughel's. . . .

— You like paintings? I have not seen many.

Her coat was pale blue, smartly shapeless. She wore fur-trimmed boots, and I could just see above them the beginning of woollen stockings on legs slim above the fur.

— So you haven't travelled much?

— I have never been away from Trondhjem. Never.

— Don't you want to?

— No. Once. Not now.

— But aren't you curious, don't you wonder what the rest of the world's like? Your own country? Oslo? The North Cape?

— I couldn't do without Trondhjem. You see . . .

She paused, I thought she was thinking how to explain herself. But then I saw her lips quietly smiling, she seemed to be listening and then turned to look at the road behind. A horse and sledge were passing. The horse was white, a short long-maned horse sturdy as a pony: it jingled its harness bells at an easy walking-pace, the sledge carried two oil-drums painted bright brown.

— There you are, she said. The horse! In Oslo it's all cars? . . . Besides, I have to stay here because of my husband.

I remember feeling then a sudden disappointment. It was not as if I had thought definitely towards that girl, it was more simply a sudden lowering of the pleasant tension that exists always, with no conscious endeavour, at a fresh meeting of the sexes. But there. She had a husband. One felt a sensation of having been robbed. Yet slight, it passed, and of course I said something like:

— Well of course that's a different matter. You're home's your home, you're right, no wanderlust can compare with building a home with the right person, the person you love—

— When do you leave?

— What? Leave—oh leave here? Tomorrow, the boat.

— He's not the right person.

— Oh.

My face felt that if I looked at her it would show too dramatic a concern, something too intimate and curious. She went instantly on:

— I don't love him. As you go tomorrow I can say that. It's good to speak sometimes, you rarely can. No, I don't love him.

As she went on, speaking in so even a voice, as if enquiring into herself, I could again look at her. Her soft and beautiful face— young, in her early twenties—had the amused look of reminiscence, whether the thought is amusing or not, a softening play of the mouth to accompany the play of thought. And then suddenly she broke off, and looked over at the ships, at the pale low railway station islanded out in the harbour, at the sky beyond:

— I used to think the station looked like a palace out there with sun gold along it's roof. Its golden now, isn't it? And the sky green between the masts?

I laughed:

— Isn't it? Why, you can see it is.

I found myself taking off my glasses to see more clearly the colours. And then realized and corrected myself:

— But of course, your glasses. No one can see properly in the damn things. Half the beauty of life goes, and half the world seems to wear them. Things look like a thunderstorm or a rose-tinted hell. Why do we wear them!

— Why! Why indeed?

Then she took off her spectacles. She turned her face full to me, and I saw for the first time her china-blue eyes. They stared full blue into mine. I had been talking more quickly about the dark spectacles—when she had said she had no love for this husband my spirits had briefly, absurdly risen. A male cunning had asserted itself, a predatory wile that leapt on the question—was she then in some way offering herself to me? Wishful thinking made it so. I had talked faster, dressing the moment to cover my true feelings. And when she took the glasses off I was so disturbed, for it cut against careful grains of reserve, that I must have seemed to have asked her to take them off: and she had assented, that made it no less embarrassing. In fact she had spoken to me first, she was assenting too quickly. Though a man might dream of such affairs proceeding without the delays of propriety, when it happens he does not quite know how to adjust himself.

But delighted beyond all that I looked down into her face, into her eyes with expectation.

She was smiling up at me. But it was no smile of invitation: it was instead a wise smile—and though her freshness of appearance made this seem unbelievable—almost a sneer. I felt immediately: Here we go. The old game. Lead him on. Get him going. Then laugh— for *you* knew all the time.

But as I thought this—I was looking still into her eyes and saw then that they were suffering, there was a mist of pain in them. So that smile of wisdom was one of knowledge of some pain, of perhaps

how tired she looked, and of a rejection of sympathy. Then suddenly
I saw that she was not looking into my eyes at all—she was looking
at my forehead, glazed, asleep, set dreaming. And even then there
crossed my mind other possibilities—the nymphomaniac glaze,
powerless and overpowering; the endreamed set stare of someone
weak in the head. But then she nodded, a solemn conspiring slow
nod. And I saw exactly what these eyes were. They were glass. She
was blind.

— You see?

— I never dreamed—

— There it is. And he did it.

The eyes, infinite in their dream, turned a little away, she stared
straight into the sun. I could see now that the flexing sensibility
of her lips moved from a reflection of other senses working—senses
of sound, of the touch of air, of other proximities ordinarily unperceived. Her eyes fixed, her face was the more alive. Then—as
though the act of play was over—she resumed those dark spectacles.
And became visibly as other women.

I could not stop myself—there was hardly a need, since she had
first wished to talk of it—from asking:

— He did it? But, how, an accident? Some dreadful accident?

— On purpose.

— But—

— If you like, accidentally. He was drunk.

— But how could he . . .

— With a broken bottle.

She must have felt then that so shocking a statement would have
made me angry: an anger to which she may have been well used. For
without pausing she drifted on, easily, with the same strange smile
of reminiscence. She might have been talking of a well-loved garden.

— You mustn't mind if I talk so. It's a little forbidden at home,
with my friends. It is awkward, you see.

— Yes. But—why—

— Oh really it is simple. It was I suppose my fault also: must not
forget that. You see, he was away on his ship: it was midsummer,
you know that is a gay time with us. To cut the long story short—I
was a bad girl. It was sudden, a foolish thing: it never occurred again.

But there—he found out.

She paused now, it seemed as if she were frowning to remember. But there was no exact frown:

— He got drunk. He was proud, he was upset and mad. He came home and held my arms, tight. I was frightened, I got away and I threw something at him. It was heavy and it hurt him: I think that must have jolted his mind—perhaps he thought he was in a real fight, somewhere else, with men, I don't know. Anyway—then the bottle, it was done in a second. He broke it in the same movement as he cut me with it, I remember his arm coming, it came across, I don't think he ever meant to stab, it was just perhaps unlucky. However—as you see . . .

She paused. Her lips suddenly lost all movement, her face grew blank. In remembering she had come across a moment too strong for her. There was nothing to say. At such times one can be quick to feel pity, sorrow: but unable to make the move of sympathy. The deeper the feeling, the more impossible this.

But she continued:

— Of course he came to his senses. I was sent to hospital. There was no chance.

— But then why do you stay?

— How can I go . . . he is so sorry.

— But—

— He feels he must make this up to me. It's all he lives for now.

— Then you've forgiven him?

— No. I don't believe in forgiveness. Forgiveness, forgetting. I have heard it so much, an old . . . distinction? 'I forgive but I never forget'. Or 'I forget, but I don't forgive'. None of such things is true. You simply grow used to a changed way of things. Time takes the sharpness away. But you are not proof against your own moods. So sometimes—not often—but sometimes—I become angry and for a time I do not forgive. Then again, in a happy mood, when things are sweet, I not only forgive but say to myself this forgiveness. But for the most I do nothing, neither remember nor blame, neither forgive nor quite forget. I simply do not care. It was four years ago.

I thought 'four years'—a short time. But then four years at twenty are long.

— Still, you don't love him. You could stay away.

— He feels he must make it up to me.

— But if you say you don't want it?

— How *could* I?

She turned those dark glasses on to me, glasses of the sportswoman and the beach. Her voice had altered. With three words it lost its evenness, its reasonability: then broke suddenly deep, as words felt deeply do, as if they are searching deep down in the breast for the heart which bore them.

— How could I? He'd think I had gone away to leave him free. He'd think I was unburdening him. He'd have no more way of making up for what he did. He'd be left alone with his conscience . . . I could never do that to him.

There was nothing to say to this. I searched hard for an answer, one must answer when looking at a blind face. I made some noise of affirmation, only that, while my own eyes searched the harbour before me. The small steam fishing boats lying still, never rocking, smooth on the river water: their sides varnished over natural wood, cleaner thus than other vessels; and themselves set in glass with their bright brass and varnish shining in that transparent northern air. The sky above so distant, glassy blue as the flesh of a seabird's egg. From one side hammering came, the curious painted pale brown and apple green of a liner rose above the houses from a hidden dock. A bird, black and white, strutted among the fishcrates, pretending to be a penguin. I could only think of the usual dread of mutilation, the story as often told—the dread of the mutilated that their affliction should imprison the loved one. And this girl. . . .

Her voice was again calm, she was smiling:

— In any case. I cannot leave Trondhjem. It's the only place I've seen, it's the only place I can still see. . . .

Later I asked whether there was some small restaurant where we could lunch. I watched her fingers select with more precision than a sighted person the numbers on the automatic dial when she telephoned that she would be out for lunch: her black, white-rimmed spectacles bent looking at the dial, it was embarrassing to be so near a woman who could not see. I found I could look closely at, say, the very fine hair at her temples without worrying about the expression on my own face, I could look at whatever I chose; and for this reason I particularly did not, I had been already punished enough for my presumption of the morning.

Then throughout the afternoon we explored and examined that strange city. It can only be remembered as a dream—no ecstatic dream, but a time suspended from reality, caught in a mirror, never properly experienced. We did not walk far. We stayed down by the quay, walked a little against the cold in the very narrow streets running back between the great wood-gabled warehouses, but always returned through the snow to the ships.

So what I saw of Trondhjem was through her eyes. She behind the blind glasses evoked again for me the picture, a picture more familiar and more sensitive of the streets I had walked that morning. I saw them in fact more freshly—as if in fact *I* had worn no tinted glasses—the pale beauty of white houses against the whiter snow, the lavender blinds of the great planked palace, the extraordinary gabled warehouses lining the rivers on stilts and painted the deep oily reds and greens and browns of a Breughel painting picked out with snow. I heard of the people, residents of this royal and merchant city—and matched their rich dull appearance with her more intimate knowledge of them as individuals and friends; so that they began to live, they ceased to be types and national puppets formed in a foreigner's eyes. Both portly and merry, their figures seemed cut from the previous century: yet they rode up the surrounding hills on electric rails, their lights at night were neon.

In mid-afternoon the sun began to set. The short day of long summer-evening light was over, and we walked back towards her home. Paused in the small square where the brilliant tall Christmas tree threw out its frosted light. I wondered whether she had ever seen it. She knew it was there, she raised her face to it and seemed to be looking. Its light flashed on her glasses black in the night. She talked of its candles. Candles! Had she ever seen that the candles were electric? I dared not ask.

We parted at the corner of her street. We simply shook hands, she turned and went along between the houses. She walked more slowly, her back a little bent. She looked like a young girl walking moody in thought.

Two men, drunk, swaying together like stage drunks as many Scandinavians seem to do, raised their hats and said something as she passed. She answered pleasantly. They watched her walking away, making gurgling noises of drunken approbation.

All that evening I could not keep myself from thinking of her— of the beauty of her very humble demand from life. The reward often of people resigned to illness, to amputation. And the next day again I woke with the thought of her. I went early to the boat, found my cabin, hung about. To the top of each mast was lashed a small Christmas tree ready to be lit at night as we would plough through the dark rough North Sea.

So it was later, when the boat sailed and I went into the bar, that I ran into my trouble. I was still exalted, still clouded by both the beauty of Nidaros and of that young girl's undemanding humility.

Two men were in the bar, speaking English. They were, I think, both pleasant-looking ordinary men of middle-age. Business men enjoying their trip. But one was already looking at his watch, comparing this with the clock of the wall:

— Well—goodbye to the North! Back to good old British Time!

The other looked up, and nodded. Nodded in sudden complacent pleasure. He nodded brightly:

— Yes! *We gain an hour!*

It was then, as if something outside myself had gripped me, that I smashed my fist with all the force I had into his smiling, nodding teeth.

The Girl on the Bus

SINCE to love is better than to be loved, unrequited love may be the finest love of all. If this is so, then the less requited the finer. And it follows that the most refined passion possible for us must finally be for those to whom we have never even spoken, whom we have never met. The passing face, the anguish of a vision of a face, a face sitting alone in front of you so endearing and so moving and so beautiful that you are torn and sick inside with hope and despair, instant despair . . . for it is hopelessly plain that no word can ever be spoken, those eyes will never greet yours, in a few minutes the bell will ring, the bus will shudder to a stop, and down some impersonal side street she will be gone. Never to be seen again. Gone even is the pain of listening to where she will book for—a fourpenny, or a three-halfpence ticket?

It is due to such an encounter that I find engaging the story of my friend Harry. Only Harry's girl was not on a bus, she passed on skis.

It was one late January afternoon when Harry was walking out at Haga. The snow lay thick, and everywhere over the fine rolling park groups of Stockholmers had sought out the best slopes for an afternoon's ski-ing. The sun was already low and yellow over the firs, it sent a cold tired dusk across the snow—and one could feel the pleasantly weary, flushed trudge of the skiers making their last climb before nightfall. Harry walked about tasting this air of a winter's day ending, enjoying the rich smell of birchwood burning, watching the first yellow lights square in the cream-coloured palace, tasting his own frosted breath. Up on the highest ridge stood the line of cavalry barracks, the fantastic line of false mediaeval war-tents—their great carved wooden folds were draped to the snow, a last glint of the sun flashed the gold emblems on their snow-domed roofs. From such an elegant extravagance it must have been fine to see the blue-cloaked cavalry ride forth steaming and jangling on to snowy hills. But now it was a ghost-house: and as if in evocation of its ghosts, every so often through the tall erect firs black-crouched skiers would glide, swift as shadows, like trees themselves flickering downward home.

It was some time then, in this bright half-light, that Harry turned and saw on the path behind him the figure of a girl trudging up on skis. He walked down towards her, enjoying the precision of her slender erect shape slide-stepping along towards him. Skiers walk with a beautifully controlled motion, feet always close together on the long hickory, pressing so lightly forward in long strides, pausing it seems invisibly between each forward motion, listening to a music playing somewhere in their shoulders—and always in firm endeavour, as on some enviable purposed unhurried quest pondering seriously forward.

Harry was looking down at her skis as she came up, taking pleasure from the movement and the slimness of her stride. So that not until she was nearly parallel with him and about to pass did he glance up at her face.

What he saw then took his breath away, he drew in a deep astounded breath and this then disappeared, so that there was nothing inside him at all.

Poor Harry did not have even a bus-ride's worth, not a three-ha'pence worth. He had the length of two long ski-strides' worth. But that, he said, was in its expanded way enough. Not as much as he wanted—that would have amounted to a lifetime—but enough to provoke the indelible impression such passing visions may leave for a lifetime.

It would be useless to describe her. When Harry told me he talked of 'beauty' and of a colour of hair and a grace of cheek-bone and an expression of lips. But what he said did not amount to a concrete image, and particularly she did not necessarily fit the blueprint of my own imagined vision, should such a one ever chance to pass. Each to his own. Suffice it that this woman's face and manner and whatever she evoked was for Harry perfection: was beyond what he thought might be perfection: was absolute.

He was so shocked he nearly stopped, he certainly hesitated and half turned his body—heavily coated and thus making what must have been a most noticeable movement—to follow his wide-eyed worshipping glance. But in the same short time, perhaps on her second stride forward, she suddenly turned her face to him. Terrified, he looked away. He never knew whether she saw him staring, or saw him at all, or looked past or though him—he only felt a surge of embarrassment out of all proportion to the occasion. He felt small, despairing, hopeless, and above all horrified that she might have caught his eye and thought it the eye of an intruder.

She passed. It was a long time before Harry could bring himself to turn round. But by then she was a black speck among others in the lengthening snow, she was irretrievable.

For the next minutes Harry walked on and out of the park, elated in spite of his distress. He was elated in the way a man is when he has suddenly come face to face with a giddying good work of art. The feeling was universal—it made to say: 'Good, good—so there are still such things in the world!' It was a feeling of hope.

But of no practical hope. He knew that he would never see the girl again. However, she had sent his spirits up . . . but soon, it was apparent, too far. For once outside the park, her park, the world proclaimed itself again. And it looked exceedingly bare and dull. The tram-ride home, among skiers now wet and drab in the electric light, was lowering. His hotel, white-walled as a sanatorium, primed with red corridor lights and reticent switches, appalled him with its sterile gloom. He took a glass of aquavit and telephoned a friend for dinner.

They went to a large old-fashioned restaurant. There were many hundreds of people, an orchestra of twenty players blared music to the farthest microphoned corner, waiters bobbed and slid like black dolphins in the white sea of tablecloth, and all around and up to the roof, high as an exhibition hall, the gilded ornament twisted and plushly glittered. There were palms, flowers, flags and chandeliers.

But here also Strindberg had kept his private dining-room: and it was with something of the same pessimist eye that Harry now allowed his spirits to sink below the level of the nightfaring populace about. A tarnish shadowed the gilt, a dull propriety seemed to stuff the people. The band played ballad music of the 'nineties—and he felt no nostalgia, but a vehement disgust at the stuffed rose-love-garden pomp the song pictured for him. The diners, sitting too erect and quiet and uncomfortably unlaughing, began to look like the awkward guests at a staff-dinner. Two Salvation Army lasses, in fur bonnets, threaded their way through the tables. When the band began suddenly to play a gay Spanish march it was no better, it sounded too slow. And there were too many fiddles.

Now if you knew Harry as I know Harry, you would know that Harry then began to worry. He began to theorize. 'The sight of that girl', he told himself, 'has coloured my whole life. By a hundredth chance I was in Stockholm, by a hundredth chance I went to Haga, by another hundredth I happened to be passing that path at that moment—and I had to see *her*. Now forever I am left with a standard of beauty which my world will always slightly fail. My relationships with women will never seem quite so keen, all other pursuits will seem henceforth without quite so much purpose. Of course, I shall enjoy myself in degree. But perfection has been trifled with. This kind of thing goes deeper than one thinks. . . . Oh why in hell did I go to Haga? And it is not as if I was as young as I was.'

He was still considering her on the train next morning at Malmö: 'The woman was always destined to be unattainable—and it is significant that I am leaving the city today. I suppose this will result in a fixation on Stockholm for the rest of my life. God knows how many superior contracts in other towns I shall discard for the sub-conscious opportunity of getting back to this blasted place.'

The train drew into Norrköping and lunch was served. It was difficult, sitting wedged with three other men, to know how much of each small dish to take for himself, so he took too little of each. But rather much of the one he liked most. In guilty despondence, he looked out at the short orange trams circling the Norrköping neatnesses. How plain life could be! And these men eating in front and to the side of him were so large and well-conditioned! He felt himself smaller against their giant, businessy, grey-suited size. None of them spoke. They exchanged the dishes with little bows, and then relapsed into their erect selves. But as the train drew slowly out of Norrköping a group of children waved from behind railings. As one man, the three leaned slightly forward and made small flutterings with their white heavy hands. And without a word readdressed themselves to their food.

Hell, thought Harry looking down at his own hand and seeing that it had not even the initiative to join in such a dull nice action. Hell, he thought, I shall have to wake myself up. And it was then that he decided on a new course of life, a disciplined course of self-indulgence. He would drink more, seek out more people, spend more money and work less.

The lowlands of Sweden rolled by. The sky hung grey and wet, the mossy turf with its scattering of huge time-smoothed boulders looked very ancient. Sometimes these boulders had been rolled to the edge of a field, but often they were too heavy to be moved, and lay still in the centre proclaiming their great, icy age. It was very difficult for Harry, wedged in now with his coffee, to see how to start on his new programme. It would have been ostentatious, he felt, to order a few brandies. But when one of the men asked for an after-dinner sherry, he did the same. One of these was enough. He felt slightly sick. The business men, in their hard girth and with their large pale faces, began to look very like boulders.

But at Malmö a difference charged the air. At first this might have passed for the ambrosia of arrival—a search for luggage, the disturbing sea-air, the genial sheds and asphalt of docks. The delight of safe danger. But no—once aboard the ferry what had come upon people was evident. A glance into the smoke-room told much of the tale. Already, five minutes after the train had arrived, they were singing in the smoke-room. Tables were already massing empty bottles. The three silent, kind, well-conditioned, Swedish business men were laughing together and sitting spread and easy. But it was not only a matter of alcohol—although the free dispensation of this, after a severely restricted country, proved in every way intoxicating. It was a broader sense of freedom. A shedding of propriety, of reserve—a change of manners, not from good to bad, but from good to good of another kind. Geniality and tolerance warmed the air.

Waiters hurried up with plates of enormous Danish sandwiches. In the very sandwiches there could be felt the difference between the two countries parted by a mile of water. Gone were the elegant and excellent Swedish confections, here were thick slabs of appetizing meat and fish piled hugely helter-skelter on a token of bread: Smörgåsbord had become Smørrebrød. And when they landed and he walked about the Danish train, Harry noticed immediately how the people had lost height and gained thickness: and how the porters wore dirtier, easier clothes. And standing in the street there was a beggar.

But although at first Harry responded to this interesting new brightness, he soon found he was the only one on the train who had no reason to be elated. He sank into greater gloom. He tried to revive his spirits with a fine meal and a night out in Copenhagen. But even when friendly Copenhageners, seeing him sitting alone, asked him to sit with them, plied him with food and drink, joked and prompted him in every way to enjoy himself—his mood remained. He felt nervous, frustrated, dull.

The next day, a little freshened by the morning, he boarded a midday boat train for Esbjærg and England. After all, he felt, things might be better. He was a fool to have taken a passing emotion so seriously. In fact, it was only an emotion and as such ephemeral and replaceable.

So that when they came to the Great Belt, and the train trundled aboard the ferry that was to take it across that wide flat water— Harry took to regarding his fellow-passengers with more interest. There is always an excitement when a compartmented train turns out its passengers to walk about and make a deckful. One has grown used and even loyal to one's own compartment: one knows the number of the carriage, it seems to be the best number of all! One even feels a sympathetic acquaintanceship with people seen through the glass of adjoining compartments and with those in the corridor. But there, on the boat, one must face a rival world—the world of other carriages. One resents their apparent assumption of equality —yet, inimical or not, it is a source of wonder that here are so many fellow-travellers of whose existence one was ignorant. One notes them with interest. One must watch and sniff.

Almost the first person Harry noted was the girl from Haga.

It could not be, it could, it was. Harry's heart jumped and his stomach sank. He turned furtively away.

He walked twenty yards down the deck, took out a cigarette and pretended that it was necessary to turn to light this against the wind. Then he backed against the cabin wall and, thus hidden, watched her. His emotion beat so strong that he imagined every passenger on the boat must recognize it, there would be a conspiracy aboard to smile about him. And consequently, though in the past days he had reproved himself for not having taken more courageous action at their first encounter—he had imagined all kinds of calm, forceful gallantry—his instinct now was for instant flight. However, common sense and a suspicion of the ridiculous strengthened him. And he was able to compromise by watching her from a distance.

She stood for a few minutes on deck, not watching the wide grey water but engrossed in her bag and some process of putting her coat and scarf and hat in order. These affairs she conducted with a tranquil efficiency. She was detached and sure, removed from all the others. She never raised her eyes to look at other people.

Then she turned and walked along to the luncheon saloon. Carefully Harry followed, pausing and looking away as if in search of somebody or something else, and chose a table about three away from hers. There he munched his enormous pork cutlet and kept her surveyed. Every time he dared to look at her it seemed a stolen, intrusive moment. But he congratulated himself on his discretion. He told himself there was time, she must be going aboard for the Harwich boat. There, with a day and a night to stroll about the large saloons, opportunity would present itself. He stole another glance. With horror he found her looking straight at him, frowning a little. She knew!

He left, and went down the steel staircase to where the train, strangely tall and of such dark heavy metal, stood waiting. He sat smoking and unnerved, alone in the carriage. But in a few minutes the ferry docked, and soon the train was rumbling out on to Jutland and the last stretch to Esbjærg.

The ship, white and clean and smiling with stewardesses, welcomed them from the smoke and cramp of the train. But the weather was beginning to blow, a freshness of pounding black waves echoed in from the North Sea and storm clouds raced ragged across a dark sky. Harry hurried aboard, established his cabin, and went up to watch the other passengers come up the gangway. He waited for half an hour, watched the last arrivals drift in from the lighted sheds across the gritty dark quay. But he had missed her. In some panic, and in her absence growing more self-assured each moment, he searched the ship. Up and down the steep stairways, in and out of strange saloons, into the second class and once, daring all, by intentional mistake into the ladies' rest room. But she was nowhere. And the ship sailed.

Harry saw how he had missed his second chance. He looked back at that hour on the ferry and cursed his ineptitude. He despised himself, as he saw himself independent and adult and assured yet baulking at the evident chance. He swore that if ever again . . . but when she appeared in the lounge after dinner he plunged his hand out for a coloured engineering gazette. All his fears returned. One does not necessarily learn from experience.

The smoking-room was large and furnished with fresh, modern, leather arm-chairs. The tables were ridged: and on that evening the ridges were necessary, and then not always high enough—for it was a very stormy night, and the ship was rolling badly. Glasses and cups slid slowly about like motivated chessmen, and more than once the ship gave a great shuddering lurch that threw everything smashing to the floor. Harry, behind his gazette, prayed that his coffee would not be shot off clownishly across the saloon. He did not think then what a good excuse that might make to smile at her. He only prayed not to look a fool.

For her part, she sat serenely writing a letter. For some reason her glass of brandy never slid an inch. It seemed to borrow composure from her. Harry concentrated on an advertisement for dozers. And, curiously, this calmed him. It seemed so absurd, it showed up the moment: life is so very various, nothing has quite such a unique importance as we give it.

The storm grew in force. High waves smashed themselves with animal force against the windows, and the ship rolled more thunderously than ever. Stewards staggered, the arm-chairs tugged at their floor-chains. Perhaps the smoke-room was half-full when coffee began: but now it was emptying, people who had resisted so far began to feel sick, and for others it had become difficult to read or to talk or, among those tilting tables, to think. As they went swaying and skidding through the doors some laughed like people at a funfair: others dared not open their mouths. And so there came a moment, in spite of the drumming sea-noises, when Harry noticed a distinct quiet in the room. He looked round and saw the room was nearly empty. There had descended the well-kept void dullness, the perceptible silence of a waiting-room. Two business men sat apart reading. Their smallest movement in that polished quiet attracted attention. The girl wrote calmly on. The panic rose again in Harry's chest. It would be so easy to go over and pick a magazine from the case at her side. There were even magazines lying on her own table! With no possibility of offence he could ask her permission to read one.

He knew it was then or never. He began instantly to invent excuses. For the first time he tried to reason. There, Harry said to himself, is this girl whose appearance has knocked me silly. But I know that a hundred to one her personality will never match this illusory loveliness. How do I know she won't be an utter fool? A bitch? A moron? . . . And then I'll have spoiled this—he could almost sigh with romantic detachment—beautiful experience. I have sipped—and that is forever more satisfying than the gross full draught. Then he looked at her again, and the detachment left him.

All right, he groaned, then at least there is the curse of classification. That has not yet disappeared. Suppose she answered me too genteelly? Or too broadly? Or in this accent or that—he heard in his ears those for which he held a deep, illogical apathy. Then he remembered she was Swedish. It would not happen.

He looked back at the dozers. He saw they were described in refined lettering as 'earth-moving equipment'. He flung the magazine aside and in pale apprehension rose to his feet. The ship gave a lurch. He steadied himself. And then with great difficulty moved towards her.

Half-way across, exactly opposite the door, he who never did began to feel sea-sick. It was as if the paleness he had felt come over his face was spreading through him, and now with every roll of the ship a physical quease turned his stomach. It may have begun as a sickness of apprehension, but it took on all the symptoms of a sickness of sea. He felt weak, wretched and unsure of what next. He turned out through the door and balanced down the stairway to his cabin. In the lower bunk his cabin-companion lay pale and retching. The room smelled richly of sick. Harry added to it.

But only a little later, weak and having forgotten all about the girl, he fell into a deep, unmolested sleep. Twice in the night he woke—once when his heavy suitcase slid thudding from one end of the cabin to the other, once when he himself was nearly rolled out of the bunk. But he was no longer sick.

He woke late, feeling well and hungry. The ship was still pitching as heavily as before. He shaved with difficulty, watching his face swing in and out of the mirror, chasing with his razor the water that rolled in the opposite direction to that chosen by the ship. Then upstairs to breakfast. The whole ship was deserted. Harry looked at his watch, wondering whether he had misread the time and if it was perhaps still early—but his watch and the purser's clock made it already eleven o'clock. The notion smiled through him that the company had taken to the boats in the night, he was in a well-equipped ghost-ship with steam up. And indeed, walking through the deserted saloons, it felt like that. But in the dining-room three waiters were sitting.

During a breakfast that he could only eat by holding his cup in one hand and both cutting and forking his ham with the other, a waiter told him they were having one of the worst crossings he had ever known. Waves, even in such a great modern ship, had smashed plate-glass in the night. A settee had broken its chain, raced acoss the smoking-lounge and had run over a steward, breaking his leg. Of course, it was quite safe, but the ship would be about six hours late. They had made no headway at all during the night, they had simply sat rolling in the middle of the North Sea.

Harry wandered out along the passages and into the smoke-room. It was vexing to be so late. He was in no exact hurry, but an empty ship in stormy weather is a most tedious ordeal, and the long tossing day stretched out grey and eventless. One cannot easily write, it is difficult even to read, getting drunk is simpler but as aimless as the crashing glasses. To be sick is dreadful, but to spend a day lurching among lurching things, with never a level moment, is if not unendurable of the deepest, most troublesome tedium.

183

For a while Harry watched the waves. Some seemed higher than the ship itself, it seemed impossible not to be capsized. A sudden wet wall of grey running water would erect itself high as a house-front over the valley of the smoke-room window: then at the last moment up would go the ship on another unseen wave. All blew cold grey, but there was no mist —a gale wind whipped spray from the waves and tore the dishcloth smoke to pieces. Low clouds scudded too fast to notice the ship, the horizon was no more than a jagged encampment of near waves. Not a bird, not a ship in sight.

Harry's thoughts naturally centred on what was still at the back of his mind. Breakfast over, he brought her foremost. And found to his surprise that he was no longer apprehensive of her. He welcomed the probability of her appearance, he welcomed the emptiness of the ship. She was obviously not the sea-sick type, she was likely to appear. And with an empty ship there would be more opportunity to speak—and at the same time nobody to smile behind his back if she snubbed him. It seemed that his sickness of the night before had proved in all ways cathartic.

He welcomed the luncheon gong, and in his expectant joy re-membered with a smile the Swedish word for this: gonggong. But she did not appear at luncheon. And gradually, his spirits falling and his stomach swelling, Harry ploughed in these difficult seas through the enormous and exquisite Danish meal.

The afternoon was terrible. Nothing, nothing happened. A few odd men came lurching through. Two young Danish fellows sat for a long time laughing over their drinks. Harry went down to pack, but was forced by the state of his companion to complete this as quickly as possible.

An hour before the ship was due in people began to come up exhausted or rested from the sanctuary of their cabins. The ship was steaming close against the English littoral, and the seas were much calmer. Disconsolate, Harry rose from his arm-chair, threw aside the paper on which he had been reduced to writing lists of all the vegetables he knew beginning with the letter 'p', and walked round to the little bar for a drink. There she was, bright as a bad penny, perched up on a stool between those two laughing young men.

His heart sank, but he went grimly to the other end of the bar,

184

with his back turned, ordered a dobbeltsnaps. He could not hear what was said, for between high laughter they spoke in the low intimate voices of people telling anecdotes: but he could watch them in a slice of mirror. And . . . so there! What had he told himself? Hadn't he been right? She was just an ordinary flirt! She hadn't talked to these men until five minutes before, and now she was going it hell-for-leather! Easy as pie, pie-in-the-sky! He might have known it! Hell, he *had* known it! And that's why (subconsciously of course) he hadn't gone up to her. . . . But through this Harry knew deeply and quite consciously that he envied the young men and deprecated his own drivelling loutish cowardice. He turned and took one last look at her. She was wonderful . . . yes, she was wonderful.

He went downstairs and made ready to leave. In a while the ship docked. He took his bags and shuffled down among the line of passengers to the rail-lined dock. It was a curious relief to feel the land under one's feet, it brought what felt like a light unheard buzzing to the ears. Then the familiar smells and a further shuffle through the customs.

Suddenly, going through the doorway to the platform, he saw her again. She was clutching the arm of a large ugly elderly man. She was stroking this man. Together the two, the elegant fresh young girl and that obscene old figure, passed through the door. Harry believed his eyes and he was disgusted.

He had to pass them. They stood in the wan light of the old-fashioned station, she fingering about in her bag and at every moment flashing her eyes up at him, he bloated, gloat-eyed, mumbling heaven-knew-what salivary intimacies. It crossed Harry's mind how strange was the phenomenon of these shipboard passengers one never sees until the last moment, these cabined mysteries—and it struck him again horribly how this applied to those two, the old slug lying down there in the comfortable depths of the ship with his fair, fresh girl. . . .

The girl looked up and met Harry's eyes. She immediately smiled, it seemed in relief, and came up to him. She spoke excitedly, apologetically in Swedish:

— Oh, please do excuse me . . . but it's funny I remember distinctly I once saw you in Haga, you speak Swedish? You see, my father and I—we've lost our seat reservations. Could you tell me what is best to do? . . . We're new here. . . .

Harry's heart leapt. The lights in the station seemed to turn up, it was suddenly almost sunny. With delight he showed them to the end of the train where he knew there were empty carriages. Together they travelled to London and never stopped talking. He insisted on driving them to their hotel.

Harry and his lady have now been married some seven years. He has never, as far as can be known, regretted the requital.

A Waning Moon

A WOMAN'S long scream cut the night, a sound sudden and curving as a shooting star. Then a splintering of crockery, a coughed sob, a scuffling, a sobbing again that rose clenched and breathless again into that high curving scream. The caravan shook itself and rattled like a giant egg bursting to hatch. And all that time a radio drummed. Yet no other voice answered the scream, it seemed that one person alone was fighting for breath in such a shut wheeled box.

It might have seemed strange indeed to those passing by—a returning quarryman, a fisherman with his day's catch. These would have passed along the lochside road where the water stretched still and deep and flat towards the island, where inland dark masses of slate-wall towered instantly above the road—and in the moonlit stillness, with not a movement for miles around, they would have seen the one eggish caravan-box yellow with light, shaking and thundering and rocking to burst.

The fisherman, a magistrate retired into those western highlands and in ways an imaginative man, might have paused and noticed the paradox of such a bubble commotion. He might have thought: This is a cartoon film. An animated caravan goes wild, soon eyes will appear on it, feet will grow themselves, and the thing will be off grunting up the mountains with puffs of steam at its skidding heels. Or he might have thought, more soberly: This great outcropping of slate, this mineral and jagged-shaped land is the moon, a dead lunar basin, and here suddenly has arrived the gondola of a space-ship yellow with the electricity of a sunnier world. But in neither case would he have been quite right—the scene was too desolate, the screams too painful for a comparison as light as a cartoon: and the loch and the slate outcrop, though dark and grave, were never as arid as a lunar landscape.

The quarryman might have been nearer to his guess. He would have thought: caravanners, townsfolk tourists, and the missus giving the old man hell. But then he might have paused to wonder—what about the old man, why didn't he give her a piece of his mind back? He listened, but hard as he listened he heard no man's voice. So he passed on, nodding his head and more then ever convinced that there was no understanding such gadabouts from the town.

Yet, all the time, there was a man inside the caravan.

Ruth Ross and her husband had driven out of Edinburgh six days before. A holiday in the Highlands. The first for two years. High spirits. And under a full moon they had driven slowly through the last of the lowlands, tasted the first stone-crop, drawn closer together as from the road they looked down from rising highland at their first wide loch—and it had seemed strangely like a second honeymoon driving together into new adventure, and with the caravan jogging behind its intimate insistent song of a home-for-two. That was the beginning, when the moon was generous and full. But some evenings later the moon was dangerously on the wane, its excitement and its pull were over, the charge in the air was weakening and they had driven that day through the wasteland Rannoch Moor. For mile after mile this sodden brownish flatness had frowned, a place of awful desolation, an endless Flandersland torn and shredded, treeless and split with sad ponds jagged as mirror-scraps, a limitless bog corrupted by the slow bombardment of reed and roving moss. As through this they motored, cramped and silent after a day on the road, the long journey to the horizon lost itself on a wraithing of the sun's last grumbling red, in a melancholy haze that offered only some hopeless homeless trudge over the end of the earth's crust into nothing. Such an emptiness echoed the vacuum in Ruth's evening throat, such a dying sunlight the sulk of boredom mounting. She lit a cigarette, difficult in the car-draught, then drew in the smoke tasteless on a dry tongue. She turned to her husband, drawn-mouthed at the wheel, opened her mouth to speak and instead turned away. The engine vibrated, shook its noise ceaselessly into her ears, into every fibre of her body. And now their road that

188

passed across the moor turned away and struck into the mountains, into the precipitous dark pass of Glencoe.

A heavy coat weighed like too many bedclothes her body, it ached like a bruise: the car's hood, canvassed and strapped, made an oppressive low ceiling; and now those mountains, peaks bent together like monstrous whisperers in caps of great conical judgment, hemmed in the thin ribbon road and its mite-sized motor. There hung still about the place a story of massacre and death. So with this claustrophobic progression, with the constriction of a day's drive, and with the old unseen moon itself dying in her veins— Ruth felt a screaming to be out of it and into wider air. The scream rose but was never uttered. Her husband's voice said evenly:

— Look—there on the right. That's where they slaughtered them, you can still see the foundations of the cottages . . . the very foundations. . . .

But there are moments in travelling when nothing is more valuable than a cup of tea, when the unique wonder there at last before one's eyes may be shrugged away for the moment's comfort—and Ruth now speeding past the bloody patch of massacre saw no vision of treachery but a few scattered stones and the mountainside split with dry stream-clefts.

— Can't you for God's sake step on it?

She saw Ross's face look surprised, then grow cold and most calmly smiling:

— *Nothing* would give me greater pleasure. One gets a *real* feeling for a place at forty miles an hour. . . .

She was then sorry, wanted to press his arm. But she could only manage:

— Thoughtless—sorry, I'm so tired.

— *Entendu.*

He had stopped that cold smile, but the posed word punctuated too drily an unpleasant moment. No sympathy, no understanding of her feelings. He drove on wrapped up in himself. Easily found words—'smug' and 'self-satisfied'—pressed her lips thinner and angrier. They drove on then in silence—the woman burning cold, the man distant and self-engaged.

But the pass at length ended, and they were out in the fresh open of Loch Leven. The lake lay grey and smooth to their right, greener hills rose wetly misted on the left; several grey ladylike houses stood surrounded by their moist girdles of fir. They drove past the hotel, past a row of dwarf white cottages, past a group of cyclists flatting along in wide plastic capes. Ruth said suddenly:

— Darling, I've had enough. Couldn't we park down here?

— But heavens—we settled on Ballachulish, it's wider there, it's finer . . .

— Won't this do? There's a hotel, it's sheltered, comfortable—

— There's a hotel at North Balla.

— I've had enough . . .

— But surely—only three or four miles more? It wouldn't hurt?

— Three or four too many. I've had it.

— Couldn't you . . .?

— No.

He braked viciously, skidded on the wet road, recovered, slewed the wheel round, lumbered the car up on to the turf. The engine cut out. In the silence, sudden and heavy after the hours of throbbing, her voice came clear and carefully deep:

— Clever.

— Indeed. And clever always to accept the second-rate by not holding out. Clever to choose any mediocre dump when what you know about can be got with a trifle of patience. Clever, too, to pass up your history at hell's god-damned miles the hour—

— Oh quiet!

— Right.

And that spoken through gripped teeth, was his last word for a long time.

In silence they unpacked. Ross got out the buckets and, carefully looking away across the lake, went off to fetch water. She was left to light the stove and prepare supper. When the time arrived for opening tins he was not back. She stood with the tin-opener in her hand. Tin-opening comes curiously into the category of 'a man's job'. Now, though not helpless, she made herself feel so. A new resentment rose.

She gave a long martyred sigh. Then, crouching a little to see out of the caravan window, still with the silver-shining baked beans and the rusted tin-opener in her hands, she looked round at where they had come to. It was surprising then to see that, though they had arrived with the lake to one side and the green hills to the other, they had in fact stopped on the edge of territory of a very different character. There rose up immediately above them no green hill but instead a high dark buttress of stone and slate, a thing mounting dizzily high as a shipyard crane and like one for the feeling of an engineering work it gave—though as she looked, uneasily, she could not quite see what it was for the dark, she only felt the size and shadow as it buttressed almost vertically out from the hillside. And on the other side of the road, opposite this thing, and forming with it a sort of gateway into some distinct district beyond—rose a high moraine of slate humped like a monstrous animal. Even the character of the lake was changed—a pier ran out, a rotting desolate wooden thing.

She shrugged her shoulders and returned to her contemplation of the lid of that tin. But now, feeling some return to normal things, she jammed in the blade and swiftly and easily made her satisfying circle round the silver-yielding surface. A rattling outside, and Ross was back with the water.

— Hello, she said.

He said nothing, only looked up at her with eyebrows arched, looked at her steadily and then away. His cheeks seemed sucked in. She shrugged her shoulders again and turned away to the stove. He sat down on the side-seat and took out his notebook. In his spare time he wrote touring articles for motor-magazines, and now he began to itemize a skeleton of the day's passage. Of the arrival at Loch Leven he wrote:

— A sea loch. Tidal. Shallow strands of orange seaweed. Cows in this, swans among cows. Pebble beach to boggish surround. Grass-grown disused jetty. Loch-water (6 p.m.) brown-grey like oiled dark armour. White cottages small enough for dwarfs (cf. Little folk, Scotland last resort of fairy kings?). Hereabouts purest Gaelic spoken. Green-bushed wet hills, half cut off by mist, how high? Clouds low like canvas-weighed balloon. . . .

Ruth passed and looked over his shoulder. She read and made a groaning laugh:

— God, is that the best you can do? Look out there!

She pointed through the window. For a moment startled beyond his reticence he glanced up, saw the dark landscape just visible beyond the curtains. But only looked her coldly in the face, moved the scalp on his head as if smoothing the thought of her away, and returned to his notes. She raised her voice:

— It looks like scree, it's all jagged and broken and loose. Scree. Is it?

He sighed, but made no other answer. He wrote:

— Along the lake lies Ballachulish, slate-quarrying town. Agglomerations of broken slate like slag heaps. Truck-shoots, harbour, railhead—

Put out, to change the subject she moved away and grumbled—just as if she had been waiting with the meal for some time:

— Well for God's sake come and have your supper. Your supper'll *get cold.*

Quietly he shut his notebook and moved along the cushions to where a flap-table was lowered. She had neither finished laying this table nor even started putting out the food—and so it was four minutes before his plate was set before him. During this time he sat doing, with much point, nothing. So that in fact he did much—he sat staring exactly at one point of the cellulosed wall in front of him, never for a moment moving his head, while on the cloth his left hand circulated in silence a wooden pepper-pot. When his plate arrived he took up instantly his knife and fork and started. No sighs of 'at last', no grimace—the rhythm of relaxing just when the plate arrived was enough.

Ruth frowned, filled her own plate; cleared up a little round the stove, rattled her meaning, and finally took the seat opposite him:

— Now perhaps *I* can sit down.

He said nothing, nor interrupted his eating. She looked at his plate and saw how he had mashed the fried potatoes wet into brown sauce. She shuddered. Together then for some minutes in silence they ate.

He had opened his notebook again, his eyes never left the page, he forked the food into his mouth sideways without looking at it. He read and ate without hurry, apparently absorbed, showing no

sign of irritation, nor taking any notice at all of her presence. But
several times she looked up at him—and now saw only those features
that disgusted her. In other moods she would have chosen to see
more affirmative features—but now there was only the odd length
of his jaw, a scurfed dryness of hairs at his neck, the fountain pen
clipped on the outside breast pocket of his papery tweed coat. She
saw the sickly hot brown mash of sauced potato going into the pink
of his open mouth—and watched the slow relish with which he
tasted and slobbered it down inside.

In such a cellulose box there was little room. The night outside,
the clear country of fresh smells stretched wide and free somewhere
far off. The polished cream walls bent down, on the narrow table
their plates touched, their bodies grew in her cramped mind to fill
the small space, there seemed not air enough to breathe. Yet even
then—worse than his physical presence was his mental absence. To
be ignored so easily, plainly with no acting effort on his part, grated
up on her the need to strike.

So that suddenly, first as a gesture but in the same second gathering true force, she dropped her knife and fork clattering and staining
the cloth, leant back heavily against the wall, jerked the table—
and his knife cutting meat slipped. He looked up, eyes blank in
remote question, stared at her long and steadily then turned again
down smoothly to his notes. She gripped her teeth, quietly swore and
flung her hand back at the cupboard handle above the cushion.
Without turning round, still staring at him, she opened the door and
had her fingers on the whisky bottle.

She poured herself a half-glassful and drank it off. Then began,
grumbling up to a shout:

— I suppose I'm not worth talking to? I suppose I'm some sort of
a dummy? I'm only your bloody wife. I only cook the bloody food.
Go on, stuff your bloody self full of it. You wouldn't sit there
like that with any other woman, Christ would you? WOULD
YOU?

He looked up, again long and steadily, then without any sign of
recognition turned back to his notes. She leaned forward, a greedy
reckless mouthing on her face:

— You wouldn't sit like that if I was your precious Elizabeth, would you, your precious bloody blonde Lizbitch. Would you? WOULD YOU?

The skin at his temples flinched back, he looked now too smooth, he was holding himself. Too carefully he turned, too soundlessly, a page. Once, discussing at what seemed a trustful objective moment their two past lives, he had mentioned Elizabeth, an early love: she had never forgotten—and Elizabeth, part of the past and unattainable, a kind of golden age myth to Ruth, had become a repeated subject of explosion. In fact, he had almost forgotten what this Elizabeth had looked like—and so Ruth's emphasis, because it had nothing to do with a truth, became on top of its dreadful repetition doubly exasperating. It was meaningless. And always on and on she went:

— It's always been Elizabeth with you, hasn't it? You wouldn't be likely to forget *her*, would you? Why in the hell didn't you marry her? Why—I—can't—think. Or was it *she* didn't want to? She saw what was coming—I'll give her that, she saw what a smug-faced, self-satisfied bore she had coming. Look at you, sitting there—why don't you open your bloody mouth?

She sat erect, back not touching the cushions, braced, eager. Bristling up like a fighting bird, breathing hard. He raised his eyes and hers were there staring straight unflinching and too bright into his—he tried to fix them but found his own instead fixed, her fury sucked the strength from him. Unjust then that he feeling guiltless should have to turn down uncomfortably his eyes—physically it gave her the truth. So—still keeping an embattled silence—he allowed himself the relief of a smile, a thin amusement of the corner of a lip.

But instantly Ruth took this as a weakness, she had been looking for it—and it stopped her shouting. She had had her effect. She leant back against the cushions, pretending ease and time, nodding. Twice, long and scornfully, she swore: 'God!' At such a moment one can act in two ways. One can act unselfconsciously, exercising the body without the mind, as one stretches purely one's arms on waking from sleep: or selfconsciously, as one can stretch one's arms imagining the stretch, romanticizing the stretching, seeing in the mind's eye how dramatically it shapes. It was in this second way that Ruth now poured herself another drink, another half-glassful.

She knew and felt every mocking expression of her lips, every breath of scorn, each snap of her eyes. Nor did these gestures suffer from their actedness, rather they were strengthened.

But they needed finality, a dropping of the dramatic curtain. That creature opposite might respond in slight ways, she could see him even now uncomfortable—but he would never break. Only by drumming, drumming, drumming on the same insistent note could she goad him inside to some sort of pain, and so draining that whisky she raised again her voice and repeated and repeated what she knew he had heard before. Beginning to move with it too, swaying on her seat, thumping the table, turning on with one flat sharp stroke the wireless switch, flooding thus the caravan with sound against his silence—so that again he moved his hand wearily across his forehead. And suddenly she wrenched herself up, pulling at the same time the table-cloth, crashing down plates and food and the mess of gravy, shaking the caravan, screaming. He looked up again, now tapped his head, made the expression of wincing from her—and this only set her screaming the louder, she took up a tea-pot and threw it against the wall, and as so much sound and violence crashed away out of her that same very need for finality overtook her own senses, the known act was flushed over with hysteria, the room took charge mounting into a headache and a blackening of light—until she could only get to the door and fling this open and, screaming, bundle down the steps into the night air.

The width of the night cleared her head—she still ran on, but stumbled little, and her lungs drew in deep cool breaths. Sobs came now like the echo of sobs, no longer forced out but dribbling like a stream that falls empty. It was quite light, still a half-moon. The two great barrows of slate rose huge and sharply black. Smells of mist came from the turf and the near wet hill, a drift of sea-smell from the salt loch. She ran on in between those great pylons of slate —and found a road snaking in between high walls of the stuff. No grass, no trees—only the metal road, the mineral slate piled high on each side, the moon-sky above—the breathless overpowering alley of a bad dream. Such monstrous piles of shattered stuff might move in: the beginnings of panic took her breath again. So that when she saw a declivity in the wall, and a high wooden gate, she broke off to it—it was shut, but there was an opening to the side and up a mound, she slipped through and climbed a few feet. And suddenly found herself out in the open, facing a great space that should not have been there, space that should have been mountain, dream-country found through a forbidden gate. A mountain-side had been torn away and in the half-mile crater left there dropped, deep and cold, a still mineral lake glowing deep green in the moonlight, bounded only by precipice, a lunar-scape of frightful width and depth. She paused a moment, unbelieving, her mind cleared, horrified. Then, drawn by her horror, she began slowly, excitedly, to move in towards it.

Back in the caravan, that husband sat for some minutes staring at the wall in front of him. Notes now forgotten. Muddled by noise and violence. Furious at her lack of logic. Angry at the wider injustice. Shamed by his own quiet cruelty. Emasculated by his failure to play a prettier and larger-hearted part.

Such rows always sucked him in—and though in a way he had started this one with his tight silence, he would dearly like to have relented, to have played the big heart giving in. But he was no proof against the goading, and now he felt too weak to marshal and examine what had been said. Thus at much of a loss he got up and slowly began tidying the breakage. This took him several minutes, he placed the broken pieces of china neatly on top of one another, for no purpose it seemed, only perhaps because not thinking he was trying to think. Thus it was a full five minutes before he found himself outside the caravan, suddenly aware of the night, and not knowing what had brought him there. He first thought of re-entering the trailer to try and remember—but instead paused, and walked a few steps further up the turf.

Why did Ross go to the door at that particular moment? Why did he take those few further steps along the turf? He certainly never knew himself: though afterwards he liked to wonder. Perhaps, without fully realizing it, he heard her faint cry coming from the quarry? Perhaps an aural sense, as with some animals, recorded sounds too subtle to be registered by the conscious brain? Or did he respond instead to a telepathic pull exerted by his wife's great danger—such energies undoubtedly existed. Or was it something less palpable— regret, now that there had been a breathing space, a move towards her? Or a feeling that he had won and could afford thus to make up? But these last two would not easily have accounted for his going out at that precise moment. Perhaps it was simply coincidence—that still exists. But however it was he did go out, and walked nearer the quarry, and from somewhere beyond those lowering pylons heard distinctly the hopeless echo of her second long wailing cry. He broke into a run, then raced in through the slate. He passed right by that door she had entered, he raced on through the slate mounds out into a wasteland beyond.

It was no wasteland, but the beginning of the quarrying village, the outcrop of the quarrying works. Everything slate—cottages roofed in slate, walled with slate, the ground about surfaced with slate-chips, small piles of slate about, huts of slate disused, old chimneys of slate. A desolate horseshoe harbour of slate-coloured water, the hills beyond dark slate and the moon-cold sky slate. Yet here in this waste people lived, yellow lights shone steady like cats' eyes from the dark cottages. But nobody was about. Ross stood there breathing hard, lost, not knowing which way to go.

But then again the cry came, now several times, anguished and failing. His name he thought he heard. He turned back, swifter now for knowing, quickly found the gateway, quickly climbed up and faced abruptly, as she had, that gigantic lunar chasm. Once more the cry came, echoing up the cliffs, down somewhere from the deeply silent water.

His eyes strained to the echo, to the wide precipitous walls. Their dark slate was flecked with white brilliant marble. Now he saw suddenly one of these flecks move. His breath went, it had moved two hundred sheer feet aloft. But then he saw further another move, and then a movement half a mile across the moon-green water. Goats. Not knowing what to do, he began scrambling down the slate-scree towards the water-edge below: and scrambling slipped: and slithering on down-flying scree, as on an erratic escalator, in his unbalance realized what most likely must have happend to Ruth.

Those slates clattered down hollowly echoing in the great lunar basin. Hearing their hard echo he felt his own danger. But for the green water so far below he did not know where his slope led. If to be any help he must clutch first his own balance—what precipice lay just below he could not see: he flung himself off his unsteady feet, he splayed his body out on the running slate and slowed himself, his eyes took in what was now more slowly passing and he saw a red projection that he could grasp. He caught it, his hand slipped on rust, then held.

He had grasped a light railway line. Breathless, bruised, he half-sat up and looked more surely round and down. In the moon it was quite light, dark shadows cut everywhere. But queerly in such a slate place and in waning moonlight some colours came out bright —the green water, and now the pale brown-red rust of rails, they led up and down slopes, they ran far round the edge of that chasmic depth of water. Rails, he saw, for small tip-wagons; and he saw standing about everywhere like the noiseless goats themselves such small reddish trucks. Derricks there were too, like long-necked birds, and rusted spiked winches lying like the husks of giant urchins. The cry came again—and his eyes went to the water. Into that monstrous green lake he saw a bridge stretched far out, a promontory more, an embankment upon which a rail of trucks stood and which ended abruptly in the centre of deep water. It was as though the embankment, the bridge had broken off—it gave dizzily the nightmare feeling of a bridge ending in the centre of space, of night, of deep water. But no cry came from there, it was far—yet it contained within itself a character of terror greater than all the rest of that place, it spoke the note of nowhereness, of indirection in a manless land where things ended suddenly nowhere, where nothing was safe and though moveless everything might suddenly lurch into motion. Then he saw that the water was moving.

First it looked as though all of it moved, then it was only a wide ripple forging out from the bank just beneath. That rail led straight down. He could see its course. Shuffling and sliding urgently he put himself into motion down the rail and to the end, where it tapered into the water—and where something clung and moved, where he was sure it was Ruth. Nearer, he saw her head in the water, saw white hands clutching the broken-off ends of the rail—and simul-

taneously heard behind a creaking and rumbling as, at first ponderously then moving slowly into faster motion, the iron wheels of a
disturbed wagon gathered momentum to pound down from above.

He could see now how on the green luminiscent water her dark
hair flowed out in a fan: now no cry—her face lay it seemed flat on
water, she hung at full stretch only by soft hands on the rail. And
Ross, who had forgotten all their differences, who felt for her so that
he could never have known them, who ached only to bring her out
of that water to himself and safe warmth, Ross who heard now the
blunt iron wagon rumbling down from above—how it had moved,
what rail might have been pulled, what slates disturbed he never
wondered, he knew simply it was coming—Ross saw how the only
way to save her was to hurt her further. Time only was important,
to get to her fast. So he let go the rail and in his last jumping slide
could not care how many slates fell sharp on her arms—until he
had his fists hitting hard on her fingers.

Silently they let go the rail and with her gently sank.

Beneath the breathless water Ross reached her and kicked his
legs in two great thrusts to move from where the truck would plunge
in after them. But that truck above wheeled in fact slower, the rails
themselves had levelled out at the end to be there uptwisted for
greater safety—the truck groaned to a tired halt. He made the
effort to the bank in hard strokes against the cold: but clutched there
only slates that loosed themselves as he grasped at them. So again
it was the rails—and by these, slowly, through minutes of cold wet
and bruising and lung-torn effort he laboured her body up against
the bank and out. It was a further time before he could get again
strength to hoist himself up. But then they were out.

She was nowhere near drowned, hardly any water loosened from
her mouth as he worked her arms about. Doing this, though, he
praised the earth—the slates on which she lay, the red-dust of the
wagon-slide, the iron wheels by her head. All that had seemed
fearful now befriended him, such elements were dry and airful
compared with the abyss of wet deep cold water.

Signs of colour showed in her white lax face. He shifted her head to
a smoother slate. Her hair dragged wet—and this too might in its pull
have helped to revive her the faster. At length she opened her eyes.

For a while they stayed staring straight up at the deep sky. She might have seen there a long thin cloud drawn like a windless line high above. This might have shown her the sky, for soon after her eyes turned slowly and saw instead of sky his head bent over above. A light came into them, a soft lightening of relief, and he murmued: 'Ruth, Ruth—it's me.'

She said nothing but her lips moved into a smile, a slow luxurious smile—and a small groan came, as if she was waking from a deep and pleasant sleep. He tried to warm her in those ice-wet clothes. He kept repeating, like some warm secret, her name, and she only smiled.

It must have hurt her, as thawing aches, when the full warmth began to come back. For suddenly gaining strength—she had not been drowned, but really no more than shocked and fainted—she forced herself up and leaning looked round. A frown began:

— . . . where, where? What happened? What happened?

She looked round fearful as that landscape dawned on her again. But it looked now more predictable, she had met it and it had acted. Ross watched her face carefully as the fear left it—and as the frown reappeared. He murmured:

— You slipped right in. I fished you out.

— In there?

— You were hanging on the edge, you sank—

— You should never have let me come. Never.

This last she said with definition, a tired bitterness in her voice. Slowly her face took on its old assurance. He watched with wonder the disapproval and the bitterness come naturally back. She repeated:

— Why did you let me come? A lot you cared. . . .

She could not, he knew, have known anything of his part in it— the truck, that time underneath the water. She was shocked, done up. Yet what allowances he might have made dissolved under the old look her face took on so easily, the look of their bad hours, the unforgiving goading disapproval of all sour evenings. Return to normal. An impossible normal. He was astonished—but his lips set themselves and beyond all other feelings a rage came. But he managed to say still softly:

— Come on, darling—up, we've got to get back, get off your wet things—

— For God's sake let me alone!

But she rose up with him, half-shrugging away his arm. Still weak she kept muttering: he heard it only as spite, words to shame him. Suddenly he stood still, his arm round her. And the idea came to him then.

Carefully he listened to the silence away for miles around them. But there was no sound. There was no movement. The village was hidden. There was no soul about. His arm gripped round her tight, his mind cold with steady anger raced back over his journey into that place. No one had seen him. Even if they had, there was nothing to show that he had not simply come to her forlorn help. He looked down at the water, it seemed to glow a deeper green, a welcome shone coldly from it as flat surfaces of water welcome what might be thrown in.

He drew in his breath and moved his arm further behind her— they were still no more than a few feet away from the deep edge— and looked for the last time round that basin of loneliness. Then, quite suddenly, she raised her free hand and made a gesture to move the hair from her eyes, to smooth open her brow. A movement well known to him, simple, a gesture both efficient and helplessly feminine.

And then it was over.

He began to walk slowly up the slate-ramp. Something like a mixture of pity and endurance, something between a knowledge of all the long time that must be lived by all people and how pitiful they must be alone in all that time, something near to compassion had come to him. As he walked up, back to their caravan, he clutched her wet small shoulder much closer to him.

A Game of Billiards

I^T is not easy to say whether this is the account of how Patten met his wife: or of why she in particular became his wife. Perhaps both.

In the mind or heart of everyone there is thought to exist an archetype to whom he or she inevitably is attracted—an archetype founded on the vision of some early strange face that once leaned down to entertain the pram with its first erotic shock. That is one belief. Otherwise—and one is tempted to think otherwise in Patten's case—a man's first meeting with a woman may coincide with a certain moment of distended nerve, of enlarged comprehension— and simply because of this the meeting assumed an exaggerated significance, personalities are photographed on a more deeply sensitive plate.

How many times do we meet and pass by those whom possibly we could love—because the moment of impact is dulled by circumstance, by a sloth of digestion, an empty pocket, a complacence of spirit! Yet—had the moment been propitious, a free moment of joy, of shock! . . . However.

That Monday Patten was forced to lunch late. It was already two o'clock by the time he had settled into his veal loaf and salad. By five past two this was finished. He refused the cheese, and asked instead for a glass of beer. The saloon bar was empty—other lunchers had already left, a few week-end drinkers had dawdled finally away. About the enamel-white counter, the tired scarlet of the stools, the yellow plaster crab-shell, the up-curling sandwiches and a last strand of parsley on an empty plate—there hovered a ticking of long, clock-long tedium. Under dark Victorian over-shelves a barmaid and a pale chef stood side by side, not talking. Upon everyone and everything was engraved one inevitable fact— that until three o'clock the room must remain open.

A GAME OF BILLIARDS

For Patten too there was an hour—a van was calling for him at three. Patten had no particular worry, nor was he unwell—but suddenly he saw the long lonely prospect and saw it so clearly he clenched his hand till the knuckle-bones flushed in their white. There were things to do—he could get a hair-cut, he could walk out on to the Monday pavements of the red-brick suburb, he could look in shop windows. But nothing seemed worth the effort. An afternoon neither hot nor cold, under a low sky, depressive and of no interest. He looked round him. Not a paper anywhere. Boredom on the barmans' face—no small talk. No cat. And so it was with relish that as he sipped his beer he remembered he had not been to the Gentlemen's for some time. He welcomed the definition of such need, put down the beer and made for the stairs.

The way to the lavatory, as with many such large Victorian houses, led through the billiards room. And on pushing the frosted glass door to this, Patten was surprised—in that emptiness almost shocked—to see there a man holding a cue. The room was never used now—it lay shrouded and in an upstairs manner deserted. He was in fact so surprised, feeling in some way an intruder, that he felt bound to greet the man—the greeting of two on a lonely road.

Like a townsman to a countryman, he turned away his face awkwardly as soon as he had spoken—vaguely perturbed too that he should have said 'Good afternoon' instead of 'Good morning'; it all depended on whether the fellow had taken his lunch or not. It seemed a long time after, when he had crossed the long linoleum past the table and had his hand already on the brass door-plate, that there came from behind him the words:

'*Good* day.'

At first it sounded like a correction. But the words were most amicably spoken, with a pleased purr to the first of them, and Patten turned and nodded back. The man had straightened upright and was looking at him—he must have stood thus throughout Patten's long walk across the floor. He was a large man—in his first glimpse Patten called to mind a type of Dutch or Scandinavian sailor, large and pale-eyed, the evocation of the 'big Swede' with solid breadth never quite controlled by his sombre suit of Lutheran grey. But this man was plainly affable; he smiled and said across the room:

'You're not going, are you?'

Patten of course laughed and went on through the door. A few seconds later he looked up at the grilled window and frowned. An extraordinary thing? Hadn't the man been leaning over the table in an attitude of play? And there had been no ball? And wasn't the table under its dust-cover? He tried hard to draw his mind back to the ball—he would have seen the polished round of white or red? It was odd? Then he shook his head—of course the man had been balancing the cue for weight, or measuring the floorspace, or so forth.

But when he opened the door again there was the man crouched across the table, now almost lying across it, his cue reaching hard for nothing. And just then the grey-suited arm gave a short jab, the man sighed, and grunting his effort lumbered down off the table. He shook his head at Patten.

'Sorry about that. But there isn't a rest anywhere.'

Patten's eye turned to the wall-bracket, looking automatically for the serrated head of a cue-rest. He stopped himself, and laughed. Then walking on towards the door said:

'I don't think your opponent will mind, anyway.'

'Oh, but he does. Binder's very particular. And rules are rules, after all.'

To Patten, reasonably polite but in no lively mood, this was taking the joke a little too far. Irritating to underline the thing. So he said nothing further, merely nodded, not smiling. But now the big man had shifted himself round to the door; to pass, Patten was forced to move to one side. The man moved to one side, too, jumbling the approach as of two people meeting on a pavement. Above all now not wanting to raise his head or smile, Patten moved the other way. The man moved too. Patten struggled a 'sorry' and then looked up into the pale blue eyes above him. The man simply stood there, eyes fixed on him, unconfused. It was plain that he was blocking the way.

As their eyes met, the big man smiled again:

'Please don't go. It's most fortunate, most fortunate indeed—you can score. It'll be a great help.'

They were still some paces apart. Patten took a step backward—now snake-cold and alert, simultaneously conscious of the position of the door, its handle, the man's size, the bare extent of that great room, the drop from such first-floor windows, the grille of the lavatory skylight. For that large man had spoken in a voice too high, too small, too excited. A loving tone seemed to coax it high, his muscular bloodless lips stretched back wide with the smile of a man relishing food; the pale eyes shone hard with brilliant, sad desire. He was mad.

At times in the past Patten had day-dreamed of this, of meeting a wild animal or a burglar or a madman. He had rehearsed his moves—and he had always shivered and sweated at the intense picture. He had always imagined that really in such a situation he would crumble instantly. But now—surprisingly—it was the opposite. He felt capable, alert, strong. After all, the rehearsals had been of use. Now he smiled as hugely, as fixedly as the man standing so still and eager above him:

'Billiards eh? Now that sounds like something. What's the game —a hundred up?'

'That's right.'

'And what's the score so far?'

'Score?'

'Yes—how many are you?'

The smile left the man's face, he looked sly—but as instantly a new smile came, faltering then pushing his lips forward in confidence. He whispered over:

'Twenty.'

Patten nodded. He was going to change the subject, carefully, from billiards—somehow get the man interested and over towards the window. He went on:

'And the other chap?'

'Binder?'

Again the slyness, and this time a huge hand, grey-fleshed but strong as the rest of him, curved up to hide a high chuckle. He looked for a moment like a man with hiccups, absorbed with some physical movement inside him. Then the eyes glittered in amusement:

'Sixteen!'

'Good for you—'

'Shh!'

A pause, while again Patten nodded. He kept nodding auto-matically. Then suddenly he looked over straight at the window, made an urgent pointing movement. He shouted:

'Lord, look at that! A ship!'

The man paid no attention. He was squinting at the tip of his cue, measuring it.

'Did you see? A ship! Sails, flags!'

Patten thrashed his finger at the window. The man looked up, vaguely:

'How could there be a ship? It's a street, you're seeing things.'

'But . . .'

'Couldn't we start now?'

Patten's arm lowered; it was no good, the man showed no interest at all. He looked only vague, as though he did not understand or that what Patten had said was so far from his world that it held no real meaning. It might take hours before the right diversion was found for such a mind. So Patten changed his tactics. He pulled up his sleeves and rubbed his wrists in energetic preparation.

'Good. Let's start. Over to the table with you.'

But the man stood still, shaking his head. Patten tried again:

'Look, I'll just slip down and get a drink. Be right up. What's yours?'

Now the man frowned. With his fingers, with a slow controlled movement, he balanced the cue in an arc so that it pointed to Patten's face. His fingers manipulated their stiff rotation, one protruded, a fetish of grace in the way muscular men, sailors and others of precise craft, hold with formal elegance a drinking-cup. He spoke softly:

'You're trying to get out of it. It's not fair. I shouldn't if I were you.'

His other hand had been holding the green chalk. Now—it was probably a thoughtless gesture, it was difficult to decide how much the man thought—he raised this hand to his face and with one extended finger rubbed the lid of his right eye. The slender cue was still pointed to Patten's face. The lid of the man's eye became

206

smeared—absurdly yet with some of the sinister mask of all grease-paint—with an ill chalked green.

Patten's assurance jumped like a gulp in the throat—and vanished. The man was violent. This had always been possible—but part of the old day-dreams and the rehearsals had implied that all danger was superable and that the dream-Patten's tactics would know a walk-over victory. Beyond this there were no resources. Now this man threatened; he imagined the point of the cue prodding into his soft eye—what had been self-command more than courage shrivelled, he backed away from the big man, shrinking with the dispirit of youth before authority.

And like authority the great grey-faced man in his sober suit strode over to the table. Patten saw his size now not only as muscle, but as schoolmasters had once been bigger than he: monuments of reserve, voracious, at a move they would spring into sharp action—contempt cold in their knowing eyes, words of ridicule on their dry lips.

Yet this was momentary, an illusion of Patten's as his chest seemed to shrink and his eyes falter, as dutifully he backed to where the little score-markers winked their varnish on the wall—for the man had already forgotten and was smiling excitedly as he stood to survey the position of balls that were not there. He shook his head and pursed his lips, acknowledging a difficult stroke. He bent over and with precision aimed his cue, paused, jabbed the air an inch from the cloth. Then straightened himself and turned to Patten in triumph:

'Cannon! My shot again, I think.'

Patten marked up the score, only quickly glancing at the figure, not daring to turn his back.

The man played on. And on and on. He made no mistake—the sequence of play became endless. He played slowly, with many pauses and much thought, with suppressed pursing of the lips as the invisible ball seemed nearly to miss its objective, with sudden chuckles of pleasure and a triumphant toss of the head when a difficult stroke was with ease achieved. He muttered to himself, grunted an occasional remark to Patten. The score rose—but slowly. Patten stood still and moved up the little markers. Sometimes now he looked at them, they took on an appearance of freedom; he envied the ease with which they bobbed so simply up and down the long slots. How different, this freedom of the little markers!

But with his captor absorbed, at least the hard tension of fear became relaxed—the room opened out again to him and he grew to know it too well. Deserted, upstairs, of solemn quiet purpose, its atmosphere hung veiled like a face from former years.

The table in the centre shrouded like the emblem of an old feast; the walls recessive with long judicial seats dreaming from their raised platforms; a monstrous marble clock dead on the mantelpiece; the cold echo of carpetless dust-aged floors; gaunt knob-headed coat-stands guarding the corners, a frayed green curtain muffling the door, no blinds on windows strutted with machinery for the winding and opening of their upper lights. From these windows a grey north light paled into the room, the door curtain denied that there was ever a door. It might have been a room far away in an empty house, with time stopped.

But Time? Time—Patten thought suddenly how it must be half-past two, how at three o'clock the last chance of someone coming up to the lavatory would be gone, the public house would close down on even the little unheard life it had, and he would be left with the long silent hours of afternoon. And then suddenly he flinched at a new thought—what when the game was finished, when the steadily growing hundred was up?

'Pocket for the red! Mother'll be pleased as Punch. You should see her when she hears about *this*. . . . There we go again, cannon and in. . . .'

Muttering always in his high voice, he moved round the table. He stood back to chalk his cue, he clambered again on the table, he winked round at Patten with his one greenish eyelid. Once he came round to where Patten stood, aimed a shot from there—so that his back was turned, his head bent down, and Patten could see the grey solid neck with its blond ash of hair. So vulnerable. A moment —then! . . . but it passed, it could not be risked, one never knew the resources of strength such men might have.

208

Watching him, Patten felt himself seeing the balls, following the play as if it had been real. Only occasionally a noise came muffled through the window to bring him to his senses. A loud lorry passing, the excited quick clatter of a woodseller's donkey racing by, and once the distant cry—so forlorn a note of empty streets—of a rag-and-bottle man. How near the street was! And it was at a moment such as this—when life seemed again so absurdly close, just beneath the window which he dared not even approach—that a sudden and so simple idea occurred to him. He gritted his teeth for not thinking of it before. He began to move the markers backwards instead of forwards.

Thus at least a respite. Time now. And once more he began to look round the room. How much time? If no one came, then till five o'clock, six o'clock, later—until some man had drunk enough to have to come? The long hours of afternoon perpetuated themselves, the colourless middle-day light forecast their slow unshadowed monotony. A line of black electric meter boxes high up on the wall stared down at him and stated they would never move; the clock stayed uninterested under its veil of dust; the screen in the fireplace dozed its faded colours.

All these proclaimed themselves so reasonably of the everyday room, the parts of the house restful and undramatized—yet there pacing round the table, muttering, clicking his cue on the floor winking and prodding, moved this one incongruous figure. Sometimes, over the distance of the table, he seemed insignificant and overshadowed by the stillness: but at others, when he came near and Patten could hear as well as the muttering a deep breathing and a near rustle of muscle straining in clothes, he grew again huge and in Patten's fear seemed to fill the room.

Then the door opened.

It moved slowly—uncertain whether to open itself or not. But Patten's eyes were on the curtain in the first instant. He glanced quickly back at the large man—he was leaning over the table with his back to the door, eyes concentrated on the table. The door swung suddenly in a wide curve open. A young woman stood on the threshold. She stood outlined in some sort of pink and dark blue, some blouse and suit and hat, against the dust of the passage outside.

She stood quite still, looking round the room, herself probably uncertain—but in the long exultant second she seemed to Patten to be standing for her own revelation, she had made some great entrance and waited now for the hushed moment of astounded eyes and raised hearts and then for the thundered release of applause. She stood like the embodiment of all heroic rescue—the figure of sudden salvation, the sworded angel, the wanded silver-shining Queen of Goodness. In her pink dressy blouse and her blue serge skirt.

He wanted to shout, but his breath was away. And when at last he caught it and opened his mouth he had already realized that he must make no sound. The man was still leaning over the table. He would turn. She was a woman—she could only be the messenger for help. So quietly, opening his mouth wide and shining his eyes in a fixed large expression of greeting, he raised his left arm high at her and there held it. She saw the movement instantly. Her eyebrows made a sign of question. Patten made a little jigging of urgency with his body. He formed a soundless message with his mouth. Then with raised hand he made large jabs of pointing to the passage behind her and downstairs.

She understood immediately. Her mouth opened in a horrified little O. She understood that she must not make a sound because the man at the table was taking his shot. So she made no sound instead broke into a silent giggle, raised her hand to cup over her mouth, bent forward her body as if to contain further the dreadful sound, and then stopped—nodded to Patten meaningfully, grimaced, and backed quietly from the doorway, closing this behind her. She understood very well that this was the way to the Gentlemen's lavatory and that the Ladies' must be back along the passage.

But for Patten she was already hurrying down the stairs for help. His ears sang an excitement of praise for her, for a woman so quick to understand, so resourceful—yet calm enough to laugh! No fright, no fainting: in exaltation of relief she became impressed on his mind

—as it happened for ever—a figure of strength and colour in the grey afternoon, after the grey fear, in the dark doorway.

He did not know what kind of help she would bring—warders and white attendants and strait-jackets and leather-aproned barrel-trundlers advanced together in his mind: but then as they massed and became more certain they receded as rapidly into doubt and urgency . . . the large man had swung up from the table startled. The door had clicked. He jerked his head round to it, then moved it backwards and forwards looking or listening or smelling everywhere in startled animal jerks. He shouted high, stifled:

'What was that? Was someone there?'

Patten shrank into himself again, but managed:

'Nobody. You're hearing things.'

The man's great muscular brows jutted together in a harsh-cleft frown, shading the eyes so that deeper back they glittered:

'My ears are all right.'

Sound abruptly burst from everywhere. A great jangling amplified electric bell, earsplitting and mechanic. First silence, then abruptly starting nowhere this huge sound! The Time bell! Still wired to the billiards room! It split into the large man's head; he threw down his cue clattering on the floor; he swelled his chest up and with one wide bent simian arm clutched the precious shroud and wrenched its placid surface into great troubled waves. Nothing remained of his game. The bell still ringing, he began to walk heavily towards Patten.

'So it's time, is it? Time to stop?'

Patten began to move away from him, backwards, backwards round the table. The man walked at every step a little faster:

'When the bell goes, it's time to begin. . . .'

At least the table was a protection. He could move fast enough. It could go on for ever—it could only be a question of who first gave in—a dizzying vision came to him of minutes, hours spent circling that enormous table.

Then the bell as suddenly stopped. For the second time the door opened—this time it was burst open and there in his shirt-sleeves stood the landlord's son, short, shirt-sleeved, able, with a clipped black moustache. He was beginning to shout: 'Time now . . . please!' —when he saw the large man and whistled:

'Lord—Moony! How in the hell did you get out? Come along, Moony, there's a good chap. . . .'

He walked easily over to the large man. And the large man seemed to have collapsed his strength. He looked embarrassed, and even in that great body, shy. He started to shuffle over to the landlord's son, dragging his hand grudgingly like a bad boy along the table-cover.

'Just having a little game, a hundred up—'

The landlord's son took his arm:

'Now, now. You don't want to be playing today; you want to be in your room, nice and quiet—'

Big Moony let himself be led easily away: his face hung and his eyes looked down at his shambling feet. As they left through the door the landlord's son turned his head round to Patten, screwed up his little moustache, and with his free hand gave three short taps to his forehead.

There are dreams of the condemned cell, of all hope lost, of a final situation where nothing at all more can ever be done and the dreamer faces nothing and absolutely nothing but the end. And then —perhaps—the weight is magically lifted; the walls recede, the pursuing beasts dissolve, the falling viaduct resumes its road. Free air returns, all is relief! But after the first sweet thankfulness, very soon after—the dreamer looks round him and finds that there he is, indeed safe, but alone also, and with nothing and no one to use his freedom upon. The first need is for another person, someone to tell, someone upon whom to begin to exercise his new-found energies.

Thus with Patten in the billiards room. His chest drew in what felt like strong fresh air as those two left through the door and he looked round at the blessedly empty room. There was no question of not believing it was over—he believed it. He relished that empty room. Then gradually as he looked round the furniture assumed other identities—the locked windows no longer looked locked, the shrouded table shrank, the hat-stands ceased to loom but simply stood plain as hat-stands, the clock looked about to tick. He began to wonder how he could ever have been so enclosed. And then the room began to lose all significance, it became a worthless empty room, a silly place to be. Downstairs there would still be people, the second bell had not rung, he could hear distant laughter. He hurried to the door and to the stairs.

The stairs led straight down into the bar. There, spread out beneath, lay the familiar lighted place. In one corner two ladies laughed, emptying their last drinks. Looking down, he felt an irritation that his release had been so easy, that others had rescued him, that he himself had done nothing towards it. This agitated a greater need than ever to speak of it, to make more of it. He hurried down: and then saw a third lady join the others—it was his saviour in the satin blouse. He remembered her instantly. And he went straight up to her, flushed and smiling and powerful, to thank her and tell her the whole story.

At first the ladies were surprised, then awed, and finally the lady in the blouse broke down laughing. The barman laughed, too. Patten laughed. They all laughed in wonder and relief. Then the barman said how Moony had always been a bit touched, always a big boy for his mum; mum had died one night when Moony was having a game upstairs. He was strong; they gave him the cellar jobs in the pub.

'He wouldn't hurt a flea,' the barman said.

In a way, instead of making him feel foolish, this made it even better for Patten. He felt that it had been all right after all. And he addressed himself seriously to the lady in the pink blouse.

On Stony Ground

ONE moment with eyes blinking into the shade of that department store, one moment entering it and with head bowed thinking how I must insist on a particular seed and on no account be persuaded otherwise, and indeed seeing already the bright-coloured flowers grown up and wrestling in heady luxuriance—and the next morning standing in front of her who seemed then unquestionably the most beautiful of all, her in the pale khaki smock among the green-handled tools and bark benches of the garden accessory department.

At length I managed:

'Carnations . . . and pansies, Hoffman's Giant.'

'Seedlings? Plants?'

'No. That is, seeds.'

'Giant Chabaud carnations, we have. But we're out of Hoffman's. Wouldn't Scrutton's Mammoth do you? They're warranted tested.'

'Certainly, certainly. By all means. Scrutton's will do fine.'

She handed me then quite simply the little coloured packets.

'Will there be anything else?'

I looked round at the pigeon cots and lawn-mowers and the green artificial grass. It never occurred to me then that I might just go on buying more and more seed. Perhaps there was an instinct stronger than the wish to stay, an urgency to withdraw from the brilliant danger? I could not bear to look into her eyes. Only when her head, her dark healthy hairy head was bent down over the little pad which she held so delicately to her breast and upon which she wrote out my bill—only then did I dare again look fearfully at her.

'Would you please pay at the cash desk?'

Dry words of parting, they were said with no emotion—with a staged softening of the corners of her mouth, a substitute smile. I took the little slip—taking it carefully at its very edge with the tips of my fingers to avoid touching hers, the pale varnished tips—and threaded my lonely way through the hoes and pergolas to where the bright light of the cashier's cottage shone, a depressive light of destination, homecoming, severance from adventure. Thus the distance uncoiling its cruel tape between us: but then as the cashier stamped the three separate parts of the bill—I realized there was a slip I must take back to her . . . the journey was not over! Walking at first quickly, but more slowly as I drew near, I returned and held out my slip. Already she was engaged with another customer, a rugged-necked mackintoshed man buying a hose-whirler, a purchase that can be discussed at length. I stood there for some time before she turned and handed me my seed. But when she said 'Thank you,' she had already turned back to the hose-whirler. I stuttered my 'good afternoon' and left, receiving no reply nor another look.

For the rest of the day, on and off, I saw her face. Why that particular face persuades me so I can't say—it is certainly a pretty face, but so are many others. We know this belief that every man is in love with one women all his life, a forgotten face that once peered down at him in childhood and whose presence coincided with some stage of early excitation. Perhaps it was so with the face of the woman in the garden accessories. It held significances incomparable with other faces, it was adored as soon as seen; it was also remote and untouchable. Round wide-open eyes, crescented beneath with deep shadows like bruises, and of a pale colour that asked sympathy for her great unguarded helplessness. Dark hair, dressed in the ordinary style of today. A mouth full and sculpted, but bloodless, almost white. A shape of face oval, perfectly regular and of a helpless strength that suggested the plastic features of a classic sculpture. Generally—it can be said at this remove—an anaemic face, but in its pale flesh crying for the manly protections.

The next day I was back buying seed.

And on each day following. I have no garden—only two window-boxes. For these I have no affection, and I love a garden too—but having none, and no gardener's knowledge, the atmosphere of such an accessory department was dry, dry and in many ways fearful.

None of the things there had any relation to the earth, they were new and shining and weatherless. Tools in real gardens are rusted and caked with earth, summerhouses and sheds are paled and softened by rain and sun and lichen, wooden sticks turn grey and even the black eel of hose takes on the softer, weathered look of old water. But here on the clean soaped floor such rustic sheds stood yellow and gummy with bright varnish, tools of steel were painted postal scarlet and locomotive green, and everywhere there flashed the white of unsoiled wood—sticks, axe-handles, fresh rakes. Stiff sacks of bone-meal stood with big tins of blight control and liquid manure—even the dark steel of spades had been stuck over with bright paper labels. For a place dedicated to the fruits of the earth, a place packed with fertilizers, it smelled only sterile. It smelled of wood, machine oil, and fish-glue.

Yet there against the false green grass, against a rotating summer-cot and a tin of creosote, there stood my pale woman in her khaki smock—and there too was life. At first I bought only seeds. The gay packets of hardy annuals began to mount on my mantelpiece at home. But after a while I progressed—I could scarcely afford a garden roller, nor did I want one, but I made careful enquiries. Together we wheeled the green-painted rollers over her polished floor. Together we discussed the endurance of dove-cots. At length I bought a long brass pest-syringe. Practical considerations were remembered—the syringe would come in for watering my window-boxes and in winter for moth-spray.

Slowly we grew to know one another. I kept a most reserved distance. I bought my seeds and went quickly away—scarcely noticing her, scarcely giving her the usual words of polite encounter. In this I hoped to be 'different': my adoration told me that day after day this woman was pestered by men trying to get her to meet them after hours—and I would be different. I would be sincere. I was not one for idle flirtation but instead he who recognized the flame of her great soul, her worth. I kept my distance—until the day when I judged sincerity to be established and consulted her upon the roller. From then on our acquaintance grew. But not apace. It may sound as if all this were coldly and carefully calculated—but nothing of the sort. My simple hopes were the companions of unbearable

terror, of failures of strength and sudden exits, of tentative pleasantries that smothered me as I stammered them—it was then like
balancing on some impelling precipice—and I was dogged by an
overwhelming distate for the falsehoods I had to tell. I had, for
instance, to invent a garden. But gradually we grew to know each
other.

And there were aspects of great charm in our development. When,
for instance, I noticed how in her very words she began to change
towards me. At first she had spoken to me only in the aloof, impersonal vernacular of gardens. When I enquired how to use an
insecticide—I was told that I must 'broadcast among the plants'.
About a carton of lime—this must be dusted along the rows of peas
to 'hasten pod-filling'. But as time went on and ease overcame her,
it was 'just scatter it everywhere'—and 'pod-filling' became 'the
peas come quicker'.

There were setbacks. Though these derived from circumstances
more than from her. Once, for instance, I thought I would alter
the quality of our discussion, seek in fact the more pleasurable
atmosphere of striped summer garden-cushions and steel-sprung
hammocks. I thought this more congenial for a proposal I promised
myself the courage to make. But it proved only a step back—I had
to be handed over to a male attendant, a hardened specialist in
garden comfort, and with him was squandered a whole day's
advance. Then again—on another day she was not there at all! It
was her afternoon off—in that store they had some system of special
afternoons. I never went on a Wednesday again.

But, how, finally, to make this proposal? What words? Every
phrase I invented took to itself a leer, the most innocent words
suggested not only sin but underhand, slimy, disreputable sin.
Several times I was on the point of speaking. But always a pre-
resonance of the phrase in my own ears stopped me. At length, quite
casually, for no more reason perhaps than that she was feeling fit
and tolerant, she herself made the breach. We had been speaking of
bone-meal. Suddenly she said:

'You ought to take me to see this garden of yours one day. I'm
getting quite to know it.'

She was smiling—and in a way that comes to those placid faces where one least expects it, her eyes flashed. For once confounding the consequences—for I had no garden—I took my plunge.

'But of course you must! Could you—could you spare one of your Wednesdays? And come to tea? We—we could drive down.'

'Well!'

Her face had fixed suddenly stiff and pressed. She fixed me with a hard astonished eye—as outraged as her voice. I started to stammer my apology—and then the coldness was as instantly gone, she broke out laughing, she had been playing.

'Well, that's very nice of you I'm sure! As it is—I don't see that I'm doing anything on the Wednesday, no, nothing Wednesday....'

'Then Wednesday it is! Here? Where?'

'I don't know that I ought, really.'

'Oh, come on—it would be fun.'

'Fun would it be? Fun for who? You, I expect.'

'I mean, you'll enjoy seeing the garden.'

'Well . . . ye-es. . . .'

'You will really.'

And after much more of this—frightening, trivial, painfully so pleasant—she agreed to meet me at three o'clock on the following Wednesday. I made a point of not coming in the next day—to show I was not too eager—but of coming in on each alternate day—to show that I was still the customer. I remember that week particularly buying Sweet Brandenburg Dianthus—and a pack of hybrid pinks called, after their breeder, Robinsonii.

Wednesday came round. At three o'clock she was there, standing by the last of the long row of plate-glass windows. At first I was unsure, I had been looking for a khaki apron. But of course she was dressed in other clothes, a hat and a coat which I noted with disappointment and apprehension. On no account of bad quality—they were well chosen and, as I saw later, they suited her: but at first they made her less attainable, reducing instantly the intimacy to which I had grown accustomed—and also they revealed her suddenly as a girl with a life of her own. Thus the cool ministress of impersonal equipment was gone and in her place there came a confusing vista of flat and kitchen and relations and friends, of a district and shops and recreations and habits. However—through all this her old attraction shone.

I came up to her flustered.

'How do you do? Am I late?'

'Oh, how do *you* do? No, not at all.'

She was more assured—the clothes—and she smiled capably. She turned a little and said:

'All my own work!'

I looked at her hat and searched for some definitive compliment —then simply stammered how well it looked. In fact, she was referring to the window by which we stood, and which was filled with a new garden scene from her department. A pink wax man in white flannels mowed a false lawn, paper doves hung in ghostly flight round a thatched pedestal, implements of all kinds were scattered about separately like giant insects—it was called 'Spring Offensive'. The sight of it put me again at ease. I said:

'I say, I've got terrible news. I'd have got here this morning to tell you, but I couldn't. I'm afraid—the car's packed up.'

'Oh!'

'*I've tried everything.* But not a murmur out of her.'

'Then what are we going to do?'

'I—don't really know. Perhaps—couldn't we have tea here in town, go to a movie . . . or what you like?'

'*Well.* Well, I don't suppose there's anything else for it.'

That was the beginning. 'There wasn't anything else for it. Placidly—never tartly said. We went to a film, had tea, and I saw her on to her bus.

'There wasn't anything else for it.' As I grew to know her better. I found those words to be the bone of her character. If I said: 'Wouldn't it be pleasant to be in the Scillies—now, with all the spring flowers out?'—the answer would come: 'Why? We'll have our own spring flowers soon.' Or if, thinking for a subject to amuse her, I would grumble at food prices, she would reply in her pale way: 'Well, after all we must make do.' Making do, in fact. And from so serene and lovely a face, a face as slow as a statue. It is difficult to convey these placidities. She was neither dull nor dumb. Nor was she disinterested, nor bored. She spoke neither from humility nor from resignation—but more from an absolute acceptance of events. A difficult manner to criticize—no ranting cheeriness to set one on edge, no lassitude to provoke one's energies. But, of course, it was at times uneasy. The temperate voice spoke and stopped. And there it was. Another conversation complete, another topic gone.

Yet for me—a magic outweighed such difficulties of communion. And on occasions there sparked from the placid face an energy of spirit and understanding that both startled and proved its constant, if unexercised, capacity within her. I first saw such a spark after we had been out together several times. We did not always meet on the Wednesdays: I had work to do, and could not often get off—so we met sometimes in the evenings. But already the evenings were growing lighter, and that fictitious car could not remain much longer in the workshops. In the end I took the plunge, I confessed there was no car, no garden, and that even my visits to the store were false. Such involved dissimulation was, when you considered it, of course a compliment: it had been taken so far that it could no longer be thought of as a means to a fickle end. But at least I expected some show of consternation, some little fuss, a period of reprimand. Whatever the reason, it is never flattering to find onself deceived. However, Desirée—Desirée Griffiths—simply sat quiet for a second, her eyes widening and her mind placidating, until she said in a voice of unusual tenderness:

'How very, *very* sweet of you.'

But there was one subject that did always animate her. This was the mention of a certain circle of her friends. At the sound of their names, and she pronounced them often, she brightened and became more affirmative. She used to repeat what they said fervently, as though she might have wished such views herself—yet was thankful she could express them at least at second-hand thus from the mouths of those she trusted. I knew none of these strangers looming somewhere within the strange citadel of her home life. They had names that grew huge in significance; yet they themselves remained formless. I could see no faces, imagine neither appearance nor manner. George. Kay. Norbert. I grew stonily envious of them. But because I could not see them, such envy remained remote and cold, I felt markedly indifferent to them, they were labelled the least important people alive.

We were at the Ideal Homes Exhibition, pressing through the crowd in the kitchen section, pressing against the ropes guarding those setpiece kitchens—those that so rack the nerves, as though they belong to someone else, and one had intruded—and she looked suddenly serious:

'You know, George is a simply wonderful cook. It's funny in a man, isn't it? He's quite the professional. You never tasted anything like George's scrambled eggs. I suppose it's a kind of touch. Yes.'

I said nothing, but took care to glance long and longingly at her profile; it reassured me to look at her.

We went to a film. It was a back-stage affair, the heroine wanted to sing in a Broadway musical and so became an usherette in a night-club in order to faint at the feet of the tall, curly-haired bandleader. Afterwards, Desirée leant across to me and whispered in great confidence:

'She's the spitting image of Kay. Kay's just like that. Honour bright—Kay'll get an idea into her head, any crazy idea—and go off and do it there and then! You can't say a word! Once it was farm-work—and now she's put her name down for Spanish at the Polly. Spanish! You can't stop Kay. Yes.'

I never felt quite so indifferent to Kay as to the others; she was a girl. She may have monopolized too much of my Desirée's worship —but she was still a girl. There was nothing of the slaphappy virile George. Nor of Norbert, who became perhaps the most sinister of the three. One suspected Norbert of having the worst appeal—an indefinable appeal. Something slow and unseen. Of Norbert she said:

'He's the quiet type. You can't fathom Norbert. But when he gets going—look out! It's always the same with the quiet ones, isn't it? Do you know—he's read all sorts of books. *All sorts.* Yes.'

George. Kay. Norbert. They assumed the legendary but remarkably real qualities of historical characters. Her descriptions defined them as the drawings in history books define kings: fabulous figures, yet possible; one believes in them, but sees them only in imaginative outline. Had she shown me photographs—as often chance acquaintances will reach for their wallets and pull forth the tired likenesses of families and friends—I would have seen George, Kay and Norbert in humble monochrome, small, remote in time, exposed in the nudity of group and grin, no longer of significance. But she showed me no such monochrome emetic. And the shapes of these three still glittered in giant and treacherous colours of the imagination.

But finally I met them.

Desirée and I had been seeing each other for three or four weeks. Once, even, we had met on a Sunday. Sunday was her special day for meeting these three, and this one was granted only because George and Kay and Norbert were away on a day trip, something on a steamer— and Desirée had desisted for lack of a love for water. Not of lack of love for them, nor love for me. I suppose I was for her a convenient sort of companion. There was—at that time—neither flirtation nor passion. A few frightened compliments from me—and from her placid acceptance. I knew this could not last for long— if it did, it would develop into a confirmed 'friendly' companionship, the requiem that begins 'dear old Clifford' and lasts for ever. But I was determined to move carefully; moreover, I was enchanted and wanted to act sincerely; moreover, I was scared.

Then one Wednesday she invited me to tea again on the Sunday. 'You must meet George and Kay. And Norbert.'

A contraction of the stomach, the doom-seizure before the dentist. Sunday tea, the special hour, George's and Kay's and Norbert's! I began to stutter my refusals; but her look of surprise—as if anyone could refuse such an opportunity!—and my own curiosity decided the affair. That evening, as we said good-night, I leaned forward and kissed her on the cheek. It was the first time. I think it was because I wanted to affirm some personal bond between us, some degree of possession with which I could defend myself when we met those three.

Sunday came. At four o'clock I knocked on Desirée's front door. Her room was upstairs on the first floor. Not until we were up the stairs, not until I had puffed up my awkward courage on the dark landing, did she say so brightly:

'No one's here yet. You'll just have to talk to this child.'

A large room, a sunny afternoon—the sun made a gentility of the fawn wallpaper, the daffodils, the tea-cups.

On the sideboard plates of sandwiches, crustless little triangles threading a line of pink paste: rock cakes as big as large buttons: a bright yellow square of plain cut cake: green tea-cups: five paper napkins. Desirée was much brighter than usual. I remember saying:

'Do you mind if I smoke?'

Quick as a dart came the response from that dear round face, palely animated:

'I don't mind if you burst into flame.'

When I was almost again calmed, the ring came on the bell. The springs of the divan echoed as up Desirée jumped. She was off downstairs—the room around me grew quiet and restless as the door below opened and a shouting and laughing as of many people crowded up with a dreadful clattering of feet. I remember standing up, then sitting down again. In they came.

To me, shaking hands with each, they loomed as large and presenceful as I had foreseen. But then as we sat down, as the first high talking lowered and slowed, as the blood cleared and the room moved into clearer focus—those three took on fresh definition. In three distinct stages. First, there had been the large looming of introduction. Then the shock of realizing that though recognizable in manner, in physical shape each of them was very different from what I had imagined. George I had seen as square-faced and crisp-haired: instead he was all circular, a circular face, with other inner circles made by a cherub mouth and hummock-round cheeks and circular eyebrows high above round surprised eyes. Kay should have been keen-faced and inquisitive—instead she turned out Scots-speaking and firm-jawed, wearing a bow in her hair, and trousers: she had the appearance of a grimly serious girl playing the kind of true-blue young housewife one sees in advertisements for soapflakes. Above her right breast she wore a brooch in the form of a telephone dial, with the inscription DIAL LOV. Norbert I had only imagined as a pair of spectacles. He had none. He was bloodless, with a yellow-

223

ish skin—his black hair grew and had been clipped far down the neck, smearing it with a shadow like dark cycle-grease. He wore at least the impression of spectacles, he kept his eyes down and withdrawn, he concerned himself secretly with the carpet by his shoes.

However—they retained their presence, for me their mastery. But as tea was eaten and variously we talked, the third stage occurred. It was as if physically they were shrinking. One by one they came into sharper focus—the large blur lensed into the smaller clearer figures. I found in fact that they were all as nervous as I was: their impregnability had been my own projection. As I caught the eye of one or the other they acted always in either of two ways— they were whipped to a quick brightness, or slowed into a surly cage of nonchalance: thus they would either chatter too brightly, or turn away purposively to show that one did not exist. They began to show, too, small individual faults. George, a lively one, enjoyed too much his own jokes—while he never laughed at them, he looked round every time for approval. I remember, for instance, how he asked for more cake:

'Desirée! Desirée, I desire you—to chuck me noch ein rock cake—'

And while at this sally Desirée was still slowly smiling, quick Kay chipped in:

'Coming over, one R.C.'

Kay was a tomboy, a boy-girl; though she never rejected her feminity, she liked to be 'one of the chaps.' When from his superior shadow, during a pause, Norbert enunciated with a sly smile:

'Angels passing overhead. Or is it twenty-five to?'

Then Kay came in with:

'Angels or no angels, says I, what's the dirt?'

'Dirt, did you say? Did I hear her say the "dirt"?'

'Come on, chaps—George, what offers?'

'Me? We-e-ll. Now if I was to say, to say that I do hear, I *do* hear how a certain party—no names—was observed at ten pip emma entering the portals of one public house not a hundred miles from one institution to wit the Polly in the company of . . .'

'George!'

'Kay?'

'Objection over-ruled.'

'Thank you, Norbert. In the company, as I was saying, of none other than the *Spanish instructor*—'

'George, that's hitting a chap below the belt! Come on, wherever did you hear such a thing, out with it—'

'At my mother's knee—or some other low joint. . . .'

Peals of laughter. And then I remember Kay, pretending to be outraged, turned on Norbert:

'Well, it's a poor story, isn't it, Nor?'

And slowly Norbert answered, after a pause long enough to wrinkle up his forehead, a pause for pronouncement:

'Mauvais in parts, like the reverend ovoid.'

Norbert, more than the others, could never say anything quite straight, his ponderous facetions leered themselves out like the editorials of cycling magazines or the weighty patter of a Lancashire comedian. Often, in fact, he assumed a Lancashire accent. With Norbert, a lie was never anything else but a 'terminological inexactitude.' Yet he was plainly considered the brains of the party— his reading, I think, came valiantly from the shorter manuals on biology, engineering, even philosophy. He could only express himself in phrases spoken it seemed in capital letters, dogma of the short road. But most often he fell below even this standard. I remember him standing up, tea-cup in one hand, another hand Napoleonic under his lapel:

'Notwithstanding sundry setbacks on the part of persons present that we shall refrain from naming—san faryan and honi-soit-qui-mal-y-pense—it is my deep pleasure to announce as a vote of heart-felt thanks to our esteemed hostess is deemed advisable by one and all. . . .'

Thus, again, George, Kay and Norbert. It was not until many days later, days after that inaugural tea-party, that a fourth development in our relationship occurred: a fourth I could never have foreseen.

But meanwhile that tea-party proceeded. Not much can be said of it. At one point the wireless was switched on and we were cheered by the violins of a Winter Garden on the South Coast. A silver band from the North took over, and was switched off. Then began a period of longer reminiscence—the first battling of tongues was over—and while George and Kay talked of their lives we nodded and smiled and smoked. I remember going over to the window. Small spring flies hurried their folded wings about the pane. I stood there for a long time looking down at the neat Sunday street. The only open shop was a tea-shop, a home-cooked establishment, its name angled in tall plastic green capitals on a black background: in the window, daffodils and saffron-yellow cakes: one could imagine, beyond the plate-glass window, on the little black chairs, the sipping of clear, violet-coloured tea. And George spoke on behind about his camping holiday near Dunoon:

'. . . smashing site we found, nice and sheltered, nice and dry. Everything in the garden was lovely. And best of all, nice and smooth—a lovely spot of turf for your groundsheet. Well. Well, then lights out. But comes the dawn and we wake up—and blimey-old-Riley you should have heard! Moans and groans. Groans and moans. You'd have thought an earthquake'd come in the night, the bumps there were. Right underneath our sheets, bumps like Mount Everest. Know what it was? Moles. I'm not telling a lie. Moles. . . .'

All the time I was conscious of the nearness of my Desirée—delighted, pale, serene. She seldom said more than 'Yes'—but that to everything. A tender, understanding sigh of a 'Yes' modulating through two long, downward caressive notes. Even when she herself said something she had to end it with the same 'yes'. Nothing disturbed her. Placid, infinitely affirmative, for me she held the room. Whatever I said, to whomsoever—I said it to her. I felt her near me —and sometimes looking out of the window, or just into the corner beneath the thin table legs, I forgot about George and Kay and Norbert and imagined her again in her khaki smock among the bright green rollers.

Later, as the ash mounted and our mouths dried, we grew quiet. At seven we hurried out to the pub.

Some nights later Desirée and I were walking back from the cinema. It was nearly eleven o'clock, dark. Her room lay off the main street and we had to cross a long square of gardens—there were few street-lamps, I remember only one, distant and speckled among the early leaves. Part of an iron railing still held a telephone box, the green of a cabshelter showed in the light and there were no cabs. With curtained windows on one side and on the other the dark trees and shrubbery, the pavements lay empty—shuffling with night, forlorn and fresh.

Since that Sunday I had seen her twice—on both occasions we had kissed good-night, it had become easily and passionlessly a routine. A routine breeds upon itself; again there was the danger of 'dear old Clifford'. So, that night, leaving the cabshelter behind and facing then the long dark pavements to the end of the gardens, I took my heart from my boots and decided to kiss her there and then.

We were walking arm in arm—joined and marching forward. To bring this to a halt, to stop, would be startling: over-alert, I even imagined that such a sudden halt might bowl her over. Also—she was talking. Without emphasis she was picking to pieces a film star we had seen that evening—and then carefully and considerately reassembling her on a consoling note: 'Still—she does as well as she can.' It seemed rude to interrupt this. Furthermore, I was carrying on my left arm an umbrella and in my hand a small parcel.

The distance to the lighted streets grew less: it was then or never. Then, to my surprise, when I was giving up hope, the parcel came to my aid. Its loop was strung too tightly round my finger. I found myself stopping, disengaging my arm from hers, and fiddling the loop looser. And there we were—surprisingly—standing about in the dark! The phrase goes: 'I woke up to the fact.' So I did, it was exactly like waking up. The tension relaxed, the night around rose darkly into shape. I remember thinking: 'Had the string been hurting all the time?'—before turning suddenly round on her and taking her shoulders and pressing down my face to hers.

She had been talking, I ate with my lips her last words. And she —she made no resisting move at all. One moment she had been talking and at the next she was being kissed. She acccepted the change as though it were no change at all. And thus for some seconds, with no word passing, we kissed.

No words passed—much else came to try us. It was an awkward, fumbling business. My hand with the parcel embraced her neck, the parcel swung against her back. The umbrella stuck out at an absurd

227

angle—its handle pressed a tourniquet round my forearm and the ferrule was caught between the railings. Her turned-up collar edged between our lips, my free hand clutched half parcel and half the folds of her coat and little of her. But such little embarrassments were mitigated by the magic—I was kissing her! She was patient in my arms! Patient, not, indeed, responsive. But that was her way.

And that was well enough. But not for long. Passion accumulates. After that first long kiss, I suddenly struggled my left arm free and dropped the umbrella and the parcel on the pavement.

That was the end. She stiffened. All the time she must have been conscious of some safety in those impedimenta. Now smoothly she turned down her head, made a rigid little fence of her arms. There came no declamatory refusal, no dramatic 'No!'—instead, in the same second, her cool voice said most reasonably:

'Clifford! You'll muss me all up.'

We hurried home.

Two days later we were to meet again—but a stroke of ill luck befell me. It had happened before, it will happen again. The spring weather was treacherous. For days it had been hot: then before midday the temperature fell abruptly, the wind rose and hurried clouds over and the rain began. I was out of town, visiting a new branch thirty miles out. And foolishly I had left off my wool kidney-band. By lunch-time the chill had got me, I was in for the old trouble. It was impossible to get home before late afternoon. I had to send Desirée a note and go to bed. I was there for a fortnight.

As soon as I was up I went round to Desirée's store. It was mid-morning, a grey day. But the garden accessories department bloomed brightly in the glaze of its own summer. Electric lights drew a fine glistening from the varnished summer-houses and dove-cots, the glossed green paint on rollers and mowers. Aluminium fertilizer-tins winked. The sacks of hoof-meal and nicotine dust themselves sat drier and more comfortably, safe on a polished floor, safe in their own weather. But Desirée was not there. However—it was eleven o'clock. I knew she would be out for her mid-morning coffee. So I waited for some time by the ornamental section, quietly enjoying the dear dry smells.

When she had not returned by half-past eleven I went over to the man in the hammocks and sunbeds and asked whether the lady would soon be back. He smiled. He was evidently pleased at this He said:

'Back? Not likely. Not our Miss Griffiths.'

I remember a little tooth sticking coyly from his upper lip, and the erosion it had made in the lip beneath. In the false interior summer a false cloud seemed to pass, the electric light grew dark. He looked at me wittily, storing up his riddle, pleased that I had to stammer:

'Why . . . what . . . isn't she . . .?'

He sucked in his tooth with a sigh of great perseverance—then as quickly perked it out again, and never stopping, jigged it up and down with words that fell damply as rain.

'Miss Griffiths, eh? Miss Griffiths's gone. Gone to be engaged. Gone and got herself married by now at the rate those two're going. Didn't you know? You didn't?'

A pause while he peered forward his astonishment.

'Bless you, only a week ago it was when the young fellow comes in and goes to her seed counter there and whisks her off pronto to a social the very same a'tnoon. Next morning she comes in—Miss Easy-Come-Easy-Go—and says she's off. Off! Quick on his pins that lad, I'll say that much I will.'

He sucked in again a whalish breath—peremptory, final, a breath that washed his hands of it all—and then, while the room was closing down on me and the future began to unreel its weary road, he added in a more reflective tone, both tender and sad:

'Nice set-up lad too. Got a lovely rose garden. Out on the North Circular, she says. Lovely roses, she said.'

I never saw her again. It took some pains to avoid this, for I began to see a lot of George and Kay and Norbert. George I had already met again once after that Sunday tea-party. He himself had telephoned me—of his own accord!—and we had taken a drink together. It was then, as early as then, that the fourth stage in my relationship with those three began. First they had been too perfect, then perfect, then imperfect: now, through these last imperfections, there formed with familiarity a more settled knowledge of them, and with it a liking. As I knew them better, they became rounded and lovable. Familiarity bred no contempt—it was otherwise, strangeness and fear had bred the contempt. As we grew more intimate, our imperfections bred affection—we became people of no mould, unpredictable always beyond a few superficial mannerisms.

They told me about Desirée. She was happily settled, and Arthur her husband was a very decent fellow, a metallurgical chemist. I liked to think of Desirée going about their evening meal, the smell of cooked meat drifting out over the garden and mingling its promise with the other succulence of the roses. He, in his sober suit, his fingers just not touching a rose, experiencing for charmed evening minutes the poetic exaltation—full and visionary as any artist's—that comes to a man who has grown his plant. And she, aproned among the clean white dishes, her eyes on the figure pursuing its soundless progress through the garden. I avoided them for fear, as with the others, of growing too much to like the bastard.

Impatience

'BEAT it off away now,' said the Dropper, 'blow.'
  'Sod you for a start,' Sally said.
'You too, darling.'
'——!'

With these remarks the two men withdrew, each a little, neither too much.

In that lovely winter weather, quiet with the first hunter's thrill of fog, sharp and curiously calm, London rose clear of long-leaved September and curled towards its fires, saw the curtains drawn over yellow windows, walked swifter among the daylit greys, dreamed through the petrol hurry of horse-leather and the evening street-lamp. Toys reddened in the shops. A church-bell no longer echoed its summer air—but now engraved the dark cold night. Black leaves gave up their wet mysterious smell. And in the ornamental districts a mist hazed the trees, graceful arches and the classic porticos of great mansions stood softly severe—it was not a white mist but silver grey beneath a red low sun, and one looked around suspiciously for the rime that was not yet there.

But the feeling struck different in the streets behind the Circus—Beak, Brewer, Lisle in their narrow grime feared winter. All those who would every day stand on corners prepared themselves to shiver, they looked up to where the chilly haze of the sky fogged down at the brown brick housetops, they saw vegetable scraps and litter in the gutters lie cold and severe, no longer moving meat for flies. Chestnut men were coming back, the Italian fruitfulness of barrows gave way to mahogany winter fare of dates and nuts and oranges. These streets were not good in winter, they smelled of raw smoke, wind blew through frayed clothes, no trees gave them grace.

The café door was closed on the Dropper and Salvatore Page. Urn-steam clouding the window patched out the street. Separately,

231

they drank their middle-morning tea. Dropper Culbertson crunched with long straight lines of teeth a dough of pastry blooded with jelly-bright jam. Sally Page ate nothing, he sulked, and in the silence now and then gave a mince of a twist-up to his shoulder, raised his chin a little like a woman offended. Culbertson fumed. His long mouth with lip mud-coloured as his face munched up and down—it was a line of lip so thin as to appear toothless above a great square bony jaw. Each wanted to be out and back to his shop, each lingered to appear not to hurry.

Matters between these two had come to a head. From the first, they had not met well. And this perhaps had affected their feeling for each other ever since. One evening Culbertson had been taking a stout and roll-mops with a big man he was close to, a man for whom he sometimes moved stuff and at other times leant his muscle. One of the boys had come in the bar with Salvatore Page. They had sat next door at the counter, and Sally had soon got going with the Dropper's big man, his valuable friend and boss. Sally was small, with sleek dark hair and thick clownish eyebrows, and his flexible mouth, humorously and charmingly resilient, could talk with the fluency and something of the note of a woman. He seldom seemed to think, the words poured out, he was easy and wiry and never at a loss, he perked always and seemed never to need to relax. He was popular among the boys, and despite his size and an effeminate nature he was a tough customer to cross. He was a barber.

The Dropper also had a cut-and-shave saloon. Both were owner-barbers: they kept their own small shops, they cut hair each day, but the shops were as much a cover and a source of other business as a means of steady income when things happened to be quiet. They were not in essence competitors, their shops lay far enough apart, but the fact of a similar profession, instead of giving common ground, had the effect of souring them further. And when at that first meeting Sally with his way claimed easily and instantly the attention of the Dropper's boss, and furthermore made him laugh, Dropper Culbertson felt a deep sulk of envy in his stomach. What the hell did this bleeding little queen think he was after? Sodding it on his territory? Not bloody likely! But in spite of one or two mean-ing remarks Culbertson made, Sally persisted. When they parted, he was on excellent terms, sinuous and hearty, with the Dropper's friend. As soon as he had left the Dropper had said something civil to his friend, civil but disparaging of Sally. And that man had swung round at him and shut him up. He asked him why he didn't smart up his own —ing line of talk instead of talking out of his —ing ——? For this Culbertson had never forgiven Sally.

The Dropper was a tall hard broad man, with a square jaw and a cropped head and small eyes wreathed in wrinkles made from squinting but not laughing. He looked a conventionally brutal man, but he dressed and kept himself fastidious. He had an uneasy reserve, deep in his big frame there was somewhere a bubble caught up. He spoke from the corner of his mouth, looking away as if for the boss on the corner, knifing a whisper always of conspiracy. Words stuck in his throat. He was sourly envious of the ease of such as Sally: and with his male size he despised the ladylike little fellow. He was called the Dropper because of his eyes. They were small, watering always, letting water as if they would dissolve. He fed them regularly with drops. He used an eyebath—but never the same one twice. The bathroom in his flat was full of them—rows of dark blue glass cups, boxes full of them. He was terrified of getting chance grit in his eyes if he washed and used the same one twice. To disguise his defect, he wore hexagonal rimless spectacles, such as jazz musicians often wear: in his long padded smooth coat he might have been a trumpet-player. He was known to do things to night-watchmen, unnecessarily, that do not bear repeating.

Months had passed, and it turned out that neither man in fact trespassed on the other's business affairs. In each establishment the racing whispers passed from barber to customer, the key-men came in for their morning shave and held court, and at night various outside jobs were attended to—but the shops were far apart, the clientèle stayed separate. However, socially brought together by common acquaintances, and sometimes by a similar choice of entertainment, the two found themselves meeting. They found themselves favouring the same café, they met at dance-halls, they noticed each other in queues for the moving pictures. They came up against each other as the strange new word comes up against the reader—a word often read but unnoticed before, but once recognized recurring with

H*   233

strange superstitious significance: just so, Sally and the Dropper had always visited these same places, but had until now glossed each other over. Sally returned all the Dropper's dislike—for he was sensitive and quick to understand contempt, and in any case Culbertson was a symbol of all the big men who throughout his life had sneered at Sally's small graces. Once or twice he had been told this was no more than an expression of envy—but telling did no good, he was against such men.

So for months the poison gathered—until on the previous Sunday it had made a head. They had both gone to a tea-dance in the same West End hotel. On Sunday the wealthy Jewish population of the East End came to that place, and for the afternoon the restaurant and the lounges were heavy with a pantherine oriental suspense. It was exactly as if a thick perfume hung and drugged the place: not unpleasantly, but drowsily, heavily. Richly dressed in styles more decorative than a northern city prescribes, the guests sipped their tea, smoothly danced, and moved from one table to another. The women with their beaked noses wore hats of fabulous overhung design; voluptuous of shape and exquisitely painted, they sat on chairs but seemed more to be lolling back on soft divans. The arrogant and pomaded men stalked about in high self-confidence, minds moving fast behind scornful eyes, bodies poised slow except for a ceaseless sculpting of hands. Culbertson sat alone at a table with his lady, a large longfaced woman with a short male haircut and the grim look of a wardress. Sally sat with a large group of Jews —and the Dropper knew that, though the fellow was Maltese, he would join the others in speaking derisively of the Dropper and his girl as a couple of goys. He sat there in a desert of anti-Aryan scorn.

It was when the dancing was over, and when the vestibule and the swing-doors strutted with overcoats and furs, that trouble occurred. For Culbertson, wanting to be away quickly, chose to pass over the commissionaire and walk a hundred feet up the street and wait there for a taxi. The taxis mostly came from that direction, and he congratulated himself on getting in first and outwitting the lot of them.

But then Sally came out with a group of friends, and they all started to stroll in the same direction. What the Dropper was doing was evident, he stood alone with his woman right on the kerb. And now these others dawdled up the same way, five abreast on the pavement. Passers-by had to skirt into the gutter as the crowd of them laughed and talked at the tops of their voices, rolling as much as walking, boastful lords of the pavement. In the cold outside air, with its winter mist and its deserted Sunday air, they looked curiously like a summer strolling crowd—with their trim moustaches and padded shoulders and spotless pale wide American hats. They came right up to where the Dropper stood. They sauntered unswerving until one of the men was right up against Culbertson—but the Dropper did not move off the kerb, and the man had to hesitate and blunder aside. Even, then, linked to the others, he was dragged off balance and brushed roughly up against Culbertson.

Just then a bus, tall and red and lighted, came busying up along the kerb. A few seconds of rattle and confusion and it was gone, the broad smooth Sunday road was empty again—but the Dropper saw what made him wild. That other lot had walked ten yards further up—and now also stood there waiting for a taxi and laughing among themselves. He swore and began to walk towards them. With childish grim determination he was going to cheat them exactly at this game and place himself a few yards beyond them. If necessary, he would do this all the way down the Dilly.

But just then he saw there was a taxi coming, squat, black, and front-lit like an ambulance. Sally jumped off the kerb and waved, waved his arms wide so his overcoat flapped like a flag, piped out high—and got it. Culbertson was also off the kerb and waving. But when he came up the others had all crammed in, and the taximan shook his head. He swore again and got his hand on the doorhandle to wrench it open—when the taxi jolted off sharply and a united burst of laughter muffled at him from inside.

It is well known that most people in the world can support hate because they can hate back—but that few people can bear the more devastating dangers of ridicule. Ridicule promotes a fifth-column, a self-espionage. Even if there is nothing to be laughed at, even if the ridicule is obviously mistaken—nevertheless, the doubt in a man's character rises to provide a target from his private list of insufficiencies. And so from the moment that laugh came from the taxi the

Dropper's dislike of Sally congealed, he stood and by the kerb silently murdered him.

His lady did not help. From her large tough face came a curiously prim voice, her down-turned lips moved small like a bird's.

'Well, I don't know. I really don't know. *Some* people know how to look after a girl. . . .'

The Dropper turned his head to her, he more hung his head round at her, not moving his shoulders. She stopped talking.

That had been Sunday, now this was Monday only when the two men stood angry with their tea. But the night had slowed down some of the Dropper's anger, he had taken much of it out on that lady he went with: but still deeply, rawly he knew he must bide his time. Among the boys it was not the custom to use violence unless some business transgression merited it. When a territory or a job was affected, or on occasions of disloyalty—there was no one hesitated to use a razor or kick the offender nearly dead. But this very stringency of method kept down casual fighting. It made a mess, a useless feud might be propagated and no commercial object was gained. And in any case, it was foolish to choose the daylight. And alone, without preparation, without a friend to gang it up.

For some of these reasons the Dropper restrained himself. Let him ride, he muttered into his cake. But he knew at the same time that this was going to be hard, he was going to have a job keeping a hold on himself—for that little incident of the taxi, which might have happened at any time, had in fact taken place the day before today, which was the day of an annual and important event, a competition of haircutting sponsored by an influential firm of dressing manufacturers. Culbertson knew Sally would be there, and Sally's table was placed near his. He felt he could skate over the whole affair—but the matter growled trouble. It growled throughout the afternoon, long after he had taken another cake and watched with satisfaction Sally leave the café first, long after the bare lights were turned up in his clean white saloon, long after he had cleaned and brightened his instruments and packed them in the portable bag.

Over the wide parks night fell, and the breath of winter came misting more keenly the shapes of trees and the pallid plaster houses. Pavements and shop-windows shone clearer, swept with cold: motors glinted warmly home, crowds hurried to the warm light of the underground or the convivial warmth inside packed and lighted buses; and here and there one saw the lonely contemporary figures of men in dinner-jackets beneath mackintoshes, and of women in coloured evening-dresses beneath short day coats, both trudging out to dinners and dances. How stimulating was this air of bright-lit winter closing in! Stamped on it in every unconscious heart was the date, somewhere in the future, of Christmas week. Without that, the prospect of the dark months would have been formidable: with it, the first months of winter seemed a prelude to a light period somewhere among the darkness ahead.

But again—none of this quality of London's life penetrated behind the Circus. And it was in one of the narrow streets, where here and there an upstairs light showed curtainless the toil of a tailor's overtime, where thin-doored cafés sided with bright blue-lit windows of wireless accessories and the curtained restaurants that sold to shiftless gourmets twice-cooked foreign foods, where there was no fresh smell of winter but a raw brown cold—it was in one of these narrow streets that a lighted doorway attracted that evening some sixty or seventy men who disappeared inside, each grasping a bag or a case, to the curious festival that beckoned them.

Culbertson set out his instruments and saw that Sally was placed obliquely from him two places to one side and over the intervening line of mirrors. Three long trestle tables ran the length of the hall, from door to judges' platform, with a shallow fence of mirror along the centre of each. And now the barbers taking part in the competition stood in rows, like guests about to take their places at a banquet, each behind his allotted chair. Or more properly the barbers were like flunkeys serving the chairs—for now the real guests arrived, men picked at random from the pubs and streets and cafés, and the barbers pulled the chairs back for them as they went to their allotted places. These guests were no ragged lot—they were simply odd men with not much to do who had been taken with the idea of a free haircut.

Up on the platform the advertising manager of the hair-cream company sat with his henchmen to either side. On a green baize table in front of them stood the silver cups, a pile of diplomas, and a jug of water. They talked amicably at their ease, there was nothing yet to be done.

Then the order to begin was given, and the hall filled suddenly with the snick-snicker of scissors. A glass-topped hall, like a billiards hall or a gymnasium, and the scissoring echoed up among the thin iron rafterwork and the dirty glass panes like the restless fluttering of a zoo-house of birds. Shaded lights hanging on long cords drew a garish glitter from the white coats of the barbers, their silver instruments, the mirrors: while high up and away the bare walls and the roof danced with giant green shadows.

The barbers talked less than usual to their customers: but habit overcame them, and soon there began a quiet warmth of chatter beneath the sharper sounds of clipping and cutting. Quiet chatter —except for Sally. Sally's voice, high-pitched and delighted, cut clear above all other noises round the Dropper's table. Sally was in his element. It was an exhibition, and he was delighted to take his part. He talked ceaselessly to the head propped dummily in front of him, his voice snaked up and down and round, and indeed it seemed to bob about like a bright light on the other side of the Dropper's mirror, never stopping, bobbing and giggling and dancing, so that the Dropper's ears began to hum with it and he rattled his scissors in hard fury.

It went on and on. It had seemed hell's own godsend that the mirror had been there to hide the sight of him. But now this voice drivelling on and on forced his presence stronger than ever, he was being sent through a loudspeaker, he was amplified, the Dropper could see his face and his movements twice as clearly as before. He saw him swivelling, all hips and elegance, round his customer, snipping expertly with precise alive fingers, arching his neck back in appraisal, arching round to look in the mirror, arching forward to flick off a stray hair—then suddenly taking the whole head in his hand and combing the lot through, sucking in his cheeks in approbation like a woman seeing herself in the mirror.

The Dropper was cutting a difficult Burlington. He had started nicely: but the voice bit at his nerves, his hands became angry, the scissors took the anger on to the hair he was cutting. He began to muff it. Impatiently he slammed down the scissors and took up the clipping tool. This made little sound—Sally's voice sounded the louder. He dragged the man's hair, the man cursed up at him. He held his tongue, took up the scissors and comb again and started snick-snickering loudly. He took too much off one side, and had to even the other side. The Burlington was a cut for longish hair, it was nearly ruined. He made as much noise as possible—yet he wanted to catch Sally's every word in case something personal was said.

Suddenly he threw down the scissors again, and holding his language, shouted over the mirrors:

'Can't you cut out that bleeding din over there?'

There was immediate quiet. All those around looked up in surprise. No one said anything. Then Sally's voice came:

'Excuse me, but did I hear a pin drop? Or is it my condition?'

They all laughed on the other side. On the Dropper's side only one or two chuckled, for standing up there, grim-jawed, his little eyes behind the glasses glittered dangerous. He grunted back, half from the corner of his mouth, invoking the conspiracy of those beside him:

'Pipe down, I tell you. You can't hear yourself work over here.'

Sally came back quick:

'Down in the forest something stirred. Could it've been a bird by the name of Dropsy-wopsy?'

Another peal of laughter. The Dropper blazed behind his glasses. He spoke quietly now:

'All right. I'll see you afterwards. I'll see you. That's all.'

'Better put a drop in 'em, Wopsyboy. Else you won't see nobody if not.'

The others did not quite catch this, they did not know who Culbertson was. And that one made no answer only pressed his long lips together and picked up the scissors again. Sally piped from the other side, in a false north-country accent:

'Let funeral re-commence. Ever 'ear what t' blind 'eadmaster said when dam broke and 'e drownded isself in school bog? "Lads, lads," he cried as he went under, "summon up Wetropolitan Mortarboard." Ha ha! Then there's the one about the cross-eyed tart and the Siamese Twins. . . .'

The Dropper never said another word. His hands shook, his hands shivered with held-in hurt crying dry fury inside him—he made an impossible mess of his clients' head.

Time went on and the judges came round with their notebooks. They looked curiously at Culbertson, and smiled to each other. Their smiles re-echoed the laughter of the others. His lips pressed tighter and he put his hand against his breast pocket to feel the little weapon there.

Now all the floor was hair, a dark odorous frost of hair sending up from among shoes and spilled lotion a smell of dry must. The barbers stood back finished, the rows of glossy heads propped before them erect and naked-necked. That shadowed upper air round the gymnasium glass and the iron rafters hung again still and quiet. The shadows stopped their green game, the birds fell silent asleep.

The judges finished their round and took their selections to the high baize table. There was a long and tedious wait: everyone watched the dais: the executives laughed easily among themselves as they made on paper their jovial ticks: the barbers talked little, for they were anxious—one of the cups or even a diploma brought prestige, and there were free deliveries of the cream and small but interesting cash prizes. Even Sally said less. The Dropper stood quiet and withdrawn into himself—he looked made of hard tough rubber.

Then the president rose to give a short address on the conservation and health of the hair. He was careful not to emphasize his own cream, but referred more to massage techniques and the need to have by one an old trustworthy lubricant. His was old. He was careful also to make his address before presenting the prizes, so that all should hang on his words. Then the time came for the presentation of the cup. This, to applause from his enemies and catcalls from his friends, was awarded to a plump Smyrnese who was known to be opening soon a large establishment. The second prize went to an old customer for the cream. Sally got a diploma. Culbertson, who had once taken the second cup and always rated a diploma, got nothing.

He collected his things quickly and made for the cloakroom. There he fiddled a long time with his coat, waiting for Sally, watching him, and then at a careful distance following him out and along the street. Sally walked with a couple of others, they tried to persuade him to come with them into a café, but Sally refused and walked on back to his shop. The Dropper kept in to the side wall, walking quickly past street-lamps and lighted windows. He felt no emotion that Sally had so easily got rid of his companions. He felt now he could wait equally for ever.

The shop was approached by steps into what had been an area. Sunk in the basement, its windows showed a yellow light frosted and thus convivial. The Dropper waited a minute up by the railings, then suddenly looked right and left up the street, saw it was empty and edged quickly down the steps. Big in his long dark greatcoat, hands deep in pockets, he was for a moment like a sudden huge shadow cast by a motor's headlights—then as suddenly as such shadows vanish he was gone.

Down by the door he looked through the glass panel and saw Sally still in his white coat bent over the basins. The room looked the emptier for its many chairs. It was very still. Through the glass no sound came. He could hear none of the noises of tidying, no little clicking of instruments.

With no expression on his face, deep in thought, his hand went to his breast pocket and drew out the razor mounted in wood. He palmed this down to his side so that his arm hung easily, and with the other hand quietly opened the door. The shop bell rang out brightly. Sally looked up at the mirror and then swung round. The Dropper jolted, surprised at the bell—then went fast across the floor towards Sally.

In a second Sally's mind had gone to his own waistcoat pocket, rejected it buttoned over by the white coat—and his hand slid across the marble behind him and grabbed a cut-throat. The Dropper's arm hung not so easily, it hung too far out and intentioned from his body, it hung wide with purpose like an ape's arm—but he knew and Sally knew and Sally knew that he knew, for he suddenly stopped as Sally flashed the cut-throat out glittering into the light.

What then happened took no more than a few minutes: but to those two facing each other it was so much longer, time pounded down as slow as the movements they now began to make. They began to move, only very slowly moving to keep moving and not be still, moving a little sideways but not getting nearer, pensive boxers circling for the first blow, stiff-legged dogs poising side-eyed: they kept at each other, never eye to dangerous eye, but with eyes curiously withdrawn and absent to listen to each second, eyes dilated wide to consider no single intention but every slight, light movement within a broader view.

Sally was out from between the fixed chairs, nothing between them now but the swept linoleum, and his razor was palmed down like the other one: it was an awkward weapon, but his hand arched round it firm, the blade was keen and he knew how to use it. Once, like a wind of leaves passing above, a car drove by. Pavement lights thudded the feet of someone walking by, the loud hollow sound brought the mist and the closeness of the street very near, and they were indeed very near—two feet only above the Dropper's head: but more than these sounds was a silence down there that rang in the ears, silence made thicker by small noises—light shuffling of feet on the linoleum, clothes rustling, a breathing that at first came light, but as the minutes passed pumped open-mouthed and heavy. Neither breathed with fear; it was rather a breath of illness, of possession, a heavy droning breath of slow-moving ritualists seized in the dance.

It was known, and not much liked among the boys, what Culbertson did to those he had to beat up. He did it not because it was necessary—but from venom, from hate without pleasure. He used the eyebaths, and nobody came away with their sight the same as before. Sally knew he carried a couple with him: but he was not frightened of this, he was simply alerted, and he watched the Dropper's big figure now with only the thought in mind to get in first. And this, with those weapons, was all that was needed. So both continued to circle.

The one shaded light struck dully down—the top of its white shade dark with dust and the yellow ceiling in shadow. But downwards the light caught a glitter of mirror, and this cast pale shapes of the two men on the walls. The barber-chairs rested back motionless, leather hard-headed creatures masked and mummied. Pink-veined marble basins lay dry, empty. But bottles gleamed deep green and redly rich behind exotic farded labels: they dreamed their heavy odours, and through teat-stoppers sent a gloomy night-lit essence on to the air. To one side a maroon-painted Moorish fret-work of wood encased mirrors, and by the frosted glass that from the street looked festive a row of brown old chairs sat tired of the torn picture papers on their knees. And still at this swept evening-time a smell of hair hung mixed with the perfume. Old enamel letters worded the mirrors: there was a methylated bottle, brass taps sprouted from pipes, and on the red and green Turkey linoleum lay the end of a burnt taper.

It was not the kind of shop one would have expected of Sally—and perhaps this proved a key to the outcome of that night's razor-ing. His shop should have been fresh, modern, plastic. But in fact Sally was tolerant, above his neatness and his nervous ladyship there straggled an easy, careless tolerance. His shop was old-fashioned, and if he did keep it reasonably clean he let the thing rest at that, and—in a London way, in a way of theatre corridors and Victorian alleys—felt it cosy and liked it. 'It's just like you, you dreary old bag,' he would say to a blowsy old pro with whom he sometimes took a port-and-lemon, 'plushy as all get out.'

But the Dropper's shop was a different kind, it was dead matt cream, and the chairs where cheap and new. There were clean white and black showcards lettered especially—the Dropper spent hours writing them out himself—and in each corner there would occur thumbnail drawings of flowers and small birds. The basins were black plastic, and in the window, arranged in attractive forma-tion, would lie rosettes of razor-blades, combs circled like fish on the slab of an art-fishmonger, neat platoons of collar-studs, and behind all an Alpine range of tiered cream-bottles. The Dropper liked to get things squared up, he liked them neat and clean. He was a delicate-handed man.

This very efficiency, compared with Sally's tolerance, probably decided the matter. The Dropper was brutal and moved with hidden angers—yet above this he liked a good job well done. Sally was nervously high and impatient for the next word and the next move—yet beyond this he had an easy carelessness.

So that finally it was not Sally's love of exhibition that forced him to move first, but his resilient easiness that made it easier for him to keep waiting. And it was not the Dropper's stealthy repression that might have enabled him to go on and on in that murderous circle but his very efficiency that forced him impatiently to clean up the job and strike first. Sally, in fact, could let things ride: the Dropper could not.

And thus after slow minutes in that dim-lit place, among the pale shadows moving like dust and the dark etherous smells—to the near sounds of the street above and the little sounds of shuffling and breathing there was added a new sound. It seemed to come first from that very breathing. The breathing seemed to get wet, as if it sweated. Then the sweat became a bubbling. And the bubbling became, from saliva, words. Words formed from the wetness, wet-mouthed words—the Dropper had begun to stream words. His mouth open, his breath dribbling, like a talking dummy the jaws began to munch up and down and from them streamed out a filthy cursing at the small man agile in front.

Sally said nothing. He kept watching. The words came out for some time—the Dropper was chanting in his heavy sleep—and then suddenly he bellowed deep like a bull and flashed out his hand. Sally ducked and knocked the wild elbow easily clear. And in the same movement he was in under the Dropper's arms, his small body chest to stomach, his head looking up at the Dropper's face, and his free arm with the razor making movements. Two movements. Left side, right side. Expertly, with care, it was exactly like lathering the cheeks before a shave.

But there was neither soap nor brush, the Dropper's cheeks suddenly streamed with blood. Two wide red curtains fell down his face, and without a sound the whole of him sank like a great draped cloth to the floor.

Sally had stepped back to be out of it. Now for a moment he stood, his dark large eyes dull, watching the big overcoat and feet mixed up on the floor.

He raised his foot to kick—then thought better of it, gave a small shrug of his shoulders, and walked over to the basin. He threw the razor in and turned the tap. He washed it, dried it, turned, still holding it, and waited. He had one hand on his hip.

After a minute the Dropper made a quick jerk with one foot as though he had just then been hit. A groan. Then nothing. Sally knew he was coming to, the shock that drops a man dead was over, he was gathering small resources, feeling and waiting there in the mess of overcoat.

A quiet second—then he was stumbling to his feet. He stood a moment swaying. Then he gripped his coat collar with both hands and held them over his cheeks. He never looked at Sally, simply lurched off silent from the shop. He looked like a man stumbling, collar up, through a storm.

Sally heard him kicking up the stairs. Then he shook his head, sighed and looked sadly round the shop. He sighed again. So that was that. Now the only thing was to get packing, to get packing everything up and get out of town and stay out for good, for town was now too hot.

Episode at Gastein

LUDWIG DE BRODA bowed as he passed the new young woman with her orange hair, her pensive grace. He bowed not stiffly, as his more military ancestors would have done, but with the ease of a new world, a world not of private halls but of the less formal lounges of hotels. His face he kept grave, it was unwise to smile too soon. And his eyes seemed after their first deep search scarcely to notice her—like the eyes on the ends of a snail's horns they withdrew their intrusion and stared seriously beyond her. Hers fluttered, there was recognition of his bow in her short glance of understanding, long enough only for this to be established: then they lowered, and with it slightly her head, as if this too were a bow, a half-inclination of the head, for it never retrieved itself.

He passed on, not pausing, a modern middle-aged man in a modern suit, with no trace of former graces but a certain recession of manner. He went in to dinner. He dined alone at his table in the white and gold, hugely mirrored dining-hall.

After dinner he walked back through the lounge, noted where the young woman sat taking her coffee, called a waiter to send a tray of coffee for himself to the adjoining table, and went into the toilet room to wash his hands, to comb his well-combed hair, but really for a minute to wait. It was more tactful for his coffee to be established at the table first, it would appear that the table was his habitually and not chosen intrusively to be near hers.

He judged his time patiently so that, when he walked out across the red carpet and past the gilded marble pillars, the silver coffee-jug already winked its welcome opposite his chair. He pretended not to notice her. He sat down, poured and stirred his coffee, chose from a new pigskin case a cigar, lit this, and stretched himself at last at ease to look round the lounge. When his eyes met hers he allowed himself a most perceptible start. He coughed, bowed again from his chair, and looked with pained disappointment at his cigar.

'I trust the Fräulein will not be disturbed by this . . . smoke. . . .?'

She seemed not to have noticed his arrival. He repeated his question. She started, noticed him with surprise, smiled and looked at the cigar as if it were a naughty but charming child:

'No, no. I don't mind at all.'

'It would be no trouble to move. . . .'

'Please—not on my account.'

'You are very kind . . . perhaps I could offer you . . .'

But she had looked away again. She closed the interchange calmly. She did not bother to pretend to fumble with her bag. Not even to look in a direction pointedly away from his table—she simply stared straight ahead, hardly at the hotel lounge at all, perhaps seeing nothing, simply effacing herself. But de Broda had reached an age when he was no longer nervous of a snub in these matters. Once he had been most fearful of this, now he was tired and more settled— for what could it matter?—and he leaned without hesitation towards her. For propriety's sake he did not turn his full face, he leaned towards her sideways like a puppet that could not rotate:

'You're staying here for long?'

She seemed not to hear. He coughed—to offer her the excuse of really not having heard—and repeated the question. Again she started, it seemed she awoke from a slight, wide-eyed sleep, and turned to him apologetically:

'I beg your pardon?'

'Forgive me—I asked only, is the Fräulein staying long? For the cure?'

'Oh—I see.' She expressed relief—it was quite as if a hand had fluttered to her heart and she had sighed. Now she could allow herself to smile easily:

'For two weeks. No, not for the cure—for a little holiday.'

'How strange! That is exactly my own position—we must be the only two unemployed by the waters.'

'You forget the ski-run.'

'Ah yes—I'm afraid I do forget that. And when I don't forget, I regret it.'

'Oh?'

'Our country teems with ski-resorts. A good thing, among other things we need visitors. But it's out of character with this old place, it spoils the—the atmosphere.'

She jutted her lower lip—he could see where the lip rouge ended and wetter pink of the real lip began. She gave a small toss of her orange hair—he noticed that it was really orange, not dyed. She grudged at him:

'Atmosphere! It's very little use having atmosphere if you haven't any money. Think of the townsfolk.'

'And vice versa. What's the use of money if there's no one to play music?'

'Music?'

'Music. Poetry. I mean again atmosphere. The music of this curious *fin de siècle*, these hideous hotels, these rustic promenades, this engineering of the waters—everything that with the years . . . is growing so much charm!'

'You do not find it oppressive?'

'No. Let me explain. . . .'

And he explained. And for an hour they talked. They agreed to walk together the next morning, he would show her something of the quality of his beloved Gastein. So the meeting was consummated, the first act was done, the game was on—with honour on both sides. Both discreet—she the withdrawer seducing, he the seducer withdrawn.

These two, then, met at Gastein in Austria—Bad Gastein to the woman, who took things as they were; and Wildbad Gastein to de Broda, who spent much melancholy time sensing things as they had been.

Wildbad was the old name, Wild Bath, and indeed the old mountain spa must have looked ferocious in earlier days. But still today, for added reasons, it is none the less disquieting. Still the wild rocky torrent falls five hundred feet from the plateau above the basin beneath. It steams and bubbles and whirls perpendicular between the dark stone cliffs of a horrendous ravine, stone cliffs that echo and magnify the awful rush of the waters with a resonance as black as the walls themselves and the sombre mountain firs that rise wet and shadowy up each side. A wild and giddying place—and now two bridges have been built over the narrow ravine, each staring straight down on to the roaring water and the long-drop deadly flat pool beneath, each with a balustrade that feels too shallow to hold a man back.

But that is not all. For part of the water jets from inside the rock itself, and this water is hot, it steams, its white radioactive steam clouds up with the spray of the cold torrent to mist an inferno of iron winches, lock-gates, great timbers and writhing waist-thick iron pipes that climb all about the gorge—such atrocious emblems appear and vanish in the hot mist like heavy instruments of torture. Meanwhile, man came to look on. And man built up and down the walls of the cliff-sides a range of violent hotels, monster edifices whose thousand windows skyscraper not only upwards but downwards too —for their main floors open behind on to mountain streets that strike about their middles. It is as though the walls of New York were placed at a vertiginous angle above no street but a hollow staircase of water: or as if the giddy buildings of Monte Carlo were transported, paler but still unsteady, high into the mountain snows. The hotels bear such names as Grand Hôtel de l'Europe, Elizabethpark Hotel, Germania—an aristocratic fusion from the *fin de siècle* playgrounds. It is from the gilded interiors of such engines of enchanting taste that men look out on to the chasm and its torturous mists.

De Broda loved the place. He was now forty years of age, a bachelor whose parents were dead, alone in a world that had greatly changed since his youth. He had himself never known the splendours of the Austro-Hungarian Empire, but remnants of the Double Eagle were impressed on his heart and he was never far from a melancholy sense sweet enough, and of a strange anticipatory nature, of those things past. He was well enough supplied with money—he had inherited houses in Vienna and land in green Styria—and he had time to spare to stay now and then in one of the older hotels at Gastein.

Recently a new experience had befallen him—he had found himself saying his name over a shop-counter and feeling the name belonged to someone else. That is, he himself had no name, and his name made the vague shape of a person in his mind—someone he had known, and rather despised, who had been close to him but nevertheless remained a stranger, something of a shadowed enemy. He tried the name again, running it over his lips—but it had obviously nothing whatever to do with the flesh and bone and mind and blood that tried to believe it fitted. He thought then of the names of friends, of people he admired—each one of them, with the concrete personalities they evoked, he could imagine bearing his own name. So I am a stranger to myself, he concluded. And then: 'Of course, this is a common experience. At one time or another, we all wake up to our names. They represent the past figure of ourselves, a sort of shadowy film actor we never quite liked, of whose acting we were rather ashamed. They represent the worst in ourselves, our knowing nasty second selves.'

But though he reasoned thus, de Broda was left with the unreasonable feeling that really—though really, too, he knew this was nonsense—he had no longer a name. Everyone else but he had a name. And this feeling, illogical but nevertheless lingering strong, emphasized for him his lack of a bloodmark in the world—his parentless, childless state wandering in winter the nearly empty halls of this summer spa. He felt spectral.

For the previous three years he had had it on his mind to marry: that is to say, to make a sensible effort to find a woman who would measure up to his melancholy and upon whom in return he longed to lavish all the affection frustrated and stored inside him. Such a lady he found difficult to find. Some were too frivolous, some were too severe: some liked him too much, many did not like him at all. He discounted the possibility of falling in love, it seemed too late: although he saw it was possible, it was impossible to foresee. But with masculine conceit and male vigour he did not discount the possibility that a quite young girl might find him attractive—and lately he had conceived the notion that, given youth and a fair intelligence, such a young person might be malleable in his sensitive fingers, she could be moulded in time into the form of a perfect consort. An ambitious plan, one with risks—but possible. And the prettier the woman, de Broda said to himself as he planned his dream, the better.

So he had kept his eyes open. And now they had noticed with interest and some intention the figure of this good-looking young woman with the orange hair, the pensive grace. She could not have been more than twenty-five years old.

For her part, Fräulein Laure Perfuss also had hopes for a profitable holiday. She was just twenty-six years old; and though she had felt on her twenty-fifth birthday a sense of having arrived at a never-to-be-experienced-again barrier of the years—the decimal system is engraved deeply in our hearts—now that she was twenty-six a different foreboding, almost a panic momentum towards the terrible age of thirty, had seized her. To be thirty—and unmarried! Laure was on the look-out for a husband: or, let us be fair, she was inclined to observe the gentlemen she met with a more deeply considerative, a more long-range eye.

And there were other reasons for this. Unlike de Broda, but like most Austrians of upper caste she had come down in the world. Her family had lost money and their home: now she herself lived in one room high up in a cold old mansion high up the Mariahilfer Strasse—her mother had long ago returned to their native Tyrol. She herself was too much now of a Viennese to leave. She worked in a high-class Konditorei—and though her wages were small, this was the one reliable pleasure of her life. Although she stood on the service side of a counter piled with trays of cakes and cellophaned sweets, it still meant for her a real connection with the old life. To that same shop she had been brought as a child by her mother. She remembered the silk blinds, tasselled, and the colour of pale creamed coffee; silver trays of sweets flashing their softness and sugar—montelimar, dragees, pralines, a hundred cellophaned marvels; most of all the polished wooden order of the yellow parquet floor and the great brass-trimmed counter and the tables with their smooth cane chairs—no gilt or plush nor coloured fabrication here, only the smooth polished woods everywhere and the cakes and the silver-trayed sweets. Now, when Fräulein Laure served her customers in the middle of the morning, when the smell of coffee, and scents of fur and perfume excited the air, when noise and a brisk draught of the street entered with the glass door's opening—she remembered autumns long past, when fresh from treading the yellow leaves outside, her own buttoned gaiters had swung under those same tables: and she remembered with pleasure, with no regret. Although she was on the wrong side of the counter, she could still smell the actuality of the sweet smells, she still walked among the elegancies of the room.

But—though one of the happiest states of life is to like one's work —she knew this could not go on. She was a woman, she feared the shelf. She had fallen in and out of love. Several times she had been near to marriage: but a certain hope had always held her back. Her young men, also poor, might have made excellent husbands. But they would not have provided excellent homes. Laure was simply holding on for her prince on his white steed. However, he had not come. And now she was twenty-six and already in the mirror of her mind heading hard for thirty.

In the circumstances, Bad Gastein was not the best choice for a holiday. The great old spa was threequarters empty, the hotel the same—but the short holiday was a gift from an aunt with romantic memories of the grand days, and Gastein had been almost a condition. As it was, this man whose card she now had in her bag, Herr de Broda, was the only unattached, the only nearly young man staying in the hotel. She assessed him carefully. He was handsome. She saw a white-skinned, dark-haired man—there was a bloom on his skin like polished bone. His hair grew thickly, it was tough and its wave oiled down, it was shaved low at the back of his neck, even beneath his collar. His dark eyebrows met to make less a satanic than a thoughtful appearance—for his eyes were large, soft, southern. Jewish or half Italian—his family had been shipowners in Fiume. He was reserved and spoke with a laboured weariness. The 'poetic type,' she decided. In his way he was charming, really quite charming. And well mannered. And well-off.

That evening she sat at her dressing-table and thoughtfully ran the sharp edge of his card against the flesh of her middle finger. She looked down at her clear-varnished nails holding the white card: then up at her face in the mirror. She tossed her orange hair and stared. Sometimes she had idled—a little fearfully—with the idea of a rich protector. Since the war several girls she knew had affianced themselves thus—and it had not seemed to make much change in them. She stared in the mirror at her face, beautiful and saddened by such thoughts. *Her* face! How tragic that it should be given away! *Tragic.* Yes, even in marriage.

The next day they walked together in the snow. It was fine January weather. The U-shaped valley lay before them many miles below, and they set out for the winding König Karol Promenade, skirting the side of the mountain along the right-hand side of the U. Above, firs rose in tiers. Their herring-bone branches glittered like marquisite. Far below, with coloured villages mapped on what seemed a flat white play-board, the valley: on foggy days from these promenades, when the valley was hidden, one felt one was looking out to sea.

But now no sea—everywhere soft snow. And soundless—their footsteps soft, the sudden shush sound of a passing sleigh, bells from below muffled, and in the immense false spring sky, blue as spring, a wide smiling sense that all occasional cries were welcomed upwards and like birds embraced in the sunlit echo of the upper air.

De Broda was well-slept, bathed, fresh, clean. Into the warmth of his big fur coat he took deep breaths of cold magical air. He felt fine. But he felt no 'countryman' feeling: he felt no temptation to become rougher, more rustic in the way of his walk. He felt, exquisitely, that he was a townsman sipping the weather, the scenery: he was a metropolitan tasting from within his warm elegance the country air. And beside him, in her green cape and her white fur hat, walked this pleasing graceful girl from Vienna. Her orange hair cut sharply against the white snow. What was it like? He wondered —then laughed deep inside his coat, for it was like nothing else but a patch of horse-urine in the snow. Or, should he try to say, the orange-iron mark of a mountain spring?

He said instead: 'And in Vienna, Fräulein Perfuss—do you live still with your family? Or have you your own—but these are hard days to find a flat. . . .'

'I live alone.'

'A career girl? What times we move in!'

'I work a little.'

'Let me guess—the arts? No? Then I have it—you design dresses! That cloak. . . .!'

'Wrong again.'

She laughed—it was a carefully light careless laugh—and put her hand up to shade her eyes pretending to look out over the valley. She could tell him about that job much later.

'You're very inquisitive,' she laughed.

He spread his hands: 'Inquisitive? No. Interested—yes! Perhaps because I hope we are going to be very good friends—it's most natural to be interested.'

'In that case I shall listen to you first. Talk to me about yourself. Tell me about the things you like.'

He was only too glad. Her education could commence immediately.

He halted abruptly in the snowy track and pointed. 'I like that,' he said.

They were just below the great façade of the Germania, golden-buff in the snow. Its terraces descended to the path, the bark-balustraded woodland promenade on which they stood. Over the near hedge of snow, on the nearest terrace, rose a small wrought-iron kiosk. Icicles hung from its summer roof. It looked like a prettily iced cake. 'You can smell the lilac,' he said.

She looked up at him and sniffed: 'Lilac?' she asked. Her eyes narrowed, peering for the joke.

'I mean, you can feel the gardens as they are in summer. But— winter has stolen the scent of lilac, time the scent of patchouli.'

'It looks pretty draughty to me,' she said.

He laughed. But he continued. His voice lingered about the ironwork, then rose up to the great hotel above. He spoke of the dresses of the ladies in the Emperor's day, of the carriages, all the wealth of leisurely fashion before the Wars. She listened, staring at the little kiosk with its eagle emblem. She found him dull. But he was careful to picture in the scene the things she might like—muffs, gloves, fans, jewellery—and once or twice she caught his mood, she felt a pleasing sorrowful pang.

EPISODE AT GASTEIN

They stood and looked back over the valley to where the hub of the spa bridged its ravine like a many-windowed Bridge of Sighs. There had been a heavy fall of snow; all around, on each separate object—a small bush, a balustrade, a rustic fence—the fall had moulded a strange snow-shape, fat and round and always benevolent. De Broda went on to tell his Fräulein Perfuss of the many famous figures of the near past who had visited the spa, and who by virtue of merely their uniforms and their figuration in a more ample age, had become figures of distant charm. He told her of Bismarck. He told her how the Emperor himself had come to open the small mountain-railway station—there was a plaque there commemorating the event.

By now Laure gave him all her attention. She was interested—at the way he spoke and possibly by what he said. For his part, de Broda felt his usual satisfaction on speaking of these things. When he spoke of them his imagination widened and they came even closer. But usually he discussed them—now he found he was teaching, he was feeding words and scenes to the upturned and—yes!—interested face by his side. He felt himself grow physically bigger.

They walked slowly back. The crisp air, the altitude, the wintry sunlight enlivened them. The very orderliness of the place, within the soft disorder of snow, was pleasing. They passed a Kurhaus, a Pediküre-salon—this was a spa for the aged, well conducted, comfortable and safe. Down past the old Straubinger Hotel, grey-green and cream against the snow: past Stone and Blyth, the English tailors: past false pink marble, past a stucco Greek mask and grapes, past a stone stag's head—each framed by the white snow: past the entrance of the old Wandelbahn, the long glazed gallery—how thoughtful!—for walking in wet weather: and suddenly de Broda stopped. By the entrance of a hotel he had found a new treasure—something he had never seen before. Excitedly, he drew Laure's attention to it.

It was a miniature copper Chinese pavilion screwed to the wall. In the tarnished copper frame of the pavilion old and dusty charts were set, and dials and needles. It was called, in retrained lettering, Lambrecht's Wettertelegraf and Thermo-Hygroscop. What slow mystery was enacted here! What an air of the diligent, hush-voiced laboratory! De Broda was delighted. Again simply the sense of something of an older decade—irrespective of aesthetic worth—claimed him. He began to speak at length thrilledly. He invented a myth to suit its solemn inauguration on that wall years ago, he described with wit the wonder, almost the terror this strange little pavilion had evoked among an ailing aristocracy of the time. '*That's* progress!' 'But what is the pen writing, what then is it writing?' 'Chinese, madam,' the General had answered.

He suddenly found he was talking to himself. Laure had moved a foot or two aside and was peering, as decently as she could, at a group of film photographs advertising the nearby cinema.

Separately, at six o'clock, they lay in their thermal baths, thinking.

'Not so good,' de Broda thought. 'A waste of time. Films!' He gave a vicious whisk to the black hoselength lurking like an eel with him in the grave-deep bath.

Along the quiet corridor, up some stairs, and down another corridor, Laure too lay naked in deep warm water.

'Wettertelegraf!' she pouted to her legs floating white, dead, detached. 'Really!' She patted the china tassel of the bellrope with a pettish groan. '*What* does he expect a girl to . . .'

'She ought to understand,' he said aloud, 'that there are other interests in life than, than . . .' He heard his voice echoing round the tiles. It sounded like someone else intoning at him. Instinct drifted his hand across the most intimate nakedness.

'Why doesn't he behave like a normal man? Why doesn't he say something like . . . like what normal men say?' She switched herself round frowning, clutching the bath-steps for support, and looked up at the brass-bound clock in the wall. Five minutes more. Five minutes to lie warm and think. She looked down her long white body and watched her hair float up like the feelers of a pale anemone.

So they lay in their big private baths and gave themselves to the warm healing water. Neither needed healing. But in such tiled seclusion, in the little tall rooms with their ample graves of water, and with the high black windows above showing the white beat of the snow outside, demonstrating as an aquarium feature all the coldness of the Austrian mountain night outside against the warmth within—in such clean tiled seclusion and such large warm water not only the body but also the mind was healed.

'Come, come,' de Broda thought. 'Don't let's be intolerant. Don't let's us be hurried. It was only a lapse—why, in any case, shouldn't she like the films? A young girl has her interests. There are very good films, too. Sometimes. She was really most charming . . . that is, earlier . . .' And alone there his lips parted in a wide smile as he remembered the pleasant feelings he had, the expanded sense of himself, before the unfortunate matter of the Wettertelegraf. Then he kicked his foot right out of the water in self-reproach, 'Vanity!' he said sternly. He stared suddenly hard at his big toe sticking up as from a separate body. There were several long black hairs streaming down beneath the nail. 'Why!' he thought in wonder, 'I've never noticed *those* before.'

Laure grew warmer and more comfortable. 'Still, I like a man to be different. He's different, all right.' She grimaced. Then, suddenly startled by all the water round her, wondered: 'Should I put my head under?' She decided not. Relieved, she thought: 'He's really rather *charming*. He'd be a credit. I can just see him at the head of the table, a party for just six. . . .' And her mind crept about silver candlesticks, a glitter of glasses, and the form of de Broda across the polished table with his polished manners so ably discoursing—he inclined a little forward to the lady seated on his right. That lady too inclined forward, her eyes never leaving his face. . . . Laure rose with an abrupt splash and began soaping herself severely. 'As for *her* . . .' she muttered decisively.

'I wonder,' de Broda mused, 'what her body's like?' He thought hard, suspended now on the water on his stomach, only his chin jutting on to one of the marble steps and supporting all. It proved difficult to imagine a strange woman's body: a known one was always substituted. 'Anyway, she's beautiful.'

'But I suppose,' she thought, 'I suppose he's hairs all over. . . .'

And he who liked most kinds said ponderously to himself, 'She's just my type.'

'Laure!' She giggled to herself as she made an untranslatable pun.

During the next few days they saw much of each other. They went for sleigh-rides up and down the mountain tracks. The sleighs were trimmed with brass and curved ironwork, their high seats were padded with green plush—and as they carved their soft-belled way through the steep alleys, as they passed fir-trees with fretted branches moulded by snow to look themselves like huge fir-cones, as they mounted to Rudolfshöhe or descended past a curtain of icicles to the lower rocks, all was romantic all most *altoesterreichisch*. The sleigh-drivers wore moss-green hats or hats of Styrian black and emerald. But once—much to de Broda's disgust—one of them wore an old leather flying-bonnet. De Broda had noticed this the moment they approached the line of sleighs waiting for hire. And he had shuffled about in the snow for a few minutes, hoping someone else would take the man. But no—and Laure had looked at him suspiciously as he made false conversation. He was about to try to explain to her— and suddenly found this impossible. It would sound like so much whimsy. Such refinements are only communicable between people of similar taste. And he had, in fact, too good a sense of humour to persist—so they had hired the man. The drive was nevertheless spoilt. He could not take his eyes off that flying-bonnet.

However, that morning produced its great compensation. They descended at one of the largest of the enormous hotels. There in the immense empty lounge they had ordered glasses of the bubbling spa water itself—for it was too late for coffee. Cold water after the brisk cold drive! They had laughed. And for some reason he had mentioned—perhaps à propos of the desolate air of an out-of-season hotel —the works of Thomas Mann. She had read them. And she had read much else. To his surprise he found she had developed quite a reasonable taste in literature. He found with joy that at last they had one taste in common.

But why? Then he thought of a girl's life, of her gentle bringing up, of the hours of careful seclusion imposed on her. He did not think of the hours of seclusion imposed on a working girl, hours in a room alone with an empty purse. However, in a way and not knowing it, he was right. For without her early education, Laure might have preferred to books the little radio, or hour-long experiments with her own face in the mirror.

Thenceforward they talked a lot about books. Once, de Broda found himself wondering: If she has read so much, if her imagination is thus so livened—why does she not respond more easily to the other things I talk about? The senses of time? Myths of the past? Could I —after all—be phrasing these things badly? He could not believe so. But then he did not know that books for Laure were in the first place a last resort. When she was out and about—and especially now on her holiday—her desire was for action and life. Though she understood much of de Broda's discourse, she was impatient of it. She listened with half an ear. She wanted to escape sentiments that in her reading she had only half-experienced, for in its way the grey page was a prison.

Still, they had a subject in common. It greased their passage. As the days went on, they became more intimate. However—it was not all easy. There was the afternoon, for instance, when it snowed again. Even the quiet air of Gastein grew quieter. Sounds underfoot were muffled by the old snow, and the new fall filled the air with a dizzy kinematic flicker. One looked up, and the white sky was black with flakes forever dropping: one looked at the black firs and the dark plastered houses and the flakes fell white: it was the sight of so much falling without sound that added to the soundlessness. In such air they walked a little—snow mounted and melted in Laure's orange hair, on the brim of de Broda's hat. To avoid getting wet through they turned into a hotel. The light was fading. It was time for coffee.

Out of the soundlessness of the snow—through the double swing-doors into steamheat and light and suddenly voices from everywhere!

'It's not!'

'It is!'

'Der Bobby!'

'Bobby! In Gastein!'

And for a moment it seemed an endless number of people in high spirits and smart clothes crowded round de Broda. He was startled, confused—and then annoyed. These were old friends from Vienna, friends from ten years ago when he had led—despite the time, perhaps because of the times—a gayer and more frivolous life. Before the worm had crept in—before he had reached that point in early middle years when a tiredness, a certain intolerant familiarity with life had claimed him. One could not call this a false tiredness; but it was disproportionate; and perhaps a little later on it would melt with the tolerance of years and he would regain some of his easier, earlier, priceless, worthless joys.

But now he had the worm. And greeted by this group of light people he felt angry, embarrassed and ashamed. Indeed, the latter he might be allowed—for this little lot were not the best kind of company. They might have been gay, but they made a strident flashy exhibition of themselves too. They talked, among the quiet coffee-drinkers, at the tops of their voices: in their actions they pirouetted and gestured with too great an ease—their absolute in-difference to the room was a conscious insult; a boordom.

'But Bobby—you must come with us!'

'Here—this table by the piano?'

'Egon's going to play!'

'Oh—the Bobby . . . how serious! . . . this way to the museum, please!'

De Broda had so many to shake hands with that he had time to plan his retreat. With his back to Laure—whom he had not intro-duced—he made his face into a mask of theirs and winked at them. He winked that he wanted to be alone with his little picce. Ah, they thought, the Bobby! The old Bobby! And instantly they acknow-ledged the formality of the occasion—it was the only convention they bowed to. They nodded knowingly and left him.

De Broda led Laure over to the furthest end of the room. He felt ashamed that he had denied his real personality, thus he was awkward.

'Awful people,' he apologized. 'I'm so sorry.'

'But they seemed quite gay.'

'I used to know them once—a long time ago.'

They ordered coffee. Near them hung a picture of a fat German Count—a famous and ferocious General—seated on a horse. He was in full hunting-dress, and from his magnificent eminence on the great stallion he held proudly in his hand a single desolate dead hare. It was entitled: 'Jagd.'

De Broda tried to find some aesthetic quality in the picture, found none, and was driven to talking again of the atmosphere of period it now described. Laure listened, but listlessly. Meanwhile the other party had grouped themselves round the piano, and the Hungarian Egon—a small round dapper man with a black moustache, an oiled and energetic man—had begun to play the piano. The others hummed, then broke into song. It was a tango: 'Küss' mich heut' portugiesisch.' One or two of the other people in the lounge looked round and smiled. An old man shook his head, but benevolently behind his paper. Plainly the room was not so insulted as de Broda had thought. Laure's eyes gleamed a growing delight.

Suddenly she turned to him: 'Why don't we go over there?'

'But Laure. . . .!'

'So little happens here—they look fun. *Do* let's!'

He felt sad and funless, clumsily and drily a spoiler of fun. He felt how much older he was. Yet persisted:

'Look, Laure—those are silly people. They're not worth while. I don't want you to know them.'

'But they're your friends?'

'Of a kind—of an old vintage, gone sour.'

'I'm not so sure who's sour.' She paused. 'Why don't you want *me* to meet them? Why *me*?'

He made an earnest expression, He made a grave, thoughtful face of care for her:

'Because, Laure, I take *you* seriously.'

It should have worked. But it didn't. It was a mistake. It gave Laure exactly the confirmation of this interest in her that she had wanted. He had never said anything like that before, and the spoken word, however often it is spoken, is important.

Power is an ugly word. Let us say it gave her a feeling of certainty, and with this of exhilaration.

'Oh how sweet!' she smiled. And then giggled. '. . . Bobby dear!'

He was still looking shocked when she put her finger to her lips and, standing up, asked him to excuse her. She went as if to the ladies' room. But on the way she passed the piano, just as 'Kiss me today in a Portuguese way' was coming to an end. Not stopping, she smiled at them unreservedly and sang out the last two bars. They clapped. And she was out through the swing-doors.

So that when after a few minutes she returned they felt they knew her and implored her to sing more with them. She did, and for a long time she stood and chatted and laughed and sang.

De Broda was left alone with the German Count and his hare. He stared up at the picture and fumed.

But later, lying in his warm appeaseful bath, he forgave her. After all, she didn't know the crowd in question. And it showed she was lively. A girl should have her fun. It was indeed, he concluded happily, a very rare combination—an intelligent girl, an *intellectual* girl with a liking for liveliness. But he thanked heaven the party had already driven off back to Vienna.

Two days later, up towards the Villa Cäcilie, a young man skied straight into them.

They all fell down.

But no one was hurt. The young man had come fast round the bend, had tried to check as he saw them, had struck a patch of ice, but then in fact had fallen and come only slithering into them on his behind. De Broda had thrown Laure back into the snow and himself across her. Now, surprised and covered with white patches, they all sat in the snow and felt themselves. Only Laure laughed.

The young man—he was plainly a visitor, he wore no local fawn or green but a dark blue ski-suit and a long peaked cap—was most apologetic. He asked repeatedly if they were not hurt? He showed not only politeness but real concern. De Broda was mollified. He laughed, shaking the snow off his coat, and assured the young man that no harm was done. He felt rather pleased that he had thrown himself in protection across Laure.

That evening the young man called at their hotel. He held some tickets in his hand. He was dressed in American clothes, but moved with European gestures of courtesy.

'I can't forgive myself for this morning's accident . . . it was really so foolish of me,' he said to de Broda. 'Please let me make some slight recompense—there is a gala dance tomorrow at the . . .'

'But, my dear fellow, don't for a moment think—'

'I would be honoured if your daught—if the Fräulein and your-self would be my guests.'

He turned for the first time to Laure.

'You must persuade him, Fräulein!'

Of course de Broda had not missed that suppressed 'daughter'. His instant reaction was to accept, to show how young he was, to show he could dance as gaily as anyone else. But reactions have their own reactions: and irritated by the youthful parade forced upon him, and moved also by his underlying dislike of dancing—he protested that he himself did not enjoy such evenings at a holiday resort. He inferred that they could be better had in the metropolis.

It was half-past seven, the cleaned and rested hour after the bath. De Broda, comfortable and thus the more generous, gestured towards Laure. 'But naturally,' he said, 'if Fräulein Perfuss would like to go—'

The young man said nothing; but he looked at Laure with a polite questioning smile. Consideratively, as though this kind of invitation occurred nightly at Gastein, Laure said: 'Well—let's see, tomorrow night. No, I'm not doing anything. I don't think—yes. I'd be delighted to accompany you.'

'Excellent!'

Then the young man out of politeness, without much emphasis, tried again to persuade de Broda.

'No, no, no. I wouldn't think of it. You two enjoy yourselves.' He held his hand up to ward off finally all protestation. Then: 'But I must introduce you—Fräulein Perfuss. And my name is de Broda.'

'Peter Hörnli. Enchanted.'

'Hörnli?'

'From Zürich.'

'Ah. And how are you finding our Austria?'

After a while the young man left. They agreed he seemed a nice enough young fellow. De Broda felt pleased and strangely possessive. It showed him, really for the first time, how intimate they had become in these few days. He knew, and it pleased him to know, that he could let her go off for an evening without fear. Besides, the chap was just a young Swiss.

Laure seemed to have appreciated his action. She grew even more charming during the next few days. She had enjoyed the dance very much, she said. It was a change. Herr Hörnli had proved a most pleasant companion.

Then one evening, two days later, de Broda took her up above Gastein to dinner in an inn on the Böckstein plateau. Plateau? It was another valley, another great U above the Gastein U. In Gastein one could think there was nothing higher, in Gastein one had touched the sky. But lo! a five minutes' walk up the mountainside that enclosed the great valley—and there one was on the ground floor of another valley again enclosed by horseshoe mountains! One felt this stepped ascent might go on for ever, it was like entering a hall of mirrors. In such discovery there is magic. Laure and de Broda, as they stepped up on to Böckstein, felt as if they had entered a dream. And that evening was indeed enchanted.

First, the magic of discovering such a valley—as mysteriously exciting as a strange garden discovered in childhood, a garden through a gate in a wall, a garden that one feels, in the instant one finds it, will disappear the next day never to be found again. Secondly, the snow had ceased to fall, and a clear crescent moon stood high in the sky, casting blue light everywhere: icicles in fir-trees flashed this light, and one saw how people had first thought of putting tinsel on Christmas trees. They went into an inn and ate trout freshly fished from the rocky river: trouts cooked in butter from the cream of the valley, herbed from the valley, and followed down by a bottle of one of the valley's cold clear rain-gold wines. Coffee, imported on a tired schilling, was hell. But then out into the moonlight, out cleansing the mouth with the smell of snow, and a wine-warmed walk to another inn just across the way. In there, a live merriment prevailed; it was the weekly zither-abend. Two squat coarse men with faces of the mountains, gnome-faces with close eyes and great noses, plucked at the little stringed boards before them. Their fingers were broad and swollen, too big for the finely-laid strings. Yet they plucked, plucked with curiosity—as if this were a strange cabalistic game and the zithers magic boards—and out sang the heavy little mountain waltzes.

More wine, and de Broda found himself linking arms and leaning close against a warm, flushed, happy Laure. Sometimes everybody in the room sang and thumped the tables, and Laure and de Broda sang too. They were closer, easier, more comfortable with each other than ever before. In that white room, clean as a dairy, and among the villagers in their sober suits and their drunken orderliness—they had touched an atmosphere removed a hundred miles from the grave majesty of Gastein. By some miracle of ventilation, the smoke of cigars vanished instantly; much wine was drunk, yet none spilled; it was unusual and dreamlike to see so many swaying wine-filled bodies and to hear such boisterous music in so orderly, so white and scrubbed a room. But this was no place of Swiss prettiness, it was heavy and solid.

De Broda was enjoying himself. He felt relaxed and blank-minded and light-headed. Occasionally he tried to pull himself—as he called it—together. How could the hour be improved? Once, he remembered that Count Czernin's shooting-box stood along the valley: and he began to speak of this. But he soon stopped.

Suddenly Laure put her arm round his neck and kissed him.

It was at the end of a song which she had been humming to herself, smiling down at the wine-flask. The song ended with three long waltz-beats. On each chord she gave him a long decided kiss on the lips.

De Broda was surprised to find himself not at all astonished. It seemed the most normal thing. Not, indeed, that it was unusual for a couple to kiss at a time of music and wine. Nor, very naturally, was it unexciting. No, it was exciting. But still—normal, as though it had been ordained, as though it might already have happened before.

As the songs were sung, as the wine-flasks emptied, they kissed again. De Broda, for once speechless, murmured only her name. Laure said nothing. She was by no means drunk: but there was about her a carelessness and a flushed bright enchantment. She seemed full of secret thoughts—secrets that made her blush and smile into herself. Now and then she held her head back from de Broda and looked at him carefully, her lips parted in peculiar interest, half-closed eyes seeming to measure him.

They left, and arm in arm walked down the snowy hill-road. At the escarpment edge Gastein came into view, they were just above the huddled high roofs—it looked a strange metropolis huddled in the moonlit gorge. Nearby the waterfall drummed. They left the road and stamped through moss-mounds of snow to the bridge over the fall. There they stood and gazed with wonder and with fear at the spectacle beneath.

Wide in front the moonlit valley—white and wide, with the mountainsides tinselling their firs into blue black distance. But just beneath only darkness and the cold roar of ceaseless water. Sound echoed from the rock walls round them, such a weight of water has a machine roar, the light wooden bridge itself seemed to drum with the sound. De Broda put his arm round Laure. They stood close together moved by the great beauty around them, close too against the beautiful greatness of the fearful thing below them.

The cold air exhilarated, it was sparkling clear and mixed wonderfully with the warm wine-fumes. A great joy seemed to swell within de Broda's breast, he bent closer to her profile, so sadly, so beautifully incised in the moonlight—and with a blessed sense of release the words of a proposal rose to his lips.

'Laure, dearest Laure. . . .' he whispered.

She turned to him.

And then suddenly the long elegant worm inside rose, the delicate worm bit him. As it bit, his lips made themselves thinner, he felt his eyes focus clearer. 'No,' murmured the cold emotionless worm. 'No. Don't be overtaken by events. You did not decide to do this yet. You decided to take exactly your own time, chose your hour, seek your setting. In another couple of days, you said.'

'Laure,' de Broda said, 'let's go.'

The next morning he came down late, enquired for Laure, and was told she had already left for a walk. It had become their custom to spend their mornings together, and he was a little irritated. However, he blamed himself for rising so late, put on his coat and went out.

It was a beautiful morning. He decided to descend the steep paths by the waterfall itself, and found himself in strange country. Great conduit pipes like sleeping boas wandered among the snow and jagged rocks; rusted winches and lock-gates draped their curtains of icicle: such a vast old machinery astounded, and steam from the hot spring rose all around against the snow. Down there, deep in the gorge, the roar of the torrent drowned all other sound. De Broda was fascinated; but not for more than a quarter-hour. Normally he enjoyed a solitary walk, normally he was delighted to escape companionship. But not that day. He began to find himself uneasy for Laure's company.

She did not appear at luncheon.

He spent the afternoon wandering from hotel to hotel in the hope of seeing her. He ended the afternoon with a book, and went up to his bath early.

But once more the comfort of those waters put him at his ease, and it was in good temper that he descended to dine.

For a number of reasons—because until the previous night they had not been on intimate but only on familiar terms, because also de Broda had been taking his time and had wished to maintain some independence, and moreover because the very size of the great mirrored and pillared dining-hall suggested a propriety that linked each table privately with each guest—they had not dined at the same table. So, since that evening Laure came down late, they did not meet until after dinner.

De Broda was careful to seem unconcerned. He waved an invitation to her from his coffee-table—the distance of manners between the lounge and the dining-room, in fact no more than an inch of curtained glass door, might have been a mile—and Laure smiled her way over.

He did not ask her anything, but entered instantly into a discourse upon his own day:

'. . . one might have been on a harbour quay, such extraordinary machinery for controlling the water, and on each side the hotel walls, like wharves . . .'

'Really?'

'. . . and far, far above, against the sky, our bridge . . .'

'Our bridge?'

'I mean, the bridge we stood on last night.'

'Oh, my dear, of *course.*'

A pause. De Broda risked a tender look. He felt truly tender: only his mind, his mind layered with experience, made it a risk.

Laure smiled brightly back. There was something inside her bubbling to come out. Suddenly it came:

'You know,' she said—and her lips dropped as though she ought not to say it—'at least you don't know, you'd never *guess* where *I've* been today!'

Desperate to control himself, de Broda made a blank, bored face that in other circumstances might have looked plain rude. But Laure was too concerned to notice.

'I daren't tell you,' she said. 'I daren't!'

He managed a smile: 'Then you must keep it a dead secret. No! Not a word!'

Laure's mouth hung still half-open. She stopped, astonished. Then a look of such disappointment came into her eyes that even de Broda saw he was being too cruel. He leaned closer, and making a play of conspiracy, whispered: 'A secret—but let *me* into it.'

She took a deep breath:

'I've been ski-ing!'

It was so much a reverse of all he wished for that he forgot himself. 'Ski-ing! Why? Who on earth with?'

'Oh . . .'

She pretended nonchalance:

'Herr Hörnli.'

'Who . . .? Oh, that young Swiss?'

'Yes. He passed the hotel earlyish—long before you were up. (How's the head, by the way?) We talked a few minutes. Then he said why didn't I ski, and he would teach me. It was such a beautiful morning I went.'

De Broda regained himself with a pale smile: 'So you went up and I went down.'

'Can't say I didn't go down once or twice too,' she giggled. De Broda laughed uneasily.

'But you enjoyed yourself?'

'Mm. It was lovely.'

And she went on to tell him all about it. She told him how fine the air was, what fun it had been, where they had lunched, how they had tobogganed home.

'It was difficult again at first,' she finished. 'But I'll soon get used to it.'

De Broda had been thinking—in the tolerance of his chair and the coffee and the lovely brightnesses of her smile and her hair— thinking how after all a day out must have made a refreshing change. But at her last words he properly flinched:

'Get *used* to it?'

'Yes. I'm going to concentrate.'

'But Laure—you've only four days left!'

'That's exactly it. Only four days. I'll have to work hard.'

'You're going ski-ing every day?'

'Oh yes.'

'But Laure—our walks together, we were going . . .'

'Ludwig dear—*please*. You know I was supposed to be having a holiday. It's as much for my health as anything. After being cooped up in that . . . in Vienna. I really owe it to myself.'

'Then I won't be seeing much of you.'

'Oh, Ludwig—yes. In the evenings.'

'It's not much.'

'So you don't want to see me in the evening?'

'You know I didn't mean that.'

'But you *said* so.'

'No. Please, Laure dearest—how can I put it—I meant . . .'

And for a few minutes they lightly quarrelled. De Broda grew more flustered and more apologetic. With fine petulant logic she undressed all his well-meaning. De Broda found himself physically sweating and gasping a little for breath.

Laure relaxed. And de Broda was so much relieved that together they spent a quiet pleasant evening.

Yet every so often de Broda remembered the kisses of the night before, and glanced at her curiously. How could she seem to forget so quickly? How retreat so easily to her earlier distance from him? Retreating to lead him on? It didn't feel like it.

The wine? Perhaps. But he thought not. And he contented himself by shaking inside his polite face a worldly wise head. 'Women!' his wisdom said. It explained nothing. It excused everything. 'Women —they're unpredictable!' he repeated, and felt much better.

Had he been alone, that is truly alone, he would have delighted in the great blue winter weather and enjoyed a long walk on the white mountainside. But he was less alone than lonesome. So the next day found him impatient of the mountains and simply drifting about the small centre of Gastein itself. He knew he was alone until the evening, the whole day was free—but he could make no decision. In fact, what he had to do was simply wait until she returned. Until that time life had no moment. It was much the same, though much magnified, as the empty endless day before a long anticipated treat, before a ball.

So he wandered round the hotels and cure-houses and the little shops. Gastein is small. One can wander from end to end in ten minutes. And back. And back again. Neither the antlers on the Villa Solitude nor the wild bulk of the Grand Hôtel de l'Europe nor the glass canopy of the art nouveau fashion arcade, nor the damask and great brass hatpegs of the Mozart any longer entranced him. Finally he thumped the snow off his boots, entered enormous swing-doors, took a chair in an immense empty lounge and ordered a glass of active water.

The waiter—one waiter for a hundred empty chairs—approached and receded soundlessly on thick carpet. He came and went like a figure projected, magnified and then minimized, on a screen of empty air. All one side of the lounge was glass. A long way away rose a splendid view of the mountains. But inside at the tables one felt more the glass than the view—which lay back removed like a picture. Glassy cold light like water filled every corner of the lounge. Nowhere the comfort of a dark warm shadow.

Far away, through pillars and down marble steps, the majestic door occasionally revolved, a hushed conversation whispered at the desk with its shaded light, and some other lonely traveller passed on quiet carpets into tall corridors and away. Occasionally a bell buzzed somewhere: one expected, somehow, a sort of answer to this discreet summons: but none was heard.

De Broda's little bottle of water bubbled silently. But it made the only movement, and a fierce one, in the room. He himself sat absolutely still. He was engraved in the solitude—any movement would ricochet painfully in such quiet. The noise of movement would stamp too severely, then echo, then vanish to reinforce the vacuum: its shape of movement would jitter slyly in mirrors all around. For there were many mirrors—the great hall was built at a time when opulence mattered more than taste. Many styles were mixed—gilt, marbles, mirrors, plushes, brasses fought for stately precedence. It was indistinguishable from the hotel hall of a capital railway terminus anywhere. And in it de Broda began to feel as lonely as a waiting traveller. Of course, he was one.

He sighed to his glass of water. He looked round for a paper: there was none. He looked round to see if, finally, the great room was empty: it was. He looked down at his fingers—it might be an idea to manicure his nails: but they were already done. He thought he would run over whatever papers might be in his wallet, and he felt in his pocket: but it was not there. He remembered, as one can know with instant certainty the difference between a lost and left wallet—leaving it in the hotel. But in this he was nearly saved. For a moment he became anxious. Ordering a drink without money! Would they think—? How would he convince them? But wearily the moment subsided, he had remembered how well known he was.

And minute by minute the loneliness grew—he could quite easily have called for a paper, but his mood and the silence forbade it—and that strange feeling of 'having no name' returned. Ludwig de Broda, he said it to himself, Ludwig de Broda. It seemed absurd—or less than that, meaningless. He looked down at his paunch. There was certainly someone there, a slimmish someone who kept unbuttoned the lowest button on his waistcoat, and that someone was, as he knew, himself. But was it Ludwig de Broda? No.

That Ludwig de Broda was a nothing. A little fearfully, the man in the chair tried to substantiate him. He racked his mind for scenes where de Broda had figured. The film, not in monotone as so often in a dream, but in full colour as flesh and clothes flashed across his mind. De Broda waving goodbye to a girl from the deck of a steamer leaving Budapest: de Broda in the Dolomites, a small lungfresh figure alone with a huge view: and for no particular reason de Broda in a narrow alley in Vienna, and again at some party, and in a room full of flowers lifting the hem of a housemaid's skirt, and so on.

He watched this de Broda in flashes through his life—until he entered the last ten years, the years of aestheticism. And now as he watched that figure of himself in picture galleries, or watching the Belvedere die in the winter sun, or standing in a railway terminus evoking its rampant days—now the character of the figure con-verged with his own actuality in the sort of railway hotel lounge where he was sitting and he grew more apprehensive as still it stayed separate. It seemed always to be someone else. He tried to shake the thought away, he sat up and concentrated on what was around him.

It was, of course, the hall of a railway terminus. That had dove-tailed nicely: so then he shook the terminus away, and made himself see that he was in Bad Gastein and nowhere else. But rather than bringing him to his senses, this instead reinforced the abysmal sense of loss into which he had drifted. For now again, examining a frieze of plaster amorini, feeling the long dusted drift of the great tasselled curtains, realizing the brass double eagle worked into the fender by the great fireplace—he was again back in the past century. And, whatever melancholy pleasures he derived from the paradise past, he suffered three distinct and almost material losses whenever he thought of it.

First, the appalling notion that he had just missed all that—not by any acceptable stretch of time, such as a hundred years—but by a single generation. He had just missed it—and this easily led to a feeling that it had been purposely done to him, that he had been left out.

Secondly, there was the suspicion that *life then had been all right*. As in our personal memories we usually tend to isolate and picture not times of distress but scenes of happiness or elation—how equally natural is it to conjure up and exaggerate the best of a whole period of the past! He saw in the decade of that brass double eagle only amplitude and finesse. It made today worse. So—*he had been robbed*, he was lost in the daylight present.

And thirdly, thinking of the *fin de siècle*, he had an impression always of people in groups, never single. The group of the family—

when homes were spacious and by whole households lived in. And the larger groups of occasion: the full house of the opera, the fashionable drives of the Ringstrasse seemed to have been peopled not by individuals about their own pursuits but by a gathering of people framed in a picture of united purpose. And in the country, or in such a hotel as that in which he now sat, he saw large groups at the tables, parties of people always, and always at some height of laughter or private festival. Now, of course, there were no groups, there was neither fulness nor purpose. *There was only loneliness.*

But already it was one o'clock. An hour for luncheon, and it would be two o'clock. The long hours until he would see Laure again were lessening. He cheered up a little.

After his bath, the day over, fresh and expectant, he was delighted to find Laure down in the lounge early.

Her orange head was bent over a writing-desk. When he went over to her she looked up happily. Her face still held the flush of the snows, she had the cool radiant certainty of a woman who has just descended from the bedroom mirror. She looked up and smiled:

'I'm just writing home—to plead for another two days.'

'Good! Excellent!'

'What they'll say I don't know! Still, I'll risk it. You didn't know I worked in a shop, did you?'

'Well . . . no . . . you never told me. . . .'

Interesting. But de Broda was too pleased by this sudden present of a longer stay to pay much attention to it. Vaguely he thought of her as the manageress, the director of the shop: though he would in fact have scarcely been troubled by the knowledge of her more humble position. It was not unusual. Besides, his snobberies were of a different kind.

'It's a cake-shop,' she said. And with a flourish of signature, 'There! Either the mine goes up or it doesn't.'

She was in high spirits. They spent a pleasant half-hour together and then parted to dine. During dinner, exhilarated by her company after the lonely hours, he decided to make his proposal that evening. He was quite sure he was infatuated, he suspected it might be love.

He considered where his words might best be said—over a bottle of wine in the Mozart? On the Wilhelm Promenade, with the great snowbound valley beneath? Mm. Or—or in a double-bath, perhaps? He chuckled. Then he thought of the high bridge over the waterfall. That was plainly the answer.

After dinner they had coffee together. Then, after some twenty minutes, Laure took out a mirror, patted her hair and said: 'Nine o'clock! I must go.'

Unconcerned her fingers smoothed the button on a gold lipstick case and the little red knob slid out. She raised it to her lips. For a moment de Broda could say nothing. He sat quite still, only his eyes widened in dread. Then he blurted:

'Going? Going? Going where. . . .?'

'I have an appointment.'

'But—but I thought we were going to spend . . . you said . . .'

'Did I? But we made no arrangement.'

She was still looking in the mirror. Her fingers moved too steadily, her face showed too little expression—it was plain she avoided looking at him.

He leaned forward, grasped the arm of her chair:

'You said we could spend the evenings together. When we talked about your ski-ing. And tonight—tonight's very important. . . .'

'Oh? How?'

'Well . . .'

'But look, Herr de Broda,—or should I say Bobby . . .?'

Now she did look at him, her teeth and the little mirror's teeth smiling bright malice, and the red lipstick point like a sweet poison in between:

'. . . look, we're not exactly living together, are we? And you never never said: Fräulein Laure, I beg you to enchant me with your company between the hours of nine and twelve o'clock tonight! No no! Nothing like that from Bobby! As a matter of fact, I'm going out to dance.'

'Laure!'

'Bobby!' she mimicked.

He got angry. He decided to put his foot down once and for all.

'Who are you going out with?'

She frowned:

'That sounds rather a demand. Really, Ludwig!'

He gripped the arm of her chair harder and leant his pale face earnestly towrads her. A touch of rose fevered his cheekbones. He said very softly:

'Tell me!'

She laughed, a little frightened: 'Well—if you *must* know, it's Peter.'

'Peter?' His voice rose. '*What* Peter?'

'Peter Hörnli.'

He raised his eyebrows—his one joined eyebrow. Then drawled, more comfortably: 'Oh him—the ski-boy.'

Her voice was sharp. 'And what's wrong with that?'

'Nothing.'

Then he leant closer towards her, he lost his anger, he spoke earnestly and sincerely:

'Laure dear. Don't go. I've got—so much to tell you. Laure— Laure darling. . . . I love you. I want you, Laure—I want you to be my wife.'

The lipstick dropped away. Her hardness dropped away. Her eyes softened, but she still frowned.

She just said: 'Oh.'

'Laure—put him off. I wanted to tell you—to ask you later. When we were walking somewhere . . . not here. But now I've had to . . . . Laure,' he took a deep and terrible breath, 'will you be my wife?'

She said nothing. Only her eyes searched his face anxiously, as though she were looking not for love but for a sign of illness—and carefully her hand was placing the lipstick on the table.

He went on, talking quickly. 'Laure—it's only Hörnli. You can easily leave a note. Do, darling, write one now, we can go out the other way—he's calling for you, I suppose?'

Slowly she said: 'But Ludwig—Ludwig—I—I can't marry you.'

His mouth pursed into a smile, as at some little puzzle he shook his head.

'No,' she said. 'I'm already engaged.'

She put her hand softly over his. It was no touch, it was a compress.

'Yes,' she said. 'To Peter Hörnli.'

His hand loosened on the arm of her chair. He looked simply puzzled.

'I'm so sorry, Ludwig.'

There was a small commotion by the inner swing-doors: a stamping of snow, beating of gloves.

'There he is already—Ludwig, you don't want to meet . . . no . . . of course. No—I must go.'

She rose and left him. She did not look back.

De Broda sat quite still. More than anything—he was seized with wonder. He simply could not understand. An old feeling overwhelmed him—of being in class and not knowing the lesson. Blankly and almost casually, as if there was no hope of solving the problem, as if that Hörnli were a puzzle of white numerals on a blackboard, he tried to examine him. Standing there by the swing-doors he looked young—unbelievably young. Could he then be not a boy but a man? De Broda had imagined him as eighteen or so. But he remembered how as one grows older ages in both directions become muddled—and saw he might be at least twenty-five, more. And his haircut—like an American advertisement. He was still in his ski-trousers, yet with some sort of belted loose coat: these were clothes de Broda could not understand, they came from another world. In fact, the New World—over his gestures, which were properly German-Swiss, there ran a veneer of American posture, frank agilities of the collegiate, laconicisms of the film. To de Broda's older culture such mannerisms were still confounding, though he had seen them extend through many European cities. But he deduced from them neither the levelling of false emotions nor the destruction of class patronage that at their best they represented— he deduced simply bad boorish manners. He saw only the bravo-me of it. It was alien to his heart.

So that now watching this Hörnli greeting Laure—with a strange nonchalant ease as if there were time only for the broadest smile, a large effusion all at once for they must be getting on, getting places —he was even more astounded that Laure should take such a man seriously. That brash boy with his easy smile? That cock-a-hoop young nothing? That figure of all unsubtlety, swaggerer of dance-halls, that sportsman?

EPISODE AT GASTEIN

That sportsman put on his hat at a gay angle and wheeled Laure, laughing Laure, through the swing-doors and out. Slim-hipped, loose-shouldered, his back covered Laure like the curtain of a play, and then that too was gone and the vestibule left empty.

For some minutes de Broda was unable to gather himself. He had not moved, his face hung almost in a smile. It was unbelievable. Then slowly he rose and walked up the stairs to his room.

He went to the mirror. He looked at his face. It looked no different. At forty he saw the face of thirty, the age-marks over the well-known shape he treated as no more than a mist on the mirror. He looked down at his hands—his slender, washed, workless fingers that could speak subtleties unknown to mouths. Further down—to the suit he wore, to its civil suavity, its politely traditional cut. To his shoes, sober and elegant. And up to the mind behind his face —a mind tutored in graces of good taste, a mind of knowledge and sometimes wit but always of culture and taste. Vain, he thought. Quite a few faults, of course. But really—how *could* she?

It all seemed so absurd. There in his bedroom, alone, he gave a shrug to his shoulders and smiled. Then suddenly—half-way between the mirror and the bed—he stopped dead. Half-way across the bedroom carpet, isolated on that carpet, the full realization of what had happened fell upon him. Its appalling echo rang round the room, sang in his empty ears. She had refused him! She had left him! She had preferred someone else to *him*! Nothing he could ever do would revise it. To him, *him*, she had preferred that boy. . . .

He grasped for his overcoat and left that room quickly. But at the head of the stairs paused—ashamed to be seen by the people in the lounge below. Then his shoulders straightened and he descended, went quickly through and out into the snow. It was a clear night, the snow glowed white everywhere. Sometimes a lighted window showed a yellow square, festive and telling of warmth within. But de Broda saw nothing, he did not know where he was walking. Through his mind there raced backwards the perspective of events —too clearly he saw the answers to questions he had chosen to ignore. The episode with that party from Vienna—of course that was what she really wanted: and her abrupt interest in the ski-run: and, most bitter of all, the way she had kissed him on that magic

277

evening in the zither-tavern—he saw how this was no more than a kind of overflow of her exhilaration with Hörnli, it had been a gesture of gaiety embracing not him but the idea of love.

The snow made no noise beneath his slow trudging boots: he felt that love for him had passed forever. Past the mauve light of a Kurhaus, past a man hacking ice from a wooden sledge—the white road leading uphill looked as uneventful and empty as his own life would henceforth be. At least the road twisted, and it rose higher to some horizon . . . but his life? Nothing appeared there—only a level road, unposted, with neither turning nor end nor anything ever to happen on it. As he watched his dark boots on their lonely procession, as if they covered no flesh of his but were boots of a warder taking him along that road, he lost the last of his spirit. He felt old and finished.

He saw sadly that those two together told no more than an old and simple tale—youth to youth. They shared together energies and vitalities he would never know again. And they shared together a spirit of the times, an acceptance of the present that he would never understand, a modern spirit strange as a foreign language. A thousand small utterances of day-to-day life separated him from that bounceful, youthful spirit: they would not think twice of, say, the look of a bottle of medicine—whereas he would long for the scrolled designs of older ointments; they would drive to Grinzing on a motor-bicycle and love it: they would accept, accept, accept— yes, they would enter into things. How simple—yet how strange! How strange that however one might groom oneself, however fine a taste and a culture and a manner and all urbanity one might achieve—and however young one still felt and even almost looked—one could never be accepted exactly as a fellow-being by youth.

The dark firs rose above him like bird-giants, their branches ridged like feathers, their topmost tufts sly as little heads. Ice on the road gleamed its cold. What might have been a magical winter's night looked only forlorn—it was a scene only of cold desolation. The wide valley stretched below, like something seen not now but in a long and snowbound time ago. De Broda lifted his eyes from his boots and looked curiously around him. He found these very boots had led him near to where that high bridge hung across the ravine and its rocky torrent.

Then two things happened. Small matters—but the kind that grow large in a grieving mind. Over the crest of the hill a motor came whirring its chains on the ice. It bore down towards de Broda. Quite normally he had to step to the side to let it pass. It passed, and, with its lights and air of company, disappeared. De Broda stood in the thick snow at the side of the road—again alone on a lonely road—and felt the motor had pushed him there with personal intent, with a jeer.

And then, when he had moved on a step, suddenly the door of a villa opened. It was a villa standing alone and the door lay along a short path. But quite visibly in its rectangle of yellow light stood the figure of a woman. She leaned forward slightly, she seemed to be peering out on to the snow, perhaps on to the road, perhaps at him. Quite suddenly, she closed the door again: and all was again dark.

De Broda turned away and hurried towards the bridge.

His mind was quite made up. He hurried with his head butting forward, with his mind in fact bowed towards the bridge and away from all light and sound and people.

But not all sound: for there came towards him the dark shuddering murmur—at first only a vibration through the snow—of the waterfall. He hurried faster to meet it. Ice caked under his heels. He slipped, he lurched as he ran. He passed into the belt of firs that with their wet dark leaves guarded that place. Then his hands gripped wide on the wooden balustrade, he looked down. It was suddenly quite dark, a cloud passed over the moon.

Foam splashed white somewhere deep in the darkness, it was difficult to see where, it was like looking down to the bottom of a well. The rock face fell vertically, stone echoed a watery roar through darkness all around; yet there grew down the sides, on every ledge, less like trees than something poisonous, the firs—darkdraped ladies suckled by rock and spray and shadows. Their arms dripped water. Sound of water echoed everywhere. Water flooded with the nightmare sound of a vast dam breaking, rearing its black smooth mass like a wall to pour down forever over everything.

De Broda stood there gritting his teeth, the muscles in his arms clenched ready. The sound below, the feel of flat water beneath hummed dragging at his mind, he leaned nearer the desirable, the terrible—then suddenly sobbed and flung himself on the ground. Breathing with fear, very slowly and carefully he crept off the little bridge on his knees.

He lurched up and stumbled into the surety of the trees: then stopped, and still breathing hard, looked back. The sound had receded, the bridge without its fall looked sure and graceful, a rustic affair among snowy firs. Without questioning himself, instantly bold again, he sneered at it within himself and began to return: but as the roaring sound grew he stopped, tried another step—then his heart altogether failed him, he turned and walked quickly away. Yet he refused to feel defeated, Vertigo, he thought. And quite natural. A matter difficult to imagine, easy to experience.

He reached the road, and heard voices. Two people were leaving the villa whose door he had seen open. Their voices came clearly across on the frosty air, he was instantly on his guard. Perhaps it had not been vertigo? Perhaps he had been simply afraid to finish what he had in mind? The doubt grew as those voices approached. He walked quicker to be ahead of them—not to be seen aimless, slinking off the road. The voices receded, he felt bolder. His figure straightened, he felt they could still see him, but they were safer and further away. He'd show them—an abrupt blood of revenge rose and gritted his teeth. And with it came a sudden idea that turned his footsteps fast down towards his hotel. Water, he thought, there was water without vertigo, the place was running with water! Revenge then, on the waters, on the voices. Revenge the proud way, a Roman revenge!

Immediately he was in he ordered the bath and went to his wash-stand for a razor. He could even smile as he remembered that of course there was only a safety razor. And the man's face engraved on the little packet of blades bore an expression hardly adequate to the situation. He tore the face off the packet and extracted several blue-black, carefully greased little blades from their envelopes. He wondered how many to take and then took two—with some idea of two wrists. He put the blades in his dressing-gown pocket and left for the bathroom.

The maid had already filled the bath. The water lay quite still. But it steamed slightly from its surface, it had a presence of movement like an animal asleep. When de Broda shut and bolted the thick white door he was alone with it, he was insulated from the passage and all sound and all people: such near-marine doors fit exactly.

Casually, almost as though he were in fact going to shave—for he moved slow under the weight of self-pity and revenge—he placed the two little blades down on the floor-edge of the bath. He took off his dressing-gown and approached the steps naked. The water in those square pools lies below the level of the floor, there are steps and a steadying hand-rail down into it: and thus de Broda had time, approaching the head of the steps, exactly to feel himself naked. He felt unprotected. He had a moment to realize that people must come eventually and find him thus. He paused in shame. He looked back along the tiles to his dressing-gown. But he had brought no underclothes in, it would mean drenching that gown. It was unthinkable. He turned again to the steps. So they'd find him naked? Well, the more shame on them, the more revenge.

And then down into the warm still water, down into the green receiver among the white clean tiles.

First to soak, to get heat into the veins. He lay back floating with his shoulders resting on the marble step. The bath was wide, the sense of luxuriance pleased him. This was fitting. He took a wrist from the water and examined it curiously. He had never noted it so closely before; so hairless, such soft flesh: he saw how blue veins crossed above the tendons—so many brittle tendons, like the thin bones in a chicken's leg. with veins crossing them like soft blue bridges. He tried to remember where the pulse was, remembered not to use his thumb, found it; and found his other hand holding his own wrist delicately as though it were someone else's. He had been five minutes in the bath. He turned to the razor-blades.

It was difficult to pick them off the tile. They lay flatly, they were sharp, he did not want to cut his thumb so he got one up with his finger-nails, his nails pincered it up like a magnet picking a weight of steel.

He held the little blade carefully. He remembered sharpening pencils with such double-edge blades, how they were greased and could slip back into the hand—and he pressed the ball of his thumb hard into the little range of slots to fasten his grip. That was in his right hand. Easing himself up to sit steadily on the step, he raised his left wrist. He turned the underside of the wrist upwards—he felt for a moment he was looking at a wristwatch—and his eye wandered over the blade and saw the second one resting on the bath-side. He saw that instinctively thinking of two wrists he had brought two blades. That was unnecessary, absurd—but it produced another problem. Which to cut first? Now that the right hand held the blade, and thus the left wrist should be the first to be cut—would not the left and weaker wrist be too weakened by the cut to manage the blade for the right? Perhaps the left hand should cut first—the stronger right one would withstand the wound better? Very carefully, careful not to cut himself, he exchanged the little blade between his fingers and thumbs.

But now holding it in his left hand—and feeling thus insecure, for the left was not used to such precise movement—a further trouble showed itself. It was very important to be both exact and quick: but that meant changing over the blade quickly and cutting fast with the right hand before it was weakened. Would it be shocked numb for those vital seconds? He thought—and then saw that after all his instinct had been right, there was no reason why he should not hold a second blade ready in the right hand. It would avoid the delicate change. He turned and, again very carefully, pincered the second blade off the tiles. Precariously holding the left hand away from his body, he nearly slipped. And that made him suddenly think: what if the shock made the right-hand fingers open and that blade dropped away down in the water?

He shook his head impatiently. That had to be risked. Main thing was to get on with it. Against his real will—which wished, since they were his own wrists, to cut carefully and tenderly—he told himself to do it quickly, to hold both hands in front in the air and then— slash quickly. With the movement of drumsticks. Like a man with butterpats. Quickly. One-two. He stretched out his hands, turned the right wrist inwards, held his breath and waited.

Waited for what?

A word of command.

From whom?

For the first time he realized that word must come from himself and no one else: he was absolutely alone with his own will.

The steam rose lightly on the water's surface, no more than a snaking of mist on the bath green. The snow pawed silently on the black window above. Movement everywhere—but no sound. He felt no longer alone, but in a crowd of movers making no sound but restlessly waiting. And supposed he would make no sound either, razor-blades made no sound. Suddenly he saw himself sliding down after it was done, a splashing of water, the dark blood clouding round him in the water. He grew greatly afraid.

Afraid of what? Because he had to make his own hands move to do it? Was he afraid of decision? No, not him! He looked closely at the skin on his wrist, soft and so tenderly his own. He saw how his finger-pads were soaked in the steamy air and ridged like fresh-waved white sand, like dead skin. Abruptly then a new thought came from nowhere, a thought suddenly from the world lost outside the bathroom. Something whispered to him that Hörnli was a Swiss. A Swiss would own Swiss francs. And Swiss francs were very valuable. And he saw instantly for the first time what precisely he wanted to see—that the Swiss francs rather than Hörnli were what Laure wanted. Not the young man's potency but the potency of money! Only that. . . . He understood well what a hard currency meant. So what was he so troubled about? *He* was not preferred, this was something quite different. . . . With abounding relief he lowered a little his hands. He let out his tense breath. And lay there feeling for the first time the old pleasant warmth of the bath.

But a doubt was there. He held hard on to this new bright belief, but deeper in his brain a dark and troublesome doubt assembled like a cloud. He held hard, he concentrated on the idea of Swiss francs. His chin came out—and abruptly and proudly a new thought came. He decided to find out. He would go against all his principles —he would go out dancing with them, to a beer cellar with them, and by God he would go up in the ski-lift! Yes, and he'd even ski! He'd stay with them at all their games and find out!

Then—he saw himself up at the ski-station. He saw clearly. He watched as the minute passed and he saw what would happen pass like a bright film through the minute. . . .

He saw himself up there by the hut, dressed for snow. He saw exactly how he was dressed, and how it was a bright and sunlit day, and how he was buckling on his skis among a merry crowd of people buckling on theirs. Much colour against the snow, much excitement: the air was crisp and the crowd of them were ready for the day's sport. Laure and Hörnli were not yet there. He himself had gone up early. He wanted to be there ready for them. And he was cunning enough to know that he needed practice, he needed quite a time on the nursery slopes. He was out of practice by a good many years.

But people were moving off, the white slopes were a dapple of gnome colour—people as small as children, suddenly a child as big in perspective as a grown-up, all dressed the same it was difficult to make out . . . and he balanced himself up on his sticks and walked sliding easily off.

But as soon as a slope came he was down. He had difficulty getting up. One ski slid one way, the back of the other caught in the snow and remained sticking up helplessly. Yet he managed to struggle upright. Then off for a few metres . . . and down again. This time worse.

He struggled with all his strength. His hat fell off. A child of five swerved easily past him. He was dreadfully knotted. But, sweating now, he did finally force himself up. He went veering on. Knees together, feet wider and wider, all awkwardness, no figure of a man. And collapsed again. Voices shouted: 'Achtung! Achtung!' And through his snow-filled eyes he seemed to see voices swear as they swerved past him. He was just in the way. Painfully again he tried to get up. He got up. But he was facing the wrong way. Then to turn. Putting that one leg awkwardly up and round. But in mid-turn the other leg slid away—and once more he was down in a baffled mess. He was finished. He knew he would never get out of this, never get back to land. He was right back in the first days of learning, humiliated and tired and useless. . . .

He sat up panting, a clown-figure tangled and snow-drenched. And just then he heard his name: 'Ludwig!' He listened and looked vaguely up back the slope and an echo came, a laughing echo: 'Bobby! Bobby! Bobby!'

Up above he saw Laure and Hörnli pointing at him and waving and laughing. Then together, as they saw him looking at them, they prised on their sticks and came sweeping down the slope.

Together, as though they were linked, they passed where he was and smiled and called good-naturedly: 'Ludwig—Enjoy yourself! Goodbye . . . goodbye . . .!' And they were past.

He watched them, the pair, sure as a couple can be, ski-ing beautifully down the long white slope, then up another, over again and across the wide snowfield, always smaller, further, smaller—until together they passed away over the mountainside and were gone.

De Broda sat absolutely still in the hot water, a little razor-blade held in each hand like the parts of a child's broken toy. And slowly two tears, two big single tears dropped from his eyes, dribbled over his cheeks, and fell down into the other water beneath.

Life, Death

O LIFE was jolly in the sunlight, splashing the cod around.
Water playing on our slab, ferns as cool as green, the whitest
tiles in town.

It was my happy job to set the fish for show. I'd take a turbot say
for central, a heavy fellow white and round. Then red lobsters, I'd
ring my lobsters round that turbot, all their noses in, to make the
petals of a flower. Then I'd take a cut of haddock, place this yellow
by the turbot's head. I don't know why I put that haddock at the
head, more than at tail or sides. I don't know what I did not half
the time. But it always came out right. I've that eye for colour: and
I'd parsley my lobsters, green to red.

Jim-at-the-Back would be out the back, sluicing his wood with
water. Back in the dark with his gas-blue jet, getting out his gut-
knives, sloshing on his footboard, thudding on his crates and whistling a song. A busy music Jim made, his hose made music—morning
music that was, music of day to begin, bright as the rattling of our
shutter when we hoisted her to let all light come flooding in. Like a
curtain, our green shutter: and opening her a chorus.

Now I had my white coat and my blue apron, and now I'd jam
my straw on pleased to greet the trade. But first I could finish off—
now I'd got my central. Mackerel, trouts and my red-spotted plaice-
lings—those coloured fellows I would take next. Striped mackerels
I'd make into a ring, and place a crab within. Two rings I'd make,
one each side to balance. Then stars of rainbow trout, all wet colours
of the rainbow dew. But my plaice—my good brown plaice with the
bright red dabs, these I'd bend tail to head, tail to head so they'd
make a round, and I'd set them plumb in middle below the big
turbot, for a braver-marked fish would be hard to find.

And right down further—though this was not the least important
—there'd be ordinaries . . . the herrings, the whiting, the cod. *They'd*

286

go on trays. But I'd range them neatly as the rest: and in their middle place a tray of rich pink shrimps. But my long fish, you'll say? My three H's, rule of three and thumb, haddock and hake and halibut? My pike if you like? Yes, they'd all come in—they'd come in squaring up the rest, they'd come for squaring up. I'd put a lemon in a big pike's mouth, lemon to teeth, and sometimes there'd be mullet like coral and bream as pink-brown babies. And soles with their faces all one side—a tearful sight.

Scallops? What with my scallops? Lump them in middle, a bunch of fresh-poached eggs? Make circles of them round my soles? Line them up to write my name? Not I! That I never would! . . . No, I'd put one of them here and one of them there, and one more there and another here—so they'd be eyed all over the place. And if Jim-at-the-Back came front and queried, 'Where's your poached, my Charley-boy, my Barley?'—I'd wink and tell him: 'Look for yourself, Jim.' And he'd look, you know, he'd look for such a while before he'd see them! But after, he'd see them everywhere, he'd see nothing but these scallops. 'You could knock me down,' Jim'd say. I'd say, 'That's art, Jim.'

Yes, life was jolly—but I'm not getting to my point of this: which was *her*.

One day I'd no idea she stepped on earth: and the next she was there with her long brown eyes and her white small face to ask me for herring in my queue. That was the time I saw her first, and I've not forgotten it from that day nor ever will. Shy she whispered what she wanted—and I had to bend my head to hers to ask her what was that she'd said. I bent my head and she looked wide of eye and whispered it again: 'Two herring, please.' Wide of eye, a baby animal.

Her mouth was twice itself with red, she had a cap-thing on her head, she had trousers—but she still was a little animal, she grabbed her shop-bags hand together more like a squirrel: and when I'd given her her two she was off bent over it and in little steps quick gone.

Me I stood there jumboed. Out of my wits awhile I was. Me, with all the skirt I have each day, fat ones, thin ones, young ones, old ones, cheery ones that pass the time of day, crabby ones all price and poke-finger. And never a tremor goes through me till that time. I must've stood there seconds looking after her; I was seized, and I see I only saw my senses when a big brown voice came in my earhole: 'Have you got *all* the day?' But then I thought I had.

All day I thought of her, all day I'd do nothing right, all day I had her picture in my eye. What was my pride in our slab, I'd never sell a fish from its place without something cut me deep. But the day I first saw *her*—I sold helter-skelter where you please, mackerel from stars, trouts from their triangles, lobsters in fours from my flower of turbotpiece.

But the next day she was back. And the day after. And the day after that! And on the fourth day, when I handed her her herring, I stuttered two extra in her hand, sleighty my hand to hers, but bold as gold with a wink for her alone. She took the herring. She did not smile. Only over her face that was so small and white came a blush spreading rose as red, and on her neck too, for she had hung her shy head. Then she was off, no word.

Yet she knew and I knew. And I was happy that day with myself for being so bold: for I had dared give away fish with Milly dark like a crab in her cash behind, and I had dared speak a first word to my love, though this was but with wink and hand.

So I was happier than for all time past. In my straw in the sun, tiles around, my good slab iced, my slab with water-spray and fern: red buses passing huge out front, and people always passing too— all busy passing in the sun, and a smile from me with my straw cocked and my heart-a-wing. Even Milly got a smile, I could smile for dark Milly. She sat in her cash all day, dark like a spider-crab taking the flies of fish and given them again for pennies and silver: or like a foreign god she was, one with six arms, taking offerings in her fat hole and chinking wealth and prayer all day, or the night that was day for *her*. But I gave her a smile. And old Jim-at-the-Back thought I was crazed with my digs and my whistles. I heard him chuckle over his sluice of slice and gut out back.

You can be sure I slipped my love some extra every day. And now one day she gave me back a smile, one day when she summonsed up the heart. And though I'm an ordinary fellow, none too hang-back, none too bold—that day I leapt in, to her smile I leapt in and whispered: 'Pictures?' Again she blushed. 'Come on!' I said. She shook her head. 'Right-ho, no fish!' I said. And all the queue behind!

So then as a small wind might have passed across her came her nod. I slapped the fish in her hand. 'Half-after-six?' I asked. Once more the little wind. 'Where?' I asked. Then she said the word, the first but for herring I'd heard. 'Gaumont,' she whispered like a thief. And she hurried away.

Now my heart sang twice. Once for her and me, together now. And once for the word she said. For she said this word like Gawmont. She never said that Gomong. And I knew from this she had no lah-da, she was one with me, we would go well together she and I.

That night I brought caramels, and in the dark we sat with these. What went on the screen, don't ask *me*. I have no recollection. With her in the dark, sunk small in her seat, arms not even on the arms, I could be only like some dynamo, some big hot engine pumping up beside her, I had fear my blood would be heard. After, we went to a fry-shop—for it seemed she was a girl for fish. Myself in the trade, I do not take to the cuts they give in those shops: but that night I ate with will, I did not know what I ate, and all I know was I knew now her name. And this was Lily.

Lil was alone, her mum and dad were far away. I was alone, I lived alone in my room. Two alone, we grew to know one another, we went out time and then again. Soon I held her hand, and soon I kissed her. Then we were betrothed.

I knew I must marry my Lil, and that was what Lil wanted too. I had few savings, though a few. I was never one for the beer, I could go days with nothing to want but my dinner and my bed. I liked a nice picture, a bus to the country. But that cost little: it was pop for me, no beer. So I could save. With me my only curse was caramels. Caramels were what I could scoff by the pound. Sometimes I went for nut-crunch—but that was but a mood, as people change their mind: and always I was back for caramels. Prices never worried *me*: I'd swop all else for caramels.

A simple taste, you'll say. But a taste the same. And that's where the money went. So though with others smokes and girls might sound a stronger vice, caramels were no less vice for me. Caramels were my sin. For each time I headed for the shop I had to think:

'Half-pound? Pound? . . .' And stop myself for money's sake. Temptation lay as strong as liquor, caramels so sweet were poison for my purse.

But now I was with Lil I had to curb myself the more. Save I must, for us to marry. Save, save hard. Lil my sweet animal saved too—though she worked only as maid, though she had little enough.

Work harder! But none could work harder than I, nor with more joy. I loved my work and where I worked. No, this meant work of another kind—work harder meant that I must try for manager. I must leave my slab and go up one.

It's from then I reckon the shade that fell on my path. Life that had been jolly no longer was. My slab I loved was no more good for me. I smiled more at my trade, but grieved the time it took to smile: I took with my slab a greater pain, but grieved the minutes spent. For all I thought was: 'Oh for the day to be done, so one more day may dawn until I'm up for manager.' I now had responsibilities who had none of these before. Sure as my Lil had come to lift my heart, so a burden came to shaden it. I lived no longer for my happy day, it was tomorrow *I* wanted.

And the weeks went by. I knew my time would come, there's talk in the trade. But it took a time coming. Though those weeks were not without their up and down. One day, for instance, my dad came to town. And I set a special tea for him, and I asked Lil. Fish-tea, seeing Lil was asked, and I took back a fine roe to cook this a way I know. Dad met Lil, and dad was stern as dads can be. I thought: 'Now we're for it, now we're off!' and set myself to rub him up his right way. But—not a bit of that, I could have spared my tongue! For my Lil opens like a flower, all sudden she starts to chat and laugh and play the pretty goat. And soon she had my dad on the reins, she has him chatting and laughing and playing the goat there too! My Lil had upped and taken charge, it was only she rubbed my dad up his right way. Who'd have thought this of shy Lil? The mischief in them—that day she made me proud and happy as kings can be. 'It's the quiet ones,' I said, but I don't know now what I meant by *that*. For who was being quiet?

Then another day, for instance, I slipped my Lil her extra mackerel—it was mackerel now for her. And off she went. But no sooner was it afternoon when Lil was back, and back beside herself. 'These fish are off!' she comes straight out all over the shop, for all ears to hear. Jim-at-the-Back pops out his head, and I saw something move in dark Milly's cash—it was Milly raised her head. Now Lil was regular those days and Milly knew each day what pence she spent. She spent for two fish, never four. But there she stood with four, all off, for all to see. 'There more that's off than fish,' I thought, 'there's my girl Lil gone off her nut.' And that was so, out of her mind she was, all else was out of her mind but that her fish was off. She was a girl standing on her rights, no less than that. 'Goodbye Manager,' I thought. 'It'll be Charley-at-the-Back and Jim-out-Front when *this* is done.'

For up went Milly's window, and Milly starts in straight that Lil had only two fish and now how were there four to be off? You could see Milly thinking.

I prayed, then took a header in. 'Lil,' I said, 'you're wandering, girl. You never got those fish from here. Those ones must be fish your mistress bought.' Now thank my stars Lil saw. 'Why!' she said, and 'I declare!' she said, and looking at those fish like strangers, '*I* beg pardon.' And we all had a laugh. But it was a creepy laugh, that laugh. And from that time on I never slipped my Lil another extra fish. Too much lay at stake for that.

Thus we had our up and down. The weeks went by. And surely came the day when I went up for manager. Goodbye to my slab, it was the depot for me. I wore no straw but a dark suit collared, and I went up two quid a week. Now I could save indeed. Through the dark winter I checked the ones that checked the crates, and no caramel passed my lips but a few for Christmas. Through wet February I saved, and March, April too. Until a month in Spring my lovely Lil I naved, she wed me in the Spring. Nor was there ever tile so white as she upon her wedman's day.

We settled in. And in the time it takes Lil gave me our nipper. A little girl, like Lil, our little nipper.

We were so happy, just the three, there was glory all around. But then it came that two of us died. Two left the three, two just wilted —but for why?—and died, Lil and our nipper passed away. A year alone we were together, then they died.

They've gone, I said, my loved ones both are gone. Please only give me back my slab—and they, who knew, did that. But I tell you this, my slab never is the same again, there's shade about for me.

No, I'm not broke, I'll crack a joke. I'll share a bag of caramel with Mill, with Jim who's gutting down the back. But life's no more the same. Why, if *you* can tell me, such happy days? Why with happy days such shade?

A Contest of Ladies

FRED MORLEY might easily have been mistaken for something of an eccentric. He was a 'bachelor', he was 'wealthy', he was 'retired from the stage'. It was not held unusual for such a man to be somewhat out of line with the rest of the world.

Nor, because he was a bachelor, was it unusual that a certain July evening found him in his bedroom wandering from door to window, from bed to fireplace, wondering what to do. Many evenings found him so—with the warm nights and in the dangerous flush of middle-age.

He looked at the metal plaque of bells by his bed. 'Chamber-maid.' 'Waiter.' But he knew that if he rang, neither would come. His eye dropped to the telephone beneath—there were buttons which led to 'Reception' and 'Restaurant' and 'Toilet Saloon': again he knew there would be no response. He wondered—as he had done so very often in the past—whether he really would have liked a response, had this been possible. But he quickly put that old idea from his mind, he was much happier as things were.

Up on the pink satin wall-paper, in a discreet position, was inset a white celluloid notice: a scramble of black lettering begged visitors to do this or not to do that. Morely's empty mind passed to all the other empty rooms around and above him, all with the same small notice bowing and begging—for the wording of these notices was polite and obsequious, a cut above the terse commercial command—by each closed door.

Downstairs the lounge would be empty. Magazines would be arranged neatly on a central table—*Country Life*, *The Gas Times*, *The Tatler*—and the curtains would be still undrawn to let a blue evening light through on to a great splay of fresh-bought lupins. Across from the empty lounge the bar would stand open and brightly polished —and empty too. At this thought old Morley brightened. Thank

293

goodness—no one in the best chair, no chattering gin-groups, no idle guests to be sauntered into. No porter on the doorstep to mar the evening with a 'Good evening' and a searching eye. Fred Morley knew he could stand alone on the step and survey what he wished, undisturbed and in silence. He brightened. Such people might have meant company. But was such company preferable to his own selected privacy? By all means no.

By what means? What sort of hotel was this—all trim and in working order, yet absolutely empty of people? Not empty as death, not dust-covered and cobweb-hung—but fresh-swept, with the feeling that a dozen servants had only a moment before left. It was as one might imagine a live hotel struck by plague, or conjured up in some ghost-tale, or in some unknown way emptied yet sailing equipped on its course like the maddening *Mary Celeste*.

A hotel bought by Morley? A hotel occupied entirely by Morley?

Almost. But in fact it was not a hotel at all. It was Morley's private house—decorated, in many of its more obvious features, like a hotel. This was Morley's 'eccentricity'. But was it, on closer consideration, so very eccentric? It is commonly a habit of furnishers and decorators to make things appear what they are not. Rooms—particularly of the well-to-do—have become escapes. The *chinoiserie* of Chippendale, sea-shell lairs of the rococo nymph, even the Greek revival—all have succeeded to make rooms what they are not. There have been Tudor cocktail-bars and Elizabethan garages, ship's-cabin beer-houses land-locked in a city street, chintzy cottage-rooms whose spinning-wheels shudder as the underground trains worm their way beneath. All of them studios of desire, each room an escape from four walls.

Morley's fancy to make his house look like a hotel was in fact less exotic than these. He had no vague wish to be different, it was a practical planned escape. A deep disaffection in him—the same that had left him a bachelor—had revolted against the idea of house-and-home. Given a homely looking home he would feel home-bound, anchored, done. But hotels! These he loved—he felt in them adventure, the passage of possibility, a lovely rootless going and coming, excitement stalking the corridors, sin lurking in the shadows of the fire extinguishers. They reminded him, too, of his touring days in the theatre. But against this stood the truth that hotels were in fact dreadfully uncomfortable: and homes were not. Hence—most reasonably—the transposition. He had dressed his seven-bedroomed mansion on the front of this rakish Channel seaside resort in a glamorous nostalgia for no-home.

Thus at six-thirty he sat and gazed his handsome eyes about the room and wondered what to do. Six-thirty is a bad hour. Hour of sundowners. Hour when the human beast, old moon-monkey, awakes to the idea of night. Hour of day's death and dark's beginning, uneasy hour of change. Bedrooms stalk with people changing clothes, drinks are drunk, high teas eaten, limbs washed fresh of used daylight. No wonder Fred Morley wondered, like millions around him, what to do. A stall at the Hippodrome? A sole at the Ship? Oysters at Macey's? A glass with old Burgess? A stroll by the Band— strains of the *Rosenkavalier* across green breakwaters, the dying sands? A tinkle to Mrs Vereker—though it wasn't really His Night?

But none of these appealed. So, old bachelor that he was, he decided to pamper himself. His hand, strong, freckled, mildly arthritic, flashed its opal ring round the telephone dial. To a waiter at a real hotel some doors away his actor's accent, from between handsome curling lips and through teeth white and strong, ordered oysters and mulligatawny soup and what—oh, pigeon pie? Excellent. And a good dollop of Stilton, thank you. Wine he had, and plenty of port. Down went the receiver—above his clean square jaws the lips silently smacked—and with erect leisurely stride his legs took him over to the bathroom. A good hot bath, plenty of lather. Then, in grace to a good quiet evening at home, the raisin-red frogged smoking jacket.

Morley had played the romantic lead in most of the more robust musical comedies. He had toured for twenty years the length and breadth of the Isles in the boots of a Hussar, the breeches of a Desert Hero, the golden robes of Baghdad. He had made his money, saved it, and retired. Now as he strode his ample carpets he was still every inch a baritone. The theatrical years had stylized every manly gesture, incised surety into every feature of his square strong face, greyed not at all the good brown curly hair brushed suavely back and half sideways. And now as he undid his stays the deep and

295

tuneful voice that had quickened hearths throughout the land broke
into satisfied strains that declared how Maud was to come into the
garden since the Black Bat Night had flown.

But, of course, the Black Bat Night was really at that time flying
in: and with it, on the evening train, there had flown in six ladies
new to the town—a Miss Clermont-Ferrand, the Misses Amsterdam
and Rotterdam, Miss Sauerkraut of Nuremburg, Miss Civitavecchia
and Miss Great-Belt of Denmark. Every summer the Town Cor-
poration organized a Contest of Beauty. This year, spreading its
festive wings, it had decided to make the Contest international.
Invitations had been despatched. In some cases accepted. Part of
the result, who had been rallied in London by their various agencies,
had been sent down by the evening train.

Now they stood in the Railway Buffet studying little lists of
recommended hotels and sipping, with wonder and weary enthusiasm, their watery-milked sweet cups of railway tea. The names of
the hotels stared up at them with promise but nonentity. There
were no Ritzes, no Savoys, none of the ordinary run. There were
Ships and Crescents and Royals and many lesser establishments,
listed as Boarding Houses, with Gaelic, Celtic and sometimes
Malayan names. All the ladies had different ideas and different
purses, and all talked at once.

A group of local gentlemen sat drinking whisky and listening.
These were a convivial lot, mixed commercials and retired front-
walkers, black trilbies or stiff-collar tweeds. They spent most of the
time ponderously pulling each other's legs; but now, with such a
sudden advent of beautiful ladies, they went further. They went a
bit silly. They giggled, they whispered, they mouthed and winked—
the ladies, accompanied by the whisky, went straight to their heads.

Thus it was inevitable that sooner or later a sally would arch
itself out at the ladies. It came very soon: an idea not indeed original,
for it involved a well-tried local joke, flashed through the black
trilby, the hair-grease, the hair and into the little grey cells of one
of the fat red-faced commercials.

Lifting his hat, he sweated towards the ladies:

'Excuse my intruding upon yourselves, ladies—but I cannot help but see where you're not fixed up with your hotel. Now if you was to ask me—that is as I am the local man, I've lived here thirty years now—I wonder if you'd know where I'd say you'd be as best fixed up?'

He paused and looked from one to the other of those girls, eyebrows raised in huge surprise. These various girls winced, or looked away, or primped fascinated at him. He then said, sharply, with lips terse to keep a straight face:

'I'd say you'd best go to Morley's.'

A gasp, quickly suppressed, from the other men. They were adept at the grave concealing face.

The ladies looked from one to the other, then at their lists. They said there was no mention of Morley's.

The man in the trilby rose instantly to this:

'And that's where you ladies hit the nail on its head. Morley's you won't find on no list. Morley's is more . . .' he waved his hands, screwing up his eyes and searching for just that one word which would do justice to the exquisition he proposed '. . . more what you call *select*.'

One of the tweeded gentlemen, removing his pipe from his mouth like a stopper, said gravely: 'Morley's is a *private* hotel.'

'Number Thirty-two, Marine Parade,' another said. 'Not five minutes.'

Those jolly men then fell to in earnest. Morley's was this, Morley's was that. Once warmed up they discovered subtleties of compliment one would never have suspected; they even began to argue among themselves. In short, the ladies were at length convinced, a street-plan was quickly sketched showing the way to Number Thirty-two, and, gamely swallowing their tea, they left for Fred Morley's house.

One or two, Miss Great-Belt for one, wished inwardly to show her personal superiority by choosing a more grandly named hotel (there was indeed a Bristol, a name as hallowed as the Ritz), but on practical thought it seemed wiser in a strange land at first to stick together.

One of the gentlemen started up to escort them: but was quickly dissuaded by a furtive shake of the head from the ringleader. Let

K* 297

matters take their course. It might be tempting to watch old Fred Morley's face; but if any one of them were seen the game would be given away.

Such was the preposterous situation when those six Beauty Queens rang the bell of Mr Morley's house. That fact is stranger than fiction has been often observed—but seldom believed. We like the ordinary, it is more restful, and liking it tend to close our eyes to the bewilderment of chance and coincidence that otherwise would strike us every minute of the day.

In the case of these six Beauty Queens, the glove of coincidence might have fitted all the more neatly if, for instance, the waiter who had brought Fred Morley's supper had just at that moment been about to leave the house. A uniformed servant would have perfected an otherwise passable illusion. But in fact that waiter had not even arrived by the time those girls pulled the bell. And it was Morley himself, in his raisin-red smoking jacket, who finally opened the door.

'*Come* into the gar—den M—' he still sang, and then stood stupefied.

'We would like some rooms,' said Miss Great-Belt, who like many Danes spoke English well. 'Have you any to spare?'

Since those girls were Beauty Queens, they were passably beautiful. To Fred Morley the vision of their six faces framed in his doorway like singers at some strange summer carol-feast both bewildered him and set his mind working at an unusual rate.

The Misses Amsterdam and Rotterdam, and the two Latins Civitavecchia and Clermont-Ferrand, now followed by saying in many mixed words that for their part double rooms would do. Morley had a further second's freedom for thought. It did not occur to him that these girls were part of a joke that had in fact been played once or twice before. Beauty seldom suggests fun. His mind instead remembered that the town was full, that these girls were probably tramping from door to door hoping for rooms in a private house, that this was difficult since they were so large a party, that it was pitiable that people should be in such a predicament, that it was the more so since they were beautiful people, that he had a large house, that it was largely empty, and . . . why not?

He bowed and opened the door wider for the ladies to pass:

'Certainly, Madame,' he said, wondering what the plural could be, '. . . I should be delighted to accommodate you.'

They scarcely bothered to thank him, but moved brusquely into what was patently the vestibule of a hotel. In fact, that eccentric decoration hardly mattered. As foreign visitors they would never have questioned an ordinary homely hall: it would simply have looked part of the mad English scene.

'La fiche?' asked Miss Clermont-Ferrand.

'Ah, oui,' Morley smiled, having no idea what this could mean. And added, as a pleasantry: 'Sanfaryan.'

'Vraiement?' smiled back Miss Clermont-Ferrand, impressed by such liberty.

But Morley then thought: By Jiminy I'll have to get moving. And raised his hand to command attention, and asked them kindly to wait a moment, and scuttled upstairs. He ran—striding now no longer—to the telephone by his bed and breathlessly called the restaurant to order not one but seven dinners. In half an hour. And then raced round the bedrooms. Fortunately these were kept made up: two double rooms, a good single room and a single dressing-room. One of these had already been slept in by guests on the previous weekend. He pulled the sheets back, smoothed out a crease or two, decided to risk it. But airing? Six hot-water bottles? Impossible. He ran round lighting with little pops gas-fire after gas-fire. Then he thought: Bathrooms! And banged open the door of the second bathroom, removing his rowing machine, a Hoover, some dirty linen and his golf-clubs: then rushed to his own to wipe off the comfortable soap-ring left only half an hour before.

In that fine old actor's frame there coursed a sort of boyish exaltation. For nearly nothing would he have disturbed the repose of his calm dinner alone: but for such a six . . . well, it hardly happened every night. He had no designs. He was simply exhilarated, flowing with the good red blush of boyishness. He felt chivalrous, too. No snake of desire but simply the flushes of virtue filled him.

He descended to take the ladies up to their rooms.

The oysters were laid out on seven plates, the ladies had been allocated their seats round the large table in the dining-room, and he himself, having seen that seven portions of pigeon pie were keeping hot in the kitchen, was at last on the point of sitting himself down—when, in the general delight at the sight of oysters, Miss Great-Belt spoke out:

'Oysters! This is very good!' she said, wondering at the same time what the charges of so considerable a hotel might be. 'But it was good luck indeed those gentlemen recommended us such a hotel!'

Morley's hand was actually on his chair to pull it back. Instead, he pulled back his hand.

'Recommended? Hotel?'

A sudden spasm gripped him where a moment before the gastric juices had begun to play.

'Surely yes,' Miss Great-Belt smiled. 'Some gentlemen in the railway bar. They said this is the best hotel we can have.' Then she added with a knowing smile, a condescension to the servant standing above her, 'But they will come quick enough for their percentage, no?'

'No?' Morley stuttered. 'Oh, yes, yes.'

The old joke! This time it had come off? His chivalry blew away like old hot air. He saw suddenly that he was in a very difficult position—he was a fraud. These ladies were deceived. They might be very angry. And more. He was a bachelor. Alone in his house, he had induced them to come inside. What would the world make of *that*? What would the neighbours, what would the Town Council, what would even the Court of Law think? Was it legal? Were there seduction laws? Certainly there were Boarding House Licences.

These and more terrors mounted in his mind. With regret he let his hand fall absolutely from the chair, then sculpted it round towards his plate of oysters, already beginning to act the part of a real hotel employee. He muttered that he did not know why an extra place had been laid and began to withdraw the oysters to take and to eat them in the sanctity of the kitchen, in what now must be his right and proper place. For he had decided to play the rôle out. For the moment it was the only thing to do. At all costs avert suspicion, a scene, the full fury of these now formidable girls.

His hand was about to grasp the plate—but Miss Civitavecchia's, lizard-like, was quicker:

'Piacere—do not trouble. It is plain,' she said, smiling round at the others, 'that we can eat some more?'

'Please place this on the bill,' she added.

Morley tried to smile and withdrew, oysterless, to the empty kitchen. Some minutes later he took care to bring only six soup-platesful of mulligatawny into the dining-room.

The dining-table had been laid with only one pepper-pot, one salt-cellar. The ladies required more. Morley, his soup and now his lonely pigeon growing cold, had to search for, fill, and serve others. Vinegar was required. And oil. And in the matter of drinks there was white wine, red wine, beer and water to be found for different tastes. Morley was run off his feet. His hurriedly gulped pigeon flew instantly back at him. And on top of all this he found it necessary, on being questioned, to invent excuses for the quietness of the 'hotel' and for the non-appearance of other servants.

Only later, when at last he had seen the last of the ladies mount the stairs—tired from their travels, they all went up early—only later when the front door was locked and with waiter-tired feet he lay in bed, did he allow himself at last a great retrogressive chuckle.

He saw suddenly how he lay there on his back like a dear old daddy-keeper, with his six young charges all tucked safely up sleeping blissfully on their six pillows. Six sudden beautiful girls at first look all of a piece. Only after a while, when the first endazzlement is over, can one distinguish between them. Now still to Morley they were banded indistinguishable, six little beauties all in a row, as if that beauty itself served the uniform purpose of a school hat and a gym frock.

And so there he lay, hoary old guardian of his exquisite crocodile, and chuckled, and gradually—not knowing what might happen in the morning, too tired now to care—fell asleep.

In the morning, reason asserted itself. Such a fantastic situation could not be allowed to continue. He considered for a moment applying for a boarding-house licence, hiring servants: but this was plainly too much trouble. And plainly it extended the falsity of the situation.

His daily housekeeper supplied the answer. He rose early to intercept her. He explained that he had given sanctuary the night before to six roofless ladies. The housekeeper froze. Morley pretended not to notice and asked her to prepare six breakfasts. The housekeeper pressed her lips together. Morley acted a laugh.

'An—er—equivocal position for an old bachelor, eh, Mrs Laidlaw?' his lips laughed. 'But safety in numbers, Mrs L., safety in numbers.'

This simple remark had a far greater effect than Morley could have hoped for. The word 'equivocal' put Mrs Laidlaw momentarily off her balance, it rescued Morley again into the status of the Master. But then that 'safety in numbers' in its turn saved her own comfort of mind, it sank her happily to earth, it was comfortable and what it said was what other people said all the world over. She served the breakfasts, hypnotized by the saying, muttering it over and over to herself. Only some hours later, when she had digested the good looks and the alien chic of the ladies' clothes, whorish to her woollen eyes, did she give notice.

But long before that Morley had waylaid Miss Amsterdam, who was first down. Miss Amsterdam was a dark-haired Hollander, possibly a descendant of the Spanish occupation. Most of her was covered with long dark hairs—but her face shone out from among the cropping like a lovely pale brown moon. She came hurrying down the stairs, and was already across the hall, between the ever-open cocktail-bar and the ever-empty lounge, almost to the door, handbag swinging like a third buttock, before Morley could stop her. But he came striding on with great actor's strides, calling: 'Excuse me! Miss . . . Miss . . .?'

'Call me Amsterdam.'

'Oh? . . . Well, by all means . . .'

Leading her aside into the lupined lounge, he made an unclean breast of it all. The word 'roofless' that he had by chance brought up to thaw Mrs Laidlaw provided his key to a happy simulation of the truth. It conjured the pitiful idea of 'roofless' ladies, it implied an open door and an open heart to all the travel-stained abroad in the night in this his native country. He explained the hotel furnishings as mementoes of his own travels, his tours—off-handedly stressing,

as a condiment of glamour, his place in the theatre—and finally
begged Miss Amsterdam to excuse this whole misunderstanding that
might so easily be taken as an impertinence on his, a bachelor's part.
Would she convey this to the other ladies, would they understand?

Miss Amsterdam's brown round lovely face went this way and
that, it made shapes of surprise and petulance and tenderness and
excitement—then finally all broke up into a wild pudding of
laughter. Brown pudge of cheeks crinkling, eyes gone, brows ridged,
red mouth neighing never-seen underteeth—no more now than a
big brown baby howling agonies of wind.

Slapping one hand across that mouth, and the other over her
stomach, she tripped her lovely legs upstairs. And Fred Morley was
left waiting—for was this laughter or hysteria?—on his uneasy
tenterhooks.

From upstairs silence.

A long silence. A silence in a lonely downstairs when the upstairs
is full but behind closed doors. Creaks of silence, rafters loaded with
words.

But—ten minutes later all was over. On the landing a door burst
open and laughter, like water from a thirsty tap, laved out and down
the stairs. Morley heaved a long and blessed relief.

With the laughter came the ladies—all six, all smiles. They milled
in and stood in a semicricle round old Fred Morley, who rose and
gravely bowed. Miss Amsterdam broke instantly.

'Mr Morley—I have told all the girls all you have told me and
all of us girls have agreed together you are a kind and a big sweet.'

'We thank you,' dimpled Miss Rotterdam, a round blonde cheese
of a girl.

'Comme c'est infiniment drôle . . .' giggled Clermont-Ferrand,
who, in trousers and a checked shirt, but with a wicked fringe and
a golden anklet, appeared to be a woman on two levels or layers—a
check-shirt cowgirl of St Germain enclosing a Nana of more liberal
boulevards.

'Such a dinner!' sighed with wondering shakes of her head the
practical Miss Nuremburg. This one, who held the annual title,
comic to the English but a beautiful reality to the German, of Miss
Sauerkraut, had in her pallid tall glory exactly the texture of that

well-prepared vegetable. A dab of rotkohl would not have harmed her cheeks.

Miss Civitavecchia took a deep breath and began, palms outstretched: 'Ma—ma Mi—a!' And went on, for a long time, expending in a tumult of Italian the full breath of her bosom. On the solid foundations of a Roman body she carried the small head of a snake: it was as if some Laocoon had been fused with the bust—the bust is meant—of a great—and great is intended—Roman Empress.

So Fred Morley stood overwhelmed by this crescent before him of beauty, smiles and gratitude. He felt, and for the moment was, loved. A pleasant sensation. But, as an Englishman, he was embarrassed . . . and through the glow of pleasure his instinct was to escape by offering them all a drink. This last was on his lips—when Miss Great-Belt at last spoke up.

Miss Great-Belt was plainly the most beautiful of all. Her present title embraced that royal reach of sea separating the Danish islands of Fünen and Zealand, and no dimension of her own. She was a dark red-head. Her skin white over lilac. Her eyes deep dark blue. Her whole face the face of a cat—round high cheekbones, nearly no nose, many small teeth curving in a long smile like the dream of a bite: yet all squared into the face of a girl. How could she have become so? Copenhagen is a great seaport through which have passed many strange fathers. Whatever . . . there she was, a brilliant cat-faced red-head, who might bite, who might smile, and who now was the only one to say a disaffected word:

'How much do we owe?' she said.

Practical? Or battle-cry? Fred Morley's interest quickened. Confused by the compliments of the others, which made those ladies into no more than lovely willing sisters, his well-tried nose sniffed Woman. For the first time one among those beauties stood out separate.

'I had hoped,' he instantly said, 'that in the circumstances you would accept my hospitality?'

Miss Great-Belt looked him calmly in the eye.

'Thank you,' she said, serene and ominously composed, 'but that is impossible. Would you please be so kind as to tell us the charge?'

Of course, all the others had now to agree with her. All their various voices rose to insist. They chattered to each other and at Morley and he could not say a word. But he kept his eye on Miss Great-Belt. She had taken out her powder-puff and with aggravated unconcern dabbed her nose: he noticed with rising spirits that she used no mirror. It was a gesture. It meant war.

Finally it was settled that the ladies paid Morely a reasonable sum per day. Later he telephoned the Town Hall to ask whether he might take in paying-guests. The clerks, for the town was over-crowded, were delighted. He arranged for service and food—after all, he said to himself, it would only be for two or three days. Then, much later, when all this was fixed, asked Miss Great-Belt person-ally whether he might escort her round the town.

'No,' was the answer. With a straight look between the eyes.

All that was on the Thursday. The Contest was scheduled for the Saturday. For three in the afternoon at the Pier Aquadrome.

Thus, for these girls, there was much to be done. Much final furbishing. Polishing, paring, depilating and all the other many measures of massage and exercise necessary to bring tissues of flesh and hair—Fred Morley was heard with a weary chuckle later to say—to scratch. For in the course of these operations old Morley's eyes were opened.

Overnight the calm of his bachelor ménage was transformed. Those girls worked themselves hard. The rooms, the corridors, the bathrooms drifted in a dry flood of cosmetic cartons: balls of cotton-wool and paper tissues mated with blonde, brunette and auburn curlings in every corner: powder flew everywhere, made solid marble shafts of the sunbeams: oil and cream made each empty surface—every table, every shelf—a viscous adventure.

Masseuses and masseurs—brisk women and strange men—came and went: Morley, to lighten the load on his new temporary staff, and because he spent much time nervously wandering and waiting downstairs, answered the door to a ceaseless stream of such visitors and the slick peremptory drivers of delivery vans. He tried as far as possible to avoid going upstairs. Things upstairs were too strange. He had found Miss Clermond-Ferrand sitting with her head in her beautiful hands and each elbow cupped in the half of a lemon. Across the landing there had whisked a blue kimono topped by a face plastered livid dry pink, with hollows it seemed where the eyes might be and naked lips huge now as a clown's, a face terribly faceless—too late he had seen that this might be Miss Great-Belt. Then Miss Rotterdam, in a bathing-dress, had come bumping across the landing on her bottom, and vanished into the bathroom: no hands nor legs, she had explained *en route*—a question of stomach muscles. Miss Sauerkraut liked to lie on the balcony on half a ping-pong table, head-downwards. Miss Civitavecchia he had found carefully combing the long black beards that hung from her armpits, a peninsular speciality: unlike Miss Amsterdam, who took no such Latin pride in the strong growth of dark hair that covered most of her—it seemed that whenever he asked for her the answer came: 'Upstairs shaving.'

So Morley remained downstairs.

He sat there with a whisky and soda, half impatient, half-amused, but more simply apprehensive of what else might come. He sat listening, cocking his head anxiously at the bumps and scufflings that came from above, and answering the doorbell.

But above all the question of Miss Great-Belt lightly, but persistently, tormented him. He was quite conscious of his middle years, and of her youth—yet after all was he not Frederick Morley, the idol of a thousand hearts? He felt affronted: a smile perhaps, a gracious gesture would have been enough to appease him. But this —what was it called—*snootiness*! Beyond the Fred Morley in him, the male rose in combat. Something must be done.

Yet was this attitude of hers exactly *snooty*? He wondered whether it might run deeper. It lacked the proper coquetry. It was the result, perhaps, more of a solid and almost matronly composure unusual in a so strikingly beautiful young girl. She had an air of remarkable self-containedness. When she walked, it was always with a sense of destination: she knew where she was going. When she carried parcels, one felt those parcels would never be undone in a flurry but would each await its proper time. There was a feeling of unhurried *process* about her. Though she bore the fiercely beautiful face of a cat, she was phlegmatic—but then perhaps a cat is, despite some appearances, the most phlegmatic of animals?

Later that evening—it had been a beautiful, if indeed a long day —he watched her leave the house arm-in-arm with Miss Sauerkraut. Their summer dresses clung coolly in the evening air to what must have been naked bodies, and the tall swanlike Sauerkraut served only to emphasize Miss Great-Belt's warm pliabilities. The two paused outside the door, then turned one way down the westering front. Two youths in padded flannels detached themselves from the group that lounged now always discreetly over the road from his front door, and at a suitable distance followed, eyes intent, mouths whetting for the whistles that would come.

The cavalier rose in Morley; but he quieted it. Then, pair by pair, he watched the others go. Each was followed by two, sometimes three, of the watching gentlemen. And then he was left alone in the house. At last—peace. He breathed a great sigh of peace. But to himself, and for himself. It was a false sigh. He knew that in a very few minutes the house would feel too empty. And so it did. He wandered for some time from room to room fingering things, sitting for a while here and then there. But he kept thinking of all those who had left, so young and expectant, to enjoy the evening—and he began to feel his years. That would never do. His bachelordom had taught him all about self-commiseration—and it was his custom to guard against it. He selected a hat, a curl-brimmed panama, pale but not too pale for evening wear, and left for the Club. The stolid usuality, the pot-belly of male companionship was what he needed.

The Yacht Club was not much frequented by yachtsmen. A few faded photographs of old racing-cutters spinnakered across the cream-painted, nautically planked walls. Well-polished brass shone here and there, and to seaward one wall of the lounge was given to good white-framed observatory glass. However, it was now a place mostly of comfortable horsehair where members, the elect of the town, might come and drink.

The warm fruity smell of gentlemen at ease greeted Fred Morley as he entered the lounge: tobacco smoke, fumes of whisky and port, horsehair and something else—starch, red flesh, woollen underpants?

—ballooned out its bouquet of security across the Turkey carpet. Here at last was escape from all feminine essences! He rang the bell for a drink and, giving a wink or a nod to various members couched in the horsehair, joined a group at the further end.

'Why if it isn't Fred!'

'Come in, Fred—we was just about to 'ave a round of Kiss-in-the-Ring.'

For it had already got about that Fred Morley had some young ladies staying in his house. Young ladies of the theatrical profession, it was presumed.

Those who now addressed Fred were a mixed bag of the livelier, wealthier citizens of the town—a couple of aldermen, a big butcher, a retired military man well-invested in beach and fairground concessions, the local brewer's brother-in-law. They were an affable, energetic, powerful lot. As far as they were allowed, they ran the town—not too unfairly. Mixed of the professional and tradesmen's classes, they forgot such differences in a close-masonry of well-to-do malehood; they even included some of the now not so well-to-do, on grounds that they had once been so—those only were excluded who had not yet come solidly up in the world. They were a cut above those other bantering gentlemen who in the first place had sent his six guests to Morley—yet they too always affected a jovial banter among themselves.

For some time Fred Morley sipped his whisky and warmed his marrow at the hands of these gentlemen. Then a Mr Everett Evans came in. Everett Evans, since he was an alderman, a prosperous draper and a local bright spark, had been appointed chairman of the judicial committee that was to sit upon the Beauty Queens. Conversation had already turned upon this coming event. Morley had kept his mouth immaculately shut. But now Evans himself had come in.

'Hallo, hallo—look who comes here!' called this group of men.

'What you having, Everett?' they then said.

'Large bicarbonate and soda, thank you,' answered Mr Evans.

'For Evans' sake!'

'That's just what. For the sake of poor Evans's poor belly, that's what.' He paused and looked mystified. Then: 'Know what I've been drinking last twenty-four hours?'

They had fallen into amused, expectant silence. Evans's chin went out, he looked at each of them accusingly, then let his eyes bulge as he blurted:

'Barium.'

'Barium?'

'No lie. Barium. Little white glassfuls of bloody barium.'

'What the hell . . .?'

'First they strip you. Then they put you in a kind of a smock affair, apron you might call it—with bloody lacing up the back. They let you keep your socks on—but them laces! Bows all down the back, bows all over your arse come to that.' He paused for breath, the others were looking startled.

And then he went on: 'That's the start of it. So you're left there all buttons and bows reading your old copy of *Punch*. Then they say come in, and in you go in a big dark black room and then you get your barium. Whole glassful. First thing down your gullet for twelve hours. Metal, it is. Tastes like ice-cream carton.'

Another breath:

'Then they do you.'

'Do you?' The gentlemen leaned forward, uneasy. '*Do* you?'

'Take your photo. The old X-ray.'

Now breaths of relief, tittering. But Evans raised his hand.

'No laughing matter, I tell you. Ulcers, that's what I've got. Stomach ulcers. You know when I've been feeling bad these last months—since Christmas like? The old sawbones says he's worried I might have something proper dicky down below and sends me along to this hospital for the photo. Well, they found 'em all right. Ulcers. No lie.

'And what's more I got more photos to be took—taken like. And 'ow the 'ell I'm going to look all these bathing bellies in the face I don't know.'

Everett Evans looked down sadly into his glass of soda. Little bubbles raced up at him, burst at him.

'Day after tomorrow it is. I can't do it. Someone'll 'ave to stand in for me.'

He looked up suddenly and glared round the company.

'Well?' he said vicious, 'any offers?'

309

All those men now looked at each other nervously. They simpered. Not one but secretly would have loved being up lording it over so many Beauties. But there had been too many jokes about the 'Bellies' already, each man saw himself up there on the platform blushing and being laughed at. So now all began rapidly to mumble excuses—jolly excuses, for seriousness would be suspect. 'The old woman'd never forgive me.' 'What—me with a grown-up daughter?' 'Think of my poor old heart.'

Except for Morley. Through Morley's mind there flashed a sudden sunlight. Here it was—on a platter! Here was the prize for Miss Great-Belt! And he—with a courteous smile—presenting it! She'd eat out of his hand! He gave a great cough.

They all looked at him. He said nothing, coughed again, looked particularly at no one and nothing.

It worked.

'The very man! Why did no one think?'

'Love's young dream! Be like falling off a log, eh, Fred? Busman's holiday.'

Everett frowned at him, the only one severe: 'Well, Fred—how about it? I can fix it—'

'Mm,' Fred said, looking out through the big marine windows. The sea was dotted here and there with little boats. Their sails took the last evening sun. He did not see them. 'I don't know that I'm doing anything that afternoon, nothing special . . .'

'I'll fix it then, Fred.' Everett pressed his lips, fixing, together.

'We—ell—,' mused Fred.

'*But*,' said the one man there who knew, 'is this right? With some of them staying there in his house?'

'What!' This was news. They all dug him in the ribs—with their eyes, their great laughing teeth. 'Old rascal!' 'There's a dark horse!'

'Yes,' Fred sighed, more than ever casual, 'I've got six of them.'

'Safety in numbers then,' hissed Everett Evans, 'that fixes it.'

'*But*,' said that one man again.

'Now look 'ere,' Evans exploded, 'Fred's had more skirt in 'is life than you've 'ad 'ot dinners. Think six little bellies mean a thing to Fred? You're off your rocker! I tell you I can fix this easy.'

In any case those other men, accustomed to the pulling of wires, were hardly worried by prospects of collusion. This now suited them. It made things easy. Fred was the man. They all agreed.

'Well, Fred, shall I fix it?' said Everett.

Morley made one final hesitation, for form's sake. He pursed his lips, ruminated, then suddenly sharply nodded. 'All right then. I'll do it.'

'Good boy,' rose ulcerous Evans. 'Lead me to the blower. This needs fixing right now.'

And so it was fixed.

It was a different Fred Morley who sat downstairs the next morning in deference to the upstairs pandemonium. From bar to lounge to front door he walked—but this time with a glint in his eye, a chuckling of hands together, sometimes the tum-tumty-tum of a little song. She may touch her toes and waggle herself and knead herself like dough, he thought—ha, *knead* herself, who'll she be needing next, eh? He blew a kiss upstairs to the invisibly exercising Great-Belt. Old Fred Morley and none other! Tum-ti-tumty-tum. And outside it was a beautiful morning, the sun shone. Old Fred Morley? Old me Aunt Fanny! Forty-eight if a day. Middle-age. And no spread.

Nor was it quite the same upstairs that morning as the day before. Those girls had had their bikinis delivered: some were too big, some too small. Tall pale Sauerkraut became too huge a goddess in hers too big: Miss Amsterdam, her brown skin cooing against the new white slips ordained by the Council but also too small, went into a corner and attached with the vigour of a true Hollander various appealing frills of her own—and of course there was a row about that. And of course the girls had by now survived their first affability —they were getting each other's measure. Some had seen others at something, others had heard some say this or that. Sides were taken, embattlements formed. But between squalls and bickering a sense of dignity prevailed. No one actually touched anyone else.

Meanwhile out on the front, on the sea—all was plain sailing. It was lovely weather and the sea lay smoothly sparkling blue. White paint of pier and railing stood freshly deadly clean against all that blue and the colours of people, boats, cars, kites—and Fred Morley had an idea. He sent, by the new and overpaid and delighted maid, messages up to the ladies Rotterdam and Clermont-Ferrand. Would they do him the honour of a stroll and an apértif before luncheon?

All he thought was: 'They're nice girls. I'd like a stroll. I've better plans for the Danish lass, let her bide (and it'll perhaps do her good).'

Rotterdam and Clermont-Ferrand—the one butterflying her arms to raise further her already sturdy breasts, the other sitting in front of a mirror practising 'facial yoga'—that is making grotesque narcissist kisses at herself to exercise the mouth, then pecking her head forward twenty times a minute like a little hen on her bright young egg—read their messages with approval and half an hour later those two were one on each of Fred Morley's arms strolling the Front. Morley in a faultlessly raffish suit of biscuit tussore, with a high stiff collar, a pin in his tie and a curl to his hat: Miss Rotterdam blonde in flowered silk that wisped round her so closely in the breeze that those following could see not only the lovely knobbles of her vertebrae but the knobbles of her suspender-belt too: Miss Clermont-Ferrand in high white shoes and a strange white belt almost taller than its breadth round her no-waist, black hair flowing, black silk buttocks a-swing, preposterously and magnificently French.

Rotterdam in her friendly Dutch way, which concealed heaven knew what guile, had taken Morley's arm to draw his attention to a group of young men playing cricket on the sands below. 'You English,' she had laughed, pressing her round lips back on to her teeth, making enormous dimples, and giving Morley's arm a niecely squeeze. All of which Clermont-Ferrand immediately, and fiercely, noticed—so that not to be outdone she had taken the other arm, pulling Fred's interest towards a sombre green-painted glass wind shelter: 'Why do you have autobus shelters,' she asked, in innocence of the normal weather prevailing on such a parade, 'when you have no autobuses?' And panted up a charming little laugh to him that also implied 'Oh, you dear mad Englishman.' But at the same time panted her mouth itself, open and eager, red-lipped and wetly pink inside, teeth laughing wide and tongue-tip pointing right out at him very close to his startled eyes.

So Fred had them both hugged on his arms. He puffed his chest with a deep breath of the good clear sea-air of morning and felt, there in the sunlight with sea to the left and bright traffic to the right, with the Cliff Memorial Gardens pine-green ahead and the white pier-dome flashing all holiday joy, good to be alive.

It was in such style that he was observed, a little further on, by those same local gentlemen who had first sent him the girls. These locals moved in a group: just then they had moved that group, bellies eased and jolly with good morning beer, from the brass-flashing doors of a near-by saloon to take a breather of sea-air before the next. But when they saw Fred they gaped, their spirits gravened and sank. For they were in that least enviable of situations—that of the practical joker who slips on his own banana-skin, that of him who is laughed at last. Yes, it had gone wrong all right. There was Fred sitting pretty, with *two*, with a blondie and a blackie, one of each kind, one to suit whatever his fancy was, turn and turn about —and they had put this in his way! They had actually been such damned idiots as to send him that choice handful he had there! Not thinking, not dreaming to keep the handful for themselves, and send it somewhere quiet round the corner where they might call later to pass the time of day. . . . Oh well, they supposed it was the booze again, that's what it was. Can't have everything. But—that it should be Fred! Fred whom always secretly they had envied, Fred who'd had it on a platter all his life, bags of it, oodles of it there on his stage-doorstep whichever way he might turn . . . while *they*. . . .

Now to Fred passing with a beauty on each arm they raised their hats and gave grim fixed smiles, new white teeth and old yellow ones flashing in the sun: to which Fred Morley, deeply satisfied, bowed and passed on his triumphant way.

Yet those gentlemen would not have been so discomforted had they seen him an hour hence. For matters did not continue so well. In the first place, those girls were young and active, they were out to enjoy themselves and not content at all simply to take the morning air. Also, as foreigners, they were inquisitive, they wanted to taste the oddities of this strange new country. So that soon Clermont-Ferrand had dragged them to a fish-and-chip booth that lay just below down some steps: and she walked now with newspaper in one hand and a chip in the other, fish-oil lustrous all over her lipstick and powdered chin. And Rotterdam had asked for a small propeller on a coloured stick, which she waved fluttering high, while firmly her other fist clasped a long thick truncheon of pink peppermint rock. They giggled bending, pointing, nudging, giving high shrieks of awe and shock at so many strange things to see. With rock and fish-and-chips they had settled their feminine differences, now they were all for fun. And having discovered the livelier scenes of stalls and crowds beneath the arches of the Parade they dragged Morley from sweet-shop to pin-table, from whelk to winkle stand, from jellied-eel to ice-cream barrow. They took him on the Dodgem cars and they had him photographed with them in sailor hats standing in front of a huge cardboard fishing-smack. (The photographer, giving his rump a resounding whack, had cried: 'Another good smack gone to the bottom!') Loudly as Morley protested, the louder they laughed and the further they dragged him. They thought these were no more than the coy protestations of an elderly man enjoying himself.

Fred Morley had planned an apértif on the terrace of the best hotel in the town, a terrace just overlooking the street and readily seen from there: he would have sat with his two beautiful guests and from that eminence with a drink in hand and a naughty glint in his eye enjoyed the envy of passers-by for the half-hour until luncheon. And then luncheon. Cold salmon, a bottle of the best, the white clean cloth, the silver and the laughter of these two pairs of lovely red lips. This had all gone wrong. Those girls had no time for luncheon. He was tired, jolted, hungry, thirsty. And he did not wish to be seen even up on the Marine Parade itself with two such high-spirited girls—who now wore each a hat with a large motto printed on it. Yet of course, when they had had enough of the beach, up they had to go.

And there, to cap everything, he saw approaching him Miss Great-Belt. Miss Great-Belt with her fine red hair and in an orange dress holding in one hand a towering stick of electric pink candy-floss, a wild mane of strident sugar which every so often she kissed with her bright carmine lips. In the other hand—and still she managed all this with no lessening of self-composure—she held the arm of a sleek young giant in a shirt of flowered American silk.

A CONTEST OF LADIES

He nearly hated her. And it was then, at a moment of shame and dislike, that she made towards him her first affable gesture. She waved her great pink floss-stick with the benign gesture of passing royalty—then gave him a huge, long, tranquil wink! And passed on.

When at last he was safely home, and when thus in comfort and at ease his temper had subsided—he still remembered that wink, reviewed it in a more benevolent light, and began to build up implications for it. Hope flowered. Wish welcomed fulfilment. It was plain her mood had turned, she had completed her feminine duties—the period of cat-and-mouse play laid down in the rules—and now she was blossomed and waiting. It only remained for him to pluck her.

So that an hour later, when he met her in the hall, he mentioned that he had a box at the Hippodrome that night. And she charmingly agreed to be his guest. At the theatre? At seven-thirty? Most kind. And supper afterwards. Delightful.

But at seven-thirty she was not at the theatre, nor at eight-thirty. He telephoned home. No, she was not in. She had gone out—to what? *What?* To a *dance?*

He slammed down the receiver and left, furious.

When she came in that night he was waiting for her. She came in early—for the next day was the day of the Contest, and she had to enjoy a long night's sleep—she came in a little breathless, her lovely red hair ablaze in the light, now with no pink candyfloss but in an evening dress the colour of the night sky. For a second when she saw him she hesitated: but instantly then gathered herself and came flouncing, almost on those tall legs bouncing, along the hall, unperturbed as usual, a glint of disdain in her navy eyes, but her lips pouted to smile. And as she came up to him she did smile.

'Good evening.'

Now it was he who played with composure.

'Good evening,' he said coldly. 'I missed you at the theatre.'

'The theatre? Of course—I'm so sorry. But you know—I really felt I could not come. To sit about all evening in a stuffy box! I needed exercise, you know. The great day tomorrow!'

315

'Indeed? And it was nothing that I waited a full hour for you?'

'I've said I am sorry.'

'And that is all?'

She said nothing. But looked at him curiously.

Then she asked: 'You really expected me?'

He looked surprised. 'Naturally.'

'Well *really*. You spend the morning with not one but *two* of these . . . these *women* upstairs. And then you expect to spend the evening with *me*? What do you think I am? What next? Shall I tell you what *you* are—you're an old satyr, that is what. A wolf! With pointed ears! With *hoofs*!'

She had raised her voice—he was so surprised he put up a hand to feel his ears—and then, having reached her climax with the word 'hoofs', which she blew at him with a mouth shaped for whoofing whole houses down, she was gone.

He stood there a moment amazed. Then his lips snapped shut. 'The Great Day tomorrow?' he said to himself. 'So be it.'

The Great Day dawned differently to those preceding. In the early hours, as from nowhere, big clouds blacker than the night had loomed up, flashed into fire, burst into water. Straight down, as if some celestial bucket had slopped over, the rains had fallen. Summer hails had swept the front. The temperature had fallen a swift ten degrees: then more. A wind had sprung up, gathering into a light steady gale. Until when dawn finally broke the Marine Parade lay drenched and grey, chilled and windy and drizzled, deserted and to remain so throughout a long wet cold day.

Morley had awoken in the night to hear the hailstones drumming and booming on the glass verandah roof below his window: and when at nine o'clock he went downstairs not at all well-slept, the house was grey and dead, no shafts of summer light livened the rooms, the blue lupins sat dusty like drab flowers in the corner of a dull boarding-house. Which this is, he savagely thought.

Yet it was hardly dull—for throughout the morning the sounds upstairs rose to a climax. Most of the girls were now not speaking to each other. But those who did yelled at the tops of their voices. Their frenzy in these last hours of preparation rose to new and furious levels. By twelve o'clock Morley could bear it no longer, he took his mackintosh off the peg and went out.

The air on the Parade was pleasanter than he had supposed. Forlorn, perhaps, the look of things—but there was a stimulating clarity abroad, a briskness of new air blown in from the sea. He looked across at the scudding waves, took deep breaths, and in between puddles stepped out briskly. Rain-soaked boats lay about the deserted beach like wrecks, a solitary figure in a mackintosh came swept by the wind down one street and disappeared up another.

This was exactly what Morley needed. He needed a change, he needed a breath of air. He was no longer angry with that Miss Great-Belt—he had lived too long to stay too deeply perturbed by such events—but only irritated: and that irritation included Miss Rotterdam and Miss Clermont-Ferrand as well, in fact the whole lot of them. He wanted his peace back. And now as he stepped out against the rain he reflected with pleasure that in a few hours it would in fact be all over. The Contest would be done and won. Not won by Miss Great-Belt, though—and a sense of justice rather than rancour filled him as he made this reservation. Yet after the Contest would they really leave? Probably—they were mostly subsidized. And certainly—if the weather held. 'Blow, blow, thou winter wind—' he hummed more cheerfully to himself as he paced along.

He went to the Club and refreshed himself. Everett Evans wished him a gloomy 'best of luck' for the afternoon—but left before the eating. Morley then had a good luncheon in the company of his fellows.

The Contest had been scheduled to take place in the open-air salt-water pool—the Pier Aquadrome, a place of civic pride. Now it had to be removed inside, into the Aquadrome's Winter Garden. This was a large white concrete modern building set like a plate-glassy liner, all decks and terraces, astern the paddle-boat old Pier.

By half-past two, in spite of the weather, quite a queue had assembled. Most of those that formed it, men and women alike, wore pixie-hoods. Tall-pointed heads leaned this way and that, chattering like a troop of fairies drenched with harebell dew—the women like wet narcissus petals in their grey-white plastics, the men in duffle-hoods like hairy great gnomes. All these were admitted slowly into a bare concrete hall brilliantly shadowed by mauve strip-lighting.

This ominous form of illumination has been called 'daylight' lighting. Yes—but it is the light of the worst day of the worst month of the year, the lilac light of a raw February afternoon. Faces everywhere lost their colour, lips turned purple-black and skins took on the pallor of long illness. Nevertheless, though soaked and drained of colour, the audience managed a certain cheerfulness: it was the cheerfulness particular to a wet seaside afternoon, when spirits soaked by the rain dribbling down windows of boarding-houses and hotels eventually make a burst for freedom—to batter along against rain and sea-wind, and thence to commingle at some echoing hall of entertainment with a cluttering of umbrellas, a thumping of boots, a wet rubber smell, a draughty gusto of raised voices.

So that now, sodden but heady with relief to be taken out of themselves on this stolen day of their holiday, the pixie audience gradually massed into seats set in amphitheatrical style round a semi-circular raised platform. On this the Beauties were to parade. And on its straight side there were ranged the judges' chairs, and their long table draped with Union Jacks.

A roar of laughter went up as Fred Morley and his four fellow-adjudicators entered. They were a great joke. Five portly gentlemen, wrested from their everyday dignities and their all-embracing wives, put to the task of examining pretty girls with hardly anything on! . . . Watch that professional eye glaze over. Watch blood pressures rise and pulses quicken! Five fat ruddy genial lambs up there on their altar . . . it was slaughter, it was murder, it was *killing*! 'Hooooo,' roared the crowd.

Dressed in their best suits, the judges simpered and blushed, dug each other in their ribs and whispered wicked chuckles in each other's ears as they settled down. One made an over-courtly gesture ushering his neighbour to his chair; another made for a brief two steps the motion so beloved of hefty hearties in their cups, he put one hand on a hip and lumbered along mincing like what he thought was a lady. Only old Fred, who was accustomed to an audience, retained his composure. He contented himself with a short, but most telling, twirl of his silken moustache-end.

A CONTEST OF LADIES

Then the uniformed Silver Band at the other end of the hall struck up—what but *A Pretty Girl is like a Melody?*—and a door opened at one side and up a long inclined gang-plank came the girls.

They came first jostling, then as they reached the raised parade spaced themselves out—a plump, slender, tall, short, round forty of them. In slow measure, with short proud steps, pausing almost at each step, hesitating just as heel touched passing heel, like primping prancing two-legged ponies they passed round the ring.

All wore the same small costume. That had been one of the rules. It had been adopted because it was time the proposer had one of his ideas accepted, so that he might remain quiet in other matters. The Contest Organization bore the cost, which in terms of the area of material needed had been slight. White rayon had been chosen— a remnant from Everett Evans's Drapery Store. Now each girl wore at her loins a close-fitting triangle, and at her breasts two discreetly billowing moons. No more. And, for sure, no less.

Each carried in her hand a card with a number. Only their shoes were their own, and these were in every case the highest they had —from great clobbering wedges to elegancies of the white summer, from shoes tasselled and curiously strapped to patent black evening shoes that quarrelled painfully with the naked flesh pressed into them. One girl, hard put, had come in a pair of tennis plimsols: she went round balancing avidly on her toes, a Shetland among the Shires.

The five judges leaned forward or sat back, pretending thus either keen judicial interest or recessive judicial wisdom. At first they were simply bewildered by so much sudden beauty. They sat in a fog of arms, legs, eyes, teeth, hair and all else. From bubble-bath and mud-tub, from pummelling-board and rubber roller came those fleshlings shining and smiling. Some had enclosed their legs in whole sheets of hot wax, from which they came hairless as ivory; others had forgone the luxuriance of mascara and instead brushed their eye-lashes with black boot polish to get a stronger set, a more lustrous shine. All smiled largely—though some by lowering their eyes achieved a sort of modesty at the same time, a redoubtable feat. All seemed not only to be following in each other's footsteps but in their own as well—this because their high heels forced their

319

knees forward, so that they hung back on themselves, as if searching out the ground before the main upperwork should follow: bended knees, mad knees stealing on tiptoe to unheard-of larders.

Miss Great-Belt hung just behind such knees when she first passed the judge's stand. Then she saw Frederick Morley—and nearly fell on them. For a second she lost her composure. Her face had been stretched into a design of radiant happy loveliness—eyes stretched wide yet with slightly lowered lids, lips stretched ovalling round their last liquid teeth. Now as she saw Morley there, Morley whom she had never expected, Morley whom she had told off only the night before, that expression did not leave her face—but in every feature it contracted, it grew smaller for a moment into an exactly reduced replica of itself. Heavens, her first thought was, what a stupid girl I am! Never to have known! (It never occurred to her how she could ever have known, she instantly blamed herself.) . . . But what a monster he is not to have told me! Then, as she transferred the blame to him, her self-esteem came flooding back, the eyes and lips opened again like the flesh of a startled anemone flowering for the attack, and never having really faltered and now with new aplomb she passed on. He would be feeling sorry, she thought, and wish to expiate his deception. Besides, deep down he's fallen for me. Besides, there are four other judges. Besides, whatever the odds I'm good enough to beat the lot of them.

As she passed him and for a moment their eyes met, Morley was able to look as though he was looking right through her.

And then round and round the girls paraded. Sometimes the band changed its tune, broke into a dreamy waltz, and then all the girls broke step, bewildered in their dancing blood by the change of tempo: they quickly regained themselves and went kneeing on.

The vast hall echoed to laughter, catcalls, whistles and sighs from the crowd. 'Irene!' some called: 'Doreen!' others. 'Git up them stairs,' yelled the lustier members, and one man throughout the long parade repeated over and over again, at most regular intervals, and on a note of despair: 'Roll me over.'

But despite such convivialities—how misfortunate those girls were! It was cold there in that hall. They shivered, and many arms and legs so smoothly cared for now erupted into gooseflesh. In the changing room the six foreign girls had shivered with cold—and with anger. They had combined in wholehearted vituperation of the English weather, and finally all things English. When they had exhausted everything else—food, clothes, weather and so on—Miss Clermont-Ferrand had summed the matter up with the irrelevant, but emphatic and somehow damning words: 'Double-decker Buses!'

Not only was it cold, but it looked cold. That hard mauve light stared down from the ceiling with the glare of arc-lamps on arterial concrete, rinsing all in varying shades of its mauve, killing all other colour. Lilac flesh, lavender crannies, purple lips, night-shade eyes— it became a circumambulation of the dead: corpsy smiles luked the way, rigor mortis was on the move, it was a dream parade of maidens killed before their time. And far away, like an old grey wardress, Life still drizzled a dustbin blessing from the windowed world outside.

The judges, first dazzled, then surfeited, had now become so used to the bodies before them that their minds, obeying the laws of curiosity and creation, began to work on them afresh. Their eyes searched those bodies as a prisoner may search his cell and find in such bareness a new world of hidden detail. Thus they began to notice that where the spine of one girl snuggled like a long and lovely dimple, the next protruded in a sweet and charming ladder of little knobs. Where one naked torso showed a broad squarish form moulded like Greek armour, the next was softly shapeless as the ribless tube of an odalisque.

Moles took on a new presence, they grew insistent as flies on a bare ceiling. Bruises—wide brown smudges and little purple nips— showed clearer and clearer, freckles came into their own, and in that light the yellowing of armpits took on a new and virulent lilac life. So too the flushed pork-crackling, the armadillo flesh at the backs of heels—this turned deep purple, so that sometimes it looked as if a girl wore the kind of stocking that had a dark reinforcement above the back of her shoe. And the light made Miss Sauerkraut's ears, which with her blonde pallor were normally bright red, black.

The veins of auburn girls stood out like nests of rivers on maps and the lines that others wore from navel to pudenda split like cheese-wire. But the navels themselves were a study on their own—dear little buttons, wicked forget-me-knots like cropped pink piglet tails, fingertip holes and penny-size pits and sometimes none at all but simply a recessive folding of modest flesh: one alderman, who had a compulsion complex, who normally had to walk between the lines of pavement stones or make countings of objects in rooms, found himself muttering a kind of permutation gamble to himself as the navels passed: 'Button-Putton. Holey-Poley. Button-Put—no, damn, Holey-Poley. . . .'

And there were the operation scars, the appendix marks. And the vaccination marks, brown cornflowers on arm and thigh. And where some had taken the sun, the criss-cross of bathing-costume straps white on brown; and the cabalist label on the wrist where a watch-and strap had been. And then all the other little marks, the little creases, and the wobbling and swinging of this and of that—all of these and so much more came to the fascinated eyes of the five startled gentlemen as that blanched and black-lipped procession passed before them.

(Yet how much more startled they would have been had their ears grown as alert as their eyes—for then they would have heard the ceaseless silent song whispered on the lips of every one of those priestesses as they marched, a song of one word only, the lip-stretched litany: 'Cheese.')

Even Fred Morley, accustomed to rub shoulders with so many ladies of the chorus, was surprised. In the theatre the light was kinder, and there was powder and paint. Here, he found himself thinking, they were like medical samples, girls in bottles, selected picklings.

Finally the moment for judgment arrived. The judges whispered to each other, passed little scraps of paper. The band stopped playing. The great hall was hushed—a murmur of whispering and tittering only, the sound of a hive of waiting bees. The girls stood in a long line in front of the judges, their hands to their sides, defenceless, offered.

Three of Morley's co-judges elected immediately and unreservedly for Miss Great-Belt. It took him some time to disenchant them. But he did. To them he stood as something of an expert, a professional man: he played on this, ironically arguing their lack of taste, making them feel silly. But instantly he raised their esteem by congratulating them on their second and third choices—with raised eyebrows and a knowing wink: 'Ho, I see you *do* know a thing or two!'

Finally a decision was taken.

Miss Amsterdam was awarded the first prize. A local lady, a blonde Miss Browne, came second, and long pale Miss Sauerkraut romped in third. Miss Great-Belt came nowhere at all.

The crowd cheered and booed, cheered for Miss Browne, and booed for Miss Great-Belt. But the judges' decision was final. There was no going back. And now Fred Morley rose to present the prizes.

A fine crocodile dressing-case for Number One, a portable wireless for Number Two, and oddly a set of pressure cookers for Miss Sauerkraut. And cheques for all. And for everybody present a few words from Frederick Morley.

'Ladies,' he began, and gave a great sigh, rolling his eyes. Roars of laughter.

'And Gentlemen,' he continued, with a sniff, as though he disbelieved in the presence of these. Redoubled laughter.

But then he silenced the laughter with measured and grave opening words. He made one of those speeches that keep the audience well on their toes—as soon as he got them uncomfortable and guilty with a passage of great gravity, he let fall a howling joke (and he was careful to make it a howler, not to serve wit in that most mixed hall). And as soon as they were howling, down he came on them hard with a passage of such stony grandeur that the air echoed a susurrus of shoe shufflings and coughs as presenceful as the laughter itself.

He had prepared this. And the reason he had taken so much trouble was to introduce a more personal condiment addressed to Miss Great-Belt. It was an address of omission. He made particular reference to the other international visitors—but not to her: and to make this the more striking he made it the less pointed by omitting one of the others, Miss Rotterdam, as well. He expressed on behalf of all present his gratitude to these ladies of lands across the sea for the honour of their visit—and then brought out some personal whoppers: of the lady from Rome's seaside ,'all roads lead to Miss

Civitavecchia'; of Miss Sauerkraut, 'my little cabbage—and not so sour at that'; of the first prize-winner, 'not only a fair damsel but a veritable *Amster*-damsel', and so on, whoppers that issuing from his presidential mouth achieved an arch and fearful force.

And that, all but the shouting, was that. There was nothing left but to go off into the drizzle.

Except—for a brief moment, but a moment which was to have great repercussion—for Miss Great-Belt.

Miss Great-Belt had her place, like all the others, in the line of girls listening to Morley's speech. But with a difference—she was the only one who somehow appeared thoroughly and properly dressed. It was as usual—her self-containedness at its magic work again. There she stood in her little triangle and her two small moons, nothing else, with her hands to her sides. She should have stood as sacrificially slavishly offered as all the others. Instead she remained composed and remote. She stood on her own legs, in her own right, occupied only by herself.

But when the speech ended, and the line of girls broke up, she simply stood on.

For only a few seconds—yet seconds at such a time that stretched in the eyes of the onlookers into statuesque minutes—she stood alone exactly as she had stood for the previous quarter-hour, her eyes fixed vaguely on the platform of judges.

Then her eyes woke up, startled. She looked around her. For a moment she hesitated. She seemed even to totter, not knowing which way she had to go. Then she saw, regained herself, turned and walked with all composure down the gangplank.

Miss Great-Belt had been thinking.

That moment of action, or of inaction, had not gone unperceived by Fred Morley. He had noticed it from the corner of his eye, not then wishing to turn his full face upon her, and had triumphantly noted it as an expression of her discomfort at losing the prize. But intuition is not a monopoly of the feminine, and far back and vaguely through his jubilation a bell of unease had tolled. An intuitive woman, in his place, would have sought for an immediate

solution, right or wrong, to such a problematic sound; but Fred
Morley had preferred to shut his ears to it, it was uncomfortable,
he had done a good day's work and wished to relax upon his laurels.

Relaxation took the form of a visit to the Yacht Club. There,
again in manly company, again among the chaffing and congratula-
tions of his fellows, there was every hope of a pleasant end to a
perfect day. But the opposite occurred. As the conviviality compounded, so did the tolling of that small bell of unease. It rang
louder and louder. He tried to be, but he could not remain, deaf to
it. And as the sound grew louder it took shape—from a vague unease
it invented form. What—he began to consider—would be her real
reaction to the afternoon's happening? How on earth could—he
thought between drinks and digs in the ribs—a strong woman like
that take such treatment lying down?

In the end he grew certain she would have her revenge. He remembered that women are said to like the last word: he considered
this afresh, and began to believe it. He remembered the adage about
he who laughs last laughing longest: he believed that too. And when
he mixed the two ideas, substituting a 'she' for a 'he', the significance
grew appalling.

But what form could such revenge take? Whichever way he looked
at it, his apprehension grew. He knew that the ways of women were
profound and unpredictable, their veiled wiles a labyrinth, their
capacity for innuendo prodigious. Yet on the other hand there was
the fact that when women fought, when the battle-cry was really
raised, then they fought with the gloves off. His mind grew confused
with visions of the Wives of Kings and Fishwives with Arms Akimbo.
But since his own capacities for innuendo were small, his mind
attached itself to, and enlarged upon, the latter conception.

She would slap his face in public! She would tear the house down
—shatter the windows, slash the furniture, flood the baths, fire the
curtains! (If that were only all . . .!) But what among these oversize
visions he really feared was that she would invent a story against
him, perhaps make some appalling charge. Assault. Rape. Or what
was that word even worse? . . . Interference! She would say he had
Interfered with Her. No proof, no witnesses? No such luck—
he knew that two women can get together, and that there would

be one or two others dissatisfied with the result of the Contest.

He became overwrought. He dared not go home: but nor could he bear the anticipation.

Finally, less from courage than from a simpler impulse to 'go and see what it's all about', he excused himself from Evans and the others ('Ho, the Homing Pigeon!' 'Bye Bye Bluebeard! Love to the Misses!') and made his way home. Less certainly from courage, for he made his way in by the back door.

Excusing himself round the maid in the kitchen, who looked at him with surprise and suspicion mixed (another black mark? 'Miss Abercrombie, a temporary domestic in the employ of the accused, was called to the witness stand'), he tiptoed into the hall and listened.

No one downstairs.

Upstairs, sounds that might have meant packing.

What voices he now heard spoke in their own languages. No more need of a common language? Getting into groups? Not too good.

Then suddenly down the stairs the sounds of running rustling skirts, heels! In panic he looked each way—impossible to return to the kitchen, no time to cross to the lounge! He was cornered! However, thank Heavens, it was only one of them—Miss Amsterdam, first prize-winner, a friend!

She gave a cry of delight, flung her arms round him and kissed him.

'Oh you dear good kind man,' she cried, hugging him, 'thank you, thank you, *thank* you!'

If anyone comes in now, Morley thought, then Evidence, Witnesses, Deeper than Ever . . . gently and quickly he disengaged himself, more formally congratulating her.

'But I am so glad you're here,' she went on to say, 'we've been looking all over for you! Now I must tell you . . .' And she went into details of how some girls would leave on the morrow, by what trains, and the rest on the following day. She made no mention of Miss Great-Belt's intention. But as an afterthought, turning her head back from the front-door: 'Oh by the way, that Danish girl wants to see you—urgently, she said.'

He was left alone with this. He went on standing in the hall, too centrally for simply standing. The maid came in to ring the gong.

He threw out a hand, giving the barometer a great thud, nearly knocking it from the wall. Simultaneously as he went on pounding that thing, the old brass gong rang out. The house echoed with huge sudden noise. And for once, all at once, all the girls seemed to pile out of their rooms together. They came tripping down the stairs at him.

He was cornered with greetings. He could not opt but to go into dinner with them.

Miss Great-Belt nearly forced Miss Sauerkraut out of her chair in order to sit next to him. And of all others her smile was the most welcoming, throughout dinner she was charming.

Naturally, he made himself most gracious to her in return. But he distrusted her, he distrusted every flutter of her lovely eyelids. It must all be a cover for something terrible to come.

And after dinner, after all valedictory speeches had been made, Miss Great-Belt went so far as to suggest that he take her our for some coffee, perhaps even to dance. 'But I know dancing must be a sore question between us,' she went on to say, 'I know it was uncivil of me to go dancing that night you invited me to the theatre. But I *do* apologize. Let's say bygones are bygones? Shall we?'

At that moment Fred Morley could easily have excused himself. His better judgment advised him to. But two other voices spoke inside him. One said that a dance-floor in a hotel was public and therefore safe; the second whispered that perhaps she really was, after all, making her peace with him. The latter voice, though in a whisper, spoke the louder. In fact, engaged again by her charms and never at a loss for respect of his own, he had already begun to believe that she was finally expressing a real attraction towards him.

They took coffee together at Morley's favourite hotel—the very terrace, glass-shaded, where once he had foreseen himself with the Misses Rotterdam and Clermont-Ferrand—and later went in to dance. He took care to act with the greatest propriety and even introduced her to his friend the head-waiter as a professional lady from Denmark, who, with her colleagues, had been billeted by the Town Hall on his house. This would put to rest any wilder speculations as to the nature of his strange and beautiful guest. The bush-telegraph would tap round the room a rational and respectable tune.

As for Miss Great-Belt, she continued to be soft, sweet, charming. All her past animosity had vanished. She seemed to throw open that invisible veil that had hitherto made her so unattainable, so much the woman of 'process', and now welcomed him without question into the privacy of her composure. A woman so self-contained is ordinarily an uneasy companion. But when such a woman decides to invite one into her private sympathies, to give exactly her laughter and her confidence in the measure one knows it is withheld from others—then she becomes overwhelming. Without indulgence, with no condescension, but purely and simply, Miss Great Belt welcomed Morley to herself. He was bowled over.

Quite early in the evening she made one point clear. 'Now I do want to say once and for all,' she said, opening her great eyes wide for frankness, leaning towards him like a large dark red cat, 'that I congratulate you on your decision this afternoon. In my view you were absolutely right. That sweet Dutch girl was obviously the winner. I can see that one of the prizes had to go to an English girl— politics are politics. And there was every reason for poor Nuremburg —she looks so pale, doesn't she? A sick woman, yes she needs encouragement, it was very kind—taking third prize. Who wants to be third anyhow? No, I know you'll suspect I'm jealous—but honestly I'm not. With me justice counts before—whatever is the word?—*self.*'

She said this with great content, purring over her sacrifice, her frank good nature. He did not notice this. His instinct rose to protect a lady in distress. He began instantly to lie that he himself had voted for her for first prize—but what could he do against so many others?

He was surprised to notice that this was not received well. She looked, he thought, even a trifle offended. Why? Ah! . . . And he went straight on to point out that it was exactly because of this out-voting that, momentarily piqued, he simply could not bear to mention so much as her name in his presidential address.

As he stumbled through these paces, Miss Great-Belt watched him keenly. She saw that he was lying, and was satisfied. They finished the evening in high spirit with each other.

When the other ladies left during the next days, Miss Great-Belt stayed on. For propriety's sake she removed to the near-by hotel but she stayed on in the town. She and Morely saw each other every day. They went to the theatre, they dined together, they took motor-trips into the country and they went sailing on the sea.

The weather continued fine, it was a memorable month. Miss Great-Belt wrote to her father and begged permission to remain a few weeks more. Morley was in heaven. Now he avoided the Yacht Club altogether: he spent all his time with his new and lovely companion in places where they might be admired by more discriminating eyes.

It was for him a flirtation *de luxe*. It complimented his years, it redounded satisfactorily to his prowess. Finally, he told himself, he had won the day. Trust an old bachelor! Sometimes, when he thought of it all, he remembered with a reproving chuckle the first days, the very first days when he had unfolded every charm to entice her, when he had sacrificed every self-respect. How had he not realized that it was the exact opposite which would win her? Why—in a dozen musical shows this very process nightly comprised the whole plot! He had played it out himself night after night, year after year—it was the very stuff of life? Why had he never realized . . .? But then why, damn our eyes, do we all spend our lives delighting in the wisdom of paradox—yet hesitate to apply the risks to ourselves?

He laughed and wagged his doggy head. Silly old fool! But then —hadn't that same silly old fool come through with flying colours? In the end? It took perseverance. He smiled, a little in love with her and himself and with everything else. 'He who laughs last,' he chuckled.

But then she married him.

An Interlude

'C OÑAC?'
    'Coñac.'
'Coñac?'
'Coñac.'
'Coñac?'
'Coñac.'
'Four coñacs please.'
Silence.
Then:
'Why, there's Peter!'
'What's your poison, Pete?'
'What the doctor ordered, Gon and sif.'

This last a reference to the brandy made by Gonzalez and the *sifón* that goes with it.

A nondescript group, distinguishable as tourists, and as tourists undistinguished one from the other. All young. All malely jocular. Some with moustaches, some without, some in shorts, some in longs. And they sat now drinking the morning away in the café under the eucalyptus trees, saying little, watching. Alert to each strange shape and habit, their eyes stared shifty shameless disbelief; or laughed as at a monkey-zoo; or narrowed with the nausea of an Englishman noting a five-button cuff. They were English.

There was not, one might at first suppose, so much to see in this one street in a small town on a small Mediterranean island. Not yet opened up to the tourist, it seemed scarcely opened up to itself. But as with all small communities, the eye gradually reduces its focus and little reveals itself as much indeed. The street of white near-Moorish houses, with closed bead-doors and blinded windows, began to look over-shut; and soon, in this very shutness, peopled itself—the houses felt near to bursting. A priest asleep, a cigarette

330

fraying his underlip, was so covered with sleeping flies that his long black habit seemed in the eucalyptus light to be covered with sequins: a black-bosomed baroness after the orgy. The green Civil Guard, and the old woman carrying the pigeon upside down, and soon all other solitary passers-by, became, as the eye settled its monotony, a successive crowd: a small traffic of carts and the eruption of a dust-greyed car made up a busy road. A few hens and their long-legged breed of chicks, emus all, and a goat, and long dogs and a turkey with the shape of a cassowary and the soul of a ghost-ship—these peopled the lower ground with their own complicated life. Blue-black bees big as birds banged by; and a frog gabbled like a shrill old man with false teeth from the irrigation stream that fed, along the paseo to the sea, a high feathering of peaceful rose oleanders.

On a slowly ruminant level, then, the place was crowded. But in ordinary terms the slow sun-shadowed street was shut and empty. With one exception. One shop-door stood wide open opposite where the tourists drank. One could just make out a dim life of dead machines in the white-washed gloom inside. Above this shop hung a notice oddly progressive for so slow-living a place:

BICICLETAS DE ALQUILER.

Bicycles for Hire! To the five young tourists, as they sat watching the street, this one shop provided a kind of balm. It was a link with the homeland, and with life lived logically. Though they had travelled a thousand miles to be on this remote island, though they had suffered a hundred inconveniences and a dozen impositions to arrive here, they somehow preferred in their eye's mind this bicycle-hire shop to all the strange and exotic sights they had spent a year's savings to see.

The owner lived and worked alone inside the bicycle-hire shop, a pale man sucked white by his machines. Rubber solution and thin-veined spokes had bled him as the multiple lens and the shutter bleeds the camera-man, the dark-oiled chassis the whole white race bred in black garages. Loving their machines, which are voracious as female spiders, they are drawn by a dark love to be sucked dry, to eschew the sun, to tinker red-eyed in the beloved grit.

That was Miguel's precise, spiritual, particularly male passion.

His greater and more general love he hung out in the sun: and this was for Conchita, the round-faced brown-skinned girl in the red skirt who sewed the dusk away with her white-bloused back to him across the street. Lace on her lap, she sewed, as was the custom, with her chair turned in towards the doorway of her home. But this was only the custom; every evening her face would turn to him over her shoulder, and smile, or call a word across the quiet street, and these smiles became a bank of smiles massing through the months like the pesetas he drew in each day from his bicycles, pesetas he saved to mass for the day, next year, the year after, when they could be married.

During the day Conchita served buns, sweets, and her turn of postal duty in the sweet-shop-post-office. Both she and Miguel had been born in this village by the sea, they had grown up knowing each other, and now that they had ceased to be children, and looked about for love and for someone to share and complete their lives— they felt the urgency for each other, and a marriage was ordained. The old, strict customs of island courtship had been abandoned by now—they were betrothed more easily in modern, though still formal, terms.

To the group of young Englishmen, who thought of their fair moustaches and their blistered pink arms as normal, this man Miguel and his woman were the strangers: Miguel's white body ran with long dark hairs, his hair was cropped short like a clothes-brush, his teeth smiled too white to be true; and Conchita, though young and fresh and charming, was nevertheless short, and round-faced as the next islander, and for all her lashes and dark-drooping eyes by alien standards a little coarse. Never to be taken too seriously.

But of course Miguel and Conchita were the real people of that small paradise whose red earth stretched its rich carpet to the blue sea's very edge: whose fig-trees gloved their deep green leaves against the same sapphiric blue: whose corn rose high and windless, like buff fur, among grey olives and green carob-trees; whose river ran fertile through reeds and oleanders to the sea, meeting it, spring water to the salt, in mysterious estuary. A rich land, a flat well-watered stretch of orchard and flower larded with white farms, feathered with palms and scented with jasmin. Rich and fertile, calm, where there was no hurry, and love might be expected to find its slow fruition undisturbed.

Rich and fertile the tourists, too.

'Hi—Peter!'

'Come on in, old Peter.'

'Sit down!'

'Pew for Pete!'

Now we have got to know our five young English better, it becomes apparent that after all they are not all the same. It was their way to call each other at every turn by their Christian names, for reasons not only of affection but it seemed also of self-assertion— as dogs urinate to convince themselves of identity. And of all the Christian names one heard, 'Peter' came loudest and most often. It seemed that Peter must be a leader or hero. Looking more closely, it was plain Peter's shoulders were so much straighter and broader, his moustache so much longer, and his smile that much larger than the others. He now came shambling over easily in his extraordinary holiday clothes—a shirt covered with drawings of the Eiffel Tower, long khaki shorts, long white plimsolls, and a long red-peaked cap on his head, stopped by the café table, stood there and laughed; and the others laughed too, five strong men echoing deep chuckles like the giggling of girls, as girls giggle simply because they are *there*.

They were there, right enough. And Peter's eye was already on the little Conchita who sewed away the evening on the kerb. He had already, between bathes and drinks and long pensión meals, found time to have a word with her in the bun-shop. On a matter of poste restante letters. He expected none, but he had established contact, with bad French and worse Spanish, on this point. The smile and the first trembling slyness had been effected. Innocently, idly, playful—with perhaps a distant darker thought, no more than a thought put quick aside. Anyway, wasn't he on holiday? And she wasn't exactly anyone particular's sister?

To be a hero is never light work. A high level must be maintained, worshippers must not be kept waiting for action. Thus it had occurred quite naturally to Peter that he ought to 'get off' with someone. 'There's old Peter at it again!' If Conchita was a bit hairy about the calves, a bit low in the shanks—nevertheless she was material. But how to manage it? He knew quite well that Spanish propriety would forbid her to come and sit in the café with him: and there was no dancing until the following week: and it would be dull and not a little embarrassing to walk up and down the street with her at their paseo time, the way they did it.

But now it suddenly occurred to him—what better than to hire bicycles, disappear with her along the road, way out of sight and around the corner, whisked! It would look fine—and of the end he could make a suitable mystery.

He rose casually, with a casual wink, and rolled his big northern body back across the road to the bun-shop. There he bought a bun. And put the question straight at her, he believed in going straight in. She refused. He appealed: he was the ignorant and lonely foreigner who wanted to be shown her lovely country. She refused.

Two hours later he was back again. He had the idea of buying some sweets, explaining how he liked to give them to children in the street. Then he asked her again. And she agreed! She agreed with no coyness, but directly, brusquely, as if she were about to iron a dress or feed a chicken. He imagined the sweets had done the trick. He was wrong. She had simply had two hours to think and talk it over with another girl, and allow herself to be talked into it. It was daring of her: but it was daylight, the main road was not lonely, and she was quite decided not to leave it. There was no danger.

Naturally though, it was important that he hired the bicycles otherwise than at Miguel's. It was so important that she forgot to speak slowly and distinctly when she pointed up the village street to another small cycle-shop. Big affable Peter did not care what she was saying and thought perhaps she was pointing the direction in which they would ride. They parted on this misunderstanding, she pointing to the time on her watch when she would be free, he proud of his lucky stars.

At the appointed time he went to Miguel's and ordered bicycles. Miguel wheeled them out, one male, one female—'for the Señora' with a big wink from Peter. Peter took them both along the street. And a moment later Miguel saw Conchita come out of the shop. He was about to call her when to his amazement and deep horror he saw her mount the machine and ride off in the company of this strange man. She never glanced back.

It is well known how a woman, or a man, can be transported by what may seem the most outlandish kind of foreigner. The solid Englishman is amazed, and honestly amazed, when one of his countrywomen shows admiration for what seem the all too feminine graces of a Latin gentleman smelling of pomades and distrust. Reverse this—and one may understand the disbelief of Miguel when he saw his Conchita with the big Englishman in his plimsolls and long red peak, smelling of pink and mad energies.

Disbelief. Amazement. But when she at length returned, and he asked her about it, and he saw the look in her eyes and a petulance of lip—he found he had to believe. He realized that here was something from which he was being excluded: and that somehow his Conchita had been swayed by this monstrous figure from the north. Why? What had he done? Could it be possible? He felt outraged: and curiously frightened.

He went back into his shop, and there among the cold machines fumed hot in his pale body. He looked at the two bicycles the Englishman had returned, and which he had taken back impassively, and cursed them. His hot blood rose at the sight of those saddles a short while ago so warm.

He saw not two patched and dusty machines, but people. Not for a moment did it cross his mind that anything drastic might have occurred. He was simply jealous of a moment's preference: and that, since no worse was imagined, was quite bad enough.

'Ah! Who's this I see? Don Peter hath returned! How wenteth it?'
'You old scoundrel!'
'Come clean, Pete!'
Big wink. No word.
'Come on. Out with it!'
'Quick off the mark, eh, Peter-boy?'
Lips uncurled to show big humorous teeth: eyes dropped modestly to enormous plimsolls. But still no word—which said so much.
'Coñac, Pete?'
'He's given it up!'
'All for the sake of a lady! Lady of Spain, I ad-o-ore you.'

335

A big sigh from Peter. And then just three words sighed with exhaustion:

'Gon and sif.'

At which everyone threw back their blond heads and roared.

Peter took care not to let on: they could think what they liked, and he liked what they thought.

In point of fact, it had been a long hot ride through a bewildering country of olives and corn and squat white farms. He had seen little of this since his eyes were on the ruts and sharp stones of a very rough road: he had taken more trouble to avoid falling off than to make this girl fall for him. Once or twice he had suggested stopping: but her strong black head shook its negation, her lips smiled but stayed firm. She had no intention of leaving the saddle: she even rode up whatever hills there were, and he was compelled by his male dignity to plod up, under the burning afternoon sun, after her. It was long, dusty, hot and tiring.

Conchita's upbringing was such that the idea of permitting any irregularity could never occur. But in spite of this, and of her determination to keep those bicycles on the road, she had encouraged him with her eyes. For her heart had indeed softened towards this romantic rich northerner: and the brain had conceived in some vast vague way something, something . . . something like a cadillac in the snow: and an altar. Such glances, together with a general lack of anything else 'to do' in such a slow place, tempted Peter down the dusty path once more the next day. And then again once more. On three successive days he disappeared along the scorched agave-lined roads. 'Into the blue' as he described it later—a waggish allusion to the colour of the agave and the questionable 'blue' itself.

Miguel threw himself on Conchita's mercy—and was rejected. One moment he entreated, the next grew angry. But she simply maintained that she was showing a kindness to the foreigner by showing him the neighbourhood. While she said this a light perversity, a small petulance allowed her eyes a dozen other meanings. It was difficult for Miguel to protest against this argument of hospitality—but he pleaded: 'What would everybody think?'

336

'They can think what they like!' a suddenly modern and progressive Conchita pouted.

'And what about me?' Miguel shouted angrily. 'What am I to think?'

She only shrugged her shoulders.

The matter came to a head on the Sunday. In the evening a dance was to be held. Miguel, telling himself to forget and forgive, asked her in a polite and friendly way at what time he should call for her? She answered that she was sorry, she had made other arrangements. Adding casually, 'with Señor Peter.'

Miguel stood for a moment shocked. He stood there in his pale skin and dark oiled overalls against the street of sun and oleanders and looked at her long and hard. At last he seemed to take a deep breath, about to say something: but then, as if it were of no use, he lowered his eyes and turned and entered the shop. He shut and locked the doors. He went upstairs to his room and lay down on the bed. For an hour he lay and smoked. He drew in the smoke hard, hitting at his lungs. His anger fired up and the little cigarette fired with it. An inch of sunlight, refracted into many colours like a medal ribbon, travelled slowly across the ceiling: it was exactly like the rainbow ribbon that the man Peter had carried once on his breast. But Miguel did not know that, he only cursed the small light for being there at all. Now everyone in the village would see and know. He lay there gritted with anger, then dull with a terrible loneliness, then hot again with pride: all feelings ran together, no one could separate them or say which rose the higher.

At first he had wanted simply to stride out and confront this pestering northerner. But there was little he could say. The man was a foreigner, presumably rich, and Miguel knew his police. Besides, another impulse moved him—he was too proud. Years before, the men of that island had fired their muskets on the ground behind the lady who rejected them, a sign of scorn. Scorn at being scorned: but nevertheless a publication of humiliation. And this need, something like the need of the cuckold to exhibit himself, moved Miguel too. He wanted to go out to the dance and sit there alone, an object of pride and pity.

He lay on his bed, and thought, and commiserated. Isolated in that small room, with the slow minutes for company, his small body grew its huge thought.

He tormented himself. He exaggerated every picture of her—of her sudden shape on the bicycle, of her face arguing at him, of her eyebrows raised in nonchalance as she said she was going to the dance with this Pee-ter: each such glimpse he made steady as a photograph, and played with it in his mind. He screwed his eyes shut and stared hard at these pictures. They took possession—the good days receded against these new, frightening, insolent impressions. The cruelty took his breath away.

A small matter, he tried to tell himself, Bicycling. A dance. But he remembered her face, a face wanting something *now*—and all the power of the present invalidated the past. He had to act. His cigarette began to gasp as the misery bit harder and faster, as the walls grew blanker round him, as this small prison he had made for himself contracted and within it an unreal fever swelled to get out. From a little seed, drenched with hot thought, the vicious plant spread its grotesque, gigantic leaves of thick grey shadow shutting out all light.

Then he remembered: A few years before a young man, unbalanced for pitiful reasons of his own, had left just such a dance, strolled into the night, and hanged himself from a tree. The tragedy had shocked the village: now it thrust its picture on to Miguel's anguished mind, it kept recurring through the long later afternoon, it moved him and it filled him with fear: but also with fascination, it was an image of hopelessness and it called him with a vertiginous drag; it held out to him the dear poison, revenge.

At nine o'clock, as the first sounds of the orchestra struck across the hot night air, summer's music carrying far, Miguel rose and began to shave. He watched his face carefully in the little mirror, wiped it slowly and thoughtfully, then turned to his suit hanging ready on a peg. His hand reached out, then fell back. He shrugged the whole idea away, and slowly went downstairs still in his working overalls: it had seemed right to dress himself for what he had in mind, then it seemed simply not worth the trouble. Anyway—he spat on the floor and laughed once, and enjoyed the feeling of the laugh—they would have to dress him later.

AN INTERLUDE

He stood in the room where he had worked for so long. From hooks on the white-washed walls there hung the dead parts of bicycles. In the gloom handlebars stuck out like antlers: tyres made a hoopla: spoked wheels and chains hung like the instruments of old torture. The bicycles themselves stood ranged on trestles, old and dusty and thin machines with wooden handlebar-holds and patched saddles. He stood looking at them for some time, head bowed, a small sad man in his greased overalls. Then he took up a knife. He went over to two of the bicycles and began to hack at the tyres. He cut with long savage thrusts, like a barber sharpening his razor, this way, that way, until the tyres hung in shreds and the bone of metal wheel shone clean. He was breathing hard now. He lurched over to the tool-bench, took up a length of rope and threw it out into the middle of the floor. Then he went at the bicycles again, and with quick, exact movements, as if he was working against time, his teeth gripped and the sweat coming, he dismantled piece by piece these two bicycles until they lay in their scattered parts by the rope on the floor. He took up the knife again and began hacking more slowly, almost with love, and now sobbing so hard his shoulders shook, at the two leathern saddles.

That was at nine o'clock—when the music began, and when Conchita, out of her red day-skirt, and now in evening white, waited brown-skinned and expectant by the door of the dance patio.

At eight o'clock those five holiday-makers had been well into their coñac at the oleander café when a large American car had drawn up.

'Yank!'

'You said it, P.'

Out stepped a middle-aged American, octagonal glasses and a Florida straw. For a few minutes the English stopped speaking. Then, since they had been there a few days, and felt thus indigenous and superior to any stranger, they began again, casually, largely, to talk. The American heard English and quickly invented a question to ask them. 'What the hell,' he said, pointing to that ghost-ship

339

turkey-bird, which was at that moment standing on one pink leg and watching them blackly sideways, 'kind of bird is that?'

The ice formally broken, they became friendly. They exchanged drinks, and finally they thought what fun it would be to drive in the big car to the port-capital and make a night of it.

'Bit of a rest from the rustic idyll, eh Peter?'

'Bit of a rest.'

'But you had an engagement, didn't you, old boy?'

'Engagements made to be broken.'

'Better fish?'

'Better fish.'

'Then what are we waiting for? Waiter, the bill!'

'Gracias, señor.'

'And grassy arse to you. Come on, let's go.'

And off they all drove.

Conchita waited half an hour, an hour. Time is supposed not to matter in Spain: to a woman, even to a village-girl waiting for a foreign prince in large white plimsolls, it does. She walked to and fro in front of the entrance to the dance, greeting her friends, watching one after another go in, feeling more and more unhappy, foolish and angry. A friend of hers, entering the dance happily on the arm of her man, mentioned by chance that the English had all gone off to the port.

Her heart fell. But somehow it was not unexpected; the big man in the peaked sports-cap had been a kind of dream, and as such could too easily disappear.

She was cruelly disappointed. But finally, more than disappointed she was angered: not only at this personal slight towards her but by such bad manners, which were in themselves to be scorned. Her immediate wish was for sympathy: and for this her thoughts turned instinctively to Miguel. It occurred that he might be difficult: but not seriously, not for long. In any case, to go to him was instinct in her: she trusted him, and a long engagement makes a man more than a man, makes a kind of brother of him.

So at nearly half-past nine she walked away from the dance patio and back along the long street, past every house she knew, past all the shops and all the lives, until she could see Miguel's closed door and the scrawled letters of his sign.

She stopped: and stood there suddenly arguing against her instinct. A reflection of resentment against Miguel rose, even then, when she remembered how he had tried to stop her meeting the foreigner. But, of course, she stood there really resenting her own guilt. Minutes passed. She felt as if the door should not be shut and that somehow he should be there to welcome her. It made her the more sorry for herself. But it was this shut door, its very barrier, that determined her to go on, not knowing then how she would behave, whether to remain cold or laugh him into forgiveness.

She knocked. There was no answer. She went round by the side, and found the patio and the inner room empty. Then she glanced through into the bicycle room and saw him standing there still as a statue.

He seemed to be looking at the dark doorway from where her knock had come: he looked taller, as if he was standing on something.

A chair? Was he up changing a light bulb? It was too dark instantly to see.

She was glad at having surprised him. A kind of mischief, mixed with sudden joy to see him again, swept away all other thoughts and she called, very suddenly, at the top of her voice, to frighten him: 'Hola!'

He seemed to stumble.

His foot seemed to miss its hold on what she saw now was a chair indeed, and then as she ran forward the foot just caught the chair again. As she steadied him, his hands were up again at the electric wire he had been mending.

Then it seemed that the electric wire was thicker than usual, it was rope slung from a beam above, and his hands were struggling with some of it that seemed to be caught round his neck—and she only remembered seeing him shake that noose free, and recognizing it as a noose, before she fell in a dead faint dragging him to the ground with her, her hands round his knees, exactly as a hangman might apply his weight to the legs of his charge.

Later, when he had got water and rinsed her face and temples, when she had cried in his arms for a long time and he had stopped her speaking of any of it—for it was all over—later they spent the long last hours of that evening and into the night sitting together on the floor, like two children over their toys, mending the two broken bicycles, stitching together the saddles, reassembling the brakes and the chain and all else that had been undone. The tyres, though, were spoiled for ever.

Question and Answer

TO Bompard, to Endoume. . . .
That was enough of a mystery, without this other.

What had happened? It seemed, nothing. Yet here was this feeling, fat as a whale, of nothing at all being right.

Even the man with the hammer had failed, his moment of laughter had petered away altogether.

He looked across the table at Miss Ponzone, at Grace Ponzone, at her his bride-to-be sitting up fresh in her evening flesh, edible, and thought how much he loved her. But it did not seem to help.

Grace pulled deeply and surely at her cigarette, all the smoke disappeared inside her, she stared for a long time at the neon moon of the church clock hanging in the blackness across the port—and then slowly let the smoke blow out thin from where in her secret lungs it had lain. He liked that. He still liked it tonight. For anyone as young and tender to take to her lips the dirty brown weed and draw upon it hungrily, kicking the lungs inside, soothing nerves that surely could not need it—this was always a shock but always most exciting, it had a look of vice. He enjoyed her show of sophistication. Somehow she still carried with her the air of one of those twelve-year-old prodigies from the poorer streets—girls who wear the cast-off dresses of their elder dancing-sisters, dresses too long and too gaudy for such stick-legged youth, so that they look like angels turned up in a brothel. Grace looked so, she was beautiful but a mouse, she had small bones and brown hair and a wan face far too young for her, and he liked her for it.

They were full of aïoli, and they had bathed in the hot sun all day. So huge a helping of thick golden garlic mayonnaise battling with the daylong sun-flush—that might be enough to tire anyone, any two people. But it had to be admitted that tonight perhaps there was more than this to make everything so flat and ominous. What had to be admitted was what few men, except to themselves, are ever heard to admit. Much in love, about to be married, he was wondering whether finally it was worth it. He was doubting the wisdom of binding himself. He sat and wondered and despised himself for so wondering. How, really, when he is without doubt in love, can a man dare to think such things? But then how, on the diving-board, longing for the swift air and the cool blue plunge beneath, can a man dare to hesitate before doing what he has plainly chosen to dare?

They sat without talking, dullness between them. Occasionally their eyes met, they smiled, and once she stretched out and pressed his hand: took hers back, though, This was no nervous dullness, nor prison-yelling for escape; nor ennui, nor apathy—and certainly not peace; it was something intolerably placid, it was flat nothingness, and quite affectionate.

All right, he thought, so we're just tired. People can't go on and on and on, this is just the pause. Cats one moment chase each other playing wild tigers, then sit down to wash. But there was something ominous about the hammer-man.

A man had come along the quay—they were sitting on the southern side of the old port in Marseilles, the Rive Neuve—selling small celluloid fairies on cards on a tray. He had stopped by a table nearest the pavement where a grey-haired man and a grey-blonde woman were dining quietly, and then stomached his pink fairies to and fro just over the edge of the tablecloth. They watched the grey-haired man raise a hand, without looking up from his plate, to wave the intrusion away. It was normal: Algerians with carpets, a couple of boy acrobats, a pregnant lottery-seller and a boatman adrift in a singing sea of red wine had already tried to entertain the table. It was normal, but it was not a table to have. Yet—thought that young man sitting with his Grace—perhaps it would have been better to have such a table on an evening such as this?

He watched as the grey-haired diner brushed away the fairies with his hand. And then suddenly the fairy-vendor snatched from his coat pocket an enormous plastic yellow pistol and fired from this a long, soundless, red carnival tongue. The fat tongue stayed stretched out quivering like a terrier's leg between the diner's mouth and his raised fork, the diner bit his own tongue, dropped his fork and grasped up at his breast.

'Dieu—my heart!' he gasped; but managed to flect a joke into this at the last moment.

The fairy-man drew himself up furiously. 'So you have a heart?' he yelled—and snatched out an iron-headed hammer, swung it high and crashed it down at the diner's head.

His woman shrieked. The smile fled from under the man's grey hairs as he ducked away from the hammer, and then that hammer of rusted iron and grey-grained wood bounced playfully up again, being made of soft rubber, and everyone broke down laughing, man, woman and vendor most of all.

As she laughed, the woman stretched out a hand and took a fairy. Her man bought it, and thereafter the pair of them laughed and joked and filled their glasses with more wine, the little episode had so enlivened them.

Infectious. Grace and he warmed to the absurdity—they had laughed with the other laughter. But then the warm night, the rattling traffic, the rock-founded rich seediness of the port slipped back into place and they too sat back again waiting, with nothing to do or say. Could two in love thus relapse against such warmth of laughter and clowning, against the warm southern evening among the crowded tables?

Perhaps they were not in love. Perhaps he was not in love. Perhaps . . . and his mind went back to long evenings as a boy when he had sat, his eyes fixed on his plate, hearing to either side his parents eating slowly through the long meal, never talking, lost to each other, graveyard meals in the lamplight when the air drummed and he was bored, bored, bored, yet never raised his eyes for fear of meeting an eye, nowhere to go and nothing to see but the enemy, and his boredom had drummed like a bat inside him screaming like night to be out.

Now could they be in for this? He looked over at her and saw how absurd the comparison was—but still suspected. He knew one thing, he knew he dared not open his mouth for fear of the words dying of disinterest. She might nod, or smile even, and that would be that, nothing would have passed between them.

Oh, they were just tired. But then—why today? The day had begun as usual. Down from the hotel early, to breakfast in the half-washed, half-open café. The sun already high, but here in the busy grey breakfast square it was shaded by tall office buildings and the fourth-storey leaves of enormous plane-trees; the sun could gear itself up golden somewhere above and beyond, but here it was still fresh and life was lived in bright shadow by the light of flowerstalls and carshine and white morning papers; water streamed the gutters gleaming in the freckled underlight of planes, the first traffic spat its blue, and to a smell of coffee and a well-slept stretch the morning was as all others in big southern towns, a hopeful fresh time before the huge arc of the day weighed in. Nothing wrong with the morning. The long blue and white buses streamed off as usual: to Bompard, to Endoume.

The day out on the rocks? Rocks white as marble washed by a sea swilling all the filth of a great port, but blue to look at and good to get into after the heat of the inner quays. So the day; the afternoon swimming among flotsam but also in a golden haze of wide-rocked magnificence, the fine blue sweep of classic Marseilles. Was there then too much sun—or too many people? Too many girls nearly naked, navel and buttock bare and the points of breasts just covered, so many, so much of it, most of it beautiful—but did the bikini, like the old brothels where so often one sat and drank and quietly left, become a prophylactic against desire? Too much fish out on the slab? And well, if so, then what has that to do with Grace? I'm not marrying womankind, I've chosen one woman and presumably for other than bodily reasons, though I thank God she has one.

Wives are like fish, he suddenly savagely stupidly thought, and they should be kept on ice. Kept fresh. Not exposed to bloat in the sun all day. . . . But he gave up that line of thought wearily, it simply led back to the sun, the heat, the long hot after-day of bathing when tired rope-soles tramp the hotel stairs to fresh themselves from sand, when stomachs call for ice. And still he knew that this had nothing to do with what really was the matter.

It had more to do with those long, long buses, Endoume and Bompard, swinging on their electric rods always up the same hills, round the same corners, and always with their quiet rubber swish, like the sound of compressed air escaping, that further defined the endless circle of their routine. And to do perhaps also with the smile he now gave her, a smile he had seen himself give only to mirrors and whose conformation he now could feel on his face as if that face were no longer flesh but only dark mercury and thin glass, as she yawned and said:

'Well, shall we go?'

She put her hand up to that yawn, gulped it, raised her eyebrows in apology and smiled a bit brighter: 'But what do you think, shall we get along? We might walk a bit.'

'Let's,' he said, also smiling, pleasantly as it must look, back at her. 'I'll get the bill.'

While he paid he watched her and wondered: Well, there's nothing in a yawn. She even joked it off with her eyes. And now look, she's gathering cigarettes and lighter and bag together and straightening her back, brushing away crumbs. You'd think it was all over. But is it?

And then it occurred to him that for all she knew he had been content with the casual night, the fullness of food, the warm air and this electric-lit quay of restaurants, sea-food, rigging and people about. Nevertheless she had interrupted without thinking, at least at first; her first words had been a yawned command. What was this, then, a taste of the future? Part of the long measure of Give-and-Take?

I'm being unreasonable, he argued, it is well known that people state things as a question and put questions as a statement. Yet . . . and back it all came to him, more indeed as question than anger, as to what was the position of a husband these days, where could he go without Mrs Bright-Smile palling along, where were the clubs of yesteryear—or the habit of staying in them—and what about the pubs, and everywhere else, and how could two normally complicated people hope to remain in sanity with each other in a three-room flat? Where had yesterday's long baize corridor, with its double-baize door and study at the end, wandered off to? There seemed only two alternatives left: to sit in the Office, or the Gentlemen's. And was that not already sometimes a synonym?

And quite apart from Give-and-Take, what had happened to the

347

one-sided myth of the bride being Given Away? Wasn't there nowadays anyone to give the poor old husband away, a practical equi-
valent? Or did he just do that himself?

But, said the mercury-smiler to himself as he took the brown bare
arm of Miss Ponzone, you do really like your own Miss Bright Smile,
don't you? And as he looked down to her, his smile broke for a
moment through its mirror and became a look of love. For you do
apply love, whatever that is, to Miss Bright Smile? You feel yourself
in love with her, you feel it so much that this could not be questioned
even by yourself, let alone by anyone else, whom you would simply
scoff off? Yes. But even so.

Was it—face it—worth the Sacrifice?

You know that you could not think of doing without Miss
Ponzone? But do you know who in future will always be there,
throughout the years, every day, everywhere, summer, winter,
autumn, spring, without fail, every minute with you and by your
side, never failing to be there, never, never, never? Miss Ponzone.

A bus travelling to Endoume narrowly missed them as in the
half-lit night they stepped off a pavement. 'Narrowly' only because
the bus squeezed its great brakes, and compressed air brought it
efficiently to a lesser speed so that they just got by. But a bus to
Endoume, he thought, would scarcely hit one: probably, also, a bus
to Bompard had braked somewhere or other in sympathy.

Just then they were passing from the more affluent side of the
Vieux Port to the other side, the Quai du Port. They were passing
the pleasure-steamers, drawn up like sea-born house-boats, that
invite you to the Château d'If; they were passing the more luxurious
cafés like Basso's on the Belges, and now once past the open end of
the Canebière they had crossed a dividing line and were approaching poorer and more notorious streets.

Something, that man thought to himself, must happen here.
Something, at least, to break our—what can it be called, placidity?
And something did.

They were entering then the tougher, brighter but darker quay,
and passing the fun-fair stood for a moment in the full yellow glare
of a large restaurant. This was again a sea-food restaurant—but it
was bigger, noisier, brasher, browner, brassier and probably better

than those on the other side. Its walls inside were mirrored, its paint
and its furniture were of a good weatherbeaten brown, its lights
were weak-bulbed and so the yellower, though there were many of
them: whereas on the other side of the port carefully printed menus
were displayed, here great black slates had been scraped with a brio
of chalk, as if something special had that very moment been cooked
or come in: in fact it was a more old-fashioned engine altogether,
its yellow glare on to the dark street was more like the light of a
naphtha flare than electric, and it was full, full, full of people
crammed together inside among its mirrors and outside under its
huge awning, all eating fast among waitresses yelling, running and
sometimes if there was time laughing. Plenty of gold in the teeth of
these waitresses, and dark strain beneath their eyes—they touted
for customers, beckoning the street at top-voice, and then had to
rush back and serve them, both making work and doing it. And two
dark moons of another kind of strain bruised round the eyes of a
middle-aged woman dressed like a pink fringed lampshade who
then passed jabbering to the street that she'd do him in for what he'd
done: and more jabbering as three black soldiers in dull khaki
swung by: and, after them, all the other soldiers, sailors, Algerians,
Corsicans, whores and pimps, as well as the greater mass of the more
respectable citizenry resident in that quarter; someone in a café
along the way was tinning a mandolin, gritty as the gutter, and a
steamer boomed and the fun-fair blazed jazz, a scooter backfired
and suddenly all the rigging crowded ahead was alight with the
wide flash of headlamps turning.

Yet in all that lively, night-lit crowd what they stopped to look
at was not people or lights or some event, but fish.

Even with their two stomachs full of aïoli and all it brings, snails,
eggs, prawns, potatoes, carrots, beans and the great white scented
fish itself mashed up with so rich a golden garlic cream—even so
they stood to look at the magnificence of dead fish this restaurant
offered as its centrepiece.

A sloping slab the width of half a dozen tables lay green with
lettuce and fern beneath a brightly shaded electrolier—and in the
downglare there glared deadly back a wilder and fatter assortment
of deep-sea and rock creatures than could be at first believed, even

on those quays, even from those markets. It was not only fantasy, it was wealth. It was not only wealth, it was art, or art plus wealth, or rich art. Scarlet, pink, grey, brown, blue, violet, green and all mixed iridescences lay piled or fatly placed on that bed of thick wet green. Giant crayfish caught the eye in a first scarlet glance, but soon it moved to thin fish with long snouts, to immense fat fish with small sad faces, to fish armoured and spiked as oriental warriors, to fan-finned fish with snaking bodies and to snaking finless bellowing eels, to old-men fish with a single long scrag of beard, to thoughtful cuttle-fish resting their tentacles forward like the feet of salivary dogs on the green lettuce mat, to furious octopuses, to brick-burnt crabs playing dead cards with their hairy front feelers held near their mouths, and cheating—in fact, to loup, saupe, dorade, rouget, langouste and all the other glum, angry, radiant swimmers of the near-by sea. And all fresh, all dripping their last wet salt on the fresh-water lettuce and all dead.

All dead—and it was with no added life that those two, Grace and her man, paused to glance at this display. They were hardly to be caught so easily by colour, light, magnificence. And they had eaten. Perhaps they rather paused because this seemed a climax to all other plenitudes of the day—as in a theatre one might be rising to go, but pause to hear for finality's sake alone the final rising richening bars of a musical finale. Or perhaps even something of the deadness had appealed to the mood between them, or even the very glum look on all those fishes' faces themselves, for those fish were certainly fed-up, washed-up, they had lived getting glummer and glummer the hardest and riskiest life there is to be had on this earth, and now they had had it, and it had been so awful their faces had not even the strength to smile relief.

However it was, they stood there for some moments observing this still, dead, beautiful, unhappy scene. Neither said a word.

Then suddenly, as if a light breath of wind had touched a lettuce leaf, or as if the lettuce itself was a sea and a deep swell had moment-arily risen, something moved.

Both of them saw it.

He saw Grace glance quickly at a waitress hurrying by—black skirts may have caused a draught; yet why then did not this occur all the time, why was not the whole green lettuce bed trembling?

For certainly there was movement now, and the waitress had passed long ago: he glanced up for an electric fan, there was none, and then looked down again to see that particular leaf of lettuce give a low heave and fall aside to reveal something dark and big and swelling beneath.

Although he had no place in the restaurant he moved forward into it, he was so startled. But then as he bent to peer closer another leaf fell away, a dead crayfish moved a moment upwards like an earth-moving grab, an eel slid coiling lower away, and all these moving apart at last showed clear in the light what was underneath. He jerked his head back in disgust. But Grace, who had come enquiring at his side, never moved.

It looked like three or four kilos of live pig's liver swelling and wrestling inside itself. It was thick as a parcel, and if it was liver it was liver dyed purple. It was wet and it breathed, oozing and dribbling a froth of wet slow bubbles. It had neither face nor fins nor legs nor feelers nor suckers, it was just a roundish wet blob of skinless purple flesh swelling and breathing. Yet after all it did have one thing, it had what looked like a big dark hole—mouth, anus, womb?—which seemed to form itself by a muscular rolling back of flesh, then to exude those long slow-blown bubbles.

'Eh! Bouillabaisse! You like to eat—' came the voice of that brass-haired, gold-toothed waitress laughing up to them '—good rich bouillabaisse? All the fish of the . . . all the . . .' And the voice stopped.

Neither Grace nor her man had moved. Now the waitress edged close beside them, her mouth still stuck open on her last words. Thus the three peered—and the fat purple thing slowly contracted its muscle and blew out another long bubble.

'Foi!' the waitress breathed. 'Eugh!' And then took a step carefully back, her lower lip squaring to bare its teeth as though she had tasted something sick.

Grace said nothing, but the man found his voice:

'You should know.'

'But I don't, I don't,' the waitress gasped, shaking her hard brass hair. 'I don't,' her work-shaded eyes, a moment before as tough as her trade, appealed in horror. How she must have worked for those teeth, the man thought, glad to be looking away from the slab—but already the waitress was in action calling 'Madame! Madame!' and the great black bulk of the manageress came hurrying through the tables.

The creature heaved again, contracting and expanding within itself in a last eyeless search for whatever it needed, water or air; it seemed to be pumping some kind of last blubbering sigh. But it still lived, and suddenly the man thought: Do they keep them beneath to keep the dead fish fresh? One look at the manageress's face told him not. Her huge old eyelids had dropped half-closed as if she had seen a snake. Now she too bent forward, carefully holding herself in readiness for retreat, stretched out a hand—and then quickly drew it back. It was a hard thick red hand on the muscled arm of a fisherman: and the man suddenly thought, that is what even a fisherman might feel like, he had seen their disgust at sea-cucumbers or fish they hated.

She pretended only to be pointing with that hand, shrugged her huge shoulders in a roll of disdain. 'That,' she said scornfully, plainly thinking of the good name of her dead fish, 'is an escargot-de-mer.'

'Escargot?' Grace suddenly said. 'Without shell? It's more a slug.' And she reached forward and prodded her small brown finger with its thin red nail gently into the purple fish. The pulp gave easily, her nail disappeared. But, disturbed, the creature began to heave the more.

'See,' she said, 'no shell.'

Then: 'What are you going to do with it?'

'Me?' The manageress looked startled. Then quickly stiffened her jaw: 'Why, nothing. It's quite—quite clean. Later, later. Besides, I'm busy.' And she looked angrily to left and right, catching a hundred non-paying customers. Already the waitress, fearing to be called upon, had found a large china tureen to carry.

'Well, let me,' Grace said, reaching forward.

She got the thing in one hand, but her hand was too small, it slithered on its own weight through her fingers, so she put both palms underneath and lifted it like a careful cushion.

To be able to do this she had carelessly handed her cigarette to

352

her man, and now he stood struck stiff with wonder holding a cigarette in either hand and seeing this small figure in smart trousers bearing in her palms the giant sea-slug as if it were a crown on sacred velvet. She stayed there a moment, looking to right and left, not knowing quite what to do.

Mighty hell, he thought, and I thought I was bored! What kind of a woman *is* this? How will I ever know what to do with a woman like this? Or what she'll do? What is she—callous or sensible? Insensible or over-sensitive? How could a woman like that ever need help? Or do I need hers? . . . And suddenly his mind went back to two others, a woman whose cat had brought in a dead sparrow and the woman had plucked and cooked the sparrow for the cat's dinner; and another, a girl in a night-club whom he had asked, to make conversation. 'What-would-you-like-best-in-all-the-world—best-of-everything?' 'I'd like to be sea-sick,' she had said, after long and serious thought. Of course, that had simply been envy, she had never been on a liner. But she had nevertheless *said* it, it the unpredictable. And that was the whole point, you never knew what they were going to do next, you could guess but you could never be sure, or nearly sure as with a man, and it was useless to deduce a state of common boredom from the faces of other people's wives and woman seen as they are on their best behaviour, it was what they did at home, or on the quiet, it was what your own inexpressible, unpredictable, ineluctable question-mark of a slip of a trouble-and-strife did that knocks the even keel into a cocked hat. . . .

Meanwhile Grace was carrying her sea-slug across the road to where the edge of the quay lay in the shadow of boats. He followed her, raving to himself and excitement growing as he marvelled: Endoume my Aunt Fanny, Bompard my foot. What do I know of Bompard and Endoume? Suburbs open up new cities, none is the same. . . . Cardiff's got a bus to Gabalfa, Edinburgh to Joppa . . . and *I* used to laugh. I could kick myself, he thought savagely—as then Miss Grace Ponzone dropped her sea-slug slopping, slithering down into dark water among anchor-chains and the iron keels of ships.

Neither saw it sink. But the light cf a ship's lantern caught the slime on her hands. She made to rub them on her trousers, stopped herself in time, then just stood holding her hands out helplessly before her.

'Messy things,' she said.

And grinning with pride, half in terror, half in gladness, he took her arm, as he thought, for ever.

A Country Walk

'LIVE in Town?' he used to say to others in the City. 'Don't know how you people stand it. Give me the country any day.'

And in his pocket, in the little card-case, he liked to think of his name engraved so steadily, so secure: Norman Harris, and Four Acres, and the name of the village, and lastly, deep and green spurning of all suburban Surreys, the rare remote words West Sussex. It was as good as looking in the mirror.

He had the face of a dog. Early grey hair, thick and stiff and occasionally yellow, he combed back straight from his small square forehead, no parting, and set the stiffer with a gummy cream: he used a wide-toothed comb, and the tooth-marks stayed set and deep, exact as the chalk-stripes on his suit, all day. Black eyebrows, pale eyes set close, and all the rest of the face pushed squarely forward, big-jowled but firm and strictly oblong, completed the mask of one of those square-faced dogs by far the greater part of whose faces gruff out beneath the cheekbone-line. His big teeth shone with the clear translucent light of dentures, but they were all his own.

'Got a little place in the country,' he would say. But when the street market became lively and he was kept late he was the last to complain: his attitude was one of polite pity to those who tried to condole with him on the long late drive south—Oh no, it was worth it every time. And he would smile broadly and strongly, as if he was full of the good gruff strong air, of beer and cheese and bits of tweed: it was nevertheless a coy smile.

Four Acres was three cottages. Good flint stuff, two thatched and one slated, and whoever had once knocked them into one had set up an old iron verandah, faded garden-blue, along part of one side: this, simply because of its age, seemed in keeping. But Mr Harris had had the windows out, new steel lattices put in, and a good coating of bright railway green put on the frames. The paths had been straightened and carefully, crazily paved. Stainless mesh netting was set along the front hedge, and a rock garden put where once hollyhocks had made a ragged jungle. Not for Harris the whimsy of those who smarted a place with coloured dwarfs and bird-coconuts: it was order, neatness and strong light modern equipment he liked to introduce—'not only sanitation but sanity' he was fond of saying. Thus there was that rock garden not for prettiness but because it was neat, low-growing, compact. He had most of the older trees down, leaving a few pruned fruit-bearers. His sheds were full of bright new lawn-mowers and newly devised clippers with springs.

In this way, although he bred no animals and grew few vegetables, and even these through the hands of a local gardener, he nevertheless caught the impression of himself as a 'model farmer'. He could be one, he felt, if he so wanted: he had the right technological attitude. Five days a week of contrasting himself with the pinstriped companionship of his city brothers bolstered this: two days' acquaintance with his neighbouring rustics did not unseat him. At Four Acres he dressed in old tweeds, but of gentlemanly cut: he had spent a whole evening battering about a new felt hat in his bedroom, going so far as to soak this in muddy water, to get it properly weathered. He bought a thick knobbled ashplant, and discarded his golfing brogues for a pair of dubbined boots.

He was not a bad fellow. These little deceptions were backed by a sincere enthusiasm for 'the country'—perhaps he was simply going a little too fast, and affectation would drop from him as the soil itself took effect. His wife was more or less satisfied: the children were packed off to school, she had friends in the near-by county town, and a motor-car. 'Of course we have "the car",' she used to say, as if she had a not too painful fashionable disease. Moreover, she quite liked gardening. Her husband was a man of regular habit, he always came home, no trouble of that kind—in fact it was she who gave the alarm, unnaturally early but as it turned out necessarily, when he did not come back from his walk that stormy summer's day.

They had been moved in two months—it was already high May —and Harris really had to face it: all this time he had never been for a good tramp. Of course, there had been much to do around the

356

house, and they had driven round the narrow roads a little—along
the narrow tar, between high hedges, canyon drives of no contact
with the fields—and he had strolled in and out the village and
round. But there, rolling out from his end of the village, and his was
nearly the end house, lay the great green question-mark—pastures,
dells, copses, streams, all the enormous green mystery compounded
of a hundred smaller ones, each hill-crest concealing he knew not
what, each path wandering where?

Accordingly, one fine afternoon shortly after five o'clock, he took
his ashplant and set out. He felt a pleasant sense of adventure, indeed
of purpose. Even a few steps away from the village, as the last
cottages fell away and the lane narrowed and the hedges grew on
each side more thickly, there fell upon him a strong illusion of entering uncharted, uninhabited territory. Green leaves high all around,
earth rougher underfoot, silence but for his own footfall soft itself
on grass and clay—a bird started from a bush and he smiled to
catch himself jump. It sounded at least as big as a badger.

How big did a badger sound? It occurred to him that he had no
idea. He remembered seeing a badger in a museum somewhere;
and feeling awed that an animal of such considerable size—thick as
a little hog—should go wild in the peaceful English countryside.
Though at night. And anyway, no one had ever heard of a badger
at bay. As he walked on he felt distinctly relieved. Animals were so
difficult.

Then the lane suddenly widened, dwindled up to a crest—and
there was the open country rolling away beneath. And a gate.

Harris paused, glanced at the latching of the gate, then leant on
it instead. He must have been walking slightly uphill, for this was a
relatively high point from which much could be surveyed. The sun
shone over a wide undulation of patched green and bright brown,
fields of all shapes flowed, nestled, sloped, rose, but always exactly
fitted together. The bright red of a Dutch barn twinkled in the
distance like a dwarf pillar-box. Trees smeared their dark patches
here and there, sometimes clustered together round some secret in
a hollow—but up on the opposite hills, where downland began, they
made immense and magnificent black shapes, like giant caterpillars
stalking across the skyline.

At one point a chalk cliff shone white—a quarry? Lanes or roads could sometimes be discerned by their thin lines of thorn hedge: but often they disappeared as the ground rose and fell. Topography, he thought. Now where are we? For a few minutes he stood and worked out his walk. He decided to skirt the low ground where he knew a small river lay and make for the crescent of downland rising above. He took another look down at the gate-latch. But the alternative path to the right was no good. He smiled at himself, and put his hand to the iron contraption.

For a time he tugged and messed about with rods and slots. He knew he must be careful to close these farmers' gates, but here were his townsman's hands not able even to open it. It was exasperating. He felt absurdly incompetent. At last he saw that the whole thing had to be lifted free of the ground—and he heaved it up, fearful of never being able to close it, or that some piece of rotting wood might simply break off for ever. But it swung quite easily; and as he replaced it he muttered 'something attempted, something done' and walked forward with far greater confidence than before.

Two black starlings were sitting on a cow's back. He saw the cow itself first, and had already begun to alter his course, before the position of the birds came home to him. Birds there on its back? He stood for a moment startled. The birds were busy pecking along the length of the cow's red back, the cow munched unconcerned. Harris stared at the birds with positive dislike, his lip curled up as at the sight of an open wound. Then he shrugged. Must be after ticks, he thought: or salt, or taking hair for a nest? Accountable at all events. But what he really disliked was the unconcern of the cow: he had never got used to the way animals got on together in the country, horses nuzzling at goats, piglets playing with geese, ducks and chickens passing the time of day. And who had once said that hedgehogs take an occasional drink off a sitting cow? Even a cat-and-dog companionship he found vaguely horrible. And now, he thought, it was blackbirds and cows.

Well . . . there was much to learn. He gave the cow a wide berth, the cow watched him moodily, following him with its eyes all the way, munching like a fat woman watching him cross the length of a long, long restaurant—and came to the opposite hedge. Briar and

358

thorn, no way out. He looked carefully at the size of the thorns: monstrous black teeth, sharp and wicked, oversize, and there was a ditch too. But . . . right over at the far corner he saw what looked like a gap. A stile? It was a good pace out of his way, but the only chance. He turned along the field, and found at the very end a large patch of mud, ending in sog, a muddy drinking-pool. But he had been right, across this lay a break in the hedge and a kind of stile.

That mud was made of hoofmarks, in each hoofmark a separate puddle had formed. He tried, sank to his welts, retreated and tried again. One boot went right to the ankle, he brought it out with a difficult squelch. But now the boots were thoroughly muddied it was not really so bad—his first instinct, booted or not, had been against mud. Then he found a kind of hard causeway, jumped the last mud, slipped, regained himself, clutched at a thorn-branch and made the stile, panting and bleeding a little at the hand.

He stood in fact on a length of low brick, a yard-long mossy quay, that dribbled. Such a wayward brick erection so far from anything was itself disconcerting. He wondered what it was, and finding no proper answer, turned to the stile. Once, he remembered, he would have vaulted it. But a true countryman scarcely vaulted, in any case he was too stout, and with some difficulty balanced himself over, caught absurdly astride for a moment in the middle, one foot too high, one too low—but then was free, rescuing his coat-tail from a sharp post at the last moment.

He was off his course, but thankful to see that this next field had something growing—although indeed cabbages like small trees, unnaturally high to his eye—and a well-beaten path along its side. His spirits rising on this substantial path, he felt he would easily find a way round. He took a direction point on three distant trees, gnarled old boles sprouting a fuzz of new branches. What were they? Poplars? Ash? Beech . . . Birch? He made a mental note to get one of those little books.

At the end of this field another gate—but this time it swung easy and clear. But then the path turned a corner and there he was faced with sudden activity—a farmyard. Or rather, an activity of build-ings: for it seemed to be quite deserted, nothing moved, though great stretches of hoofmarked mud, troughs, litters of hay, and the dark eyes of byres and sties and stalls suggested a meeting-place of considerable herds. But now—not even a chicken.

The problem was—could one pass through this, which was plainly private property? He hesitated. He saw the small farmhouse itself further on, saw the curtains unmoving and the door shut, and because there seemed to be thus absolutely nobody about, walked casually forward. If he walked slowly enough nobody could accuse him of using the yard as a right-of-way, he was simply strolling and had not realized. In any case he saw, as his eyes grew accustomed, that the path did really continue, all these outbuildings and the farm simply lay to one unfenced side of the path.

He continued along, swaggering rather—if he had had a switch he would surely have swished it—and the great consoling smell of dung fattened the air: somehow this heartened him, this was the round odour of life, fatstock, folk . . . but a moment later the stench of mashed swede-stew and a pile of acrid fishy fertilizer made him take a second thought.

He had just drawn level with the farmhouse itself, and was steadily looking away from it, when the dog began to bark. At first two short hairy coughs—like a man disturbed from sleep behind his paper— but then as obviously the dog grew certain of its trespasser this rose into a long quavering wail, one could hear the dog's head pointed to the sky. Harris quickened his pace. Then slowed it—it was vita not to show fear, animals smelled it. His ears strained for the clank- ing of chains. His eyes searched the sides of the farmhouse, fearful to see this snarling ball of hair come hurtling round a corner, teeth bared, furious, certain master of his own ground.

But nothing happened. After all, the dog must have been chained up. He quickened his pace again—the dog was making enough noise to wake the countryside, at any moment someone was sure to appear. Yet he passed the house and came opposite a kitchen garden without trouble. He breathed more freely.

What then happened was a piece of pure bad luck. Certainly in the country something or other mildly disconcerting, or exhilarating, is likely to happen: one finds a mole, a dead crow, gipsies, a steam- roller—any number of minor interests to liven the outwardly placid scene. But Harris's lot, for a man like Harris, was indeed hard.

Suddenly, from nowhere, screeching like an angry bird, a small pink pig flew at his ankles. It came at a low run, he had never seen a pig run, like a heavy pink obus it came screeching low across the mud at him and its snout was at his boots before he really knew.

Memories flashed in a second—maddened boars, pigs nuzzling up dead bodies, an awful story somewhere of an ailing hermit, too weak to move, being devoured by his own famished pigs. They had inward-bearing teeth like rats. And now he saw this muscular pink body beneath him had long gristly white hairs, whiskers on pink rat-body.

He gave a great skip—and took to his heels. The pig came squawking its mad bird-sound after him. How could he know that piglets run as nimbly as little dogs? Or that this, the runt of a litter, nuzzle-tripe as some said, had been raised on the bottle, and indeed on buttered toast in the very bedroom of the farmer's wife, and in its newfound strength thrilled with such affection for anything human that now it was simply squawking with love to cover Harris with kisses from a wet, adoring snout?

It was bad luck that it had somehow got loose: and that perhaps the dog's barking had excited it. In effect, it chased Harris a good hundred yards or more, Harris's dog-like face gritted like a pointer towards the barred gate ahead, his legs kneeing like bounding wheels beneath him. He cleared the gate with an agility unknown for years, and stood breathing heavily as the pig rammed its snout at the bars, wicked small eyes glinting beneath ears saucy as little hats, pawing the ground with high heels, suddenly switching sideways and butting the gate like a bouncing foal.

Hell—would it burst the gate? But now behind bars it looked its size, much smaller indeed—yet Harris turned and quickly made off in case it found a way through the hedge. He was breathing hard and thoroughly upset. However much one liked to eat pork, being bitten by a pig was nauseous, far worse than feeling the teeth of a dog, even of a horse, even a bull's horn. Perhaps the similarity was too near—long pig? But all the same he could see now how small the thing really was, a baby—and felt foolish.

No doubt now that he was upset. As he walked along this next field he felt there were eyes watching him, and put his hands in his jacket pockets to give himself a firmer appearance. Once his foot struck a hard rut, and he stumbled and nearly fell. Nerves out of balance, he lost some of his physical balance. A horse's head appeared over the high hawthorn and stared at him inquisitively: he looked away, the beast was playful, and now followed him slowly thudding along the other side of the hedge. They all seemed to want something, these animals.

And suddenly he thought: Pray God I don't meet a wounded beast. Pray God I don't meet anything limping or in pain, a horse or a cow or a stoat or even a bird. The animal would implore help, he would be utterly powerless to give it, he simply would not know how. Once he had found a wounded thrush in the bushes of his old garden in London: its back had been bitten by a cat, he had chased the cat away and then found himself alone, eye to eye, with this mauled bird. The bird had looked at him blearily through lizard-lidded eyes, and hopped a little further away. What in heaven's name to do...? Bang its head on a tree? A penknife? Take it in and foster it . . . but it was too late. He had peered down, thunderously alone with that little scruff of feather, and had seen to his horror that white worms were already milling among the bloody feathers. The blue-bottles had been there before him! He could scarcely bear to remember what finally he had done—he had lifted his boot and stamped on it, squashed it dead. And only through clumsiness, only because he had not known what else to do.

He plunged his useless hands further into his pockets—and an awful vision arose of a sad-eyed spaniel caught in a trap. Then suddenly he saw a dozen cows walking with interest in his direction. He did not know that cows were liable to do this, mistaking him for their boy—and once again had to quicken his pace. They lumbered across at him, a surprised look in their eyes—perhaps they were in calf, or with newborn, enraged. He quickly checked over their udders, just in case it was even worse.

Again he got to his gate in time, and this time steeled himself, having judged the distance and the cows' pace carefully, to open it slowly and surely. But it was barbed and chained! He had to climb it, the barbed wire ripped a sleeve. He stood cursing. By the hedge he saw a patch of giant docks, they were far too big. He thought:

Time I was getting back. And he looked round for his three gnarled trees, his location mark. They had disappeared.

But straight ahead, and curiously near, for he seemed to have gone no great distance, the downland began. Distances were deceptive. He decided to go on, achieve higher ground, and find his trees again.

The thorn hedge changed to a stone wall and he soon found himself on turf. Up here the sky seemed to have grown much bigger —a clearer air blew across the rough ancient stones littered about. The sky's great width could be felt all around, the clouds themselves seemed to hang nearer, a feeling of the immensity of the heavens befell.

Harris took a deep breath. But instead of drawing relief, his upset nerves went their shaken way and drew even greater unease from this vast new desolation that lay everywhere around. He glanced over the stones and turf up to where a monstrous ring of black trees gathered on the rim of the hill making a dark mystery of their depth.

He did not like to look at them, he looked away downward and back. He searched for a long time for his own trees, his landmark, and at last found them in what seemed an utterly changed position. They looked very small and far away. He must have veered round in a half-circle? Yet this could still be no more than a mile or two from his home.

The country lay like a map beneath him. He could see a main arterial road cutting across like a white line, and the winding road home, a long way round: and in between the lower-lying fields which he could cross as a direct cut. His home village lay hidden behind a kind of escarpment. Then suddenly, as he was gazing over the wide sunlit vista, his nerves quickened, he held his breath, that whole undulation of rising and falling ground had seemed to move, heave itself.

The shadow of a cloud was passing over the map, it came towards him like a fast-moving tide, heaving the hills as it came.

A simple matter? Not so simple. He watched it, he began to judge whether it would envelop him or not. It came at a fast windblown pace, eating up the fields, blotting out life like the edge of a dangerous sea moving in.

The whole countryside grew more inimical. Every deep acre of this ancient sleeping earth breathed a quiet, purposeful life—and it was against him. Not now the simple material conflict with animals —the grave earth itself and the green things growing in collusion with it took on presence and, never moving, breathed a quiet hatred on to the mineral air. He tried to shrug the feeling away—but it was too strong: and just then the light seemed to blank out, the cloud had reached him and the earth grew grey and more than ever foreboding.

The turf at his feet lost its sunlight, it looked immensely aged, it had a Saxon tread. Winds had blown across those same stones for a thousand years. And above on the hill the ring of trees looked even blacker. Had they been planted to make a sacred grove? The whole pagan mystery, so far from his apparent world of metalled roads and garages and garden fences—yet always so near, always alive just on the other side of the hedge where the field is alone with itself— that great and awful mystery gripped him with its panic force. The graven stone, blood on the stone, dark rings on the pale green grass, bones of old sacrifice sleeping the old terror out over thousands of years. . . . Harris, not an imaginative man, felt all this, as he would in a dream when unknown instincts rise. And his feet seemed fixed to the spot, he could not run for there was nowhere to run, simply because there was too much of it everywhere, it was all-enveloping: just as in a closed cupboard there is no escape, only the stifling dark, here it was all air, giddying, stifling in its very wideness and its spreading everywhere without end.

He was giddy as a man on a ladder—but then that same cloud saved him. For he looked up. And he saw that not one but several clouds were travelling high, they were in fact massing, and this imminence of storm and rainfall brought him to his senses, he had the ordinary fear to grip on of being caught in the wet. He looked again to where the high-road ran, but it was too far—the best chance was what seemed a short-cut across fields. There was a wood, too, to shelter in: a simple copse set in a kind of dell.

That storm massed quickly, it blew up mauve in the sky—in such a wide sky its full turbulence was seen to grow, it was not like watching a small expanse of clouds form over rooftops. To the left and right the air still clear—but away in front, just over where that escarpment hid his village, this great dark purple mass formed, a monster like a giant jelly-fish hanging dangerous teats of vapour in the sky.

The whole earth darkened. What was green became mauve—only the chalk-pit flashed into white baleful light. But Harris suddenly looked at his watch—this was not only the storm's darkness, it was late and the sun was falling. Beneath the high purple mass the horizon showed a line of brazen light, a yellow floss of dying fire, apocalyptic, like a plain strip of light beneath a purple stained-glass window. He had to hurry. He glanced once back at that ring of trees above him—they lowered darker than ever, black as storm now against a dark sky—and hurried downhill to where the fields began. He marked his way on the other cluster of trees below that might afford shelter.

Was it a valley he now entered? Technically yes—a river wandered low-lying among its reeds somewhere in those flat miles: better to think of it as a basin, a wide flat circle of meadowland ringed round by the sudden cliffs of the downs. All this lay to the left of the fields by whose roundabout route he had arrived—now he seemed to move more easily, there was indeed a long lane that led exactly in the right direction. Moreover, he was walking downhill. Then the lane suddenly stopped: fields stretched ahead with marsh-grass growing in high green tufts from what looked dangerously watery earth. But there was a kind of raised embankment. He followed this. It led to the little wood.

All this time the sky grew darker, the clouds massed huge above, the dying sun cast shafts from the immense cloud panoply and ringed it with poisonous light—it seemed that up there in the heavens a vast battle was already begun. But not a drop of rain. The air held itself breathless: the whole country lay in the bright gloom of a steel engraving.

Harris hurried along the embankment towards the little wood. As it grew nearer he saw that it was not a little wood at all—but a gathering of ancient ivy-grown trees, some very tall, others of a drooping, stick-branched watery nature, alders and willows. The embankment entered into them, in an almost human way they seemed to be trying to get a foothold on it. Certainly now the grass to either side was wet and boggy, no cows grazing, probably treacherous underfoot. A sluice suddenly appeared—moss-grown mouldering wood barred with rotten iron, its two struts upstanding like a derelict instrument of torture. He passed it quickly, not liking to imagine for what secret purpose of mud and water this engine had been erected. Visions of imponderable masses of floodwater slowly seeping, of dangerous messages—Close the Sluices!—came to mind.

But now also—it was something to do with the very flat meadowland round and the approaching branches, gnarled and twisted, of the first tree—his mind suddenly returned to a picture seen in a story-book years before, perhaps before he could even read. It was a picture that had filled him with terror. It was the picture of an oak-tree: but an oak-tree that ran on castors, that could be seen racing over the fields at eventide, one moment a dot in the distance, zig-zagging nearer at tremendous speed, until its great flying arms came hurtling towards one, clutching all around and far higher than the little cottage, the little boy's eyes . . . he could not remember what it had ever done, or how the story went; perhaps in the end it had been quite a kindly castor-tree but it had struck a chill of terror that had never been forgotten.

Remembering this, he even paused for a moment before following the embankment into the wood. He looked uncertainly into the greater, greener gloom arched by the branches: cast his eye once more back at the grey fields, overcast and still, wet and empty—ridiculous, of course to think of crossing them—and then the first heavy splashes of rain came down, each a few yards apart and thudding the grass, and he ran for it.

Inside the wood, darker still. Now ivy and rotten roots exposed like old bones where the earth had dropped, long strands of briar, and everywhere a thousand young leaves speckling everything like giant green lice: so many little leaves dazzled, and now very slowly they moved, shivering and creeping, and began to rustle, as outside the rain-wind rose. Yet these were small movements—up above where the full force of the wind struck the high branches a great thrashing and swaying began: and down below the rotted old trunks, some split, some already fallen, began to creak and strain terribly.

And indeed dangerously—some had already half fallen and hung inclined like tall ship's booms against the upright masts of their ivy-clad fellows. These trees were immensely tall, their thin trunks branchless until very high above; a forest of ivy-sick masts, creaking and straining below, but in dreadful converse above where the wind swayed their foliage to make giant heads talking together.

Harris knew they were talking about him. Alone with their vegetable enormity, with nothing human near him and his nose filled with the smells everywhere of rotten leaves and mould and green decay, his responsible middle-aged middleman framework of tweeds, mackintosh, tobacco, moustache and all experience ceased to matter at all, it faded and he was in mind naked, a soft nut of human flesh small and childish and vulnerable . . . and suddenly, for these trees were so mastlike, with the weight of leaves beginning very high up, there came to his naked mind some fearful thing he had read about a giant race of palms, on an island in the Indian Ocean, a unique Seychellian growth whose manner of fertilization puzzled botanists, and of whom native superstition rumoured a silent shifting after nightfall, those monster trees moved together in the tropic dark to embrace in giant and terrible vegetable loves.

He hurried on with the baleful whispering ever louder in his ears. Ridiculous, he said—and hurried the faster. At least the path was clear. Or it had been. It was getting too dark properly to see. A wall of rain was falling somewhere outside—no light appeared now between the tree-trunks. Yet it had looked such a little wood.

Then his foot caught in a root, and he was down. Or had the root instead moved, caught at his foot? He put a hand out to scramble up, and a long arm of thorned briar clutched at his sleeve. He tore it away. Another fastened on to his trousers. He managed to get himself upright and plunged on. More briars took him, the ground slipped thickly underfoot. Then he realized what had happened— the root in that brief black instant had turned him off the path, his mind black with struggle had plunged him thoughtlessly on into the thicket, he had lost the path.

He stood still for a moment breathing heavily in the dark. The wind roared above, the rain rustled its wall somewhere away, the smell of mould rose everywhere—nothing, nothing but wet dark all around and no way of telling where that path was.

But no good standing there. Anything might happen. He pushed on. More briar caught at him, he heard his coat tear, as soon as he freed himself other arms caught at him, he was using his weight now, pushing through, yet all the time getting in thicker and thicker. Nor did he know what ground was beneath . . . a sudden ditch, a patch of bog, old rabbit holes with earth mouldering loose all round them . . . appalling words came to mind—hornbeam . . . creeping osiers . . . sedge. . . .

Fear mounted on fear. Not only the vegetable conspiracy, but the acute possibility that the storm might really fell a tree, an immense mast of timber crashing black as the dark down upon him . . . and as he thrashed harder at the briar and the briar clutched him more closely he lost more and more of his balance, sound everywhere giddying his ears, and then the blood pounding inside them roared up to meet it, all rushing and drumming in him like a man lost in the giant thrum of a weir. . . .

And visions of the whole dreadful day came back, all things conspiring against him, gates, animals, the stone menace of the downland, that low water-land and its sluices, the storm, this dreadful wood and all the terrible life around—and there flashed back to him things he had never much noticed: a white horse cantering up a field, unsaddled and too free, a classic beast upon some purpose too much its own; the remote and faceless siren song of telephone wires; an old iron wheel half devoured by high nettles; and a pinprick man away in the fields who had paused in what he was doing to follow Harris round with his eyes, even at that distance an intruder.

There in the dark, caught by thorns, he suddenly stopped: and like an animal bared his teeth.

Then, snarling with fear, sweating, now beginning to shout Help! Help! Help! he blundered further into the blackness, the cruel strands of thorn caught deeper at him, twisting right round him, in their wild state overgrown so that he was like a man caught in a gigantic rose-bush, he could go no further, and sinking his weight on them only sank deeper in, until he was hanging there powerless to move . . . and then and not till then did he see straight in front,

only a few yards further, a wide stretch of dully gleaming white—
the chalk-pit, the precipice?

His heart rocked, he raised his eyes up to where the wind howled,
raised all his wild dog's face to heaven to mutter a prayer of thanks
—'O God, O God', and fainted right away.

It must by then have been getting on for nine o'clock—about the
time his wife began telephoning to neighbours and finally the police.

But he hung there for most of the night.

No proper search could be made. The country can easily swallow
a man.

It was only by chance that a mobile police car found him towards
dawn. Only by chance—for the motor would have drowned the
sound of the exhausted cry he put up as gradually he regained
consciousness: but at that point the broad white arterial road
descended in a long gradient, and the officer driving had shut off
his engine, very slowly coasting.

He was found quite easily only a few yards from the road itself,
almost on it.

He was drenched through and badly shocked when they brought
him home. He developed rheumatic fever, and it bent him double
for the rest of his life.

The house was shut up and they returned to live near London.
Fear is quickly forgotten—he still talks with some air of the time he
lived in the country, regretting that affairs of business forced him
back to the suburbs. They still have 'the car', and sometimes drive
to the country: but he stays inside, bent with his new disease.

Formerly, people would have said that darker forces than nowadays we recognize had cast a spell on him that night. What is a
spell? Was it so?

A Last Word

T HE house was owned by Henry Cadwaller. It was tall and grey
and windowed black; it rose, and was now falling, in the Fulham
area, and its presently visible name, DWALLER HO, suggested much
of its function—a dwelling-house where people might dawdle to
death, with a Ho to summon the aged and weary to its door.

Henry Cadwaller was a man of thrift, and the old gold letters lost
from the fanlight of the original HOUSE had never been replaced, nor
had half the black-and-white tiles on the steps, nor the stained-glass
lights to his hallway. These red and yellow and purple panes,
patched nowadays with wood and cardboard, shed a more Gothic
gloom than ever: indeed, the whole house was patched, its large
Victorian rooms were partitioned with papered three-ply—each
lodger lay and stared at his own piece of ceiling frieze, coming from
nowhere and disappearing with mad purpose. And the curtains of
many of the windows had once patently been tablecloths—or why
the ink-stain at the top, why the vertical fringe? And the bedcovers
were unmistakably made from old curtains—or should bedcovers
have ring-slots, and widen towards one end? Plaster fell freely from
the grey façade, and was helped on its way by abandoned wireless
aerials that flapped wearily down the walls from window-sills lined
with meat-safes and milk-bottles; the garden at the back was a rot
of thistles, crates, cans and the shattered glass of the old conservatory,
now a plywood bathroom; on the roof the chimneys chatted in all
directions, and cowled ventilators sprouted anywhere on the walls
like an iron mushroom growth; in the old hallway the little fireplace
once used to warm the footman's rump now held empty bottles and
a pair of goloshes, and on the front door there were pinned, like the
notes of a white up-ended dulcimer, thin strips of card announcing
the names, against bakelite bell-pushes, of fifteen lodgers.

These bells were a source of much irritation to Mr Cadwaller: a long time ago he had had them fixed to save himself trouble at the front door—but had overlooked the fact that each time a bell rang the cost of a small electric impulse went down on his bill. There were some days—on Monday morning when various laundries called, or on Saturday when the coming and going was something appalling—when he sat in his front room holding his hands over his ears to deafen this costly tolling. And sometimes, driven to absurd measures, he would run to the door when he saw a van arrive simply to save that insistent ringing whose every vibration cost money—yet never without his pan and brush, in case a horse had passed to drop manure for his window-box. He liked milk-carts, and only ordered coal from a company that still employed the old drays.

Of all these bells, one angered him more than any other: and that was Mr Horton's. Mr Horton, a retired merchant, seldom had visitors; but always—and Mr Cadwaller knew well by now that it was out of malice—he rang his bell before entering the house. To test it, he explained.

Mr Horton was the scourge of Mr Cadwaller's life: and thus perhaps its main stimulus. A feud had begun months previously, shortly after Mr Horton had arrived, in the bathroom. Throughout the house, Cadwaller had had the overflow-holes in each bath reset three inches lower: expensive, but a reasonable outlay thus to lower authoritatively the level of each lodger's bath and save on the cost of hot water. And then one morning he had entered a bathroom just quitted by Mr Horton. And he had seen the dark ring left high up above the overflow line.

He studied it, had the overflow tested, and then lay in wait. Each time Mr Horton had a bath he left the same high ring. At length Cadwaller could stand it no longer. 'You put your foot over it!' he said, catching Mr Horton in the passage.

'Beg pardon?'

'Your foot!' He pointed through the door to the bath. 'You keep it there.'

It was a second of enormous understanding. Each man sized the other, recognized his intention, grasped his game.

Mr Horton made no attempt to prevaricate, he closed his eyelids and sighed, before passing along the passage.

'I cannot, Mr Cadwaller, help my sponge floating to the further end of the bath. If,' his voice rose, 'you can call it a bath.'

From then on it was war, cold and subtle war. Cadwaller considered, of course, serving Mr Horton his notice. But the rooms were not all full, it would be his own loss; and did he really want Mr Horton to go? For that flash of mutual understanding had been of deep significance—as though twins of some kind had found each other. Each recognized his brother in thrift—and both were as suddenly aware of a physical resemblance. Their thrift, their almost acrobatic thrift—what others might call 'meanness,' though where does meanness begin and thrift end?—might have been apparent before: Mr Cadwaller might have noticed the amount of free samples that made up most of Mr Horton's mail, and Mr Horton might have taken more notice of Mr Cadwaller's brush and pan. Indeed, idly they must have remarked these and a number of other matters; for now, in a sudden retrogressive flash, each totted up the other's account—and such was the intensity of the moment that each realized for the first time something else, they recognized their more than strong physical resemblance. Standing in the dim, daylit, room-smelling passage—the one in an old brown dressing-gown, the other in his tweed jacket fortified everywhere with leather—they faced each other like mirrors, two tall stooping grey-haired gentlemen each mumbling on a long jutting, petulant, prognathous jaw. On a long pale turnip of a jaw, on small bottom teeth monkeying forwards and under a drooping grey moustache disguising the short hare-like upper lip. It was as if, in the pale light of some curious asylum out of time and place, Valentin-le-désossé had met the Habsburg Charles II.

The formation of Charles II's jaw compelled that poor man to eat no solid food, he was fed on liquid hominies. Not so Mr Horton: he liked his liquids, and the stronger the better, but he liked to eat too. This proved a matter of further contention; for Mr Cadwaller ran a profitable dining-room downstairs, and Mr Horton liked his food, when he ate it there, very well done. But Mr Cadwaller liked his guests to eat their food half-raw, it saved gas. And here was this Horton consistently sending his back to be burnt! That is, when he ate it there. For upstairs there was a no-cooking-in-the-rooms rule:

and from beneath Mr Horton's door there crept into the linoleumed lincrustaed passage the most eloquent odours. Yet how could this be done? No trivet for the gas-fire, no gas-ring. Cadwaller even looked outside the window, as if Horton might have been an alcoholic hanging out his bottle, his gas-ring on a nail. However carefully Mr Cadwaller searched, he never found the answer. For Mr Horton cooked, beneath a tent of sheets, on an electric blanket.

Thus these two long-jawed gentlemen went to war: finesse of economy became their touchstone, they tried to outdo each other at every move—and the sphere widened, they openly criticized each other's tactics in fields outside any personal engagement. Thus, when on one morning of strong sunshine Mr Horton looked in on Cadwaller and found him sitting in a chair in front of which was spread newspaper to prevent the sunshine fading the carpet, and moreover moving round the room with the newspaper and his chair as the poisonous beautiful sunlight travelled round, and moreover trying to do his pools at the same time—Mr Horton was able to scoff at him for dispersing his concentrative powers. 'You'll never hit the jackpot that way,' he said. 'Why not spread the paper all over?'

'Because I like to look at my carpet,' Cadwaller growled. 'What's the use of buying a carpet and not looking at it? Besides, I need the paper for the boiler.'

'You could burn the paper later.'

'Eh?' Cadwaller hadn't thought of that. But quickly, 'I suppose you want me to go out and *buy* papers to put on the carpet?'

'Chuck away seventy thousand quid if you like. I don't care.'

And for a moment Mr Cadwaller would think he was really losing seventy thousand; and they would pause facing each other wildly, big turnip chins raised and trembling like the masks of warrior-ants.

All such arguments, absurd as they always became, were distinguished by the cardinal difference between them: Cadwaller's thrift was immediate, the act of expenditure itself gave him unbearable pain; while Horton held the long view, he never minded shelling out if finally profits might be reaped. He liked to foresee things. Thus Horton would with much misgiving pay the registration fee on a parcel, realizing the payment that otherwise must be made in time, fares and shoe-leather: but Cadwaller could not put that shilling on the counter—and took instead tenpence worth of bus fares, and lost time and shoe-leather into a bad bargain. And while Cadwaller wore his old coat out and stitched leather into the elbow-holes, cuffs and neck—Horton foresaw the necessity of this and simply had the arms from his chair removed. (Trouble there, they were Cadwaller's chairs; but Horton made him a footstool of the arms, to save the wear and tear of bedroom slippers.)

As is natural, this common ground brought them much together, not as friends, not exactly as enemies—perhaps more like passionate chess-players. They could never resist each other's company. Their blood rose to each meeting. They went to the Sales together, where there was much argument as to what was true 'clearance' and what was cheap stock brought in for the sale: and whereas neither bought much, Cadwaller would fall eventually for something he did not want at all, simply because it was so very heavily reduced, while Horton bought necessities, seeing the heat of summer through a winter's fog, or even buying two things, like a piece of mirror and a picture-frame, which he could put together to make something of three times the original value.

On such expeditions they would sometimes lunch together, and both, as often happens with 'mean' people, wanted a taste off each other's plates. And so after a few hair-raising encounters when one or the other was served a larger or more appetizing helping, they agreed to order two plates of different dishes and two empty plates as well and then divide exactly both taste and helping. It proved an efficient solution—and if a more plentiful helping of something else passed them on its way to another table, then it was bad luck, it was painful and as pain must be forgotten. What could not be forgotten was a difference between them on the matter of alcohol. Needless to say that they paid for their own: Cadwaller always ordered mild beer, slow long pints of mild beer, perhaps three, but each occasioning an equally mild outlay and each worth its weight in drinking-time: but Horton ordered a small whisky in a large glass, believing in the greater toxic value of spirits, and watched with joy the publican's knuckles whiten as he pressed home the free soda-water. His joy was thus only confined by Cadwaller's presence, for Cadwaller too enjoyed the publican's discomfort, but at his, Horton's, expense.

Thus life continued, in and out of Dwaller Ho. The two great chins, the downdrawn moustaches faced each other and fiddled, fought it out. Ring up TIM? Nonsense, ring up a friend, combine a chat with the time. Take out your sister? Take her in a *taxi* to a cheap restaurant—the taxi'll do all the plinthing she needs. Keep the veg: water for soup? But what of the reducing costs, the expanding gas-bill? Tip the waiter a bit more to get a bigger helping next time? But what if all that money goes in a common pool? Switch out the hall-lights when no one's there? But the poor filaments they make these days—and what of the switches anyway, what of *deterioration*, wear, my God, and tear? And keep the Ascot pilot flame going to warm the place.

As time went on, and in early summer, that fruitful time that follows the mortal months, Cadwaller killed himself.

They had argued about horse-shoes and motor-tyres: shoeing a horse cost exactly twice the cost of motor-tyres over the same distance. Four treads each. Deep in this and adjacent problems of shoe-leather, Cadwaller, during a particularly wet April, refused to have his walking-shoes repaired until the holes achieved a reasonable importance, like the size of the yolk of a flat-fried egg: one could walk on inclined welts. But welts or no, those holes let in water, he caught cold, it lingered, he refused fires and hot-water bottles during the deepening bronchial troubles, there were developments, and in the latter middle of a starless night he died all by himself in the dark, not wishing to turn the light on or ring for his nurse.

Birds were singing in those days. The guests at Dwaller Ho were upset, despite the discomfort to which, in their creaking partitions, amid their personal sounds and their occasional smells, they had always been put. But even so most of them felt more for poor Mr Horton than for the dead Cadwaller himself. For they knew that neither could live happily without the other. They had all recognized how much each had meant to the other; neither old man had ever tried to hide their curious rivalry, and it was a local joke. Yet not only a joke, it was touching, too, in its way—and now there was poor Mr Horton alone, bereft of his adversary, his playmate. He sat at his window, the early summer sunshine too fresh for his worn skin and his grey hair, and more than ever that long jaw seemed to press his mouth closed, always as if he were offended and refused to speak, as if he were the little boy left out of the game, alone and with no one to play with.

But if the sight of him then was touching, his fellow-guests were really moved on the day of the funeral. For early that morning Mr Horton was seen to pick his way through the broken glass and old crates and rubbish of the garden to a single flowering bush at the end wall. He carried a knife. He stood by the bush for some minutes, staring at it, then looking at the knife in his hand, as if he were considering whether it was worthwhile to risk the blade. Then his shoulders suddenly shook—the poor old fellow couldn't be weeping? —and he bent down and cut off a branch of flowers. Another and another. And finally turned, his head bowed, and carried back to the house an armful of blossom.

Everyone knew his intention. And though they smiled to see this final economy and murmured that Cadwaller would turn six feet beneath when these, his own flowers cut free of charge, touched his grave—nevertheless they were deeply moved by old Horton's thought.

The day of the funeral was one of sunshine and fresh warmth, a pale and lovely day of early flowering summer. There were few mourners: but when the hearse drew up at the cemetery gates, and the little file of people came in ones and twos up the asphalt path, lost and at a loss among so vast a civic sea of marble and granite— Mr Horton was already there standing at a respectful distance away from the yellow mound of new-turned clay. The grave was like any hole in the ground—only the mourners, and they much more than the coffin, gave it presence and meaning. And of the mourners, Mr Horton, a sad figure and the older for the fresh blossom held in his hand, seemed, in his resemblance to the dead man and in the memory the other had of the two together, to sanctify the moment more than the priest, the fair weather, the grave.

A short service was read, the coffin lowered, and then, when the carpet of green grass had been finally placed over the grave, Mr Horton went forward alone to place his flowers on his old companion's last resting-place. He stood for a minute, head bowed, in silent prayer. Then turned and walked, a solitary figure, away into the years of loneliness.

A LAST WORD

They watched him go, they saw the last of him turn out through the cemetery gates. But nobody, naturally, saw the giant chuckle beneath Mr Horton's bowed shoulders: nobody knew the true nature of his last tribute, his bloom, his last word, *Rubus Idaeus*, the common raspberry.

A Woman Seldom Found

ONCE a young man was on a visit to Rome.

It was his first visit; he came from the country—but he was neither on the one hand so young nor on the other so simple as to imagine that a great and beautiful capital should hold out finer promises than anywhere else. He already knew that life was largely illusion, that though wonderful things could happen, nevertheless as many disappointments came in compensation: and he knew, too, that life could offer a quality even worse—the probability that nothing would happen at all. This was always more possible in a great city intent on its own business.

Thinking in this way, he stood on the Spanish steps and surveyed the momentous panorama stretched before him. He listened to the swelling hum of the evening traffic and watched as the lights went up against Rome's golden dusk. Shining automobiles slunk past the fountains and turned urgently into the bright Via Condotti, neon-red signs stabbed the shadows with invitation; the yellow windows of buses were packed with faces intent on going somewhere—everyone in the city seemed intent on the evening's purpose. He alone had nothing to do.

He felt himself the only person alone of everyone in the city. But searching for adventure never brought it—rather kept it away. Such a mood promised nothing. So the young man turned back up the steps, passed the lovely church, and went on up the cobbled hill towards his hotel. Wine-bars and food-shops jostled with growing movement in those narrow streets. But out on the broad pavements of the Vittorio Veneto, under the trees mounting to the Borghese Gardens, the high world of Rome would be filling the most elegant cafés in Europe to enjoy with apéritifs the twilight. That would be the loneliest of all! So the young man kept to the quieter, older streets on his solitary errand home.

378

In one such street, a pavementless alley between old yellow houses, a street that in Rome might suddenly blossom into a secret piazza of fountain and baroque church, a grave secluded treasure-place— he noticed that he was alone but for the single figure of a woman walking down the hill towards him.

As she drew nearer, he saw that she was dressed with taste, that in her carriage was a soft Latin fire, that she walked for respect. Her face was veiled, but it was impossible to imagine that she would not be beautiful. Isolated thus with her, passing so near to her, and she symbolizing the adventure of which the evening was so empty—a greater melancholy gripped him. He felt wretched as the gutter, small, sunk, pitiful. So that he rounded his shoulders and lowered his eyes—but not before casting one furtive glance into hers.

He was so shocked at what he saw that he paused, he stared, shocked, into her face. He had made no mistake. She was smiling. Also—she too had hestitated. He thought instantly: 'Whore?' But no—it was not that kind of smile, though as well it was not without affection. And then amazingly she spoke:

'I—I know I shouldn't ask you . . . but it is such a beautiful evening—and perhaps you are alone, as alone as I am. . . .'

She was very beautiful. He could not speak. But a growing elation gave him the power to smile. So that she continued, still hesitant, in no sense soliciting:

'I thought . . . perhaps . . . we could take a walk, an apéritif. . . .'

At last the young man achieved himself:

'Nothing, *nothing* would please me more. And the Veneto is only a minute up there.'

She smiled again:

'My home is just here. . . .'

They walked in silence a few paces down the street, to a turning that young man had already passed. This she indicated. They walked to where the first humble houses ended in a kind of recess. In the recess was set the wall of a garden, and behind it stood a large and elegant mansion. The woman, about whose face shone a curious pale glitter—something fused of the transparent pallor of fine skin, of grey but brilliant eyes, of dark eyebrows and hair of lucent black —inserted her key in the garden gate.

They were greeted by a servant in velvet livery. In a large and exquisite salon, under chandeliers of fine glass and before a moist green courtyard where water played, they were served with a frothy wine. They talked. The wine—iced in the warm Roman night—filled them with an inner warmth of exhilaration. But from time to time the young man looked at her curiously.

With her glances, with many subtle inflections of teeth and eyes she was inducing an intimacy that suggested much. He felt he must be careful. At length he thought the best thing might be to thank her—somehow thus to root out whatever obligation might be in store. But here she interrupted him, first with a smile, then with a look of some sadness. She begged him to spare himself any perturbation: she knew it was strange, that in such a situation he might suspect some second purpose: but the simple truth remained that she was lonely and—this with a certain deference—something perhaps in him, perhaps in that moment of dusk in the street, had proved to her inescapably attractive. She had not been able to help herself.

The possibility of a perfect encounter—a dream that years of disillusion will never quite kill—decided him. His elation rose beyond control. He believed her. And thereafter the perfections compounded. At her invitation they dined. Servants brought food of great delicacy; shell-fish, fat bird-flesh, soft fruits. And afterwards they sat on a sofa near the courtyard, where it was cool. Liqueurs were brought. The servants retired. A hush fell upon the house. They embraced.

A little later, with no word, she took his arm and led him from the room. How deep a silence had fallen between them! The young man's heart beat fearfully—it might be heard, he felt, echoing in the hall whose marble they now crossed, sensed through his arm to hers. But such excitement rose now from certainty. Certainty that at such a moment, on such a charmed evening—nothing could go wrong. There was no need to speak. Together they mounted the great staircase.

In her bedroom, to the picture of her framed by the bed curtains and dimly naked in a silken shift, he poured out his love; a love that was to be eternal, to be always perfect, as fabulous as this their exquisite meeting.

Softly she spoke the return of his love. Nothing would ever go amiss, nothing would ever come between them. And very gently she drew back the bedclothes for him.

But suddenly, at the moment when at last he lay beside her, when his lips were almost upon hers—he hesitated.   .

Something was wrong. A flaw could be sensed. He listened, felt—and then saw the fault was his. Shaded, soft-shaded lights by the bed—but he had been so careless as to leave on the bright electric chandelier in the centre of the ceiling. He remembered the switch was by the door. For a fraction, then, he hesitated. She raised her eyelids—saw his glance at the chandelier, understood.

Her eyes glittered. She murmured:

'My beloved, don't worry—don't move. . . .'

And she reached out her hand. Her hand grew larger, her arm grew longer and longer, it stretched out through the bed-curtains, across the long carpet, huge and overshadowing the whole of the long room, until at last its giant fingers were at the door. With a terminal click, she switched out the light.

Among the Dahlias

THE zoo was almost empty. It was a day in late September, dry
and warm, quiet with sunshine. The school-holidays were over.
And it was a Monday afternoon—most people had a week-end's
enjoyment on their consciences and would forbear to appear until
the Tuesday.

An exception to this was John Doole. He could be seen at about
two o'clock making his way quietly past the owl-houses.

Doole is what may too easily be called an 'ordinary' man, a man
who has conformed in certain social appearances and comportments
for a common good; but a man who is still alive with dreams, desires
whims, fancies, hates and loves—none particularly strong or fre-
quent. The effect of a life of quiet conformity had been to keep such
impulses precisely in their place as dreams or desires, writing them
off as impracticable.

Doole would also have been called a phlegmatic man: at least,
the opposite to a nervous type. When Doole compulsorily whistled
to himself, or pulled up the brace of his trousers with his left hand
while his right patted the back of his head, or took unnecessarily
deep breaths while waiting for a train, so deep that he seemed to be
saying Hum-Ha, Hum-ha with his mouth contorted into a most
peculiar shape, or went through a dozen other such queer acro-
batics during the course of his day—these gestures were never
recognised as the symptoms of nervous unbalance, for too many
other people did exactly the same, and Doole knew this too, he
found nothing odd in such antics. In fact, he had just as many
'nerves' as a Mayfair lady crammed with sleeping pills—only his
manner of outlet was different: also, since he never recognized all
this as neurotic, it was the more easy to control.

Doole was a man of forty, with a happy pink face and receding
fair hair, a little paunch, and creased baby-fat round his wrists. He

had three dimples, two in the cheeks and one on his chin, which gave him the happy, merry look—but his yellow eyebrows flew up at angles over pale lashed eyes, arching out like a shrimp's feelers, and this gave him a little the look of a startled horse, his eyeballs rolled and seemed to shoot out, while those dimples had the effect of stretching the lip over his teeth into an almost animal fixity. He wore a richly sober brown suit, a little rounded over his short figure; an eyeglass bounced on a black ribbon against his paunch; his tawny shoes were brilliantly shined. The paunch seemed to pull him forward, and he threw his arms back as he walked, fingers stretched taut, and his whole body rested back on a very straight, backward-pressed neck. It was easy to imagine him in a bathing costume: one knew he had thin, active legs.

He was in business, in fireplaces. But he would often take a walk in the afternoon between two and three. 'Nobody comes back from lunch till three, you might as well not have a telephone,' he often said. 'I'm damned if I'm going to sit there like a stuffed dummy while they stuff the real man.' He himself was principally a vege-tarian, ate lightly and often alone. He loved animals. He often visited the zoo, though he shuddered a little at the hunks of raw meat dribbling from the vulture's beak and the red bones lying about the lion's cage.

Now he stood for a moment discussing a large white owl. The two appraised each other, Doole's eyes with their appearance of false anguish, the owl's with their false wisdom. The owl had its trousered legs placed neatly together. Unconsciously Doole moved his own into a similar position: at any moment the two might have clicked heels and bowed. 'Just a flying puss,' Doole said to himself, con-sidering the owl's catface of night eyes and furry ears and feathered round cheeks. 'Likes mice like puss, too,' he thought with satis-faction, forgetting in the pleasure of this observation his vegetarian principles. It is satisfactory to come across a common coincidence in the flesh—and Doole expanded for a moment as he nodded, 'How true!' As if to please him, the owl opened its beak and made, from a distance deep inside the vase of feathers, a thin mewing sound.

Doole smiled and passed on. All seemed very right with the world. Creatures were *really* so extraordinary. Particularly birds. And he

383

paused again before a delicate blue creature which stood on one long brittle leg with its nut-like head cocked under a complicated hat of coloured feathers. This bird did not look at Doole. It stood and jerked its head backwards and forwards, like an urgent little lady in a spring hat practising the neck movements of an Indonesian dance. Doole took out his watch and checked the time. Nearly half-an-hour before he need think of the office. Delightful! And what a wholly delightful day, not a cloud in the golden blue sky! And so quiet—almost ominously quiet, he thought, imagining for a moment the uneasy peace of metropolitan parks deserted by plague or fear. The panic noon, he thought—well, the panic afternoon, then. Time for sunny ghosts. Extraordinary, too, how powerful the presence of vegetation grows when one is alone with it! Yet put a few people about the place—all that power would recede. Man is a gregarious creature, he repeated to himself, and is frightened to be alone—and how very charming these zinnias are! How bright, like a consortium of national flags, the dahlias!

Indeed these colourful flowers shone very brightly in that September light. Red, yellow, purple and white, the large flower-moons stared like blodges from a paint box, hard as the colours of stained-glass windows. The lateness of the year had dried what green there was about, leaves were shrunken but not yet turned, so that all flowers had a greater prominence, they stood out as they never could in the full green luxuriance of spring and summer. And the earth was dry and the gravel walk dusty. Nothing moved. The flowers stared. The sun bore steadily down. Such vivid, motionless colour gave a sense of magic to the path, it did not seem quite real.

Doole passed slowly along by the netted bird-runs, mildly thankful for the company of their cackling, piping inmates. Sometimes he stopped and read with interest a little white card describing the bird's astounding Latin name and its place of origin. Uganda, Brazil, New Zealand—and soon these places ceased to mean anything, life's variety proved too immense, anything might come from anywhere. A thick-trousered bird with a large pink lump on its head croaked at Doole, then swung its head back to bury its whole face in feathers, nibbling furiously with closed eyes. In the adjoining cage everything looked deserted, broken pods and old dried droppings lay scattered, the water bowl was almost dry—and then he spied a grey bird tucked up in a corner, lizard lids half-closed, sleeping or resting or simply tired of it all. Doole felt distress for this bird, it looked so lonely and grieved, he would far rather be croaked at. He passed on, and came to the peacocks: the flaming blue dazzled him and the little heads jerked so busily that he smiled again, and turned contentedly back to the path—when the smile was washed abruptly from his face. He stood frozen with terror in the warm sunshine.

The broad gravel path, walled in on the one side by dahlias, on the other by cages, stretched yellow with sunlight. A moment before it had been quite empty. Now, exactly in the centre and only some thirty feet away, stood a full-maned male lion.

It stared straight at Doole.

Doole stood absolutely still, as still as a man can possibly stand, but in that first short second, like an immensely efficient and complicated machine, his eyes and other senses flashed every detail of the surrounding scene into his consciousness—he knew instantly that on the right there were high wire cages, he estimated whether he could pull himself up by his fingers in the net, he felt the stub ends of his shoes pawing helplessly beneath; he saw the bright dahlia balls on the left, he saw behind them a high green hedge, probably privet, with underbush too thick to penetrate—it was a ten-foot hedge rising high against the sky, could one leap and plunge half-way through, like a clown through a circus hoop? And if so, who would follow? And behind the lion, cutting across the path like a wall, a further hedge—it hardly mattered what was behind the lion, though it gave in fact a further sense of impasse. And behind himself? The path stretched back past all those cages by which he had strolled at such leisure such a very little time ago—the fractional thought of it started tears of pity in his eyes—and it was far, far to run to the little thatched hut that said *Bath Chairs for Hire*, he felt that if only he could get among those big old safe chairs with their blankets and pillows he would be safe. But he knew it was too far. Long before he got there those hammer-strong paws would be on him, his clothes torn and his own red meat staining the yellow gravel.

At the same time as his animal reflexes took all this in, some other instinct made him stand still, and as still as a rock, instead of run-ning. Was this too, an animal sense? Was he, Doole, in his brown suit, like an ostrich that imagines it has fooled its enemy by burying its head in the ground? Or was it rather an educated sense—how many times had he been told that savages and animals can smell fear, one must stand one's ground and face them? In any case, he did this—he stood his ground and stared straight into the large, deep eyes of the lion, and as he stared there came over him the awful sense: *This has happened, this is happening to ME.* He had felt it in nightmares, and as a child before going up for a beating—a dread-fully condemned sense, the sense of *no way out*, never, never and *now.* It was absolute. The present moment roared loud and intense as all time put together.

The lion, with its alerted head erect, looked very tall. Its mane—and he was so near he could see how coarse and strong the hair straggled—framed its big face hugely. There was something par-ticularly horrible in so much hair making an oval frame. Heavy disgruntled jowls, as big as hams, hung down in folds of muscled flesh buff-grey against the yellow gravel. Its eyes were too big, and shaped in some sharp-cornered way like large convex glasses more than eyes—and from somewhere far back, as far away and deep as the beast's ancient wisdom, the two black pupils flickered at him from inside their lenses of golden-yellow liquid. The legs beneath had a coarse athletic bandiness: the whole creature was heavy and thick with muscle that thumped and rolled when it moved—as suddenly now it did, padding forward only one silent pace.

Doole's whole inside was wrenched loose—he felt himself pan-icked, he wanted to turn and run. But he held on. And a sense of the softness of his flesh overcame him, he felt small and defenceless as a child again.

The lion, large as it was, still had some of the look of a cat—though its heavy disgruntled mouth was downcurved, surly, pre-datory as any human face with a long upper lip. But the poise of the head had the peculiarly questioning consideration of cat—it smelled inwards with its eyes, there was the furry presence of a brain, or of a mass of instincts that thought slowly but however slowly always came to the same destined decision. Also, there was a cat's affronted look in its eyes. A long way behind, a knobbled tail swung slow and regular as a clock-pendulum.

Doole prayed: O God, please save me.

And then he thought: if only it could speak, if only like all these animals in books it could *speak*, then I could tell it how I'm me and how I must go on living, and about my house and my showroom just a few streets away over there, over the hedge, and out of the zoo, and all the thousand things that depend upon me and upon which I depend. I could say how I'm not just meat, I'm a person, a club-member, a goldfish-feeder, a lover of flowers and detective-stories —and I'll promise to reduce that profit on fire-surrounds, I promise, from forty to thirty per cent. I'd have to some day anyway, but I won't make excuses any more. . . .

His mind drummed through the terrible seconds. But above all two separate feelings predominated: one, an athletic, almost youthful alertness—as though he could make his body spring everywhere at once and at superlative speed; the other, an overpowering knowledge of guilt—and with it the canny hope that somehow he could bargain his way out, somehow expiate his wrong and avoid punishment. He had experienced this dual sensation before at moments in business when he had something to hide, and in some way hid the matter more securely by confessing half of his culpability. But such agilities were now magnified enormously, this was life and death, and he would bargain his life away to make sure of it, he would do anything and say anything . . . and much the most urgent of his offerings was the promise never, never to do or think wrong in any way ever again. . . .

And the sun bore down yellow and the flowers stared with their mad colours and the lion stood motionless and hard as a top-heavy king—as Doole thought of his cool shaded show-room with all the high-gloss firestone slabs about, the graining and the marble flow, the toffee-streaming arches, and never, never again would he feel dull among them . . . never again. . . .

But it *was* never again, the ever was ever, at any minute now he would be dead and how long would it take him to die, how slowly did they tear?

He suddenly screamed.

'No!' he screamed, 'No, I can't bear it! I can't bear pain! I can't bear it . . .' and he covered his face with his hands, so that he never saw the long shudder that ran through the whole length of the lion's body, from head to slowly swinging tail.

In the evening newspapers there were no more than a few lines about the escape of a lion at the Zoological Gardens. Oddly—but perhaps because no journalist was on the spot and the authorities wished to make little of it—the story was never expanded to its proper dimension. The escape had resulted from a defection in the cage bolting, a chance in a million, and more than a million, for it involved also a momentary blank in a keeper's mind, and a piece of blown carton wedged in a socket—in fact several freak occasions combining, including such as a lorry backfiring that had reminded the keeper of a certain single gunshot in the whole four years of the Kaiser's war—the kind of thing that is never properly known and never can be explained, and certainly not in a newspaper. However —the end of it was that the lion had to be shot. It was too precarious a situation for the use of nets or cages. The animal had to go. And there the matter ended.

Doole's body was never found—for the lion in fact never sprang at him. It did something which was probably, in a final evolution over the years, worse for Doole; certainly worse for his peace of mind, which would have been properly at peace had his body gone, but which was now left forever afterwards to suffer from a shock peculiar to the occasion. If we are not animals, if the human mind is superior to the simple animal body, then it must be true to say that by not being killed, Doole finally suffered a greater ill.

For what happened was this—Doole opened very slowly the fingers that covered his eyes and saw through his tears and the little opening between his fingers, through the same opening through which in church during prayers he had once spied on the people near him, on the priest and the altar itself—he saw the lion slowly turn its head away! He saw it turn its head, in the worn weary way that cats turn from something dull and distasteful, as if the head itself had perceived something too heavy to bear, leaning itself to one side as if a perceptible palpable blow had been felt. And then the animal had turned and plodded off up the path and disappeared at the turn of the hedge.

Doole was left standing alone and unwanted. For a second he felt an unbearable sense of isolation. Alone, of all creatures in the world, he was undesirable.

The next moment he was running away as fast as his legs would carry him, for the lion might easily return, and secondly—a very bad second—the alarm must be given for the safety of others.

It was some days before his nerve was partly recovered. But he was never quite the same afterwards. He took to looking at himself for long periods in the mirror. He went to the dentist and had his teeth seen to. He became a regular visitor at a Turkish Bath house, with the vague intention of sweating himself out of himself. And even today, after dusk on summer evenings, his figure may sometimes be seen, in long white running shorts, plodding from shadow to lamplight and again into shadow, among the great tree-hung avenues to the north of Regent's Park, a man keeping fit—or a man running away from something? From himself?

Outburst

LIGHTFOOT his name, but not Lightfoot my ruddy condition he thought as he faced his lop-sided one-and-a-half-size queue on a warm September afternoon, for his feet ached so.

Mothers and their sons made up his queue, as they did other small queues formed towards the assistants behind their counters in this wool-smelling, carpeted School Outfitter's; and it was surely a credit to some British sense of fair play that even among these the almost-rich, with pearls about their necks and sometimes cairngorm thistles pinned above well-supported left breasts, and at such an hour as four o'clock in the afternoon when they wanted badly their teas—that they should in every instance have formed patient, fair-minded, unembattled queues.

However—Mr Lightfoot hardly considered that this afternoon, his feet ached too much: he had been standing since nine o'clock that morning, with only half-an-hour for lunch, for the school holidays were ending and there was now the usual last-minute rush for outfits, nobody having seriously considered that they were not the only persons in the world, and his feet ached; moreover, a veal-and-ham pie in his pocket for his tea was slowly melting, the jelly already sopping into its lardy crust; and on top of all this he had troubles at home, and in his conscience. One could not say whether feet or pie or wife or conscience afflicted his usually equable temper the most. Possibly each exacerbated the other, so that feet ached more and pie melted faster and conscience nagged harder and wife's voice boomed louder than would singly have been the case: for, singly, would any have been so much noticed? Not such, in any case, for Mr Lightfoot to compute—his hot and heavy head only ached muddled with all these troubles, and he dearly wanted his own tea, let alone pie. Yet it was four already, and his queue steady and demanding.

The hot smell of new grey flannel, trousers and jackets and caps, stifled the air; clean glints of plate glass and polished brass cleared it. The atmosphere was thus not overpowering, yet it might have been subtly the more poisonous for what went unseen—who knew what massed particles of stuff a sunbeam might not have revealed, who knew how wetly furred his lungs? Years ago toilet-saloons had been forbidden the old-fashioned machine brushes that ran on leather bands—you never see them now—because the particles of cut hair sucked down into their lungs gave the barbers pulmonary consumption: now who knew what wisps of cotton and wool might not be the innocent-seeming cause of a lingering death? But no sunbeam came to reveal the thousands of floating wisps, the sun had wandered away with the afternoon, and through the window the sky over the chimney pots had already a distant, evening set about it: the day was gone—yet still all these people pressing, wanting, choosing, chatting. . . .

'Now his towels, can they have their hoops sewn on here?' a lady was saying, the hard afternoon light creasing her face with all anxiety, the years pressing suddenly forward: 'I mean, do you do them . . . here . . .?'

'Hoops, madam?' Mr Lightfoot quietly questioned.

'Yes, it says here'—and the lady crumpled her school list the better to see—'require hoops . . . no, loops, I'm sorry, loops.'

'Oh *loops*, madam.'

'So silly of me. Now who would think of sewing a hoop to a towel?' the lady laughed.

'Who would indeed?' answered Mr Lightfoot, his eyes carefully downcast.

'You don't see many hoops about these days, actually,' the woman continued. 'I mean, do you?'

'No,' said Mr Lightfoot. 'Now—he wants some rugger shorts, doesn't he?'

He angled round the counter neatly to avoid crushing his pocketed pie—why not return it to its place under the counter, with what absurd hope had he pocketed it some twenty minutes past?—and measured the boy.

'A bit long for John I think,' he said grating into his voice a kind of joviality.

'Too low on the knee for Eric,' the woman said, and repeated it, Eric.
Slipping, thought Mr Lightfoot, saying: 'Eric, of course. Of
course, young Eric. Where am I?' But he knew where he was, his
tape was at the boy's knees, and however dissimilar that small grit-
smeared knob of bone to the plump dimpled joint whose memory he
could not thrust from his mind, he thought: Knees! And guiltily
his mind jabbed at him wicked glimpses of the majorette he had
followed, like a man in a hangdog raincoat, like a man who writes
on walls, through the amusement park only last evening.

The nights were beginning to chill, though the days were still
warm: and, if one could bring one's mind, stifled as it was by the
grey flannel atmosphere in the shop, to remember the fresh smells of
weather, last night had a breath of winter about it, even a mist had
seemed to haze whitely over the park's still green but drying, dying
leaves, making all too still, as if it were a fuzzed dark print of a park
—as he had rounded a clump of painted wooden girders to see, in
cold lantern light, the lovely military figure of a half-naked lady in
a feathered busby.

No one could accuse Lightfoot's mild and married eye of easy
prurience: he was neither shocked nor excited by this abrupt appari-
tion. The world of film posters and lingerie advertisements had
accustomed him to the probability that half-naked ladies stood or
strode round every corner, and only by chance were rarely seen, so
that this lady in the cold blue light seemed to him little more than
part of a usual pattern, with her tasselled boots, her high busby, her
long naked legs and her frogged bust. He was only a little surprised;
and then mostly by the surrounding trees and the wide grass, for
these dwarfed her, and usually such ladies were so large. It was
probably a simple reflex, man to woman, not consciously interested,
that made him look her way twice.

But the second look caught her knees—and then he found himself
trapped. Were they really blue, or was it the light? Pretending to
be interested in the euphonium carried by a wizened hussar in the
band slouched at rest behind her, he edged closer. He saw that her
knees were braced back, noted their dark navy dimples, slunk his
eye higher to see indeed goose-pimples powdering fine round thighs.
Such was the intensity of the light that each small pimple was deeply

shadowed, giving the thighs themselves something of the perforated appearance of well-rounded cheese-graters—you could flake off a tasty bite of cheddar there he thought, startled into irrelevance. But he pulled himself up sharp, and forced his eye away to the bandsmen who were now spitting at their instruments and shuffling into position to play. Heavens, he thought, she must be cold! Pray heavens, he wished, that they march off! Just then, from the lady's light-blacked lips, a little jet of pure white steam escaped. No wonder those knees were braced back! He saw her thighs, the pale blue lovely cheese-grinders, suddenly shiver like the haunches of a thoroughbred horse.

Then, alone round their hidden corner in the park, the band raised instruments to lip, the lady gripped her silvered baton, she laughed for a moment round at them and suddenly heaved her bare arms across her bosom like a frozen cabby—then to spread them wide and take the first prancing step forward as twenty brass instruments and drums behind smashed instantaneously into sound, and they all swung off to the old march, that some people hum like 'Da-da, and the same to you,' and others something else.

Lightfoot went with them. The cold had done it. His eyes had settled on her knees, and he would never have more than briefly noticed them but for the cold. But the cold had shown him her real intimate knees beneath the simple cursory idea of knees—and it was indeed the knees that had got at him, not the thighs with their frightening pantalettes and their eye-averting intimations of intimacy, but the big fat-muscled knees with wide hollow holes in them more like the eye-sockets in a pair of chubby skulls than dimples: and he had gone forward, hurrying up past the big-drum and the heavier brass to the cornet row so that he could walk level with her, pretending a jaunty joining in the march, but glancing ever down at these fine live joints he slyly savoured so.

Round the amusement park they had marched, others joining in. Lightfoot had worked out the hairpin bends, and hurried skilfully across, so that he was there waiting with a good view as the band came swinging towards him, the knees prancing upwards first and foremost of all. He shuddered now with shame, and with secret delight, to think of it.

He had been late home for dinner. When his wife had reminded him at some length of this, he had given the excuse of a beer at the buffet. That was also a sin—but how light, how innocent against this other! Normally he would have lied about the beer, she always made such a fuss. But now last night she had capped it all by saying: 'No need to tell *me*. Your breath came in the door before you, thanks very much.'

When he had not touched a drop! The injustice! Somehow doubly unjust—since the knee-following was, in all the more practical senses, innocent. Why shouldn't he? Other men did. But dark thoughts tapped at him saying: Better not start that. Not at your age. Dangerous.

'Now will these do him? With the wash to pull them up a bit?' he asked these other small knees belonging to Mrs Arbuthnot's boy before him.

The mother agreed. He touched the knees with his tape and pulled it away as if he had been stung. Upright again, he turned to her further orders. Guilt, hunger and injustice made a black circle of the soft shop around him. He concentrated on the white patch of his order book, while the air whispered carpet-softened conversations and a machine somewhere quietly clicked.

The boys wanted their teas too. Most of them, being from different schools, stood silent from each other, and silent from their mothers too, for fear of some embarrassing endearment. They stood about bored as dummies, dreamily hungry, faces showing no expression whatever, for so young the set lines of character had not yet engraved them. Yet there were two brothers whispering near Lightfoot's ear. Licking their lips and mouthing the words voluptuously, they were discussing food:

'A nice plate of boiled pull-overs, now, how about that?'

'Toasted ties for me. And plenty of sauce all over.'

'Lovely thick sock-sauce!'

Mr Lightfoot murmured: 'Now boys!' quite sharply, yet smiled up quickly for the mother to see all his teeth. This particular mother was more than usually trying, she had the exact printed list of what was wanted in her hand yet misread it every time: did she disdain spectacles? She certainly disdained him, Lightfoot. She wore on her

head a curious nigger brown hat shaped like the hull of a racing-
yacht, its prow extending far forward over one eye: perhaps this
was worn to overcome her masterfully beaked nose—but that was
impossible, and now the nose and this cocked-looking hat and her
two cold grey eyes only managed for her the appearance of a faded
but still formidable field marshal. Yet, however formidable this
Mrs Arbuthnot, who knew what lurked behind in the other mothers?
What fearful pleasantries, what chatty passings-of-the-time that were
finally far more to be feared than this field marshal's stare?

Setting his teeth, his mind whirling, he wrote and measured and
smiled and wrapped. Once he glanced up and saw all the hats before
him, perched at such odd angles to the faces, unrelated whorls of
felt or straw that primped nevertheless a certain pompous assever-
ance, an I-am-ness, into the faces beneath—and these hats brought
his mind again to his wife, and to injustice. His empty frame burned
with indignation. What a situation! Why should *his* marriage have
turned out like a cartoon-joke? All the old clichés prevailed—the
voice carving through his morning paper, her acute suspicion of
alcohol, dress bills, everything. Somehow she managed to make him
feel clumsy and male, while assuming herself a masculine authority:
he could not now do the simplest thing, neither take a glass of beer
nor an odd hour's walk, without explanation, examination, judgment. Conditioned to authority by school, by his father, and by the
hierarchy of his work, he felt easily guilty: he felt his wife's eye and
her voice everywhere, and nowadays more often than not he hesitated before taking some simple enjoyment, then desisted—quite
absurdly, and he knew it. But knowledge is no palliative—and here
he was again torturing himself unnaturally about last night. It was
all so mixed in his hot muddled mind, guilt and innocence clashed
together, sense of sin and injustice brewed in conflict to make an
ever more fevered broth boiling up and almost over in him.

His mind shouted. But outside it, in the crowded shop, everything
was strangely silent. Among so many assembled, few spoke but the
assistants and their immediate customers. The figures of wax boys
in glass cases smiled silently at real boys bored and unsmiling. The
mothers were of too refined a class easily to engage in small-talk
with their fellow-queuers, and when sometimes they did, nervous

assurance made the words so loud they quickly died, to be sucked swiftly away into the thick-piled carpet.

Through the window, by a chimney high in the afternoon sky, a little white cloud passed free in the free blue air. And everyone still stood, getting hotter, hungrier, breathing their patience more heavily, while the electric clock moved steadily on, its awful red minute hand racing round. Fresh-pressed flannel shorts lay in quiet grey stacks, cellophane glinted round coiled garters, pants and vests were piled under glass like a museum show of dry fluffed tripe—all was quiet. And the minute hand raced round like a magician's thin red wand.

Lightfoot suddenly thought: Did they all wear sweat-pads? Looking up swiftly from a woollen sock caught somehow in his carbon paper, he swiftly undressed all the women nearest to him, and saw them with those strange white pads in their armpits, white straps everywhere, a contraption in which he had once surprised his wife looking as if in waterwings. All these women, then—were their well-found suits and dresses merely a smooth deception to cover such wide white balloons? His mind wandered on, aching and light. And how was his pie doing? And when, *when* would there be tea? A wonderful vision suddenly arose—to soak his feet in a bowl of strong, fresh tea!

'Stewed vests, with lashings of custard,' one of the boys mumbled, distinctly licking his lips.

'Plimsoll custard,' the other agreed.

'Hot pants!' the first boy abruptly shouted, it seemed irrelevantly.

When then suddenly Mr Lightfoot said at the top of his voice: 'And here are your Rugger shorts, Mrs Arbuthnot. I trust they fit snug and you'll run a mile in them!' When this momentous pronouncement rang on the air there was a sudden silence, which previously one would not have thought possible, so quiet was the whispering shop. But now certainly a silence cut hard and heavy, one could scarcely breathe, it was as tangible as if an overflow consignment of blankets had entered the shop above all the other cloths. Even the machine stopped its quiet steady clicking, as if clogged.

'. . . and Mrs Arbuthnot's sports stockings? Many a pretty game with *that* leg, I'll be bound,' rang out Mr Lightfoot, an awful smile fixed across his face.

Everybody stared. The other assistants along the counter stood stockstill, garments in hand, eyes obtruded with horror. Their foreman, the shopwalker, in black coat and decorated trousers, had been telephoning and now stood with mouth open not speaking into the mouthpiece, a bewildered general flank-attacked, knowing a decision must be made, not immediately knowing how. And the other assistants knew that Lightfoot must have gone mad. None knew what multiple frustrations had burst, but they knew Lightfoot, and now they watched him paralysed, as now speaking in a kind of high comedian's falsetto, and in caricature of a shop-assistant's ingratiating manner, he went on holding his stage, grinning his teeth out over stretched lips and spitting hard, hard irony, all poison suddenly erupted.

'And, Mrs Arbuthnot,' he minced, 'would you like the school number *nailed* into your instep?'—he extended wide a generous arm —'It would be a pleasure.'

Then the silence around was broken. Somebody laughed. It was no more than a titter. But it humanised the silence, it was the lonely titter in the audience that liberates laughter pent-up for a joke suspected but not quite understood, and it was a titter, not a snigger —it was affirmative. It was infectious. Other titters began, and one lady's bell-like laugh sounded quite prettily and loud on the air, clearing it.

Mr Lightfoot had opened his mouth again, continuing: '. . . the delicate question arises, Mrs Arbuthnot,'—hearing the titter, mistaking it in his fevered liberty for a snigger, as the others had mistaken the wild light in his eyes for one of fun—'of your pants, your little winter vests. . . .'

. . . when something too dreadful occurred, the field marshal's glare on Mrs Arbuthnot's face began to fade, even the prow of her nigger hat seemed to recede from its pointed aggression, as between thin ever-so-nicely rouged lips a little tooth poked its way, and the lips themselves rose daintily at the corners to form a shy baby melon; far away at the back of Mrs Arbuthnot's pale eyes a little light began to dance: rogue dimples, one each side, like the shadows of two pearled lobes, appeared from nowhere—and like a snowdrop pressing shyly through the frost, the girl inside the field marshal came into the full view of everybody.

And the whole shop relaxed. Even the floor-walker beamed—he was not quite sure yet but in any case this unusual situation, however improper, had somehow been saved: from the looks of his custom, it might even be a good thing: 'I want this shop to be a happy ship'—he remembered his avuncular address at a salesman's meeting.

Then Lightfoot, continuing but feeling his voice weaken, heard a woman's whisper: 'You'll never get a good cockney down.'

So that was it! He looked round the merry circle of eyes, and at Mrs Arbuthnot's coy tooth, with growing horror—they were patronising him! Patrons indeed they were, and in the full measure of their removed class they were unbending so much as to treat his great anger as a barrow-boy's quip, a performance, a cordiality! A smile and a joke whatever the burden . . . how easy to sit back more comfortably if the poor laughed, all well with the world, conscience appeased . . . oh God in heaven, *cockney wit* . . . and desperate in the face of such laughter, he the irrepressible tried to blaze with anger, but found instead all his spirit deflating, for there he was after all circled with smiles, hemmed in by a rubbery compound of goodwill against which all would bounce back, whatever he tried; and he opened his mouth once for the swear-word that at least might do it —but the word never came, it was not his way . . . and instead a pepper of tears came to his eye, dry tears that would never truly appear, a burning of eye-ducts echoing the despair that racked his whole body, as he bent down again to his order book, his moment of rebellion over, drained of all further fight, and went on in a quiet voice:

'And now Madam . . . the boy's bedroom slippers?'

To the Rescue!

YOU'D best go by train,' said this healthy-looking lady in overalls and some kind of cap, 'if you ask *me*.'

Tressiter, who had asked her, looked vaguely about him at the trees heavy with summer, at the model engine bright blue beneath, at the miniature rail disappearing in a miniature curve into green thicket. He remembered the map. No railway. He looked down at high-stepped lizard shoes pointing like a porker's feet out of the woman's overall trousers.

'Train?' he said, puzzled.

She pointed down at the engine, half the height of the man oiling it. 'There,' she said. 'In five minutes.'

A mixed mob of Brownies and Cubs poured in and out of the miniature carriage doors, little folk in exact proportion to the size of the carriages. At a more distant perspective they might have been a crowd of scout instructors and gym mistresses mobbing round a real train. But just behind them a real and giant scoutmaster and a huge sort of gym mistress stood, bringing a dream unreality to the scene. These two shepherding their last charges into the coach suddenly followed, their heads bowed, their giant shanks dragging after them to disappear finally, satisfactorily within.

Tressiter raised his black homburg and smiled: 'Well if you say so, Madam,' he said. 'Many thanks.'

He descended the stairs and put an uneasy hand on the door of an empty carriage. It felt quite solid. He doubled himself down and entered. Inside it was surprisingly capacious—he could sit up straight without bowing his head! Yet the station steps, the plat-forms, and of course now the carriage windows—all these were definitely undersized, half-sized? He remembered how during the war his battalion had been stationed in a school built for very small children: washbowls, lavatories and so forth were low-down and exactly half-size. It had been strange bending to such dwarf appliances, but possible. It had given one an oddly child's-eye view of life. A curious sensation. Yet he had noticed that the opposite worked too—here were little things making you feel little, yet big things made you feel little too, he had noticed that, for instance on his Sunday afternoon walks in London, it was only when he passed a really immense house that he felt it to be like the houses of childhood, its size proportionately large to his grown eye. There must, he thought looking out at the real countryside cantering past, be other dimensions at work than those we know.

He looked at his briefcase and saw the initials M.R.T. with some reassurance. Mervyn Ralph Tressiter on the way to see some silly old—to see Mrs Miriam Albee in her summer cottage about a few wintry old bonds. Travelling on the light railway out to Dunromin on Dungeness. Definitely. Yet the initials? The resounding MERVYN RALPH? During his schooldays those initials had meant a great deal—he had carved them everywhere, written them in red ink at the top of clean blue-lined pages: as with the two Christian names, never used since in such sonorous order. Here they were with him again, full-size in a half-size train.

What then occurred through the window was not more reassuring to Tressiter, who had arrived at London Bridge and his office quite normally long, long ago that morning. For the high June grasses and the heavy-leaved branches above suddenly ceased; one moment he had been softly curtained in country green—and now here was the train running through what seemed to be an endless desert of pebbles. He craned round to see what was to come, and saw the little black rail track curving on indeed into desert distance—into a kind of nothingness. Overhead the sky hung hot and solid blue. Beneath stretched nothing but a vast pinkish-grey plain of little stones. He remembered the map, this must be the Ness proper, a monstrous long snout of silted shingle prodding into the channel. Now the sea could be seen—or at least that hollow look of unobstructed air that indicates the sea beneath: the horizon proper was hidden by a raised motor road upon which a bright blue motorcycle raced along slowly with the train, while just beyond, as though also on the road, there crawled the white fretted upper-works and orange-banded funnel of a cargo-steamer. Gravel-covered villas with brilliant red or green roofs now dotted this road—and among these the slow-travelling superstructure of the steamship looked like a white rococo casino left over from the turn of the century. An arid place, sea-blown and open—Tressiter wondered how Mrs Albee could have chosen such a spot for her summer residence. Now there came into view a holiday camp with deserted hard-courts, a wired-in corral of empty chalets. The train stopped, and the Cubs and Brownies milled out to disappear almost instantly, swallowed somehow by the very emptiness. Once more the train started—Tressiter felt he must be the only passenger, alone in the tiny train, and now even the villas receded, there remained only shingle and lonely wooden huts, creosoted bungalows on whose tarry verandahs sat solitary figures in deckchairs, tattered rugs about their knees. Occasionally a woman in an apron would be seen standing with a basin, absolutely alone, near one of these shacks. Each bungalow had a fenced surround of ground: inside the fence it was still pebble, no difference. Cocoa and strong tea must be drunk here all day, Tressiter thought, from enamelled tin mugs.

There hung over everything a desolation of peace—the kind of peace that follows war, when everything is tattered and the earth scourged dry. No cafés, nothing but shingle and these huts lonely from each other. Nothing grew but weeds. Sometimes the startling pink of valerian started up but even this looked unreal, no green to soften the hard plastic pink. The whole place of black huts and nothingness was as quiet as death.

The train stopped at its weedy terminal and Tressiter descended to visit Mrs Albee at Dunromin. It was simply another creosoted bungalow. He concluded his business quickly. Among washed-out curtains over a cup of strong tea—in fact Mrs Albee served him with a china cup, uncracked—he found his mind worked the quicker simply to get away: if she wanted to hoard her little nest-egg in such circumstances, it was—well, one could not say it was none of his business because it was his business; nevertheless Tressiter had not to reason why. Mrs Albee's grey hair was dyed in parts red, and she settled herself to talk. She stroked him with her eyes, there was the urgent desire of loneliness about her. Against these importunities,

Tressiter worked with precision: he did two hours work in one.

So that shortly after noon he stepped free from the bungalow into the rest of a day that had no precise purpose. There was not really time to get back to London and the office; and it was certainly time, his stomach rumbled, for lunch. He had been told about a café by the lighthouse on the tip of the Ness. It was a sunny day, and he thought he would go and sit a bit on the beach afterwards. To get to the end of something, over a hill or to the very tip of such a promontory, was a familiar compulsion.

In the asbestos-lined café there were baked beans to be had. 'The stores haven't arrive yet,' the woman said, when he enquired for eggs or meat. She spoke softly, slowly, with an almost beautiful content—they might have been on an island far off the coast of Scotland. He ordered baked beans, and then ordered them again. He did not quite finish the second portion: fortified by hot coffee he left for the beach.

It was not far. A few weeds straggled like dull green paper streamers among the pebbles; then they too died away, the last black hut was passed, and only the pebbles, cleaner, yellower, remained. They rose and fell in two steep silted dunes, and suddenly dropped away shelving into deep blue water.

To one side stood the lighthouse and its buildings, to the other a single solitary hut: otherwise the yellow-pink pebbles stretched in their millions, a mighty bank as far as the eye could see, cutting exactly against the blue sea under its blue sky. A light breeze opened out the air all around.

The lighthouse compound, bright white and black, stabbed clean against the blue, its line of black-tarred chimneys as clear-cut as the white tower itself. No gulls, no refuse. Tressiter opened his lungs and breathed in the great clarity. You could smell the tar. He took off his homburg and sat down: he stuck, he had sat on a patch of tar. So most of this wonderfully clean-looking beach was fouled with tar and ship's oil! He was just piling his briefcase and homburg into a careful castle—when a voice suddenly piped from behind:

'Messy, ainit? I bring it in when I go ome.'

He shot his head round. He saw a thin white boy of about ten in a dark bathing-dress.

'You—you bring it in?' Tressiter said, startled that in such empty space a person could approach shadowless, unseen, from directly behind; and especially as no sound had come from pebbles that looked so resonant. But now a loud near pebble-crunch embodied the voice: and, after all, it was only a boy.

'The tar of course,' said the boy.

'But what do you want to bring it in for? Is it valuable?' he asked.

The boy looked vaguely out to sea, not a trace of scorn on his face for Tressiter's obtuse confusion.

'I bring it in on me feet,' he said, his voice like a rising and falling aerial whine, without human direction, blank.

There was silence as the boy sat down. Here was the whole wide beach, yet the boy chose to sit just beside him, a few feet left in between so as not to be actually *with* Tressiter! A little essay, Tressiter thought, in human gregariousness—grouping against the elements but taking care to remain individual, the lone wolf and the herd in the same veins.

And I'm an outsize essay, he thought again, in the misapplication of metropolitan man to the free littoral—here I've covered a forty guinea suit with good indigenous tar; also every brace and lace and buckle about me irks to be free: now if I did not feel in the board-room the delightful and reassuring pressures of suspenders and braces and waistcoat strap and the back of my collar, let alone my well-fitting teeth and the smooth texture of a shaven jaw—why, if I did not feel all these armours exactly attuned I would never be able to pull my weight in conference, I'd be acutely demoralized. Yet here I want to throw them all off! It's not hot, and I don't want to sunbathe—it's simply some fearful association of ideas.

'You don't half like baked beans,' the boy said vaguely to the sea. He added: 'I'm a guts too.'

So the news had got around already! A sensation in so remote a spot—that a man should have two helpings of the same! Once again he sensed that here was a place so solitary, with so few things moving in its lonely space, that anything could happen: that something *would* happen.

'I can throw a stone into the sea,' the boy said, his slow dreamy eyes on the near deep water. His mouth hung a little open—no purpose it seemed, in keeping it closed. Tressiter waited for him to say, 'Can you?'—some normal inclusion of himself. But again the boy said nothing further. He was vacantly content with a plain statement of his personal, slow direction. Tressiter saw him suddenly as some awful kind of snail-boy, blindly slithering through life over an interminable vista of baked beans and pebbles without destination or purpose, except occasionally to surmount the barrier of a tarpatch. But at last the boy tossed a stone into the sea. Tressiter watched it throw up a small web of water, heard its resonant plonk-sound, and the stone was gone forever.

The boy stood up. 'I'm going in,' he said, 'I'm going in plop like my stone.'

Now Tressiter lay beneath and the child was standing above him. It reduced him to child-level—once again on this strange day—and it seemed even insolent of this boy, now grown up there, not to look down at him.

'I can swim,' the boy said and began to walk off.

Thank God at least for that, Tressiter muttered under his breath. Then in sudden despair for some sort of communication, he called after him: 'Where do you live? Is that your Mum and Dad back there?'

But the boy never noticed, broke into a run crunching sudden brittle thunder from the pebbles, and then, all arms and pony-stepping legs, windmilled a white spray into the sea. 'Arms like little white sticks,' Tressiter thought, looking back to the distant hut where perhaps the boy had come from, and where he had noticed two figures sitting wrapped up in the sun. 'He couldn't have been here long, no brown on him. Perhaps it's his holiday, his first day.' He remembered the slight red flush beginning on the boy's arms, showing the skin whiter beneath—and found this rather touching.

The thought took him back to his own holidays as a child, to smells of sea and sand long ago. That miraculous secret land of rocks and sea-weed left by an unusually low tide! The gritty feeling of sand from his feet in the bath as evening fell and the long salty day was over!

He shook his head regretfully and looked down at his grown-up paunching stomach in its adult lease-holder's season-ticket suit.

Again he was back again thinking of himself small, the whole day seemed to contrive it—and he looked over at the lighthouse, and even this, in the big simplicity of its patterned white and black, looked more like a giant model than a high windswept tower. He squinted at it, solitary against sea and wide shingle. 'I could have built that myself,' he thought as he reduced it, 'with my bricks.'

And close inshore there passed model ships, perfect in all detail. Heavy-tonned cargo-steamers came right in to round the point of the Ness: the sea was deep here, and from the little hill of shingle shelving sharply down it looked the deeper, one could imagine the angle continuing straight down like the side of a basin—and somehow in the clear air the ships looked nearer even than they were, and in his eyes reduced in size, for one seldom sees a ship so, it is more usually either a speck in the distance or a high wall of steel at a quayside. The breeze blew their smoke to nothing: moving slowly past, with no visible effort to be seen, they might have been drawn on underwater strings. Tressiter felt his heart jump as he saw the bright orange and black paint, and the white deck-works, and blocks and rigging and bollards and capstans: long ago he had pressed his nose to the toyshop window and seen such ships in all their miniature detail, each item priced . . . how he had yearned for those little brass knobs, how his pocket-money had loved out at the window. . . .

A faint cry came from the water.

Idly, not lowering his eyes to the sea between his pebble-dune and the ship, he left the cry unanswered. If the boy ignored him on the beach, he'd be damned if he'd applaud whatever he was up to in the water.

Again the cry, louder. The letter L seemed to curve up on the wide air, then blow away. Casually he looked down. The boy was waving at him.

Well, he could wave. Then a vomit of hard fear raced up to catch the breath in his throat—the boy was struggling, waving for help, 'Help!' the cry came, '. . el . !' and he saw the stick-arms thrashing lop-sided and the boy's chin thrust urgently up as if he were being strangled, gasping for air.

For a second urgency paralysed Tressiter. He felt the taste of salt-water in the boy's mouth, he looked back at the two doll-figures sunning in the tarry verandah back up the beach, he stood up and waved wildly. Neither moved.

He looked down with horror at his suit, his shoes. The boy was absurdly close inshore. No more than twenty or thirty feet out: but in deep water; and with what currents pulling down?

He thought wildly: They take off their boots, they take them off and fling their jackets off and plunge over the embankment wall . . . he struggled with a lace, then heeled the shoe right off, then the other, and his jacket —in the last second he rolled this up and put it not on tar but on the homburg-briefcase castle—and then stood again milling his arms in a wild semaphore to the sunning rugs up there.

'Ell!' piped loud now from the sea, desperate as a gull's cry. The dolls sat on staring at him, not a movement. Once sunlight seemed to flash on glasses. Asleep? Sun-blind? Spectators immobilized in the sun, quiet as insects . . . and the lighthouse, the black and white coastguard's house impregnably walled—no sign of life . . . and on a ship passing he could see decks and rails and lifebuoys so near, but impossible . . . he ran down the shingle, not feeling the stones, nor then, as he dived in, the sudden chill of the water. Only when he was swimming, a heavy-breathed breast-stroke towards the stuggling bob of a head—only then did he realize suddenly a kind of hopelessness, a smallness about himself alone among waves. Not waves only wind-ripples, but at water-level waves higher than the eye . . . and now his soaked trousers weighed him back, his own breath was going . . . and what would he do when he got to the boy? If he struggled? The thing was to hit them? Hit them in the face? But where in the face?

In the long few yards pushing through the water he saw the hull of the oil-tanker, wondered if he should go back and signal it from the beach, knew he shouldn't . . . and then half way to the boy he saw the head disappear. Had he gone under or was it a wave in between? Suddenly he thought for the first time: Is it worth it? Is it worth two lives? And though hitherto during that day a specious sense of being small again had struck him, in the little train, then on the beach—now much more darkly and deeply he felt it, he was right back again like a small boy with big things round him and the old guilt worming up, he was doing wrong and he would do it knowing it and there was a shadow of punishment above though he would find a tale to tell himself out of it . . . and, so thinking, tears burned in his eyes as his helpless breath came and he turned and started to dog-paddle back to the shore.

But on the beach a figure came, bounding enormously alone down the shingle an old man in striped pyjamas, grey hair whisking in the sun, shouting something, now plunging straight into the sea and coming fast with an overarm crawl. And Tressiter, gulping down his guilt, turned slowly round and began his hopeless dog-paddle back towards the boy.

But even then he trod water, hoping the man would pass him, hating to lose more distance from the shore, hoping with fear even greater than fear of water that he had not been noticed.

The boy's head was clearly to be seen again, and this strong swimmer flailed swiftly past him: Tressiter trod water a little nearer, wanting to appear at hand to help, yet not moving far, calculating each foot . . . and the man had the boy safe and had turned on his back and was frogging hard to the beach. Tressiter turned and kept pace, paddling fast now. At last they stumbled up the first wet shingle, and the man stooped to gather the boy firmly in his arms. Tressiter found his own arms outstretched round and under and a little way off this burden, as if to catch it if it fell—but a cautious inch or two away, useless yet looking useful as crabwise he trod up beside the man to the dry shingle above.

He stood by uselessly as the man got the boy's arms moving and water trickled out from his bluing lips. He felt he must say something. The man paid no attention to him. He might not have been there. Yet now he felt he ought to be congratulated—the lie had formed in him, he had never *really* turned back, he had gone in after the boy and risked his life, he who was a poor swimmer had done this.

'How is he?' he said.

The man took no notice, working away concentrated only on the body beneath. The thought came to Tressiter that it would have been uselsss if he had brought the boy in, he had no knowledge of these respiratory exercises—and this too excused him. Yet he could have carried the boy to the coastguards? No time, no, there would not have been time.

A woman was stumbling over towards them—he saw that now the verandah of the hut was empty, they must have seen him go in after he had waved, and a little hope clutched at him as he thought how purposeful his back must have looked—and now the man raised his head and yelled: 'Cocoa, Ma! Hot cocoa, get back quick!'

Then as she turned, the boy made his first movement. The man muttered 'Thank God,' and gathered him up again. He stood up, breathing hard, with the boy in his arms. Tressiter urged forward a step: 'Can I help?' he said.

He saw the man's eye take in the pile of homburg and briefcase. the coat neat on top, and then the man looked at him, from his feet up to his eyes, a long look from old wise eyes. 'You've helped,' the man said. 'Haven't you?'

'Yes, but . . .' Tressiter stuttered, wanting to explain, wanting the man to see how hopeless it would have been, and above all wanting now to act in some way—so that he stumbled after the man up the shingle to the hut, thinking that perhaps the old eyes had not accused, that he had misheard a note of sarcasm. As the man passed through the verandah, Tressiter said: 'Can't I get you some brandy?'

The man said over his shoulder, 'We've got brandy.' And he was left standing there in the porch. A moment later the door, rattling all its glass, was slammed in his face.

He stood there soaked through, dreadful tears of injustice rising. Now the boy was all right shouldn't he, Tressiter, have some brandy too? Hadn't he gone in after the kid? Here he was miles from home, wet, cold, exhausted . . . he went down the beach to his clothes, picked them up and started towards the distant huts. Mrs Albee, he thought, Mrs Albee. He could have gone to the café—but it was too near the beach, they would hear about it. 'Mrs Albee!' he cried, 'Mrs Albee!' stumbling through the weeds and the old cans and wire to her safe, creosoted door.

Eventide

SIX o'clock. A cold summer's evening.

The bar was empty. Polished linoleum slid over the floor and the clock was stopped—not a tick to disturb the dustless quiet of dark shamrock curtains, dark-varnished wood, windows paned in neat squares of frosted glass: nothing glittered; all only shone dully in the grey evening light, and such gloom could not even be called subaqueous, it was so dry and dead. Yet this was the saloon bar of a public house; and now at six o'clock sat waiting, its clock stopped, for time to pass.

After a long while the door pressed open. The door never swung, there was a compressed air device screwed to the top, and a rubber wheel ensured further quiet. A man came in. First he was a shadow against the street light, than a man in a creased grey suit walking to the bar —as the door, his accomplice, bowed to a rubbery close behind him.

From behind the bar half a woman shot up, a cardiganed torso on a sudden spring-lift, glasses masking her eyes, cheek-bones gleaming white, a net dowsing dull brown hair. She stood facing the man, thin-lipped. Neither spoke.

The man stood chest-on to the bar, feet placed astride, planted like a passenger on a ship. He now sighed, as if a journey had been completed. He took a big sheet of a handkerchief from his pocket, buried his face in it, and blew. With no more than a quick glance at what he had blown, he braced his shoulders again and sucked in air through his teeth. Glancing sharply to left and right at the emptiness, making sure they were alone, again he faced the woman, who had been waiting, rigid and woolly, all this time.

Finally the man said: 'Good evening.'

He cooed the 'good' high and the 'evening' low, so that it made a little song—but not so much a song of greeting as a lullaby of condolence.

The woman made no spoken reply. But her head inclined in the shade of a small bob, recognizing the greeting as an item ticked off on a list.

The man then took a pipe from his pocket, looked at it, shook it, and set it into his teeth so that it stuck out upside down like an odd piece of brown plumbing.

It must have given his molars a clenched, manly feel—he sucked in air again with a big-chested hiss: and now he said, as if it were all one long slow word:

'Nice-glasser-best-Mrs-S.'

He spoke as if he had turned the condolence in upon himself: he ordered this beer not as if he desired it but as if he deserved it, and that it was not all he deserved, but he would be quite satisfied to accept it, he was not the man to ask for too much, his demands were reasonable and modest. Enough was quite enough for him. For the present. And nobody should deny it.

He was balding a little, thin sandy hair looked stranded over red ears, and his pale office-whipped face had a pleasing mildness. He received his drink, paid for it, fingering out the exact money, and remained standing, not touching the glass, satisfied simply by its presence.

Then again silence.

As he contemplated the glass, the woman returned to her evening paper. The clock stared paralysed. Only the little pipe, upside down cast a note of brown caprice into a scene otherwise still as death.

There would be hours of daylight yet. Double summer time had stolen the sundown hour. Day's work ended, evening begun had lost its proper definition of approaching darkness: it was a neutral time.

The saloon bar had been furnished in the 'thirties in an attempt to be homely and be cheerful. A note once modern had impaled itself on the air once and forever, delineating time the more strongly for its recent passing—sad and near as the death of a promising child, and, in terms of the world and the passing years, as expendable.

The hopes, the abundant feeling that must have gone to make such a place! A horizontal oval mirror hung on thin brass chains over the fireplace. The fireplace itself had square mauve tiles that shone but did not reflect, and they were surrounded again by dark stained wood. A gas-pipe, bright-polished, fled like a killer-snake from the ladylike fender. The fire itself bared its boney sockets like a death-trap.

The dark wood that everywhere predominated had a cheap brittle texture, a sense of varnished creosote. Even the dart-board was nicely enclosed in a dark wood cabinet. Someone had had the ideas 'sunny' and 'cheerful'—there was a dado of whipped-up copper-brown plaster waves and above this a wallpaper of embossed gamboge shells: the effect was of the awful yellow glow that precedes a great tropic storm, the colour of the end of the world.

Spattered about were cheerful trifles: paintings of Cornish fisher-villages, a gold basket sprouting paper flowers, cardboard beermats. Advertisement cards mounted on their own props snapped and yelped.

But no room could be so uniformly dreadful as this: there was indeed one note of relief that might have cheered the trapped customer. On one window appeared in bright red letters the lightly mad, enchanting message: TUOT?.

Suddenly the woman behind the bar closed her paper with a rustle like a thunderclap.

'You don't know my biggest boy,' she said. 'He's grown a beard.'

The man looked anxious. 'There now,' he said, and clutched the pockets at the side of his coat. And then the woman began to fish urgently in a bag. Her breathing got short. The man looked more than ever anxious. He peered over. Would she find it, what was it, would it be lost forever?

But she suddenly snapped out a bruised brown wallet. 'Here we are,' she said and bent her glasses down fingering at photographs inside. She drew out two of these. One she put on the bar for the man to see. It showed a young cleanshaven sailor smiling against a brick barrack building.

'That's how he is really,' said the woman and then showed him the other photograph, of a similar young sailor, but with a beard.

'And that's how he really is,' said the woman.

The man nodded. They both gazed at the photographs, at little grey different worlds somewhere far away where the sun had once shone.

'He's a sailor,' the woman explained.

'Ah,' the man said.

And the silence like a hungry black spore came gliding up from nowhere and gathered itself hammering huge. It had waited like dust in this room where there was no speck of real dust, and now it rained down dry dew all over them. The man struggled to say something—but the silence was falling too heavy.

Then at the last moment his eye caught a picture in the paper she had put down. His short fat forefinger came from his pocket and like a squat sausage held in his hand pointed all by itself at the representation of a kingfisher.

'We had one of them come in the garden once,' he said. 'Little blue bird.'

He raised his eyebrows and smiled straight at the woman. Her glasses stared back reflecting nothing. The silence began to shroud over again.

'Went away after a couple of days,' the man sighed. 'Never saw it no more.'

And down clapped the silence. The man raised his glass and slid some of the beer down inside him. It made no sound whatever. The woman picked up the photographs and tucked them away. A thin sunbeam slid in over a patch of linoleum, shivered, turned grey, and disappeared.

But twenty minutes later the door opened and one, two, three, four quite separate people came in. A train might have arrived, disgorging sudden passengers. Yet there was no train near, nor any particular bus.

However, men with briefcases and umbrellas and hats and a woman with a string bag bulging tins all came in and scattered themselves everywhere, there was a shuffling of shoes and a cracking of papers, a tinkling of glass and a fizzing of soda-water; and the little light of cigarettes lit; and talk.

They exchanged civilities. They said about the weather. One of the men winked and murmured, 'Mind how you go' to the woman with the string bag raising gin to her lips.

There was nothing said that had not been said a hundred million times before. Yet how precious, how preposterous a load of lovely human litter, like a confetti of coloured bus tickets! How warmly and lightly these simple communications hit upon the air!

Even the death of the furniture died away.

The man in the grey suit coughed, eased his shoulders as if throwing off a chill, blew out a deep breath of relief and suddenly winked and leaned across to the woman behind the bar.

'And how is that boy of yours these days,' he said, 'your sailor-boy with the beard?'

Cat up a Tree

A WILD, glassy morning—all winds and glitter . . . the sun glared low between the chimneys, through black winter branches, blinding you at a slant, dazzling white and bright straight in the eyes—it made a splintering dance of everything, it made for squints and sniggering. . . .

Winds swept from nowhere, scooping up leaves and hustling them round the corner, knocking little dogs sideways, snatching and flapping at your trouser-legs. Cold nipped at noses and pinched ears red . . . it sang with cold in the keen bright light. Under a white sky the walls, roads, people, trees shone brightly coloured, red, green, blue, grey colours, as in a folk-tale, as if everything were made of coloured glass. Behind white cloud the sun hung and fiercely glowed, a monstrous incandescent mantle. A gentleman crossing the road moved like a puppet, parts of him glittering—one feared that by his own tread he might smash to smithereens his polished boots on the brittle macadam. . . .

Gentleman? He was no gentleman, he was a fireman. A jerky, puppety fireman, in blue trousers piped red, black jogging topboots, and in his braces and white sleeves. He carried a broom. He looked like a puppet because he was then crossing the road in the light—he walked so slowly against the hustling and swirling of the leaves, the dust, the winds, the shattering light.

Hindle Rice, alias Pudden Rice, number sefenty-too-fife, going then through the big red door into the Appliance Room, white-tiled like a scrubbed lavatory for motor-cars, where big top-heavy engines stood and waited, where now Pudden Rice would sweep together over the tiled floor a few small piles of dust, leaving these neat pyramids for the officers to see as they passed in their peaked caps, while in the shelter of such evidence of work proceeding Pudden Rice would for the rest of the morning lean on his broom and think

or chat or smile to the good-mornings, or break-for-tea, or perhaps
if he felt brave drop the precious broom altogether and abandon
his alibi to collect and break up twigs for firewood at home.

Rice soon dropped the broom. Out in front of the station the
black wintry twigs cracked and snapped in his hands. That sunlight
caught his eyes, so he could see nothing in front but bright light, as
of a halo; and to each side things moved too quickly and glittered
like glass. A cat went dashing past, its fur ruffled forward by a
following gust of wind. Up the street two navvies were hitting at a
metal spike with steel hammers—the blows came ringing on the
wind like sharp bells distorted. An old woman in black scurried by
with her veil blown fast into her teeth: she mouthed as this tickled
under her nose, grimacing at Pudden Rice with her head tilted
queerly to one side. Yet in a little garden opposite a girl sat reading,
sheltered by a bush in a warm pocket of sunlight! A paper bag sailed
like a wingless pouter suddenly out from some trees and on over her
head—then disappeared abruptly over the top of a bush. The girl
waved at its shadow, as if it might have been a fly, and remained
throughout reading unconcerned.

Rice smiled to see the girl sitting so quietly. Then he saw a pile
of leaves on the pavement in front form suddenly into a single file,
trickle round in a wide circle, then run for the shelter of a tree-trunk.

A window above banged open and a voice piped: 'Rice! Rice!'

Pudden dashed for his broom and then carrying it walked slowly
to the stairs. He climbed the stone steps, circling with them the
black-barred well down which hung long grey hose-lengths and
ropes, and muttered to these shiplike hangings: 'Now what's the
matter? Now what's up? I swept the tiles, didn't I? I done my job?'

He had reached the landing and was about to turn in through the
green swing doors—when the whole station leapt alive with sound,
sudden as a thunderclap, high-pitched and vibrating for ever, flashing off the tiles, reverberating round the brass, BRNNNNNNNNG
—the deafening alarm bell gripped in its electric circuit and ringing
on and on for ever. . . .

Rice flung down his broom and dived through the swing doors.
Across the room and into a passage—to a sudden end where two
brass rails stood flanking a steel pole. Now the clatter of footsteps

everywhere, and the alarm bell still jangling. Rice stamped his foot on a brass doorknob, a spring trap-door shot open upwards—and there was the hole! He jumped over it and gripping the smooth steel pole disppeared flying down. A rubber mat at the bottom, and all around suddenly the Appliance Room's white tiles again, with the engine of the Pump already roaring, men scrambling into boots, and more coming sailing down the pole, on that light-headed morning like a rain of heavy angels. But angels with funny faces— Nobby redhaired and pointed like a fox. Graetz with his comic round moon-face sprouting high up like a sunflower, Sailor with no neck and like John Bull washed white by a bad liver, Curly with his bright bald head, fairhaired Teetgen like a fresh blank Apollo with black teeth. These all came sliding down and scrambled for the Pump, Rice among them. He jumped up on to one of the high side seats and started to pull up his leggings. The automatic doors flew open and the Pump clanged out into the sunshine, as into a fog of white crystal, so that as they turned and roared off down the street light struck up from each brass fitting and from the axes and silver buttons—and somehow the heaviness was washed away.

Perched high up on the side, Pudden struggled into his coat. It flapped and blew out its short tails. He was just able to see the girl in the garden smile—and then his helmet fell down over his eyes. One legging flapped loose. The engine tore along, accelerating faster and faster, until it seemed to Pudden high up above the windshields that perhaps they had left the ground and were scudding through the air itself. The officer in front clanged the clapper of the brass bell as fast as a hand could move. Up England's Lane they tore, down Downshire Hill, through the Crescent, up Flask Walk, down Well Walk, sweeping along the middle of the wide roads like an angry brass beetle, roaring up the narrow streets and scattering dogs and cats and barrows and once an old lady carrying even in November a lilac parasol.

That morning the weather had made poets of the people. It sometimes happens—an angular trick of the sun, a warmness of a wind, something stirs an exultation in the most unexpected hearts. Not in the heart of all the people ever, but sometimes in those ready to be stirred, and sometimes also in dull hearts of which this would never have been imagined, but these people too receive a sudden jerk, a prod in the spirit, a desire for more than they usually want. Memories arise of things that have never been, tolerance arrives. They laugh—but perhaps that is only because they are nervous at the odd look of things. A trick of the weather has transformed the street, the hour, life. Perhaps this trick is a more powerful agent than the liver or even the libido. Perhaps one day it will be agreed that finally the most critical words of all are 'good morning'.

The passers-by smiled, one waved his hat, and a middle-aged butcher brandished a chop at them. Pudden still struggled with his uniform—how it eluded him! The belt and axe caught in the hooks behind him, his round helmet kept falling over an eye, an ear—and once his foot missed its support on the running-board and he nearly fell off the machine. He gripped the brass rail just in time. Yet, awkwardly as these things tugged at him—the wind, the clothes, the belt—he began to grin: 'What an odd engine—how peculiar that on most days it seems so heavy, so oiled and dully heavy with its iron extinguishers, its massive suction pipes, its hard wood ladders —yet today . . . all I can see about it is light, and how high it seems, how topheavy, and most striking of all are the brass rails and the red leather cushions! It's as upright as a queen's coach! And here we are—Nobby, Graetz, Teetgen, Sailor and me and the officer—all sitting and standing high up on top, like exuberant boy scouts, or tin soldiers, or travellers packed up on top of an old-fashioned coach! Ridiculous!'

But it was really so. The engine was built higher than cars are built usually, and brass rails armed the erect leather seats, vestiges of the horse days, a tradition to be surrendered unwillingly.

The bare trees skidded past. Rows of front doors approached and receded, innumerable windows winked and flashed in the fierce glare. The skyline of roofs and chimneys stood out black, giantly as against a milk-white sunset. Far off there appeared a church spire, it grew into a pointed little church, into a large grey church, and then this too was gone, veering off to the left. At last Pudden got himself straight. He then stood up and faced the wind, one leg crouched up by the ladders. This made him feel a dashing fellow. Phlegmatic usually, this pose in the wind and this clinging to a precarious rail excited him, never failing to rouse in him old postures of bravado learnt from early adventure books. Then, in the sharp sunlight, with the little houses flashing by, he thought suddenly: 'Good Lord— we're going to a fire! Perhaps to a real fire! It may possibly be a false alarm pulled by a boy or a drunk or someone. (He saw a sheet of figures—over 1,000 False Alarms Malicious last year—one of them fatal—a fireman was killed, crushed against the garage door in the rush for somebody's funny joke.) But . . . perhaps it really is a fire, this one time, by chance the real thing? Asphyxia, boiling, frying— I saw a fireman frizzled up in burning oil till he was like a little black monkey, a charred little monkey wearing a helmet several sizes too big for him. And when Sailor tripped in the molten rubber —his arm. Andy's neck after that sulphuric acid job. . . .'

Rice looked down at the two shining round helmets primping up in front of him. He laughed, and felt the corners of his mouth split and all the teeth catch in the wind, he laughed and seemed inside to shine with laughter; how could frying and falling walls happen on this kind of a glass morning? Hot smoke in this pure air? Such things happen to a rosy-cheeked crew of bright tin soldiers? The wind echoed in his ears like a sea-breeze, thrumming past as regular as telegraph wires, and still the sun shot pinpoints off the brass and glared whitely from the chimney-tops ahead. Suddenly Pudden began to hum a march, a high-pitched jigging march for dwarfs stomping off to the forest and the anvils—as joyfully repetitive as train music. . . .

They skidded round a corner and braked to a stop. They were in a cul-de-sac made up of small white houses with painted doors. Trees growing behind showed above the roofs, an effect peculiar in a large city. These looked like country cottages, and the windows were in each case so cramped up and warped that the houses seemed to be no more than a pack of doors and windows clustered together, balancing for breath. A few trained bushes stood in tubs like sentinel birds before the black and pink and primrose doors. And there on the pavement corner stood the fire alarm post, singular and red, as bright a red as when the snow is on the ground.

They leapt off the machine, the officer ran up to the alarm and then stood by it, looking right and left, uncertain, while the broken glass twinkled beneath his polished boots. Rice thought: 'Bright as the day Teetgen went to the paint factory fire and came away with his boots varnished, bright for days!'

The officer peered into the alarm—it had certainly been pulled. But no one was there to direct him. He looked up at the windows, then behind him—searching with his eyes anxiously for smoke. 'That's the crazy people they are,' thought Rice, 'pulling the bell and then running away expecting us to find the job by magic. That's them.'

A small boy appeared from behind one of the bird-bushes. The officer frowned and strode heavily towards him in his big boots.

'Well, son—and who pulled it?' He looked like a giant wooden soldier towering above the suddenly real boy. Blue coat splashed with red, silver buttons and axe, round red face as neat as a doll's, shining black leggings stiff-legged.

Ignoring the question, the boy said: 'Is there a fire, mister?'

'How long have you been here?' the officer asked, his voice sharpening with suspicion—then turned his head, so that his face shone brightly in the sunlight. He yelled over his shoulder to the firemen peering about: 'One of you—scout round the corner.'

Attracted by the sound of bells and brakes and the stamping of boots, there had by then collected a small crowd of onlookers. Half of these were boys, carrying rifles and swords, or driving small pedal cars. One wore on his head a top hat peaked with half a brim only, painted blue and labelled *La France*. Two painters in white overalls looked sadly at the fire engine. A tall man with a thin face clouded with red veins asked if he could lend a hand. A smartly dressed woman dragging a trolley laden with shopping smiled and smiled, as though she was the mother of all and 'she knew'. A man in a blue uniform winked at Teetgen, because *he* knew too—he knew it was just another bloody exercise, mate. Three Jewish exiles passed hurriedly, twisting their necks round to keep the uniforms in sight, frightened, round-eyes as owls.

By then Graetz, a tall white sunflower with his round face drooping off his long neck—Graetz was standing isolated in a circle of boys and saying aloud for their benefit: 'It's a false alarm—and from now on we've got our eye on this post. Got a policeman on it, we have, so in future . . .'

When suddenly in a garden wall between two houses a door burst open and a fat woman in a broad white apron came bustling out. She ran towards the Pump with her arms outstretched, as though the Pump might at any moment recede and vanish. She began shouting as soon as she appeared: 'Don't go! Don't go! Oh, I'm so glad you came! Milly's up a tree.' Then paused for breath as the officer went up to her. 'It's round the back, round the back,' she panted, 'and I pulled the alarm, you see. They told me it was right —you see, she's been up there since last night. She mews so.'

The officer said, 'How do we get through?' And at the same time shouted back to the men, 'Cat up a tree. Bring the ladders.'

Teetgen and Nobby jumped up to the front of the ladders on top of the Pump. Graetz and Rice began to pull at the bottom. The straps uncoiled and then the long ladder came sliding out. Once again Rice felt like a puppet, a wooden soldier clockworked with the others into an excited, prearranged game. The sunlight seemed to blow by in bright gusts. Now everybody was laughing—except one of the lugubrious painters, who began to grumble loudly about the bleeding waste of petrol and men's time. But the other onlookers found it great sport, and in the laughing dazzling light began to shout: 'Pretty Pussy!' and 'Mind it don't bite you now!' and 'See you keep her nightdress down!'—this last from the thin man with the bad veins.

Pulling at the ladder Nobby said: 'Last week an old girl called us for a parrot up a tree. But we wouldn't go. Cat-up-a-tree's legal, parrots isn't.'

Now the fat woman in the apron bolted back through the garden door with the officer following. The four men carrying the ladder squeezed through at the double. Rice at the rear end nearly jammed himself between the brick wall and the heavy wooden ladder, catching his fingers in the extension pawl, nearly coming a cropper and laughing again. Then they were in the garden—apple-trees and young beech saplings, a black winter tracing of branches everywhere against the glowing white cloud beyond. The sun glared through this filigree, striping the litter of dry leaves, striping the air itself with opaque lightshafts.

'There she is, lads,' shouted the doll officer, pointing upwards.

The other dolls doubled up with the ladder working like clockwork, raising their knees in a jocular movement as they ran.

Above them, isolated at the very top of a tall sapling, crouched on the tapering end of this thin shoot so that it bent over under the weight like a burdened spring—sat a huge dazed cat.

In a book of children's stories this cat would have seemed improbable and amusing. Its position was as improbable as that of a blue pig flying. It looked like a heavy young puma borne by what appeared to be a tall and most resilient twig. In real life a branch so thin would have snapped. Yet here this was—happening on a bright November morning, a real morning though rather light-headed. In children's books too there are pictured with vivid meaning certain fantasies of the weather—lowering black storms, huge golden suns, winds that bend all the trees into weeping willows, skies of electric blue with stars dusted on them like tinsel, moons encircled by magical haloes. These appear highly artificial, drawn from the inspiration of a dreamland: but they are true. These skies and suns and winds happen quite frequently. So that on the morning what appeared to be unreal was real, apparently richened by association, but originally rich in its entity that had created the fairy association. Thus this was a witches' morning, a morning of little devils and hats popping off, of flurry and fluster and sudden shrill laughter.

Teetgen put his weight on the foot of the ladder and the others ran up underneath so that the ladder rose with them until at last it was upright. It was thicker by far and heavier than the sapling—but as its head crashed into the tapering sprout branches they supported it easily. They swayed precariously, then sprang back into position, while the cat, refusing to be disturbed by these alien perplexities, looked away scornfully—or, as animals often do, pretended to look away, keeping an ear cocked sharply towards the new varnished ladder-head now extending towards it.

The officer began to climb at the run, stamping on the ladder as firemen are taught to stamp, to punish the ladder and thus to control it. More than ever he appeared to be playing a game with this deliberate kicking of his boots. Pudden and the others held the ladder firm at the bottom. They were thinking: 'What if he breaks his neck? A man for a cat? What a life . . .' Through the rungs of the ladder a line of gaily coloured underclothes flapped and danced their strange truncated dances. The fat woman stood a little way off, chequered by sunlight, her hands clasped, talking all the time. Some birds started singing, and in the middle of the city a cock crowed.

The officer pranced to the top and picked off the cat by the scruff of its neck. He stuck it on his shoulder and climbed down. The crowd now jammed in the doorway cheered and whistled. They all wanted to stroke the cat. So did Pudden. But as the officer reached the bottom rung the cat jumped from his shoulder to the ground. It was a black cat, fully grown, with white whiskers and paws. As it collected itself on the ground, several of the firemen stretched down their free hands to stroke it, somehow to congratulate it also upon its narrow escape.

However, the cat never even looked at them. With deliberation it stiffened its legs, so that it seemed to stand on its toes, flung up its tail straight as a poker—and walked disdainfully away from the firemen, leaving only the bright adieu beneath its tail.

THE END